T0103816

Collage

Collage

Subhankar Banerjee

PARTRIDGE

ISBN: Softcover 978-1-4828-8355-8
eBook 978-1-4828-8354-1

Print information available on the last page.

To order additional copies of this book, contact
Partridge India
000 800 10062 62
orders.india@partridgepublishing.com

www.partridgepublishing.com/india

This is work of mine is dedicated to that man only. My strongest support, fiercest critic, toughest teacher and best friend, my Father – Late Anindya Sundar Banerjee.

At the same time I must thank my wife Puja who has always inspired me on writing this book.

Mangal was standing on the open part of the first floor beside the cabin in the nursing home. This small area has been kept free for future construction but in the current situation it was so vast for him that he was feeling lonely. It is end of November and he has put on a thin round neck T-shirt and a blue tracksuit but not feeling any chill. Perhaps the conditions he has gone through in last half an hour has killed all his earthly feelings. It is almost 7:30 in the morning and he was looking down there on the road which is just waking up now but in next one or two hours the same would become one of the busiest road in the area and at the end of the day it will become free from all the hustle bustle again and go to sleep. The phenomenon is no different than that of a human life, it born, slowly becomes busy and then fully occupied with duties and responsibilities, finally one day goes to sleep, endlessly.

Is he becoming emotional? Mangal asked to himself. It is not the proper time to become one, he told to himself. Very soon he will have to stand in front of his family members who are still in a dilemma. He looked back at the cabin. Life will never be the same again for him. He can clearly see the face of the man lying on the bed. He seems to be sleeping, peacefully. The feet of the tall figure are hanging outside the general sized bed.

Mangal became occupied with various reminiscences again. When he looks back to his own life he just gets stunned about what he would have done in life without that man. The person whom at that point of time he used to be most afraid off? The man from whom he always wanted to hide himself. The man who used to ask Mangal all those terrible questions which he did not have answers for. The man who had solutions for those toughest mathematical problems from his text books of his student life. The man who was always used to be angry with him due to his mistakes, wrong doings and fickle mindedness.

Mangal still get astonished thinking about the level of dedication the man had regarding the education for his children. He was so crazy about education, may because of the hurdles he faced in his own student life, Mangal said to himself. At the end of every month he used to visit the private tutors he hired for his kids, to get their progress report and attentiveness towards education and studies but unfortunately always used to return home with every possible negative reports and remarks from them about of Mangal. The man was always worried about the future of his children. The man with his limited belongings and capacity had always stretched himself beyond his best to provide his kids all possible facilities, even some times before they actually had asked for. The man who actually was so farsighted that if he would not have planned the career path then today Mangal would have been somewhere that he probably would not have the capability to dream of a good life, at least the life he is living in all respect today.

Dr. Kundu is asking for you, please come with me, a female voice broke in to Mangal's chain of thoughts. He turned back and found a nurse standing right behind him. Yes please, Mangal followed her inside the cabin.

We will have to observe for one more hour and then only we would be able to certify, Dr. Kundu said to Mangal, standing in front of an electronic medical equipment, which was showing a straight line of light on its screen. Mangal was in no mood to answer, he just gestured his approval and left the room. He came downstairs and out of the nursing home. From a small shop just opposite of the main gate he bought a packet of cigarette, probably the first customer of the day. The cigarette again drove him back to his thoughts.

How could a child who lost his mother at the age of 2 and a half years and literally became an orphan turn out to be a person with so much of strength? Mangal really gets astonished when he think about the mental strength that child had. Luck also played perhaps the coarsest game with that abandoned child when it gifted him Typhoid at the age of 12 / 13 years, that too in a remote village of Bengal in the early 1950s. He fought back and not only survived with mere Homeopathic medicine and zero care but eventually by physical exercising consecutively for years built such a muscular and manly physic that became a point of discussion for others.

There was no one to inspire or support the education of that boy, even no one to ask whether he is hungry or not but the boy was so determined towards education that he started providing private tuitions at the age of 14. Whatever he used to earn he kept half to support his personal education and rest half he used to give to his family, where in fact one day he was humiliated and insulted for not earning at the age of 14 years and taking foods two times from the family. After two years the boy lost his father too. At the age of 18 years he had to take a Porter's job in a Railways shed in nearby locomotive but did not leave his studies and completed graduation in Accounts Honors from the University. He did not leave it there and started his Masters' degree in Commerce and completed that too successfully.

Within this time the young man also had involved in to social works and politics. Very soon he ascended as a popular as well as supportive person for the needy and poor people due to his selfless services. At the same time his enormous courage of standing against all those powerful and greedy people of that time in support of those poor people had made him a trusted name among them.

Hello, your cell phone is ringing, the shopkeeper informed Mangal. Mangal took the phone out of his pocket, it is Babul, his childhood friend who today morning helped him to reach here at the earliest possible.

Is there anybody with you? Babul's voice from the opposite side. We are arranging the things that will be needed and will be there in half an hour. No, it is okay, Mangal replied. Have you talked to your mom? Babul asked again. Yes, I have depicted them about everything and suggested to stay at home, Mangal replied. Just wait there, we are coming, Babul completed and disconnect the phone.

Is everything alright, asked the shopkeeper? Mangal did not notice that the man was deeply listening to him. Hmm, Mangal looked at the man, are you asking me? Yes, it seems something serous has happened, is everything alright the man replied. Yes, to the maximum possible, Mangal replied and left the place. He crossed the road and enter the thin lane between the nursing home and its boundary wall. He lighted another cigarette, the only companion who will never ask a single question and would not disturb him to be alone for some times.

Though Mangal had tremendous differences in views and thoughts with the man lying on the bed in the cabin about more or less in each and every subject but still he always admits that the man was his first and till date best teacher of humanity, equality, politics and sociology. He was Mangal's strongest support and at the same time greatest critique of his views and thoughts. There used to be always a fight between them even on the discussion of the smallest issue, but he has taught Mangal how to argue with respect to your opponents. He has taught that unless you respect your opponent even your peers will not respect you. He has taught how to acquire knowledge before you argue. He has taught the power of regimentation and unison of people in everything. He has taught the strength of the unity of people when standing against powerful people who are corrupted and harmful for the masses. He has taught how to maintain placidness and at the same time sharpness of mind in life, especially when the situation is adverse. He has taught how to laugh at and avoid those people who try to abuse you and want you to do the same so that they can drag you down to their level. He has taught how to support and fight for the needy and poor people. He has taught that only your blood connections are not your family, it is eventually much bigger and includes all those whom you could help without any greed of direct or indirect, material or non-material gains. So many things he has taught to make Mangal a man.

Even after so much of his lessons and teachings I must admit that I am not as good a student as he was. But still I promise to that I will always try to be a man like him, a human like him. I admit that neither I have the level of mental nor physical strength as he had and acquired through extreme dedication, but I promise today to my toughest teacher, greatest critique, strongest support and best friend ever that I will give my best shot to be like you, Mangal looked towards the sky and told to himself.

The mobile rang again. Where are you? We are at the main gate.

This time Mangal's youngest uncle from the opposite side. Wait there, I am just coming, Mangal replied and came out of the lane. People from family and friend circle have started gathering. They came in front of the cabin. The man is still sleeping.

You seat here and don't leave the place. We will arrange everything, Mangal's uncle said him and left the room.

Mangal looked at the face of the man. As if he is sleeping so peacefully and don't want to be disturbed.

A CHILD MAKES A MOTHER ...

1940, in a chilling cold night in the month of January, in a rural area of Bengal a young man was helplessly walking to and fro outside the outer most room of his house. It was as early as 2:30 AM but the day has not yet started. Though the night is full of moonshine as it a full moon and the sky also glittering with innumerable number of starts but Brijendra was in no mood to explore or at the least enjoy the beauty of the nature around him. He is restless to know what is going on in the room where he has not been allowed to enter. Within the room his wife Bimala was trying her best to bear with the tremendous labor pain but the sound of her cry was clearly audible from outside. She was going to give birth of her fourth son and fifth child. After fighting the battle for nearly one more hour, almost at 5 o'clock when the dawn was approaching and the sky has already changed its color to saffron, she successfully gave birth of the child. The elderly village nurse came out of the room with new life wrapped in cloths in such a practiced way that the chilling cold could hardly reach the skin of the just born baby and announced with a wide smile of her face, it is a son. Brijendra leaned forward to see the first glimpse of his son, happiness was clearly visible on his face. Then he turned his face to the nurse and asked, how the mother is.

The nurse maintaining the same smile replied, both the mother and the child is ok.

The young man looked at the sky and expressed his gratitude to the Almighty.

Some days later, Bimala was lying by the child in her room when Sumatibala entered the room with mouthful of betel leaf, which she is addicted to and almost always keep on chewing. Sumatibala is a distant relative of Brijendra and after the demise of her husband she used to live alone in a nearby village. What is his name? She asked to Bimala.

Not yet finalized, Bimala answered with a smile and tried to let herself seat on the bed. You don't need to seat on, Sumatibala directed Bimala and came forwards. Let me see the face of my grandson once, he is so good looking, just like an angel, name him "Sundar", the elderly woman said. Okay, I will convey this to his father, Bimala replied.

Why, is he elder than me in the family or am I afraid of him? When I have decided the name for the child "Sundar" then no one could change it. Convey this to your husband. The elderly woman replied but this time with a sense of order. Bimala shook her head to show that she will act in accordance with the order.

Bimala was more attentive to others and neglecting about herself. Due to some complexities in the delivery she became so feeble that for nearly six months she could not go outside the home. But other women of the village used to admire her due to her helping nature and attitude and she was an important member of the group of women in the village. She was dear and near to all other women in the locality and a well-accepted point of consultation for them in their household issues. Everyday some of them used to visit Bimala as the physician prohibited her from any kind of stressful outdoor activity and recommended her to take complete rest for some more days. Out of everything Bimala used to miss most the women's ghat in the river adjacent to the village and where each and every woman of the village used to take bathe, wash cloths and clear utensils because that was the only place where the women of the village had the access and freedom to spend some time together every day and enjoy various gossips.

Do you know a witch has come to this village and she is so dangerous that even if that witch touches any kid that kid will die in three days? While gossiping on various things suddenly Sucheta told to Bimala. One such day when Bimala was seating in her room some women came to meet her and Sucheta was one of them.

What? Witch in our village? Bimala asked with surprise. The other women supported Sucheta and one or two even told that they know people who have personally witnessed the phenomenon.

Have any of you witnessed that in your own eyes? Bimala asked. No body answered but they said they know people who have witnessed the same and they are so honest that none of them have ever lied in their life for a single time even for their personal gain. Bimala did not answer.

SOME MILES AWAY

You unlucky witch, don't you dare to come in to my kitchen. Seat out there and when the time will come, foods will be given to you, an elderly lady screamed from inside the kitchen. She did not stop there and continued, you have eaten up three children in three years and till so hungry? Or waiting to eat up my full family and then only you will be satisfied? You cannibal witch, when so many people dies every day why don't you die.

Parbati was standing like a statue outside the kitchen and the woman from inside who was offering her such beautiful words was her mother-in-law. It was almost 2 PM and no one has asked Parbati for a grain of food from the morning or even a glass of water. She was starving as usual since morning but did not have right to enter the kitchen of the house. Parbati did not reply as she has become used to such languages for herself. She does not have the right to enter the kitchen as she is an unlucky witch, at least as per her in-laws and others in the society. She does not even have the right to touch any kid in the locality because it is believed that if she touches any kid the kid will die. Parbati, a fourteen year old girl has become used to all these.

Parbati still reminds that day when she was married with Janardan even before she could have reached her teen age. More specifically at the age of 11 years. This was a very common phenomenon in those days. Janardan was young, well behaved and gentle man. He used to love his wife very much. He was working in a big organization and was doing well enough to maintain his family. Janardan's ancestral house was in a village far away from the nearest railway station and due to his job he had to travel to the city every day by the early morning train. Janardan had to start daily early in the morning to reach his office on time and used to return home late in the evening after attending his duties and responsibilities there. So it used to be terribly tough for him to carry his daily journey especially in the monsoon and winter seasons. He knew what kind of behavior Parbati receives from his other family members but as the youngest son he did not have the right to support or stand by his wife openly or to oppose the elderly of his family.

Due to her too young age and physical immaturity for carrying out normal married life the first child Parbati conceived in the next year of her marriage was miscarried. She was broken but got no one to stand by her in those days when she actually needed someone to share her grief with. She needed a shoulder on which she could rest her head and indulge the tears to come out freely. But she had none, she was left cruelly alone in the darkness of sorrow. However the people in the family started condemning her for that accident. No one considered her age and not even tried to understand the unbearable agony through which the little girl was going. That was not all, she was forbidden by her in-laws to visit or meet people from her father's family as a punishment for the crime of miscarriage. She became terribly alone in her day to day life. In such a condition when that little girl was fighting her excruciating condition of life by counting hours and minutes, her family members mounted extreme pressure on that little girl and her husband Janardan to conceive again. In those days it was in fact robustly implemented more than any other system in the society to blindly follow the suggestions provided by the seniors of the family which used to be treated no less than the final decisions. Unfortunately this little girl was no different and she again conceived in the following months but due to her extreme weakness and ill health the baby she gave birth of was so immature and week that it did not survive more than some days, which was more agonizing for that young mother. She was broken from the core of her soul but there was no one to understand her agony and the reasons for that accident. On top of that everyone was more interested in insulting that little girl for the unfortunate happenings.

The same thing happened again in the next year for three consecutive times and the little girl came to the doorsteps of her death, when by the grace of the Almighty, finally her husband decided to do something to save his wife. But at the same time it was not possible for him to rebel against the seniors of the family directly. Janardan applied his intelligence and discussed with his father that he is facing tremendous problems in carrying out his job from this distant village as it is far from the railway station and also could not employ his time properly in the office which in turn affecting his professional career. He acted with the maximum possible seriousness and created a situation that this could even lead him to losing the job. This trick worked and Janardan finally managed his father to permit him for purchasing a piece of small land and building a house in the vicinity of the railway station. At the same time he promised that in every weekend and other holidays he with his wife will visit the native village to stay with the family.

In those past three years the girl had earned the ultimate of human pain as a woman and a mother. At the same time she had also earned the humiliation in that prejudiced rural society of being an unfortunate witch, who if touches any child that child will die. This tremendous insult became so well-known so fast that all the women in that village and surrounding villages started avoiding her. Even other women within her in-laws also reacted the same way.

So Janardan finally succeed to take his beloved wife out of that netherworld and took her in his new house in the village where Bimala and her family was living.

Though Janardan changed his place but before they could have reached their new home the unfortunate humiliation that was stamped on his wife Parbati reached their new locality. In her new home though Parbati was free from any humiliation as she used to face in her in-law's house but two things was constantly haunting her every moment she was living through. The first thing is the painful three years and what she had to tolerate with, and the second thing is the behavior of the women in the neighborhood of her new residence. Janardan again became busy with his office and used to return in the evening which again created an intolerable loneliness in the life of Parbati. To deal with the loneliness she started going to the bank of the river flowing out of the village in the morning and again in the evening. She used to seat there in the banks under the big banyan tree for hours. Seating there Parbati used to keep watching with blank eyes those women who used to come to take bath in the river with their kids in the ghat which was especially for the women and no men were allowed to use that ghat. The women also noticed her but used to avoid in the unrealistic panic about what they had heard about her. It was terrific throbbing for Parbati but she had become habituated with such neglecting eyesight and hurting avoidance of people. She had almost become a sculpture of stone and lost all her senses to react or feel the pain.

LET'S STAND UP

Nearly after nine months or so on that day Bimala visited the river ghat with her youngest son Sundar for taking bath with other women. She was so happy to be there with her friends after spending a long duration confined within the house. Suddenly while gossiping with other women her eyes fall on a young teenaged girl seating mournfully under the banyan tree and for the first time she noticed Parbati seating at a distance and looking at the children who came with their mothers and were playing on the adjacent ground. Bimala very minutely noticed the melancholy face and blank eyesight of the teenage girl and it was heartbreaking for her. At the same time she also noticed the behavior of the other women who were accompanying her in the ghat, towards the lonely and depressed girl. She found that all of them are feeling sad for the girl but at the same time all of them somewhere in their inner mind were considering the prejudice so seriously that they were afraid of even talking to her. That day Bimala did not say anything to anyone and just returned home with many questions and also started searching for the answers for those questions within her mind. In the afternoon when all the women again gathered in the ghat for cleaning their kitchen utensils Bimala noticed the girl seating at the same place the same way she found her in the morning. Bimala returned without discussing anything with anyone but someway or other those eyes were haunting her. Once I was also a girl of that age and with time I have become a woman, now if I don't understand or stand by her then there will be no shame more penetrating, Bimala uttered to herself.

In the late evening when Sundar's father returned from his business Bimala went to him as usual with a cup of tea and asked him, have you heard about a new couple who have come to live in the neighborhood?

Sundar's father raised his face and answered, I had not only heard about them but I had also met the boy personally in the market place. He sipped the tea and added, the boy is good and very obedient kind. Then Brijendra depicted every details about Janardan and his family, his job and so on and so forth.

Bimala before asking the next question studied her husband's face and found it satisfactory. She then asked her husband, have you heard about what people are saying in the village about the girl. This question created irritation in the mind of her husband and that was visible on his face. Then with a crocus sound Brijendra replied with another question, who are those people in the villagers talking about such rubbish about the girl? Are those people capable enough to decide who is what and who is not? Worthless fellows, he completed.

Bimala carrying the same seriousness on her tone asked again to make it a bit direct, tell me one thing what do you think about these rumor what people are talking about?

This time her husband stared at her and calmly replied, I have many important jobs to be done and I generally spend the day working hard so I don't have time to discuss such idiotic matter with those worthless fellows who neither have any work nor they are willing to work. He paused and added, and I believe such things are simply thoughtless and of no value. Those people who do not have any constructive things to perform used to spend time on discussing such stupid things. He returned the finished cup back to his wife and continued, you know Bimala two questions have always haunted me and I have though tried my best but never have reached the answer. Firstly the unscientific prejudices and the by birth caste system in the Hindu society has always divided the society in several parts and never did anything good for the society or the culture but till date those two same old dividing in nature and fully unscientific baseless rotten things are existing in the society and that too in full fledge, but why? We have been worshiping who have fought throughout their life and sacrificed everything they could easily have enjoyed in life to educate the people of the society to unsubscribe these two disgusting things but at the same time when we are searching for bride or bridegroom for the marriage of our son or daughter we are mentioning our caste and asking for bride or bridegroom from the matching caste for them. There is hardly any difference in culture or sentiments in people from different caste of Hindu religion but we love to forget the same when the time comes to take decisions, why I don't understand? Secondly the question that I have not found any answer is whether a woman becomes a mother by giving birth of a child or the child that born gives birth of a mother in a woman? Perhaps both are equally right. He completed and left the place for his drawing room.

Bimala understood that her husband is also not taking that decision about the girl and it was more than what she expected. Now she was indomitable about her next step.

The next day as usual after completing the daily works in the house Bimala came to the river ghat with her youngest son Sundar. Some of the other women of the village were already there and some were yet to come. She looked at the spot where she saw Parbati seating yesterday. Parbati was seating there as usual and was looking at the field where the kids came with their mothers were playing. Bimala suddenly called Parbati in a loud voice, hey girl come here. Parbati was shocked that someone was calling her. Initially she could not believe her own senses but when Bimala repeated pointing to her, I am calling you, come here. Parbati had no other choice but to follow the instruction. The other women were also shocked and one of them from the Maiti family asked Bimala, what are you doing? Why are you calling that condemned girl here in the ghat where our kids are playing? Bimala did not answered their question as her eyes were fixed at Parbati who in turn was till in a dilemma that what she had heard is right or wrong. Bimala again shouted and asked Parbati, do not you understand what I am saying to you.

Parbati appeared almost in a shivering condition in front of Bimala with the slowest possible steps and watching the faces of all the women who were standing beside Bimala. She was feeling tremendous nervous about what is going to happen. Probably she will not be allowed to stay in the village anymore and she again will have to go back to her in-laws house. All possible negative thoughts were creating a shattering sensation in her mind.

I have never seen you here in this village, Bimala said to Parbati. What is your name and where are you from? Bimala asked her. All others were looking simultaneously at Bimala once and at Parbati next.

My name is Parbati and I am from a distant village, Parbati paused for a moment and added, I live here with my husband. We have recently shifted here from the village for the ease of his service, she answered the question. Bimala then asked some other questions which were more womanly in nature. Parbati answered all of those with her eyes on the ground. In between she has not raised her eyes even for once.

The next question Bimala asked was no less than a quake that vibrated everyone present there, so you are married for almost four years, do you know how to manage a naughty kid?

Everyone was stunned. For the first time since she has appeared she raise her eyes. She tried her best but could not hold her emotion or the pain she has been going through and all that agony flowed out of her eyes in the form of droplets. She either did not know or was unable to answer this question.

Had I rebuked you? Then why are you crying? Bimala asked placing her hand softly on Parbati's shoulder. This broke Parbati in to tears more immensely. Bimala waited for some time and let Parbati manage herself. She again asked her whether she had rebuked or bitten Parbati so that she is crying. Parbati gathering her entire strength replied, I am forbidden to touch any kid as I am unlucky for the children.

One of the women standing there could not hold herself anymore and asked Bimala that does not she know that if Parbati touches any kid, it might be severely fatal.

That is what today I want to witness in my own eyes, Bimala replied without looking at the women and fixing her eyes on Parbati. Her eyes were depicting her determination to challenge the myth and to break it once and forever. She added, I believe that my son will leave as long as the Almighty have decided and a mere touch of any man or woman could never have the strength to exceed the will of the Almighty.

Parbati was shocked probably the maximum possible and had become a mute spectator. Bimala suddenly placed Sundar on Parbati's hand and said quite in an audible voice so that everyone present there could perceive her words, from now he is your son as much as he is mine, take care of him unless I come back, with a smile on her face she moved towards the river for taking bath. Parbati did not understand what she should say in reply or probably she was more interested to the child in her hand than to any other thing in the universe.

After returning from the river Bimala took her son back and in front of everyone said to Parbati, from now on whenever you want, you could come to my home and adore your own son as long as you wish.

From that very moment Parbati became a mother figure for Sundar and though she successfully gave birth of her own son after some years but till her last breadth she used to say that Sundar is her eldest son and it was Sundar for whom she became a mother for the first time in her life.

Going to his in-law's house ...

Sundar's father had become a well-known businessman in the locality because of his hard work and business intelligence. He was successfully running his old business as well as had started some new ventures like metal sheet, cloths and grocery items. Atanu, his youngest brother was helping him in all his businesses and the two brothers were really doing well in their professional life. The house they used to live had also been expanded and renovated. A new section with two big rooms and associate facilities has been built for Atanu's family. They had purchased quite a good amount of farming lands also in some neighboring villages.

Sundar, now a boy of two and a half years, was playing with his toys and friends when he found Sarala aunty calling him. Sundar please come with me right now, your mother wants to see you, Sarala's voice was clearly showing the tension she was in but for a two and a half years old Sundar it was not conceivable to understand the urgency. It was almost 10:30 AM and Sundar was more interested in playing than going home back.

I will not go home now and not bath also, tell mom, Sundar was stubborn. No son, you won't have to bath now but please come with me, Sarala requested Sundar and almost convincingly lifted the boy in her hands and started walking as fast as possible for her, back to home. The boy has started throwing his small hands to stop his captor but Sarala does not have time indulge or rather waste, so she kept moving.

Sundar when entered the room found his mom lying on the floor on a straw mattress and his father seating on the floor by the left side of his mom. Many other people have also gathered in the room. His youngest uncle Atanu and aunty Sarojini was also seating there. There are tears in their eyes. Sarala took Sundar near to his mom and sat him down there as close as possible to the pillow on which Bimala's head was resting.

Bimala was not saying anything, she was just looking at Sundar. Suddenly a drop of tear came out of her eyes. Why are you crying mom? Who has rebuked you? Good kids don't cry, Sundar tried to wipe the drop of salty water with his small palms while telling all those lines his mom use to say to console him when he cries. Mom did not answer, she was still looking at Sundar without blinking her eyes. Sarojini aunty came forward and gave a small glass filled with water in Sundar's hand and guided him to pour some slowly in the mouth of his mother. Sundar stared at his aunty once and then followed her. Suddenly Sarojini broke out in to tears with a scream, holding Sundar in her hands. Suddenly all broke out in to tears and the priest closed the eyes of Sundar's mother who was lying in front.

Is mom sleeping? Why all are crying? Sundar asked to himself. He could not comprehend why mom is not opening her eyes. Most likely she is sleeping. After some time he was taken out of the room by Sarala.

Where is mother? Why is she not coming to me? After some days when Sundar enquired his aunty about his mother. Sarojini replied, your mom has gone to meet the God son and she is seeing you and all of us from there, Sarojini pointed towards the sky. Sundar could not understand why mother has gone to meet the God when every year God comes here at the time of puja?

18 MONTHS LATER

Sundar has just joined the primary school. He is a boy of 4 years now. In last 18 months everyday he had tried to find out his mom in the sky but failed. Sarojini one day had showed him a star and said that his mom has become that star. Sundar still don't understand how his mom had become a star. He always try to see his mom in that star but could not find her.

One of Sarojini's main job now is to take care of Sundar and her own son Noni who is just six months elder than Sundar. Noni is also started going to the same school with Sundar. Two brothers always used to be together. People use to call them Kartik and Ganesh, as Sundar is good looking so he is called Kartik and Noni is chubby so he has been named Ganesh by the villagers. In the morning Sarojini prepare them for school and in the evening when the two naughty kids return from there, it is again Sarojini's duty to arrange foods and everything for them before the two left for playing.

It was a Sunday afternoon and Sundar was playing with Noni in the field when he saw Sarala coming towards him. Come with me your mother has come, Sarala uttered to Sundar. Mom has come, where? Sundar asked to Sarala. She is waiting for you at home. Before Sarala could have finished his words Sundar started running vigorously towards their home, Noni followed him.

Sundar stopped at the door of the room. A woman, wearing a beautiful sharee was seating beside his father but certainly she is not his mom. Sundar though could not remind the exact face of his mother but he can remind her eyes very much. Those two eyes which were looking at him without a blink, those eyes which were telling so many words to Sundar, those eyes which were feeling the pains yet to come in to her son's life, those beautiful eyes full of agony not for herself but for her son she was leaving behind. Come here son, meet your new mom, Sarojini called Sundar inside the room. Sundar was not clear about what to be done. Noni has also reached the place and now standing beside him. Sundar waited there for some moments looking at the woman, then suddenly turned back and started running. Sarojini called him back but he did not stop. Noni stared at his mother for a moment and then followed his brother the same way he followed Sundar earlier. Sundar finally stopped reaching the stairways of the old temple of the village. Why did not you talk to your mother? Noni asked his brother. Sundar gazed at Noni but did not answer, actually he is also not very clear about what he has done and why he has done so. His mind was blank, totally blank.

Within this 18 months a new family has come to the village. Actually they have rented the house next to the house where Sundar and his family lives. A newly married young couple. Abhay Mukherjee, a very well behaved, soft spoken, calm and quite young man came to the village few months back with his newly married wife to live. His native place was in a distant village of Purulia, faraway district of Bengal. His wife Uma was from an affluent family of the same area and was the youngest and only girl child of the family after her four elder brothers. She was highly adored and pampered by her father as well as elder brothers. Abhay was living in Purulia until he got a job in a big manufacturing unit in an upcoming industrial town approximately five miles from the village where Sundar and his family lives. As he was new in the job and not affluent enough so it was tough for him to rent a house there in the town. That is why he decided to take a house on rent in a nearby place which will be cheaper and at the same time where from he could daily attend his office without much of long and tiresome journey. He finally settled in a two room small house adjacent to Sundar's ancestral house. Both Abhay and his wife Uma was very decent type of persons and within quite a short time they became well known to the villagers for their gentleness and beautiful behavior. Abhay was at the age group of Atanu, they became close friends and so Uma and Sarojini. Abhay used to call Sundar's father as "dada", means elder brother and used to respect him like the same.

Abhay was a student of Printing Technology in his graduation but in his job he did not have any opportunity to use his knowledge of that. He was keen to use the academic knowledge in to practical works, so he decided to do something on his own and started a small printing press in one room of his rented house, which actually was the first printing press in that area. He indeed worked hard to bring all the parts and parcels of the machineries from Kolkata and assembling those on his own. For every bits and pieces he had to go to Kolkata to procure which was really tough after maintaining his office but he successfully achieved that. Due to his knowledge, hard work and scarcity printing press in the area, within a short period of time it became a profitable business. Though Uma's new settlement was far from her paternal house but her bothers used to visit her new house in every occasion. They were also very happy seeing their sister and brother-in-law in well established in their respective life. So everything was picture perfect till then.

Good time does not last for long. Suddenly one day a news came to Abhay's house that his father-in-law, i.e. Uma's father has encountered a severe heart attack and the doctors have informed that he is in such a serious condition that he might not survive for long. Uma lost her mother just one year before she came here in this village and still was not totally out of that shock. In such a situation this unexpected news about her father just trembled her from the core of her heart. One of Uma's elder brother, Sachin came to inform Uma about this and at the same time to ask for permission from his brother-in-law to take his sister with him as Uma's father had wished to see his only beloved youngest daughter for the last time. Next day Uma went for her paternal house with her brother. Sachin requested Abhay also to be with them but it was not possible for Abhay to join them right then as he had many pending jobs and also had to apply for leave in the office. He promised Sachin that within next two to three days he will complete all his pending jobs and also apply for leave in his office and certainly will come there. In a small village this type of private incidents becomes public very easily. Next morning all the women from the neighboring families came to solace Uma on the eve of her journey back to her paternal house in Purulia.

For the next one week life was too tiresome and hectic for Abhay. In one side he had to complete and deliver all the pending business assignments to his clients and on the other side he had to manage his office jobs including a leave. Abhay was not a veteran in the office yet, so he was not entitled for a leave more than three days at a stretch as per the office rule. Whereas he need a leave for at least five to seven days. He actually had planned to visit not only his in-laws house but also at the same time to spend some days with his own parents and other members of his family as after joining his job he had spent almost an year here and had not have any chance to visit his native village so far. So to get the approval for his leave application Abhay had to manage many things including working overtime for four days to satisfy his boss.

Finally in a Wednesday he came to Sundar's father to inform him that early in the next morning he will be going to Purulia. May I come in dada? Abhay asked permission before entering the room. Sundar's father was seating in the drawing room with his business related documents when he found Abhay asking for his permission to come in from the door. Please come in Abhay, you are nothing less than a member of my family, Sundar's father replied to Abhay.

While Abhay entered the room, Brijendra gestured him to take his seat. Comforting himself on the chair Abhay wait until Brijendra raised his face from the Business documents and asked him, tell me what you have come for. Dada as you already know Uma has gone to see her father, tomorrow early in the morning I am also setting out for Purulia, Abhay informed Sundar's father while seating on the chair in the opposite side of the table. By the way how is your father-in-law now, do you have any news, Brijendra asked Abhay. Abhay shook his head to show that he does not have any news from there. When will you return from there? Atanu who was seating there and helping his brother asked his friend. Actually I have planned to visit Uma's father first and will stay there for two days and then I will go to my native place, Abhay replied. He added, there I will stay for two to three days more as I have been out of my village for almost a year. And if everything goes as planned then will return by next Thursday, Abhay completed. So when are you starting tomorrow? Sundar's father asked Abhay. Abhay turned his face from his friend to Brijendra and replied, I have planned to catch the first train towards Burdwan which is at three thirty in the morning so that I could reach Purulia early. You have worked overtime last night so will it be possible for you to catch the first train? Why don't you take the next train? Sundar's father suggested Abhay. Dada the problem is the next train is after two hours from the first one, he paused for a moment and continued, and when I will reach Burdwan there will be no connecting train from there to my native place so I will have to wait in the platform. The second train will take two more hours compared to the first one to travel the same distance, Abhay replied.

Okay as you think better, you are more conversant than any of us in this regards, Sundar's father replied smilingly. Abhay requested him and Atanu to take care of his house in his absence. The next day, i.e. Thursday was weekly off for the business for Brijendra and every week on that day he used to visit his suppliers in Kolkata. He was busy on his business related accounting jobs as next day he will have to make payments to his suppliers, order for new stocks and manage the existing inventory so on and so forth. So he could not discuss the matter with Abhay for long and directed Atanu, who was helping him, you go with Abhay and take care if he needs any help. Atanu accompanied Abhay and also asked Satyendra, the eldest brother of Sundar to be with them in case any help is needed.

Reaching at Abhay's house Atanu and Satyendra found three big metal trunks filled with printed papers were in the corner of a room. What he will do with these trunks full of papers, Atanu asked Abhay. Ohhh those trunks, Abhay looked at the trunks and said, I had an order from one of my clients from Burdwan, so I thought that I will deliver the items to my client as I will have some time between the connecting trains. This will not only save my expenditure of sending those materials there and also two jobs will be done at one go, Abhay replied. But the question is how you will carry all these heavy trunks to the station tomorrow that too so early in the morning when there will even be no porter, Atanu asked Abhay. His worriedness for his friend was visible from his expression. Abhay looked worried too thinking deeply about what Atanu just said, as he have not gave any thought about it and now it is too late to arrange something. Actually I have missed this point, but is there any way out now? Abhay asked for help. He paused for a moment and then added, I think you are correct, I need some porters. But how porters could be arranged now, Abhay asked Atanu. Atanu replied, let me check if some of those porters could be arranged who work at our stores. Atanu turned towards his nephew and directed Satyendra, you go to the godown right now and see if at least one or two of them could be agreed. Satyendra went out and came back within half an hour with three porters.

Tomorrow morning you will come here and take one trunk each to the station, Atanu directed those porters. Remember Abhay babu will take the first train at half past three and you must be here sharp at three, Atanu explained, you will be paid separately for this job. The porters in unison assured Atanu that they will do the job and also will also maintain the punctuality as directed by him.

After completing all required job when Atanu and Satyendra came back it was nearly the time for dinner. Sundar's father asked Atanu about the status and Atanu narrated in details that he and Satyendra have done all the necessary things and tomorrow Abhay will not face any problem in his journey. Sundar's father appreciated and asked them to join the dinner.

After dinner Atanu and Sarojini went to their portion of the house with their son Noni. Sundar's father used to sleep in one of the two rooms in his portion and all the four brothers Satyendra, Narendra, Mukunda and Sundar used to sleep in the other room. The second room was adjacent to the lane connecting their house with the house of their Abhay uncle. Suddenly in the middle of the night a hissing voice broke through Sundar's sleep. He woke up and found Narendra, was calling Satyendra. He was talking in a mild voice and trying to draw the attention of Satyendra, the eldest of the four brothers, Dada, dada please wake up, listen to the sound of the footsteps in the lane. Satyendra did not wake up. Narendra again tried and this time pushed his elder brother. Satyendra was in deep sleep and was in no mood to entertain his brother. Why are you disturbing me in the middle of the night? Tomorrow I will certainly complain to father on this, after a long try Satyendra wake up in a typical drowsy mood and said to Narendra. Please listen carefully, there are some sounds coming from the lane, Narendra tried his best to make his brother understand that there must be something wrong is going on. As if some metallic items colliding with each other, Narendra drew Satyendra's attention towards the sound of people walking in the lane adjacent to their room and at the same time there were very low but still audible whispering sounds of some people talking to each other. Sundar's eyes were moving from one his elder brother to the other.

Satyendra did not even try to listen to what his brother Narendra was actually pointing to and with the same drowsy condition told, don't worry Abhay uncle is going to Purulia. Narendra again tried to draw the attention of his elder brother by mentioning the metallic sounds. This time Satyendra almost furiously replied, I personally with Atanu uncle have done the arrangements in the evening and if you still have any doubt then you can personally go and check. He paused and added, but if you disturb me again any more then it will surely be the worst for you, this time Satyendra became angry with Narendra and bitterly uttered. Narendra was neither mature enough to go and check personally nor he was sure enough to approach his father so late at night, so he silently back tracked. He looked at Sundar who was silently looking at and listening to the conversation between two of his elder brothers. Narendra thought for a while whether he should take Sundar with him but then he thought that he himself is young and Sundar is even younger and finally decided not to venture the risk outside. The kids fall asleep within some minutes.

After sometimes a hue and cry drew their attention and it was enough to wake up all the brother. Dada, dada, please wake up, I have been looted, it was Atanu's voice and he was calling his elder brother. Within two to three minutes they also heard the voice of their father talking to Atanu. The boys came outside their room and found Atanu was telling their father, dada I have been looted, thieves had stolen everything from my house. He was almost crying. Sarojini was also standing there with her son Noni on her hand.

How have you entered not only this portion of the house but also have reached up to my room, Sundar's father asked Atanu? He paused for a moment and then added in a low voice as if he was saying something to himself, the door in between was closed from this side. It was a question nobody thought about before but this question created a shivering temptation. Ohhh God, we have been crushed, Brijendra almost screamed and both Sundar's father and Atanu ran towards their drawing room where they kept the money from the business, which they will have to pay to their suppliers the next day. Satyendra, Narendra, Mukunda and Sundar, all followed them. The damage was done, the lock was broken and the door was wide open. Most shockingly the metallic wardrobe in which Sundar's father used to keep the cash from his business, was totally broken and looted brutally. Another metal trunks in which the family ornaments and other valuables were kept was also looted and lying empty in a corner of the room. In a straight and simple ward, every single valuable and costly thing was ransacked. Sundar reached there after all his elder brothers and found his father seating on the ground of the room speechlessly and his uncle Atanu was nearly at a stage of crying. Listening to this hue and cry the neighbors arrived and more surprisingly Abhay uncle too was there.

You are still here now? Have you not left for your scheduled train? Narendra approached Abhay uncle and asked him. NO son, the porters Satyendra arranged yesterday have not yet arrived and I have missed the first train and have no other option but to take the next train, Abhay replied.

Narendra returned to his elder brother Satyendra and just said, Abhay uncle was going to Purulia, right?

Satyendra did not look up and in a timid voice replied, how did I know?

I told you but you were so overconfident that you did not even bother to listen to me once, Narendra replied.

Everyone present there was busy in calling the police or consoling Brijendra and Atanu. Nobody heard what the two young boys were talking about in such an unforeseen situation, except another younger one, Sundar, who was standing behind his elder brothers.

The Boy Had His Mother ...

Good boys always abide by their mother, I promise tomorrow I will bring fish for you, Sukanya uttered to her elder son. She added, today please you eat what we have. It was nearly 3 PM and Sukanya was trying to manage her elder son Rajan, who have just returned from his school and was seating with his lunch. The plate had four things in it, some rise, some mush of boiled potato, a piece of onion and a pinch of salt. She knew very well that tomorrow when Rajan will ask for the fish or something better she had just committed, then there will be no other way for her but to make another excuse to the kid. Sukanya understands that for a 6 years old boy it's more than pathetic to eat rice and boiled potato almost every day, but how would she arrange something better in such a condition is the biggest question without any answer in front of her.

You promised yesterday also but you have not bring it today, Rajan complain to his mother reminding her the same promise she made to him yesterday. I remind son but today I was so busy that I could not go to the market, Sukanya replied, tomorrow I will surely go and bring something for you, today please manage with this, Sukanya said and started comforting her son by the palm leaf made hand fan. At the same time she tried her best to resist her tears from coming out. Okay, but tomorrow I will not eat if you don't keep your promise, Rajan replied and started his lunch. Hunger is perhaps always more important than promises made. I knew, you are my good son, Sukanya console her son with a smile. Sometimes even false promises gives so much of enthusiasm and peace of mind that even at the toughest situation of your life you will be more than happy to fight with the situation and feel that there is at least one person in the world who cares for you, who feels for you, who cries for the pain and agony you feel, who would extend even beyond limits to arrange the maximum possible for you and most importantly who does this just because of one thing which is called affection.

Many scenes were coming in to her mind. Poverty is not very new thing for her. She is from a poor family and witnessed scarcity all through her life from childhood but situation was not as helpless as it has become in last one year. She still reminds the day when she got married to Anjan, a daily wage laborer, and left her father's home to live with Anjan in this one room mud house. Anjan was poor but very hardworking and caring husband. There was inadequacies but life was nice. After two years of their married life Rajan came in to their world as a happiness. Sukanya still remind Anjan's passion when at the final days of her pregnancy she was invited by her parents to live some days in her paternal house so that she could get some relief from the day to day household jobs. Anjan denied and promised that he will not let Sukanya do any household job unless she becomes fit for that. He kept his words and for next three months he managed both the household and his daily work in fact more efficiently than his wife itself. If you would have been a girl then certainly you would have been much better a housewife than I am, Sukanya even used to tease her husband seating in a corner of the room. In one such instance she asked Anjan, how do you manage both your daily work and the household job so competently? Anjan in reply just smiled and said, don't worry, if you just love someone then you could also carry all the duties and responsibilities exactly like I am doing these for you. In that instance Sukanya mocked him but now a pale smile appeared in her lips. You were true, exactly true, she uttered to herself within her mind.

Mom give me some water please, Rajan intrude in to Sukanya's stream of thoughts. Yes son, surely. Sukanya stood up and moved to the other end of the small room where the waterskin was kept. She came back with a glass of water for her son in few moments. Rajan after some sips again concentrated on his lunch.

Past moments again gathered to round Sukanya's mind. For the first time in her married life she witnessed tears in Anjan's eyes when he took his son in his hand for the first time. The way he adored Sukanya, is still alive in her mind. Rajan was a boy of two years when Anjan and Sukanya became parents of their second child, Debashish. This time Sukanya was not ready to put the burden again on Anjan's shoulders. When I have done for my first child then I will do exactly the same for my second one, Sukanya reminds the way Anjan argued with her to not let her go. I know you will but my parents also want to feel the pleasure of nurturing their grandchildren and this time I request you to allow them to enjoy that, she managed with such an emotional logic to agree Anjan to let her go to her father's home with Rajan for few months. Though initially Anjan was not ready but finally agreed with his wife and one day went to his in-law's house to keep his wife and son there for few months. He came back next day. Every week Anjan used to visit Sukanya and his son once. Life was scarce but Anjan's love made it fulfilled and it was just like a dream came true for Sukanya.

In due course of time Sukanya mothered her second son, Debashish. So now we need to have another room in the house, otherwise it will be tough in near future, seeing his son Anjan said to his wife with a smile on his lips.

Monsoon came within few weeks and Anjan got busier in his work. This is the time that gives the most income to any daily laborer in a year. Anjan started working from sunrise to sunset to earn some more money this year so that he could finance to build up the second room in his house. But the dream did not come true. One day while returning from field in the evening Anjan lost his life in a venomous snake bite. The neighbors tried their best with the local thaumaturgy but nothing worked. When the news reached Sukanya it was too late. It took two more hours for her to return to her destroyed life in her house with her two sons. Anjan's lifeless body was lying on the ground surrounded by the fellow villagers.

Sukanya was changed. A softhearted, casual and romantic young girl at her early twenties died with Anjan that day. A strong, determined and tough mother was born who is not allowed to give up at any point of time and situation. The struggle was begun from that very moment. She became more than determined to fight the war of life with all her capabilities and strength against all the odds yet to come. She started trying her best with keeping her honor and dignity intact to make her two sons educated. She started working in other affluent houses of that village as a housemaid. Not that only but whenever she got some time after such entire day's hard works, she started to make paper packets which she used to supply to the shopkeepers of the local village market to earn a bit more to bring up and take care of her two beloved responsibilities – Rajan and Debashish. Words like relaxation or rest vanished from her dictionary.

With her gargantuan mental métier and fortitude she never got tired, she never got frustrated, she fought briskly and never showed her back to the challenges she faced.

ON THE OTHER SIDE OF THE VILLAGE

I told you not to finish all the oranges yesterday but you did not care and now we have nothing today, Patru accused his elder brother.

How do I know that they will deploy guards for the mango trees? I thought today we will have access there, Biswa replied with a visible expression of guilt of not understanding on his face. Let us search a bit more, I am sure we will find something somewhere here or there, he added.

"We will find something somewhere here or there", Patru mocked Biswa. You may enjoy touring in hungry stomach but sorry to say I don't, Patru replied almost bullying his brother.

Would you guys please stop fighting or should I leave, Sundar asked to both oh his peers. He added, let us see if we could arrange something. The quarreling brothers ignored each other and followed Sundar. After searching for sometimes in various potential places the boys incidentally found some coconuts in a tree.

I think these are the only option we have today, Sundar spoke to the two. Biswa and Patru both nodded in agreement. Sundar stared at Biswas and requested, only you know how to climb a coconut tree amongst us, so it's your turn now. Biswas acknowledged and moved towards the tree. The strongest and eldest of amongst those three musketeers Biswa started climbing the tree to get some of those coconuts. The rest two, that is Sundar and Patru kept waiting under the tree at a safe distance and watching for if anyone comes or was near.

Sundar, by now a boy of 10 years has finished his primary education and started going to the high school. He is almost free to do whatever he thinks good for himself and there is absolutely none either to guide or to rebuke him. Now what he feels is good to do, he is free to in his life. Sundar is now much more mature than any other boy of his age. Life has matured him to that extent. The more he is growing up he is becoming a boy who talks not only less than expected from a boy of his age, rather only when he is directly asked to talk. He has learnt to camouflage his emotions and feelings in within his mind and not to express those in front of any one, whether a friend or any of his family members. The only time his eyes burn when every night he somehow manage some time to go to the roof top to look at the sky and find out the star that his Sarojini aunty showed him years back. The star that aunty told him his mother has become. He tries to remind whether he has ever spoken to his mother or mother has spoken to him. He asks himself what could be the words that his mother had uttered to him. How she used to pamper him or even how she had taken him in her hands? He knows there is no one whom he could ask all these questions except Sarojini aunty but he always had failed to approach her to ask these questions. Many times from many senior ladies of this village he has heard that his mother was a very beautiful and respected woman but he had been afraid of asking them anything more about his mother. He indeed has portrayed a sketch of his mother in his mind but had never tried to verify the accuracy of his thoughts from anyone on this earth.

In the school Sundar has also got two classmates from the contiguous village, Biswa and Patru, two brothers. Though Biswa is some years elder than Patru but they were in the same class. The two brothers have become very close aids of Sundar. They were also from a poor family and sometimes it is very natural and evident that someone's economic status automatically makes him or her a friend with people from the same status and it specially happens in the childhood when you get to understand the divergences of bare feet and feet with shoes or no lunch box and a lunch box in the school bag or same pair of shirt and pant every day at school with changing pairs.

After returning from school that three musketeers used to threw their school bags at home and get out of there in search of coconuts or oranges or papayas whatever were available and suitable to eat in the nearby areas, not because of having somc fun but to fulfil their day long hunger. Yes because of satisfying their hunger after whole day at school, because there was no one in the family to arrange for a plate of rise at home for Sundar. There was no one to wait for that 10 years old boy with a welcome smile on lips and affection in mind back there at home. There was no one to say "come, first seat and eat something then go to play, you must be hungry after whole day at school" or "this is what I have managed for today, eat this and I promise tomorrow I will arrange something better or tasty for you". Sometimes even false promises are much more than no promises at all.

In one of such beautiful hungry afternoon Sundar and two of his friends Biswa and Patru after returning from school and leaving their school bags at home was roaming in the village and adjacent areas in search of anything available and eatable. You keep watching that side, I am taking care of this one, Patru uttered to Sundar pointing his finger to the right side. Sundar nodded and turned his eyes towards his responsibility.

While watching suddenly Sundar's eyes fall on a scene which was present in his eyes even after four or five decades from that day. Actually he never forgot that. Just like them Rajan was also back from school and at the porch of their mud house he was seating on a straw mattress. He was looking like waiting for someone or something and the doors of the only room of that house was half open. Biswa was a seasoned climber and within next few minutes he dropped two or three coconuts from the tree. Now it's the job of the other two to collect the fruits as quick as possible within the time Biswa climbs down. In the meantime Patru called Sundar and asked, Sundar please help me to collect the coconuts. He added, Biswa has dropped at least three from the tree top. Sundar's concentration shifted from Rajan to Patru and he joined his friend in collecting their prizes for that day. He looked at the tree and found that after completing his job Biswa was climbing down. He started collecting the coconuts.

Biswa climbed down to the ground and the three musketeers with their prizes got out of the garden and moved for a safer place where they could peacefully consume the fruits without any interventions. Within few minutes they reached their favorite place, a small area covered with deep bushes behind the house where Rajan lives with his mother and brother.

How would we peel these, Patru asked Sundar? We need something to crust the coconuts, bare hand this no way possible, remarked Sundar. So they started thinking and finally Biswa requested Sundar, ask for a dagger from Rajan, as it was the nearest house and you are also well known to his mother. Sundar thought for a moment and then decided to go to Rajan's house to ask for a dagger. Opening the front fence gate he was just thinking of calling Rajan and his eyes attracted towards Rajan, seating on a straw mattress at the porch of their mud house with a plate in front of him containing only some rice and a boiled potato. He was eating that with highest possible satisfaction and his mother, that poor noble lady was seating in front of her son with a palm leaf fan in her hand and blowing it slowly to comfort her son. She was telling Rajan something indeed. What she was telling to her son Sundar could not listen to but he stared at that mother and son for some times without speaking a single word. Actually he was not able to speak because he was looking at something which he desired for whole of his life knowing the truth that he will never get it, he will never get his mother back, he will not be able any more to make the first ever call a child makes – "Ma". The call that gives you all your joy, the call that gives you relief from all your pain, the call that comes automatically at all your happiness. He kept watching for some moments without being noticed by any of those whom he was watching and then he silently came out of that home without asking for anything. He forgot to ask for the dagger, he forgot the terrible hunger that was killing him just some moments before.

Where have you been for so long? Where is the dagger? Patru asked Sundar.

I could not ask for anything, Sundar replied.

Now how would we crust the coconut? Patru asked again.

Biswa sensed something unusual looking at Sundar's face. He raised his hand to stop his younger brother from asking any more question and then he asked very politely to his friend, anything wrong with you Sundar?

Sundar did not raise his eyes from the ground. You know Biswa, today I realized I don't have "Ma". Sundar continued, you know Biswa, today I have realized seeing Rajan and his mother that a child even from the poorest family lives a human's life even if that child loses his father but a child from even the richest family will hardly live a human's life if he loses his mother. Biswa and Patru was not only shocked but speechless. They have been knowing Sundar for long but first time ever they are realizing the agony of their friend. First time ever they are witnessing their friend losing the battle to stop the droplets to come out from his eyes.

ONE IS ENOUGH FOR ...

You are really leaving your studies for ever and will never ever return to the school? Sundar asked Biswa staring at his friend with sheer astonishment. He still could not believe what he has just listened from Biswa himself. He could not believe his own ears. Patru also did not say anything to Sundar and stood with his head down. Sundar, Biswa and Patru were returning home from school when all of a sudden Biswa has declared some moments ago that he is leaving his studies and joining a job from tomorrow. That verse was enough to stop Sundar from walking and asking his mind. Biswa and Patru had also stopped by the road and now was standing beside Sundar.

Yah, Biswa's answer was short and clearly depicting that he does not want to talk on this matter anymore. He did not even looked at Sundar and fixed his eyes on the ground with his head down while answering. He has become tired of answering the same questions for uncountable number of times to various people including teachers and friends. If this would have been anyone except Sundar he would have ignored the question in fact, but Sundar is not merely a friend but rather a childhood soul mate. He can't ignore him or avoid to answer his question, irrespective of the subject which might even be something Biswa hate to discuss. Though his answer was the minimum required but his facial expression was telling the tale clearly that he himself even not very optimistic with this decision but anyway he is bound to follow this.

But, my question is why now when we are just two years from our final school leaving exam, Sundar asked with the same surprise in his eyes as well as in his voice? He added, you would certainly pass the exam as far as I know you. Your preparations are also up to the mark, even our teachers said that in the class. Why can't you wait for just two more years Biswa? Sundar unknowingly touched the most paining chord in Biswas's mind. Till the decision was finally burdened on his shoulder by his father he had argued on the same point with his father. But unfortunately there was none to listen to him. This time Biswa could not hold his temper back in within and almost screamed more on his own frustration than on the questioner. Because I have a good developed and strong physic that looks like an adult and fortunately or unfortunately I am the eldest son in the family, he did not stop and continued, so such a strong and capable boy should not waste his time and energy by going to school and spending the whole day there by studying books. He paused for a while and continued, but this time with a lower voice and controlled emotion, rather it is very much evident that the boy will help the family to earn its bread and butter. Why don't you understand and keep on questioning? Biswa turned his eyes from Sundar and stared at the other side and uttered, yes Sundar, I am leaving my studies, and yes just before two years of my final school leaving examination which I am confident that I could pass with an honorable results. Does it make any difference to anyone on this planet? Biswa stopped, he was breathing intently.

Both Sundar and Patru was shattered by such devastating reply from Biswa. They have never seen this attitude of their friend before. Biswa had always been a silent and well-mannered boy and generally never loses his temper even on many other much more important or serious matters. Biswa himself has also understood that his unmanaged behavior has shocked not only his childhood companion but his own younger brother also. He stopped for a while, breadth deep to manage his anger and sat down under a tree beside the road they were returning through. Sundar and Patru stared at each other and followed Biswa silently.

For some moments none of them uttered even a single word and then Biswa first broke the silence. Sundar, nothing is hidden to you. You are well aware of the economic condition of our family. Biswa paused for a moment and continued, there are seven mouths including myself, my brothers and sisters and my mother and only two hands to feed them. My father is a porter in the nearest railway workshop and use to carry the wooden or iron made sleepers for the railway track from one place to another, which are necessary for regular maintenance of the track. You know those wooden or iron made sleeper are so heavy that it required two porters to carry one sleeper from one to another place on their shoulders in the track. Do you know how much he earns after such a bone breaking day long work? Not even enough to arrange a daily proper square meal for all the members of the family. By the way, by the word "proper" I meant just one vegetable item with a plate of rice, Biswa paused with a line of smile on his lips and then again continued, we all in the family are well aware of all these. Now in such a tough and terrible condition that man, my father wants me, his eldest son to share his shoulder with him to carry the burden. Is this something you call tremendous expectation? At least I can't say that. Sundar I always keep one thing in my mind that there are people blessed by the God that they see only the better side of life but unfortunately everyone is not so blessed. In my situation, rather in our situation we have three choices, either we could die or we could escape but I am a strong man and would not die or escape so easily but I will even fight with the destiny for my rights and I promise that I will defeat destiny to take care of my family". Sundar was speechless, he looked at Patru.

Don't worry brother, I will be there to be with you in next two years, Patru said. His eyes were moist.

No, a strong and bold voiced reply came from Biswa. The other two was surprised. He replied to his brother with burning eyes, every one of us will not sacrifice for the same cause. You will have to complete your studies at any cost. I am doing my duty and you will have to perform yours. One of us will has to stand out to prove that we were capable of changing our destiny if a single chance would have been offered to us. And even without any such offer we will defeat destiny to prove ourselves.

There was silence, pin drop silence. For some more time the three sat there but no one had anything to talk about and then they slowly stood up to return home.

Next day Sundar and Patru started for school without the third of the group and in the entire journey they did not speak to each other, actually both of them was missing Biswa. Just before entering the gate of the school Sundar asked Patru, when Biswa left today in the morning? Patru raised his eyes and replied, nearly at half past eight in the morning. After that none of them talked anything about Biswa the entire day. The class, the playground, the return journey, in fact everything was incomplete to Sundar and Patru.

On the other side Biswa was indeed stronger than and healthier than any normal young man at his zenith of youth. The railway sleepers that used to be so heavy that it required two porters to carry one sleeper from one to another place on the track. Biswa was so strong that when he was given the job to carry one wooden sleeper with another labor he first tried to lift that on his own and successfully lifted and carried the same to the destination point without taking help from his partner. So in that instance he became a "good laborer" to the contractor who offered Biswa a pay of one and a half times more than any general porter. It became a win – win contract for both of them, the contractor was happy that he is making a profit of half of a porter's payment and Biswa was also happy of getting 1.5 times pay for the job he was doing very easily.

AFTER SOME MOTHS

Life has thrashed Sundar tremendously in between. He has suffered from a deadly typhoid. Sundar has become so feeble these days that he was not even capable of walking for long on his own. He has spent nearly six to seven months on the bed and fought with the lethal disease just with the help of medicines offered from the local health center free of cost. Nobody expected that the tiny boy would make it possible to revive from the typhoid. Nobody in fact was interested even about his fate instead. But sometimes your destiny proves everyone wrong and establish something unbelievable and we the people call it miracle. It was absolutely miraculous that Sundar revived. He lost all his possessions except life within these few months.

After recovering, Sundar now is so weak physically that he was no way in a condition to play in the ground with others or go faraway places from home with his friends. Every afternoon he used to walk 300 meters from his ancestral house with all his strengths to come to the bank of the small stream passing by their village and seat there looking forward aimlessly just to spend some time out of the clumsy room and that bedding on the floor which had been almost an integral part of his life for past few months. Patru used to accompany him and update him regarding various events happened that day especially in the school. He also share his notes and other study materials with Sundar which in fact is a great help for the boy. Biswa used to join them often, if only he is back from his job a bit earlier than normal. Life was unbearable but Sundar was stubborn to win the battle.

It was the winter of that year and the time of the worship of the Goddess Saraswati, the Hindu Goddess of knowledge and wisdom, which generally happens in the month of late January or early February. Every school in India and especially in Bengal organizes the worship of the Goddess at school and generally the students of standard ninth or eleventh are given the responsibilities of the arrangements as because the students of standard tenth and twelfth are usually busy with their forthcoming final board exam in the month of March. In the day of the worship all the students come to school in the morning as early as possible and spend the day in worshiping Goddess Saraswati. Finally lunch is being provided to the students by the school authority and after lunch they return to their home back with hope and belief in mind that this year Goddess Saraswati will surely bless them with great marks and particularly in those subjects, which they are weak in.

This year Sundar and Patru was in standard ninth and their batch was responsible for organizing the event this year. It was not possible for Sundar to attend school or to take part in those activities, so for him Patru was the only source of updated information about this year's planning as well as what are being done and how. Everyday seating on the bank of the small stream Sundar use to ask Patru about every bits and pieces about what is going on in the school regarding the event and Patru use to depict everything in details to his friend. As if Sundar was living those enjoying moments of student's through his friend.

In one such day excitedly they were discussing about the upcoming event, seating in place where they used to meet in the evening when a voice intruded in to their discussion.

So what are you people arranging for lunch this time? Sundar sensed a manly palm on his shoulder. It is Biswa.

Luchi and Alu Dum, Patru replied instantly with a smile of pride on his face as generally Khichdi is arranged but this year they had managed to arrange Luchi and Alu Dum, one of the most beautiful and tasty Bengali delicacy and combination of food that not only delicious but also there is hardly any Bengali on this planet who does not fond of. You know how many times we have to go the head master and all the other teachers to get the permission from them and what kind of efforts we have put in to manage such a huge expense to replace the same boring Khichdi with such delicious food items, Patru was more interested to describe boastfully the level of achievement that the students of their batch have achieved.

There is no doubt that these items are far more expensive than normal Khichdi and used to be very rare collection in the meal of any poor family. So it was a lucrative thing for Biswa not only because he loved to eat but as he hardly had the affordability to arrange the same foods on his own. See I know presently I am not a student of the school and should not be part of the lunch but as you are the organizing batch so could you afford me for the lunch, he could not resist himself from asking this to his friends?

Obviously, why not? After all you were also a student just some days back, Sundar replied. Neither Sundar nor Patru even think twice whether it will be permissible or not and decided that they will take Biswa with them. As per Sundar and Patru the logic was very simple, as Biswa is a friend of their so if to anything they have right, then Biswa should also has. So it became obvious that they will take Biswa with them in the lunch. Perhaps real friendship is more valuable than any dam thing in this universe. At least boys like Sundar and Patru who have not yet been polluted by the sense of profit and loss thought that.

THE EVENTFUL DAY

Finally the day came, Sundar and Patru started for school in the morning. Sundar was walking with the support of his friend and Patru to support Sundar was walking slowly. It was decided beforehand that Biswa will attend his job earlier than his usual time and complete his tasks before the lunch time and will come directly at the school from his workplace so that he won't have to bunk his job and sacrifice his one day's income. In the lunch time he will join the other two at the school gate where the duo will wait for him. Sundar had to take several breaks for resting in between the walk of almost a mile. Finally when they reached at the school the worship was just started. The two attended the event and waited for the time when the third of the team will come as they will have to go to the main gate so that Biswa don't face any problem to find them out in the gathering of the students.

There he is, Sundar pointed his finger to draw the attention of Patru. They were standing by the main gate of the school as per planning. Sorry huh, a bit late due to work pressure, Biswa said to his friends. I though you people might have entered the school after waiting so long for me, he added expressing his gratitude.

It's absolutely okay, Sundar replied with a supporting smile on his lips. He then added, don't waste any more time standing here. Let us move to the dinning straight way and the boys moved in.

The lunch was started and the boys had to wait a little for the present batch to complete their lunch. When the new batch starts they sat together in one corner and within a few minutes the delicious luchi and Alu Dum was served to them. As usual Biswa started his performance. The head master was monitoring the event as the guardian of the school so that everything be properly managed and no boy left dissatisfied about anything and some other teachers were helping him. As if it was his duty to feed each and every boy of his school appropriately with best care and affection. The other teachers who were also present there and were taking note of everything minutely. They were inspiring all the boys to eat as much as possible to them. Students were no way less than the own children of the teachers those days and the teachers were no less than the most honorable guardian to those students too. The students also were trying to prove their capacity to the teachers to be appreciated.

Biswa while eating was not satisfied with the lack of promptness of the boys who were serving. He was eating faster than any other boy in the hall and was actually getting idle very frequently due to lack of the speed in serving. So he had to seat idle with bare plate in front of him and was getting irritated also. At the same time while monitoring, the head master also noticed that one boy in the group is eating much more than others and that too very fast and also with tremendous an affection for the food. He also noticed that the boys who were serving were giving four luchis at a time to everyone but that boy was actually completing those four luchis in less than half of the time taken by other boys and many a time he was seating idle with nothing in his plate and due to that was getting irritated. Why are you seating idle? The head master approached to Biswa slowly and asked him.

How long will it take to eat four luchis sir? They are giving only four at a time, Biswa replied. The next question the head master asked was dreadful not only for Biswa but for his other two of his companions. By the way, which class are you from? Then suddenly he recognized his past student and said, hey you are Biswa, right.

The three started looking at each other. Other boys were also staring at what was happening. The three had no answer for the question. Sir actually he was a student until last year but not a present one, but he is a very good friend of ours and that's why we have taken him with us in the school, finally Sundar stood up and replied. Both Biswa and Patru had also stood up with pale face and fear in mind that the head master will surely rebuke them and punish for this immensely wrong job. In the hall it was a pin drop silence, as if all the boys were just waiting for the tsunami which is going to strike any time now. The other teachers were also speechless and watching what the decision the head master takes.

The head master looked at Sundar and replied, you don't need to say anything. He paused and added, I know my students, both past and present. He then placed his hands one on Sundar's and the other on Patru's shoulder and with appreciating voice said, I am proud of your friendship and truthfulness. Then he turned and looked at Biswa and smiled. Seat down and complete the lunch, he directed the three boys calmly. Serve not four but ten luchis at a time in his plate, he called the boys who were serving and directed them pointing his figure to Biswa. Then he turned at Biswa and said, today I will see how many luchis you can eat. As if the entire hall breathe out and started enjoying the show. Though no one actually counted the number but Biswa certainly did not stop before at least fifty to sixty luchis and when he finished of his show the head master told him to come again in the next year and the other students – see that is what I expect from all of you.

Now after such a great performance the trio were headed towards their homes with highest satisfaction and joy. They were more than happy and discussing the day's events. This time Sundar was walking with the support of Biswa in one side and Patru on the opposite. They were joyfully discussing that day's event. But suddenly the condition changed. Sundar and Patru stopped seeing one of their old foe Shyama coming from the opposite side of the road with his friends. Shyama was a student of the same school and was going to school with his friends. They were seven or eight in number. Just before some days Shyama was packed down by Patru in the football ground and in that point itself he promised that one day he will avenge that. They were all from the well to do families of the locality and nearby. In the meantime they had also seen Patru and the other two. The three musketeers were so deeply involved in their discussion of the day that they have not even noticed the people coming. Now the distance between was such that it was not even possible for them to run away. Even Patru could have tried running but for Sundar it was no way possible to run in such physical condition. He was so feeble that he had to seat after standing for half an hour at a stretch.

What happened to both of you? Why have you stopped walking suddenly? Are you feeling tired? Biswa was actually unknown about the football ground issue so he thought Sundar might be tired. Patru and Sundar told him about the incident in as brief as possible. Biswa thought for a second and replied – don't be afraid, come with me, I will see. In the while the other team had approached the trio and Shyama came a step further and asked him, now who will rescue you? Do you remind the day?

Biswa came forward, it was his call now. He replied Shyama, if you have courage then come one by one. He paused and added, and make a deal if anyone is down once he will accept the defeat and will not fight again.

Shyama looked at Biswa, though he was a bit doubtful as he knew Biswa beforehand but then it is a matter of prestige so there was no turning back. He accepted.

Shyama was down very soon by Biswa. Then one by one all the other boys tried and eventually shared the same fate of Shyama. But they kept their promise and once down no one came to the field again. Now when all the seven or eight were down and finally accepted defeat, Patru came forward and made the million dollar comment to them. He stood in front of Shyama and uttered with a boastful attitude, see one of us is enough for you, we two have not even participated, and then with a tremendous winners' attitude asked Sundar and Biswa, let's go home.

THE SWEET DISH … …

Everyone will now start running with me and complete five circles of the ground without any break and after that we all will return to the Akhara to practice, the middle aged man uttered with a heavy voice and unmatched personality to the teenagers of the village and other nearby areas standing surrounding the man. He paused for a moment, stared at Sundar and added with comparatively milder voice, you will complete only two circles as you are not yet fit for five. Then he turned to the other boys again and announced with the previous heavy voice, don't disremember that the tournament is going to be announced very shortly and like previous years we have to defeat everyone to be the champion again. The tall and muscularly built man directed his young students. Everyone including Sundar nodded and followed their trainer Madhab Chandra Chatterjee.

This is perhaps one of the two most important things of Madhab Chandra's life, Bodybuilding and Wrestling. The other thing that drives his life and keep him happy is good and tasty foods. He also has a vow of bachelorhood for throughout his life and is utmost serious about keeping his vow stand out. His family people, mainly consists of his elder sister and sister-in-law, tried many times for his consent for marriage but every time they had to return with bare hands and finally out of sheer frustration when they got to understand that there is absolutely no way to agree Madhab Chandra, they dropped their idea and left Madhab with his vow. As per Madhab firstly a feeble man is even worse than anything in this universe, so the parents of each and every boy must inspire their son in body building and wrestling. He always used to say that, secondly to have energy for the first you need to eat a lot of foods. You must remember a week young generation is the reason behind a week nation.

After the deadly typhoid Sundar had joined Madhab uncle's Akhara and within few days due to his discipline and dedication has become a dear student to his trainer. Madhab also feel sad for the feeble boy and his loneliness. Sundar's trainer also trying his best and encouraging Sundar that very soon Sundar will certainly overcome the weaknesses if he keep on practicing with the same effort.

MADHAB CHANDRA CHATTERJEE

I was thinking to take Madhab with us in our house, but only if you think this would be proper, Krishna Chandra was seating on the chair by the window when his wife Surobala intruded in to his thoughts. It was late in the evening and dark outside. Krishna Chandra was lost in his thoughts as he has been here in his in-law's house for almost last one week leaving all his business back there in his place. His mother in-law was at her death bed and yesterday she had passed away. Krishna Chandra raised his eyes and looked at his wife with a querying sight. The same though was running in his own mind also, he did not reply and kept staring at Surobala.

If you think this would not be right, in that case he will have to be here, Surobala uttered. She paused for a moment and added, but who then will take care of the child? He does not have anyone except us.

Krishna Chandra gestured his wife to come in and seat by his side. I don't understand how do you read my mind so accurately, he asked Surobala? You know, I was thinking the same thing when you arrived in the room, Krishna Chandra added with a smile on his lips. He paused for moment and completed, go and tell Madhab to pack all necessary things by tomorrow, he will be going with us day after.

Surobala thanked her husband with her eyes and almost ran out of the room to inform her younger brother.

Krishna Chandra took his only brother-in-law Madhab with him in his house at here in this village when Madhab's mother passed away and left him alone without any guardian. Madhab then was not a child as Surobala used to say about her brother but was a teenage boy of sixteen years. Krishna Chandra was respected man here in this village and also was well to do and educated. He took proper care for the education and wellbeing of his only brother-in-law. Madhab was admitted in the local school and also teachers were arranged for his private tuition. He was also an attentive boy towards studies and did not disheartened his brother-in-law and successfully completed his education. When after completing education

Krishna Chandra asked him whether he will join any job or go for higher studies, he answered, I would like to start my own business because there is always a scent of servant in any service. May be small but I will be my own boss.

Krishna Chandra did not say anything and finally Madhab joined the business of Krishna Chandra to help him as well as learning how to run a business. Within few years he learnt to business and Krishna Chandra sponsored him to start a new business in the same area. Madhab stayed in the village with his only sister and sister-in-law. He had two addictions in his life, firstly wrestling and secondly food, and in both of these two he was really a great performer.

Once Madhab started earning the first thing that he did, he established an Akhara in that village, where the young boys will learn wresting. He personally hired a trainer for the same from his own pocket. After one year on the first anniversary of the Akhara he arranged a competition. From then every year he used to organize the same wresting competition his Akhara in which many boys from different areas started to take part and that event became very famous within a short period of time in the locality. People used to wait for the competition and cheer up the boys. Madhab Chandra was actually the sole sponsor for long time of the Akhara. He always used to start his day just after dawn practicing there for hours. After practicing in the Akhara he used to go to swim in the river for nearly half an hour and then worship Bajrangbali ji and read the entire Hanuman Challisha. In the meantime he had also built a small but very beautiful temple in the house and dedicated it to Bajrangbali ji. While he practices in the Akhara and swim in the river, Surobala and the other women of the family started to work their hardest to prepare the breakfast for Madhab, which as per them is in fact more than enough for a heavy lunch for two men. The same kind of enormous arrangements the ladies had to make for four times a day for Madhab but they used to do it lovingly.

Madhab due to his muscular physic and love for games and sports was very popular and also close to the young chaps of not only his own village but also from the nearby villages. He became an idol figure for many young boys who indeed joined his Akhara with a dream of having a physic alike him. Those young boys used to dream of being their Madhab uncle. For those young boys, any kind of necessity like purchasing a football or organizing a sports event, their Madhab uncle was the first person the boys used to approach for help and truly speaking they never had to return with empty hands. So due to these kind of activities and his love for food made Madhab well-known in the locality, which in turn created a situation that whenever there was any celebration or events in any house of the locality Madhab used to be one of the important persons to be invited. Madhab too never disheartened any of his hosts in any occasion for lunch or dinner. He always used to be the showstopper and people around him not only was fond of watching him eating but also inspired and cheered for him which actually used to let him feel like a hero. Many a times Madhab also attended more than one invitation on the same day and unbelievably there is no such record which would prove that he had underperformed and disappointed his viewers in any of those invitations. Everywhere he just not only tasted rather enjoyed each and every item offered to him to the maximum possible. He was so fond of foods that winter used to be his favorite season as he always said that, marriages might be made in heaven but receptions are planned on earth and generally on winters.

THE WINTER MORNING

Today all of them had to practice under the guidance of Bhootnath da, the senior most member of the Akhara after Madhab and was almost the right-hand man for Madhab regarding any Akhara related issue. Bhootnath was no doubt a very helpful and cheerful young man but everybody missed the appearance and vocal inspirations injected by their Madhab uncle. Due to Madhab's absence today the tenure of the everyday practice was cut short and after completing their regular exercises while leaving Bhootnath said to Patru, today I will go with you to meet Madhab uncle, wait for me. Patru waited and started helping Bhootnath to rearrange the exercising equipment they have used, whereas others including Sundar also left for their home.

Sundar has just returned from the Akhara and after washing himself he was seating on the straw mattress on the roof top under the warmth of the morning sun with his books when Patru approached him almost hopping the stairways perhaps two or might be three at a time. It was clear from his deep inhalations that he was running frantically. Come with me, Madhab uncle is seriously ill, Patru anyhow conveyed the message to his friend.

It took some moments for Sundar to realize what Patru is saying. How do you know that Madhab uncle is ill? Sundar asked in reply.

My father and all others have gone to see him. Bhootnath da asked me to inform you and all others right now, Patru completed in one stretch.

Yes, I think this is true because first ever from the day I joined the Akhara, today Madhab uncle was absent in the morning and we practiced on our own,

Sundar uttered more to himself than to his friend. Let's go, the two did not waste time in waiting or discussing and started running towards Madhab Chandra's house.

THE ULTIMATE PERFORMANCE

Life for Madhab was going smoothly and absolutely as he wished for. He did not wanted to and never even tried to change himself even at the age of his late fifties. He was carrying out all his age old daily routine of wrestling in the Akhara, swimming in the river, worshiping Bajrangbali ji, reciting Hanuman Challisha for hours, organizing wrestling event in his Akhara, sponsoring various games and sports events in the locality, enjoying foods and attending invitations and finally for supporting all these he was running his business well. He never had any desire to make his business any bigger or to earn a lot. He was happy with his earning and never planned for any savings. Today in such a chilling winter day when he left his shop late in the evening he was very cheerful not because of having good businesses but the reality is on that day he received invitations for marriage reception from three of his clients. The only negligible issue was all the three was on the same day and one out of those three was in a little distant place of half an hour walking distance from his house. Other two were in his locality so he planned that he will attend the distant one first early in the evening and then the other two one after another.

After an week on the specific day of invitations Madhab Chandra kept his shop close in the second half of the day as he had to start early in the evening to attend his first invitation of the day. He started from his house as early as six o'clock in the evening so that he could complete it and come back to join the others. He reached the place as per his planned schedule.

Welcome, Madhab babu, the head of the family welcomed him at the main gate of the house. Madhab replied with a wide smile and approached in. The man guided him through the inner pathways of the house and took Madhab to the place where the program was actually going on. After initial introduction given by the head of the family to the people present there, Madhab looked forward to meet the bride and the bride-groom seating on the ceremonial chairs. He wished them fortune and prosperity, gifted them as per the custom and did not waste more than half an hour on all these formalities and courtesies and directly came to the point, i.e. the place where dining was being served to the invited guests. The head of the family personally took care and asked the serving boys to arrange a suitable place for his special guest and then asked them and said, look boys, he is my special guest. Then he turned at Madhab first and then to the boys again and directed them I will personally watch your performance and his plate should not be empty for even a moment.

Many of the boys there knew Madhab and they heartily accepted the direction and replied, don't worry uncle we will not give you any chance to complain.

Madhab smiled back to the man and sat himself down comfortably on the chair. He started slowly and humbly with the initial items, but as the time passes people started enjoying his innings unknowingly that it was his first innings for the day and he will be playing two more such all-encompassing and enormous innings just after that. The boys serving foods were mainly from various adjacent villages and Madhab was also a well-known person to them. Many of them even in the past have approached Madhab for various kinds of helps and support regarding sports activities. So they were requesting him to have some more for each and every item and Madhab did not neglect or disrespect any of those requests from his fans.

After an hour or so when he finally completed with the sweet dish it was no less than the completion of a great show. Some from the people who were enjoying the show appraised and congratulated Madhab. Some other started pushing him up by comparing some of his own previous performances with this one and was trying their best to prove that the previous one was even better. Madhab always used to enjoy such kind of appraisals and with a mild smile he was replying to them that as he is getting older day by day so could not eat like young days of his life. At the same time he was adding that due to the same growing age he has recently started eating less than what he used to even just before some days. Finally before leaving that place to attend the next he met with the head of the family, express his gratitude and ask his permission to leave.

His next destination was nearly a half an hour walking distance back to his place so he was happy that while reaching there this walk will help to digest and also he will regain some energy which will help him in turn to prepare for another performance. He reached to attend the second invitation with full of enthusiasm. Here also he followed the same schedule from meeting the head of the family first, then meeting the bride and the bride-groom and congratulate and wish them luck and finally gifting them as per the custom and then wasting no more time anywhere he directly approached the dinning place accompanied by his host. The scene here also was of hardly any differences from the earlier one. The same kind of introduction, flattering and energizing, then a humble starting by Madhab, same type of people's encouragement and same instigation and requests from the serving boys. It was again almost a same kind of show as the previous one. After the show even the comparisons and appraisals were also of no different than the previous one. The only difference was Madhab did not have time to enjoy and cherish those encouraging and appraising words people surrounding him there were raining on him as he had in the previous one as the time was running out and he had to attend the last one. He was keener to know what the arrangements will be there in the third one. Though it was nearby but the clock was also in the verge of touching the eleventh rank for the second time of the day.

Madhab after completing the formalities left the place in hurry and started for attending the last invitation and he reached there in next ten to fifteen minutes. He met the head of the family in the main gate as he was completing the formal send off for the invited guests. It was time when some guests who arrived early in the evening were leaving and the head of the family and the host was doing his duty of send them off smilingly.

Hey Madhab babu, why are you so late, busy in the shop? He asked his guest. I expected you to be here earlier, he paused and added. Whatever, please come in, he welcomed Madhab with full gratuity and expressed his mind that he was worried that Madhab might not come and if that happened then it would have been a disappointment for him. Madhab smiled and replied, I actually got a bit occupied with some other jobs otherwise I would have been here earlier. He added, but how could you think that I would forget your invitation. I could forget anything but could never forget or overlook an invitation from a friend like you. The man asked his eldest son to take Madhab inside the house and arrange everything he needed. Madhab completed the formalities and reached the place of his desire, the dining hall. He was one of the member of the last batch and that was even more satisfactory for him for two reasons as the arrangements were more than sufficient and secondly there would be no next batch so there would be no disturbance for him and nothing would compel him to hurry.

Madhab gave his best shot of the day from the very beginning till the last sweet dish. He was completed when the head of the family and Madhab's friend entered the hall after completing his other responsibilities and requested Madhab for one more piece of *Sandesh* (a very unique and testy sweet in Bengali delicacy). Madhab felt that was really impossible for him but the man kept requesting for the same and Madhab finally accepted. It was matter of prestige so he took that sandesh and put it in his mouth but did not gulp that. He thought that once he will be out of the place he will either swallow it if possible or through it out.

Madhab, when started for his return journey towards his home it was no more PM. It was almost a fifteen minutes' walk from there to his home. He was in a very cheerful mood and was walking in a moderate pace without any imperativeness. But this cheerfulness of his mind did not last for long. Suddenly he started feeling an uneasiness in breathing. He stopped for a while and let himself sat by the side of the village path on a culvert for some minutes. But the feelings did not improve, rather it was getting worse. He has started perspiring in that chilled winter night. He was also started feeling more intense breathing problem as if he needs some more oxygen in each of his breath. The uneasy feeling was increasing in a rapid speed. Madhab thought for some moments and decided to start again to return. He stood up and started walking slowly. He realized that he could not see everything clearly and also he has started feeling a disturbing gyration in his head. As if everything, even including the road is undulating in front of his eyes. Every passing moment the walk was becoming tougher for him but he was determined to reach his home as only then he would get some medicine or treatment that could help him to get out of this trouble. Madhab was stopping after few steps and recollecting all his energy to carry on the rest of his journey.

Finally after a terrible experience when his home was nearly hundred meter he started feeling an acute pain in his chest. The pain was so pinning and intense that the muscularly built figure of Madhab was getting tattered in it. He stopped again and looked back and forth with the hope to find someone who could help him forgetting that it was past midnight and no one would be there on the street on this night of winter. He as expected found no one on the road except some street dogs. Madhab stretched himself to the maximum possible and took nearly twenty minutes to cover that last hundred meter. The outer most gate used to be opened so he just pushed that to open and entered his house. He had no more energy or strength to call any one from the home to open the second gate. There was the small Bajrangbali temple that he built for worshipping. He any how reached that place by not walking rather creeping and laid down there on the platform of the temple.

THE WINTER MORNING

Sundar entered Madhab uncle's house with Patru. Many people from the village were already present there including some senior most to boys even junior than Sundar. He found his father is also standing there with a dimmed face, near the temple. Due to Brijendra's tallness Sundar could clearly see his father from the place where he was standing with Patru. It took a while for Sundar and Patru to make a path through the gathering towards the temple where Madhab uncle was lying.

Reaching the spot Sundar saw Madhab uncle was lying on the platform resting his head on the lap of Bhootnath da. His eyes were closed but his mouth was opened. Sundar and Patru both were astonished seeing for the first time ever in their life that their rough and tough Bhootnath da weeping. The local doctor was seating by uncle's body with his face down. Everyone present there was speechless, as if they have forgot how to talk. There was absolute silence except some sound of crying in women's voice which was coming from the inner portion of the house. They boys in the curiosity of knowing what has happened, approached one elderly woman who was standing in front of the gate that leads to the inner part of the house. When they enquired what happened to their uncle, what the woman depicted was shocking. Early in the morning when the women of the family discovered Madhab on the platform, he had already breathed his last quite sometimes before.

The news of his death sprayed in the small village like wild fire and people started coming to see his dead body. Sundar and Patru stayed there with their Bhootnath da. Madhab Chandra's lifeless body was kept on the platform of the temple with closed eyes but his mouth was wide open as if he was trying beyond his capacity to breadth but the most shocking thing was discovered by the doctor who came to check. There was a piece of sandesh in his mouth till then. He did not threw that last sweet dish out and tried till his last breath not to waste that.

Too good, always bad ...

SOME YEARS BACK

So Brijendra, everything's okay? The tall fair skinned man asked the question to Sundar's father while entering in to his shop.

It was early in the afternoon and Sundar's father Brijendra Narayan was seating in a comparatively sluggish manner as there was no customer and was enjoying the time. He promptly got out of his indolence seeing his senior and respected friend Biren. Yes dada, it's alright here, Brijendra replied and offered another chair to the man standing in front of him. You must be returning from school, he added.

Ramu, go swiftly and arrange two cups of tea for us right now, while Biren make himself comfortable in the chair Brijendra ordered one of his employees to arrange some tea for both of them. It was very clear to Brijendra that there must be something very important otherwise Biren would not have visited, at least not at this time.

Biren babu was a teacher in the local school and was such a man with tremendous persona that even the bravest and the most notorious students used to shiver in front of him. His actual name was Birendranath Mukherjee, but he was more well-known to people in the shorter form of his name, that is "Biren Babu". Though he was not the head of the institution but was the eldest amongst the teachers and used to be respected most by all others. Some of the teachers were even his students once. Mainly a teacher of Sanskrit but that man used to be requested to teach many other subjects also because of his extensive and in depth knowledge in those subjects. Birendranath Mukherjee was senior in age but that respected person was almost friendly to Brijendra.

So, dada, anything urgent? Brijendra asked while the tea arrives.

Hmmm, I have to share something with you. Brijendra since last week I was teaching your son in the school and I must say one thing that he is exceptionally brainy and at the same time attentive and last but not the least he is an obedient kid, he continued. If proper care is taken, I assure you that he will one day become a boy to be proud of. Biren babu paused for a moment, sipped the earthen cup full of hot tea he was holding in his hand and again started saying what he was talking about, I am here actually to request your permission to teach your eldest son Satyendra as a private tutor, obviously if only you don't have any restrictions. I would prefer to teach him many other things which might not be covered under the general school syllabus but very much important for higher studies, Biren babu completed while sipping the tea again.

What are you saying Biren da? Brijendra promptly reply in a humble tune. You have asked to personally teach Satyendra and I will have restrictions? It's an honor for me as well as for my son also, he added. Just tell me at what time Satyendra should reach at your home. Brijendra told his mind joyously.

Thank you Brijendra, that is what I expected, send him from tomorrow after his school, Biren babu replied and stood up to leave. He threw the cup in the dust bean and moved forward. Brijendra accompanied him to the staircase.

Out of all the brothers of Sundar, Satyendra, the eldest amongst them was probably the boy with the simplest mind and best academic record. He was very soft spoken and submissive kind of person from his childhood. His obedience, brilliance and at the same time attentiveness towards studies, made him very affectionate to the teachers of his school and also within the family and friend circle. Not only Biren babu but all the other teachers in the school also had affectionate feelings for him because of his nature and talent. Except Biren babu, the head master of the school Manabendra babu was another prominent appraiser amongst all others. Manabendra babu was at his fifties and a bachelor. He used to live with one of his nephew Jagannath, who was more famous as "*Jaga*". Jagannath was senior to Satyendra but just the polar opposite of him regarding obedience, talent and attentiveness. After failing several times in different classes and examination he finally became a classmate of Satyendra and next year he maintained the same terrific performance and became one class junior to Satyendra. He was no less than a headache not only for Manabendra babu but to the entire pool of teachers in the school. Jaga used to commit all possible mischief a boy of that age could ever even think of but at the same time he was so clever that there used to be hardly any material evidence to prove his involvement in that. In many cases he had been doubted by several teachers but he could never be condemned due to lack of proofs.

THE GREAT EXAM

Satyendra was in standard X and preparing for his final school leaving examination. All the teachers were not only hopeful rather sure about a milestone result from the best boy of the school. Satyendra also was preparing with all his strengths and attention. On the other side Jaga was in standard IX and was trying desperately to pass his annual examination this time, as otherwise he would be expelled from the school due to failing in the same class for three consecutive years. In desperation of passing the examination Jaga did the unthinkable. He chalked out a plan in his mind which could be a bone chilling suspense thriller for any other boy of his school. He asked his closest friend in the school, Subinoy to help him in his plan. Subinoy was his closest friend and confidant but was a classmate of Satyendra. Subinoy was from a well to do family and may not be as good as Satyendra but was a mediocre student who used to pass all the examinations with fare kind of marks. His father was a very famous businessman in the area.

Subinoy, I need your help this year in the annual exam. You know if I fail this time, even the Gods of the heaven would not be capable enough to resist my uncle from rusticating me and I don't want to get back to that boring life in the village I have come from. Jaga and Subinoy was seating in the bank of the river when Jaga depicted this while throwing small pieces of stones in the river. Though he was saying something to Subinoy who was seating beside him but Jaga's eyes were fixed on those small wavy circles that were being created due those small stones he was throwing in the river water. He was deeply thinking about and searching for something that could help him getting out of this critical situation. He was well aware of his personal preparations and also knew that even he is allowed for an open book test then also he would not be capable of passing the examination as he does not even know what is where in the book.

Subinoy was also looking at the river. He turned his face and stared at his friend for some moment, the tension was clearly visible on his face. If you know all this then why are you still wasting time doing all such foolish works? Subinoy asked his friend in reply. He added, employ your time in your studies to the maximum possible at least now onwards, so that you could at the minimum pass the exam. Jaga after a long time turned his eyes from the river and looked at his friend with a thin mocking smile on his lips. If I start studying right from now and study for 24 hours a day, then also I could not pass the exam in next seven days, Jaga replied. I don't even know which book is for which subjects, he paused for a moment and then continued. I have planned something else and if that plan works no one on this planet would be able to resist me from passing the examination and that too with remarkable marks.

Okay, may I know what that mighty plan is, Subinoy asked him.

Certainly, Jaga replied with a smile and added, after all you would also have a very important role to play there. Jaga continued, look I will attend the exam but once the question paper and answer script is distributed I will replace the same with previous year's question and some white sheets that I will bring to the hall with me. Then I will pass both the current year's question and blank answer script through a window to you.

And what would I do with those questions and blank answer paper? Subinoy almost screeched at Jaga.

That is what I am going to tell you now, Jaga replied with a visible irritation of his face due to the unwanted intervention from Subinoy and continued. You will be waiting there for the same unless I pass those to you. Then you will have to take those to Satyendra to write the answers. Once Satyendra finished it off, you will again take it back and pass back through the same window to me.

Do you understand what the hell you are planning and what will be the consequences if we are caught? Subinoy replied. He continued, with you I too will be thrown out of the school mercilessly. Have you gone crazy? And moreover why involving a good boy like Satyendra? I can answer those for you.

Jaga looked at his friend for a moment and then said, firstly you will have to be with me as I have supported you many times in the past in your needs and this time when I need your help, I will not allow you to quit. Secondly I can't take a chance this time to let you write the answers, Jaga replied to his friend.

Subinoy thought for some moments. It is absolutely true that in many cases when he was in problem, Jaga has always been his first support. But how could you be so sure that Satyendra will agree to this? Subinoy asked.

Don't tell him anything in details now, Jaga paused for an instant and continued, just assure him that this is an urgent requirement for someone who is in a life and death situation, and also say that you will tell him everything in details once the urgency is over. Also don't tell him this is for any exam or something, just say the answers of the questions are needed, Jaga directed Subinoy. He continued, one more thing, tell him not to share this with anybody as this is a matter of utter seriousness.

The next day Subinoy came to Satyendra and told him everything as he was directed by Jaga. Subinoy tried his best to maintain the highest possible seriousness he could though his words and facial expressions. He added that this is a matter of life and death for someone and only Satyendra could help that person to come out of this despondent condition. It was more than enough for Satyendra to be ready to help someone in need.

After the first exam Subinoy said to his friend, Thank you Satyendra, you don't know what a great work you have done to support a needy person. He added, please wait here for ten minutes unless I return, don't go anywhere alone. He asked Satyendra to stay there and left for Jaga. He came back quickly and took Satyendra back to his home. Please don't share this with anybody, it will be fatal for the person, Subinoy requested Satyendra before leaving him at home. Satyendra silently nodded.

The same phenomenon continued for all the papers.

On the days of the examinations Subinoy used to come to Satyendra's home and took him to the preplanned place in his bicycle. He requested Satyendra to wait under the big banyan tree just in the opposite corner of the big playground behind the school and used to go to the window of the class room to collect the question and blank answer script. He then used to return within ten minutes and passed it to Satyendra with the same request to him to answer the question within two and a half hours. As the exam was of three hours in total so he kept some time in safeguard so that he could return the paper to Jaga within time. Satyendra always with a smile used to start his work and he also used to complete answering by the stipulated time and returned that back to Subinoy.

It was unbelievable. While checking the answer papers all the teachers were surprised by Jaga's performance. When they discussed amongst themselves, it was revealed that the same surprise is common for all the teachers. Unfortunately paper for one of the subjects was being checked by Manabendra babu and he was almost quacked to the route by seeing the quality of answers in Jaga's script. He was no way ready to agree that those were anyway written by his own nephew. He knew him from the very beginning.

I can bait to anything on earth but this could never be his own, there must be something wrong, Manabendra babu uttered to himself. He was seating in his desk in the office room and checking the answers scripts of the students, currently in his hand he was holding the answer script of his own nephew, Jaga.

Madhusudan, Manabendra babu called his attendant loudly. Yes sir, Madhusudan was seating outside the door in his wooden chair and entered the room almost within a moment. Go and call Jaga, tell him I am calling, I don't care even if he is middle of any lecture in the class, just tell him to be here right now. The loud voice of the head master coupled with his angry attitude was more than enough to make Madhusudan run for to fulfill the order. In next five minutes Jaga was standing in front of the head master, in his chamber. Manabendra babu stared at Jaga silently for a while and then he spoke with the same weighty voice but this time without shouting, tell me the truth, how have you managed to write such extraordinary answers to all the questions?

This time I studied for the exam seriously, Jaga replied placidly staring directly to the eyes of Manabendra babu. There was no sign of excitement or tension in his eyes.

Jaga I know you from the moment you were born, don't try to befool me. It can never be the outcome of your studies, tell me the truth. Manabendra babu almost screeched at his own nephew but could not make Jaga to say anything other than what he said at the beginning. Get out of here, but remind I will see it to the last, Manabendra babu dismissed Jaga for then.

He did not say anything on that time but a distrust was raised in his mind. He enquired with all the other teachers who were examining the papers for other subjects and what he received was almost the hardest to believe for him. Jaga has answered all the papers with the same outstanding quality and this time he is going to be the first boy in the class. Now when all the teachers were saying the same thing the distrust changed in to certainty and he again called Jaga in his office room but this time in the presence of all the other teachers who have examined his answer papers. Manabendra babu threatened Jaga in utter desperation to either reveal the truth or it might have the worst consequences for him. But Jaga was unbreakable, he gave the same answer he had already given, this is my performance and I have worked hard to achieve this.

It was now beyond limit. Manabendra babu announced that the examination for class IX would be cancelled and there will be a re-exam for all the papers and at the same time he also declared that this time he will personally see that the question papers to be the toughest ever.

Manabendra, what am I listening to? You are going to re-arrange the final examination for the Class IX students, is that right? Biren babu entered the head master's chamber while asking the question. Manabendra babu stood up to show his gratitude and welcome him. He seat again only after when Biren babu sat himself in a chair on the opposite side of the table. Biren babu was not aware of this situation as he was out of station for some days. Today he has returned from there and also has attended his duty in the school. Once he got the news he came directly to the head master's room. Manabendra was ashamed of his failure of not finding out any other means to prove the relevance of his doubt on Jaga.

Yes Sir, actually I am helpless. I don't have any other option to stop the crime that has already been committed by that felonious boy, Manabendra babu replied with his eyes down in shame. I am ashamed that he is my nephew, the dignified man added the last line almost being shattered in within.

Crime committed, will you please elaborate what happened to you? Biren babu asked his junior to describe.

Sir, can you imagine Jaga has got highest marks in all the subject in the last examination? Sir, you know him no less than I do, is that any way possible without committing some extraordinary mischief? The terrific distress he was feeling was absolutely clear from his voice.

Biren babu though for a while and then asked, Manabendra have you talked Jagannath? What is his reaction on this?

Manabendra shook his head and replied, as you know him sir, he is no less than a seasoned criminal. First time I asked him personally and then again in the presence of all the other teachers, jointly in various other ways. He added, we actually interrogated him to the maximum possible for us as teachers, but got the same answer from him every time, Manabendra babu replied helplessly.

And what did he answer, Biren babu asked?

He lied to us and boastfully responded, "This is my performance".

Hmm, Biren babu stopped for sometimes and then asked, Manabendra, can I see his answer papers once?

Why not sir, anytime. Manabendra babu called the clerk and ordered him to bring all the answer papers of Jaga form the respective teachers.

The Clark returned with all the papers in a while and passed the bunch to the head sir. Thank you, you may go now, Biren babu asked the clerk to leave and pick up one of the answer script from the bunch and went through the entire paper. Then he took the next and did the same. The same way he went through all the papers with a gentle smile in his lips.

Manabendra babu was a silent spectator till then. When Biren babu completed his task, Manabendra babu could not resist him to ask, have you seen sir what a liar he is? Is it possible for him to answer in such a manner for all the questions with so much of quality?

Biren babu in return answered with the same smile in his face and said, No Manabendra you are half right. Manabendra babu looked at him with surprise. It was evident from his expression that he was eager to know where he is right and where he is wrong. Biren babu continued, he did not lie, it is obviously his performance and no doubt about it, but he had not answered even a single of all the questions in any of the papers.

What does this mean sir? Manabendra babu asked his senior, I can't get your point.

Okay, Manabendra, do one thing, send someone to ask Satyendra to come here and you will get to know where you have failed.

The same Clark was sent to Satyendra's class and within next five minutes Satyendra was standing there in front of the two teachers. Have you called me sir? He asked Manabendra babu.

No son, Biren babu want to ask you something, Manabendra babu replied affectionately to his beloved student.

Biren babu passes the papers one by one to Satyendra and asked, is not this your handwriting Satyendra?

Certainly yes sir, Satyendra replied.

The next question Biren babu asked to his favorite student, when did you write this? And who told you to write this?

Satyendra depicted in details, sir actually Subinoy came to me and told me that he needs my help for someone. When I asked what kind of help is needed, he told me that I will have to come with Subinoy and there he will give a question paper, which I will have to answer. So I used to come with Subinoy and seat under the big banyan tree there, in the opposite side of the ground, he pointed his figure to the location of the tree and continued, and he used to take one question paper and blank answer script each time and asked me to write the answers. I used to write all the answers and return it to him then he used to go somewhere and after returning from there he used to take me to my home in his bicycle.

Have you never asked him who and why you are writing for, Biren babu asked Satyendra?

Yes sir I asked Subinoy once and he told me that he will tell me everything in details once the work is completed and after that I forgot to ask him again. Should I ask him now sir? Satyendra replied.

Manabendra babu intervened this time and said to Satyendra, no son, you don't have to ask him anything. You may go and join your class.

Have I done anything wrong sir? Satyendra asked looking at both the teachers with anxiety.

Not exactly Satyen, Manabendra babu replied, I have made a mistake which now I will correct.

Satyendra nodded his head and went back to his class and the next person to be called was Subinoy. He actually had nothing to hide because already everything was clear to all. He just begged for pardon but had to face a guardian call notice and one month suspension from the class.

The ultimate blow was waiting for the mastermind, Jaga. He was rusticated from the school for ever. He finally dropped his studies and returned to his father's house and joined his ancestral business. Perhaps he was not even sorry for what happened. But before going back to his village he met Satyendra for the last time. Jaga hugged Satyendra and laughed loudly a lot, finally he told to Satyendra, I will never forget you. You are too good a person I have ever seen and probably will even found any in future.

Satyendra answered, please be attentive to your studies and stop doing these nonsenses this time. Otherwise you will again face such teething troubles.

Jaga laughed louder, nodded his head, patted on Satyendra's shoulder and left the place without saying anything else.

TIME MOVED ON

Satyendra was totally occupied with William Shakespeare's "Macbeth" when Sundar entered the room. Dada Subinoy da is waiting for you in the main gate, Sundar informed his brother. Satyendra turned towards his brother, but his facial expression said clearly that he has not listened to or understood any of the words what Sundar has said to him just now. Sundar repeated again and wait for the instruction. Yah, call him in, Satyendra replied softly to his brother and again got back to the marvelous piece of Shakespeare.

After the Jaga's episode time moved on, Satyendra was now in his 3rd and final year of college education. He was doing his bachelor in English honors. As attentive as he had always been and categorically as beloved to the professors as he used to be throughout his student life to his teachers in the school. His old friend Subinoy, who was also studying in the same college but in pass course was his only companion to college. After that Jaga's incident Subinoy had never done any mischief may be either for being afraid of rustication or his father. Subinoy's father, Narottam Chowdhury was also a businessman and friend of Brijendra. Narottam was a very successful, established and wealthy businessman in the area. He started his life with one small garment shop which he received from his ancestors but he made all the other businesses by his own intelligence, hard work and dedication. He not only had many types of businesses but at the same time he had purchased huge amount of farming land in and around the area. Subinoy was his only son but Narottam used to be a strict or sometimes an autocratic kind of father for his only son. He never indulged Subinoy in any respect, rather he was a kind of very authoritative father with strong personality. Narottam Chowdhury always wanted his son to be a good student and attentive towards studies and that is why he used to cite example of Satyendra to his son. Subinoy was not as talented as Satyendra but after the Jaga's episode he became more attentive towards his studies. Satyendra was his main inspiration as well as instructor at any point of time. The fear of his father in his mind always used to compel him to work harder than possible to at least pass all the examinations with standard marks.

Narottam had a belief that nothing could be more harmful for a young boy than liquid and nonessential cash in his pocket. This typical thinking of his father had tremendous effect on Subinoy's life. Whenever he asked for money, he had to answer so many questions to his father to clarify the necessity of his requirement. Subinoy as a grown boy used to feel humiliated for the same sometimes and to avoid this types of terrible circumstances he took a short cut and used to steal the amount from his father's cash box kept in the private chamber of his father where the man used to keep cash for the business. Subinoy mostly used the dine time of the day to commit the sin when his father used to return to home for lunch. This is the time when all other employees used to be either busy in lunch or were taking rest after the lunch. Subinoy used a broken window in the backside of the main room to get access to the cash box and the same way to return after completing his secret mission.

Sir, may I have the pleasure to know what are you concentrating on right now so thoughtfully? Subinoy mocked his friend while entering the room.

Satyendra turned to his friend and asked in reply, have you read Macbeth Subinoy? He paused for a moment and then continued, it is such a beautiful piece that you will hardly found another in English literature of all time.

For your kind information, whenever I am compelled to study any piece of Mr. Shakespeare I generally sprinkle some water on the pages, Subinoy replied while seating on the mattress his friend was seating.

Why do you sprinkle water on the pages? What purpose does this solve? Satyendra asked with astonishment staring at his companion. Subinoy with a naughty smile on his lips replied, with the hope that the water will soften the words at least to some extent so that my teeth don't break.

You incorrigible idiot will never understand how much feelings are needed to script such literary masterpieces, Satyendra answered with sheer disgust.

Sorry my dear friend if I any way have hurt your emotion about Shakespeare or English literature, please pardon me, Subinoy replied again with the same teasing smile and continued. I have travelled nearly ten minutes to reach at your doorstep to seek help from his majesty to teach me how to solve this grammatical issues which are very important suggestion for this year's exam. More importantly I just need to pass the exam and I must mention here that I do not have any intension to become the first boy of the class, sir. With so much of irritation Satyendra said his friend to open the book.

This was a very common scene for everyone who were aware of the friendship between these two boys. Satyendra always used to help his friend Subinoy in his studies and Subinoy was also very much dependent on Satyendra regarding the same. At least four to five days a week either Subinoy used to come to Satyendra's house or take him to his house and spend long hours together in studies. Satyendra was more than happy to help his only friend.

The final exam of the graduation appeared. During exam days the world use to become the worst place for the boys. And once the exam gets finished astonishingly the same world becomes the most beautiful thing, at least until the result is declared and the boys have to face their parents with the same piece of paper. After the exams, Subinoy started enjoying the life at the fullest. No pressure for studies, no scheduled class, no lectures from the professors, no tedious study time that he has to attain unwillingly. An absolute freedom from all such boring and disturbing issues. Life was smooth and going in a very satisfying way for the boy, but every good time that has a start also has a finishing line and the finishing line came suddenly one day in Subinoy's life. The day was when the result got declared. Satyendra as usual had a champion's result. He was greeted by not only the professors but also by the other people in the neighborhood. Subinoy did not expect a result like his friend but at least somewhere in a corner of his mind he was hopping a result which will provide him a chance for the entry in the master level course. That did not happen, though Subinoy was promoted but with such a feeble marks that there was no hope for him to get any option for admission in the masters' degree course. He was devastated but not disheartened.

WHY MARRYING NOW?

I have discussed with many people and found that there is absolutely no chance is available in the university level for you with the kind of result you have for the masters' degree. From tomorrow morning you will be joining my business to help me, Narottam directed his son in the dining table. Subinoy also expected the same from the day he received his result and silently nodded his head. Narottam paused for some moments and continued, another important information for you is that, I have arranged your marriage in the coming season with one of the daughters of Bholanath Roy. He is a very good friend of mine and also a very nice man, he added to complete. If I am not wrong, you also know him well enough. Subinoy was not ready for this. It was no less than a punishment for him. He looked at his mother to help him out of this but the way she turned her eyes made it clear that she does not have the courage to stand against her husband on this issue. Subinoy also could not say anything in front of his father as it would have been a suicidal attempt for him but once his father left the room after completing his lunch Subinoy started shouting and tried all that was possible to his mother. Tell father that I am ready to join the business but I am not going to marry that girl and that too within such a short notice, Subinoy told his mother to convey this to his father.

Okay, in a convenient time I will try to discuss the same with your father but I can't promise you anything at this stage about the decision that your father will take, his mother replied to calm her son down. I suggest you not to say anything to your father as you know your father no less than I do, she continued. Once the man decides something then there is hardly any chance that the decision will be changed or even modified, she added to complete.

Why don't you let him work in the business for some days and when he will become accustomed with all these responsibilities, then the marriage could anytime be arranged, at night in the dinner table Subinoy's mother raised the issue with a slight inclination that has support for what her son is saying. Subinoy had boycotted the dinner by asking to serve the food in his room to show his discontentment on his father's decision.

When I was married to you I was younger than him and had almost nothing but one small shop. Today I have earned all these out of my hard work and people respect me because I never break my promises, Subinoy's father did not even raise his face from his plate and answered with a deep and weighty voice. He continued, if I had done all these maintaining all my responsibilities of my family life, then what problem could your son even have? I have promised to Bholanath and your son would never have to face all that I had to, he has his father to guide him. Narottam paused for moments and added, it would be better if you tell him to be prepared for what I have said, He completed. His wife did not have the courage to say anything to counter him.

After dinner when Subinoy's father went to his room to smoke his hukka Subinoy came to the kitchen to meet his mother, who was busy rearranging the utensils and asked, what did he say? His mother while working replied that, nothing has changed, he is stubborn on his decision.

Finally Subinoy played his last card of emotion. I warn you, if the damn marriage is arranged I will leave the house for ever. Tell him that he will get a daughter-in-law but in the cost of his son. His mother tried to console him but finally became the postman and conveyed the message to his father.

Hari, go and tell Subinoy that I am calling him here right now, Narottam called his attendant and directed him. In next few minutes Subinoy was standing in front of his father. Your mother said you have decided to leave the home for ever if the marriage is not cancelled, is that right? Narottam asked his son.

Subinoy from the corner of his eyes tried to see the expression of his mother but failed. She was seating at the extreme corner of the bed. I don't want to get married now, Subinoy answered in a hardly audible voice.

If you have decided to leave the home then leave it right now, but the marriage will not be cancelled, Narottam did not bother to wait there anymore and left the room. Subinoy was the only son of his parents and thought that emotional trick might change the wind in his favor, but now after this he is proved absolutely wrong.

The discussion was over but Subinoy returned to his room with more desperation and started planning to any how stop the decision of the marriage. It had then became a matter of prestige to him. Finally what he did at that night was mesmerizing. He planned to loot the cash box of his father to put him under financial crisis and thought that will force him to change his decision. At least for some days he will be busier in something other than this dam marriage.

Subinoy woke up from his bed in the middle of the night and came out of his room. He had not slept till now. He came out of his room and moved towards the kitchen to survey the situation. He thought that if anyone notices him he could make an excuse of thirst. He crossed the bedroom of his parents with slow steps and raised ears. Everything was calm and quite. He entered the kitchen, took a glass of water and came back to his room. So far so good, no one is awake. He again came out of his room and this time walked towards the staircase. Subinoy came down through the staircase to ground floor and went towards the backdoor of the house. Now he could feel the bubbles bursting in his stomach quite eminently. Subinoy opened the door as quietly as possible without making even a cracking sound in that old door. He came out and locked the door from outside. Finally jumped cross the boundary wall and walked towards his father's office.

It was an unruffled night, no one was there in the road to spot him except some street dogs who were lying under the sheds of those street side shops. He appeared in front of the office building and entered through the way he had used many times before also. Next day was the Hat so the cash box was at its paramount condition. Now looking at the amount Subinoy became a bit scary. Previously maximum amount he had ever theft from there was used to be negligible but now it is a hefty amount lying in front of him in the cash box. He could feel that his hands are shivering, but at this point he had no other choice as he had already broken the lock of the cash box. He did not think any more and picked up the bundles, placed those in his pocket and got out of there almost running.

Subinoy returned to his room the same way he got out of it just few minutes before. Everything was as he left half an hour ago. He hid the bundles under his bed but could not sleep for the night.

Next day the news of robbery spread like wildfire in the surroundings. People came to survey the actuality of the news and when found that to be true they were also traumatized. That was the first time ever in that locality such an incident has taken place. In that placid rural area it was no less than an earthquake, so automatically it raised the eyebrows of everyone.

LETS PARTY

Two days passed, Narottam was worried and distressed but probably his son was in more dilemma about the stolen money. Narottam and his son both were tensed about the whereabouts of the money, but just in opposite sense. Subinoy was spending more time in his room than ever being afraid that if anybody anyhow finds out the stolen money lying beneath his bed in his absence. Finally he decided to spend the money so that he could get out of the tension of seating on that in the room. Now spending so much of money in a rural area was not only impossible but there was risk also. So he decided to go somewhere to spend the amount. Going alone was again another problem so he decided have companion. The only name came in to his mind for this purpose was none other than Satyendra, which will shoot three apples in one arrow, firstly his parents will not doubt him, secondly Satyendra is a person who hardly ask any question and thirdly the burden of money will be over. As per plan he approached Satyendra.

Satyendra was sleeping when Subinoy entered his room. Come on, wake up first boy, I have good news for you, Subinoy woke his friend up.

What happened? Satyendra asked with lethargy.

As you already know I am going to get married very soon, Subinoy paused for a moment and then continued, and once I get married I will not get chances of enjoying life, so I have decided one thing, Subinoy told his friend.

May I know what you have decided, Satyendra asked.

Surely first boy, I have come here to share that with you. I have decided that one day you and I will go to the city and enjoy a movie, how is that? Subinoy asked his friend.

But recently there was a robbery in your business and you are going to ask for money for watching movie from your father, Satyendra asked his friend with surprise. He will definitely rebuke you, better we should wait for some days, he added.

Look, I am not going to ask for anything from anyone, I have been saving these money from long back, Subinoy answered. He added, you don't need to break your head on that. Day after tomorrow I will come to your house early in the morning to call you. Be prepared, he completed and stood up to leave.

On the scheduled day in the morning the duo caught the first train to the city from their native place. Subinoy bought the tickets. Reaching the city railway station Subinoy started searching for a Taxi. Wait here, let me hire a taxi for the entire day, he said to Satyendra.

Do you know how much will it cost you, Satyendra asked his friend in anxiety.

Subinoy turned to Satyendra and said, you don't have to think anything, I am here at your service, sir. You just enjoy, he added.

Seating in the taxi Subinoy ordered the driver to take them to a specific hotel, which was really costly. They reached the hotel in next fifteen minutes and there Subinoy booked a room for the day and ordered for breakfast. After breakfast they took rest for some time in their room and then sat out to the biggest theatre hall and purchased the costliest tickets. They watched a movie and after that they returned to their hotel room and ordered an expensive lunch. They actually were living a king's life for the day.

When are you planning to return home? Satyendra asked his friend. The departure time for the last train is not very far, we must leave now, he added. They were lying on the big soft majestic bed after their extensive lunch and Subinoy was in no mood to waste this time.

We are not going to take any train, we will go by the taxi itself, Subinoy did not even bother open his eyes to answer. Satyendra was amazed, he again asked about the expenditure and Subinoy just replied that everything will be managed. After some time they came down to the hotel lobby. Subinoy paid the taxi driver a double fare to agree him to take them to their place.

When they returned back to their place Subinoy ordered the driver to stop the car before a kilometer from their village so that no one spot them getting out of a car but he did not tell that to his friend. Why are you stopping it here, we will have to walk a mile from here, Satyendra asked his friend.

Mr. first boy have not you read that one short walk helps to digest foods better, Subinoy replied to Satyendra. The reason was quite logical to Satyendra and they walked back to their respective home.

It was the dinner time and Satyendra's father and all his brothers were taking their dinner when Satyendra entered home. Get fresh at the earliest and join the dinner, his father said to him.

Actually father we have taken so much of food the whole day and I don't have any place in my stomach for even a single grain, Satyendra replied to his father. He continued, you know that for better digestion Subinoy left the taxi one mile before and suggested me to have a walk to home. He has become so health conscious this days, Satyendra completed.

His father was a bit shocked, really, tell me in details what you guys have done the entire day, Brijendra asked his son in a friendly voice. Satyendra did not hide anything and with a great joy he told what they had done the whole day in details. When his father asked about the expenditure, he simply informed that the entire trip was sponsored by Subinoy. Okay, no issue, get freshen up and go to bed, Brijendra directed his son.

The next morning Satyendra's father came to Subinoy's father and depicted the entire story. The curtain was raised and the scene was more than clear to Narottam. Hari, call Subinoy and tell him I have ordered him to come here right now, Narottam ordered his attendant.

Narottam our boys are not kids anymore, so I would suggest you not to be rude to Subinoy, Brijendra suggested his friend. Hmm, let's see, Narottam answered in the shortest possible way.

After a while Subinoy entered his father's office room and the first question he faced was, how much have you spent and how much are you left with?

Subinoy was shocked, he started mumbling. His father asked once again but this time with a louder voice and that was enough for Subinoy to tell the truth. He was ordered to bring the rest amount right then. Subinoy had no other choice but to serve the order.

Should I call the police for the crime? The next question Narottam asked his son. Subinoy did not answer, he was just standing still with his eyes fixed on the floor.

You may go now, Brijendra rescued Subinoy. Calm down as otherwise the family matter will become a spicy gossip in the society, once Subinoy was out of the room he said to Narottam. Narottam nodded his head and thanked his friend to rescue him from this great problem. I would like to call your son once more, Brijendra asked to Narottam. Subinoy came in with permission in next moment. He was just waiting beside the door. Subinoy, one thing I could not resist myself to ask you, what actually instigated you to loot your own business, Brijendra asked the boy.

Subinoy described the entire incident and the environment of the room suddenly changed by the sound of laughter. After laughing for some moments Satyendra's father finally told his friend, we are perhaps the first two old men ever in the lines of history who are witnessing a young boy became a thief to stay bachelor. Both the guardians started laughing together again.

Though the incident made Subinoy a funny character in the neighborhood but the only good news for him was that his marriage was postponed for some years then.

ALMOST KILLED THE GODDESS ...

I will show the people of the village and especially that ridiculously egotistical old moron Bishnupada that I am far a better artist tan him. I will show that old idiot that I could make sculpture much better than him, Mukunda uttered to his brother Sundar. Mukunda was the third of the five brothers of Sundar's and just elder than Sundar and the youngest of all, Anil. His complete disgust was evident from his expression but it was no way clear to Sundar about what his brother is so much irritated. The two were seating in the room with the lantern in between them and books opened in front of each of them to demonstrate that they are attentively studying.

What happened to you, Sundar raised his eyes to ask his brother. Why are you so angry with Bishnu uncle, has he rebuked you, Sundar added.

You know what that selfish narcissistic man had told to me today, Mukunda replied. He continued, I have worked so hard this year and especially when he was suffering from fever and lying in his bed. I have rigorously worked to make the sculpture of the goddess Kali that will be worshipped this year but he did not allow me to draw the eyes. I requested him so many times that if I fail I will replace the head of the sculpture but he did not even think twice to say that I am a novice and it is a matter of excellence that only comes through experience, he completed with a rage quite visible on his face.

He is a veteran on this and perhaps knows things better than you do or any other does, Sundar tried to stand a logic.

Veteran! Knows things better! Mukunda was in no mood to listen to any logic and mocked his brother. Don't tell me all these worthless words, he is jealous of my creativity, he added. But don't think I will seat idle, I will show him what I could do, he added.

Then what would you do, Sundar asked his brother.

I will make another idol and this time totally on my own and show that old jealous man that I can do much better than him, he completed.

THE REASON BEHIND

There was an age old temple of the Goddess Kali in the village and from the time unknown the villagers had been organizing the worship of the goddess every year. Perhaps nobody was aware of the fact that who established the temple or started the ritual but it was a very important part of life to carry that with affluence and honor in that small village. It had always been and still being organized very flamboyantly in the village. It is basically an event of one night, which use to start in the evening and completed by the end of the night, but for that few hours the entire village gathers in the temple where the event is being organized from time unknown. Though the young batch of the village takes the lead in organizing the event but the elderly women of the neighborhood actually direct them as per the rituals and requirements which the boys have to abide by and they do very wilfully. This also use to be a very special day for the kids of the area who are neither yet enough mature nor allowed by their parents or guardians to stay outside their home after the sunset in their everyday life. This is the only day when they are allowed to stay outside their home till the midnight unless the event is completed which actually offers them a lucrative chance of playing with their friends from the afternoon till the midnight. Another very interesting thing for them is generally the worship of Goddess Kali is organized on Saturday so the next day there is no going to school, which means no waking up early in the morning. So this specific day and the event becomes a kind of all-round celebration time for them.

It was the responsibility of a very aged man from the village name Bishnupada to make the idol of the goddess every year. He has received this responsibility from his ancestors, who used to carry out the same job year after year, generation after generation. Though many kids gather around to watch him when he works on the idol but Mukunda was not alike the others in this context. Unlike other kids he was always eager to help Bishnupada in his work. Mukunda, from his childhood had a sheer interest about making earthen sculptures. He had always been very much interested about this event and used to spend his time there from the day Bishnupada started working on the idol. Mukunda used to spend hours watching the person making the idol from a load of clay to a magnificent idol of the goddess Kali and was always ready to help Bishnupada in his work. While helping for years he also have learnt to make sculptures. He had an artistic sense in him and also tremendous interest.

This time you will make the idol and I will help you as you used to do for me, Bishnupada said to Mukunda. You know there is only some more days in between and tomorrow I will start working on the idol so come sharp, he added.

Really, this year I will make the idol? Mukunda was surprised hearing the same.

Yes, this time you are the main artist and I will be your assistant, Bishnupada replied with a smile on his lips. Originally Bishnupada was suffering from fever so he needed Mukunda more than previous occasions which actually made Mukunda happier than anything else. He was at his thirteen and was feeling very proud of his job.

So when should I come tomorrow, he asked his guru.

Come in the afternoon, after returning from your school, Bishnupada suggested the young boy.

From next day Mukunda joined Bishnupada and was happily following each and every order given by Bishnupada. The elder was actually just directing the boy seating on a place and all the jobs were being carried out by Mukunda. In fact Mukunda has really become the main artist this time who was making the idol.

The boy became disheartened when after working so vigorously he was not allowed to perform the most important part of the job, drawing the eyes of the idol. Bishnupada did not allow Mukunda to do this part rather he did that by himself. Mukunda was keen to draw the eyes as that is counted as the main job of making any idol. He requested Bishnupada many times, he also said that if he fails then he will replace the head section of the idol with new one by working for some more hours but Bishnupada was stubborn. He did not say Bishnupada anything but he was hurt. So he decided that he will make another idol of the goddess and will do all the things that should be done for the event on his own.

To complete his mission successfully he watched the event extremely carefully taking note of everything that was being done by the people for the entire time of the event and refused to leave that place even after called by his friends several times to join their games.

Once the event was completed the next day Mukunda started his own arrangement. The first thing I need is a safe place which is out of the sight of the elders of the house, he confirmed to himself. He choose the area behind their home and adjacent to a pond as he will also need water to work on the clay for making the idol. That small area is used by the kids to play and the pond used to be visited just twice a day by the housemaid to wash the kitchen utensils, once in the morning and once in the evening. So the place was safe from any kind of unwanted interventions. The next most important thing he needed was clay, which he collected in small loads to avoid any curiosity of the others from the riverbed. Now Mukunda was in a dilemma as the next requirement was an assistant because he was the main artist so an assistant is needed to help him in supplying small bits and pieces every now and then he will need. The only obvious choice was his younger brother Sundar, who will obey him as well and keep things secret from others on his direction.

Would you like to be my helper in making the idol, Mukunda approached Sundar one day while going to school in the morning. I can also make it on myself but as I have already shared the idea with you, so I thought I should ask you once, he added. There was no question of "No" and Sundar joined the mission.

Next day the two brother started their job silently at the scheduled place after returning from the school. The problem irrupted when their cousin sister Arati suddenly saw them working there. She was almost at Sundar's years. What are you two doing here with so much of clay and bamboo sticks, Arati asked her elder brothers? The two boys stared at each other and started searching for a suitable answer. They have been caught red handed and that too on the first day. I will tell this to aunty that you guys are playing with clay here, she added.

We are making an idol for the goddess Kali, there was no other option but to share the truth with her so Mukunda replied.

Idol of goddess Kali, but why now, the event is over, Arati enquired.

Mukunda thought for some moments and then depicted exactly what truth is and why they are making this idol.

Then I would also be a part of this, Arati replied.

There was no other option for Mukunda but to accept the proposal. He then ordered his assistants to take a vow in the name of the goddess that they will not disclose about this to anyone. The oath was taken without any question and the mission started. So Mukunda needed one but got two helpers, Sundar and Arati. The other important items like straw, bamboo, ribbon, etcetera that Mukunda has seen Bishnupada to use while making idols were also arranged by the team from various places of the households but without being noticed by anybody. Sometimes kids are more united for a cause and also more efficient and effective in doing something silently than their matured seniors. So all the things which will be required at the initial phase were collected and it was the time to start the actual job. You will have to leave all your games for some days until the idol is not ready and also have to help me until then, Mukunda knew from his experience with Bishnupada that making an idol is not a one day job so he decided and ordered his assistants to attend the workshop every day after returning from school until the job is completed.

Arati used to reach the place before her elder brothers, as she was in the primary school and used to return earlier. Mukunda and Sundar joined after some time. Mukunda started his work and Sundar was helping him as he was being directed by Mukunda in various works like fetching water from the pond, pasting the mud or clearing small bit and pieces of imperfections mixed in the mud, so on and so forth. Arati was feeling a bit neglected and less important as she was not being given any job like her brother.

You go and arrange for some small pieces of old cloths, sensing the feelings of Arati, Mukunda suggested her and she happily went in search of the same.

In a very few days Mukunda proved that he not only has the talent but really learnt the art of making idol from Bishnupada also. The main structure is ready and now what we needed is the readymade silhouettes for making the face for the idols, Mukunda uttered to his companions while washing his hands full of mud and dirt in the water of the pond. He paused for a moment and then almost uttered to himself, but the problem is those are available only with the professionals in the field who need these every year for making idols for various occasions. I have to try to collect it from them, he completed.

Why don't you ask for that from Bishnu uncle? Sundar asked him forgetting that his elder brother was actually competing with the man he mentioned.

So you want me to beg to that old moron, the obvious reply was a piercing look and some harsh words from Mukunda. I will manage this without his help, you people don't need to be worried about that, he added.

To collect that readymade silhouettes, the very next day Mukunda fled from his school in the tiffin break and reached the village where those people used to live who have been making idols for generation for various gods and goddesses. While helping Bishnupada he was well known to some of them. He approached all but no one was actually ready to share their business credentials which they have received from their ancestors to a little boy like Mukunda and made many excuses to avoid the same. Still he successfully managed one old guy to lend him one silhouette for some days. He put that silhouette in his bag with the utmost cautiousness and started walking back to his home where he knew his companions were waiting for him. He returned with an expression on his face like the conqueror of the world.

Have you got it? Arati could not help herself from asking the question when she saw her elder brother coming. Sundar has also approached and was standing behind Arati with unmanageable excitement.

Yes, I have, Mukunda declared with more satisfaction than pride and cautiously bring the silhouette out of his bag and show it to his brother and sister as if he has won a cup some competition. Now, nobody on earth could resist us from making the idol, he said more to himself than his companions.

Within next few days the idol became ready except the coloring and cosmetics part. I must say the idol we have made is much better than Bishnu uncles', Sundar said to his brother and sister standing by him proudly and profoundly. Arati supported him with joy. Mukunda did not say anything but his face was glowing in thc pridc of victory. Hc was looking at his own creation with widely opened eyes full of consummation and dream. Yes I have done it, the boy whispered in within his mind.

The more the venture was progressing the more it was becoming tough to arrange resources. In those days kids were not allowed to have cash in their pocket, so there was no question of purchasing anything on their own will. Mukunda and his two associates, Sundar and Arati started collecting basic household items to produce various colors that too without being noticed by the seniors of the family. For example they collected turmeric powder from the kitchen for yellow color, kumkum from their mother for red color, coal dusts from the store for black, so on and so forth.

The coloring of the idol was done by next three to four days and first time Mukunda draw the eyes of any idol and it was really outstanding. The toughest question arrived in front of them when the team was at the happiest point with their success in the venture. Where the sharee for the idol would come from? The problem is, as per ritual when you have made an idol of any god or goddess you have to worship the same and you are not allowed to use any old or used piece of cloth for an idol that would be worshiped. So the kids had to arrange a new piece of sharee for their idol. Buying one was beyond possibility.

We have only one option left with us, Mukunda uttered to his helpers. They were seating in front of the idol. Sundar and Arati stared and him with hope. We have no option but stealing one from the stock of father's cloth store, he completed. The other two looked at each other. There was more frights than surprise in their eyes.

You must have gone crazy, father will beat you to death when he will come to know about this, Sundar tried to create the same horror he was feeling in the mind of his elder brother.

Absolutely, Arati supported him. Mukunda did not reply, he had already decided.

Unbelievably in one Thursday he stole one from the store. as the store used to be closed on Thursday and no one used to visit the area on that day except an old servant who was directed by Mukunda's father to open it once in the morning for clearing and rearranging things. Mukunda followed the old man silently and when he was clearing the rear side of the showcases, Mukunda without a sound collected one sharee, put it in his school bag and came out of the store without being noticed by the old man. He was successful.

IT'S UNIMAGINABLE

After returning from school when Mukunda and Sundar reached their workshop the situation was shocking and heart breaking. The two boys were shattered. What they were witnessing was no less than a nightmare for them and especially for the elder one. In the name of Rudra, who did this and how, Mukunda screeched to himself rather than anyone else but the question got its place to Arati. The little girl was crying seating in the same place where they were making the idol. The idol was lying on the ground, broken badly in to pieces and was in irreparable condition. Mukunda burst out of sheer frustration and this time directly asked Arati with a shouting voice, how has this happened? Who has done this?

Arati did not reply and keep on crying. She took some time to stop. She finally started to describe what happened, today just before some minutes when I came here I thought that a platform is needed to place the idol for worshiping as it is done in the pandal. She snorts twice and continued, I started collecting some bricks from the adjacent area, as you see. Arati pointed her finger towards some bricks lying there. The other two members of the team were eagerly listening to what their sister was describing. Then I made a platform. She while weeping pointed her figure towards the platform she had built just before sometime, which now has turned in to no less than a mess of bricks. She continued, after building the platform I decided to place the idol on the platform. When I was lifting the idol from its place suddenly two street dog ran to the place and the second one, which was chasing the first bumped with my leg and I fall down with the idol in my hand and the idol got damaged. She also showed the wounds in her left elbow and left knee, which was having scars and a little sign of blood too.

Sundar had a great affection for Arati and was frightened about the reaction of Mukunda but there was more tension and grief in Mukunda's face than anger. He was totally devastated witnessing the dream of his young mind lying destroyed and scattered on the ground for which he had many plans. Which in fact was his answer to the humiliation but his affection for his younger sister was more than that distress he was in. He did not rebuke Arati for her over excitement which had actually been the cause of such an accident. Sundar go and fetch some water from the pond, the scratches and strains of blood in Arati's elbow and knee needs to be washed right now, Mukunda directed his brother and helped his sister to stand up.

After everything became normal the three were seating with the broken pieces. Arati was still whipping slowly. There was a feeling of guilt hurting her from within. It is a must to complete the ritual of worshiping when we have made an idol but the issue is again broken idol could not be worshipped, Mukunda said with enormous tension to his other companions. He continued, secondly we have just one day in our hand as the worshipped was planned on next Saturday, so it is absolutely impossible to make another idol within one day. He looked at his second in command, Sundar, for a possible way out but Sundar had no answer for the question.

I think we should now inform the seniors of the family about this in details and they will surely come up with a solution for the problem, Sundar finally suggested to his elder brother.

Doing this will surely invite a terrific punishment for all three of us and I am afraid of that, Mukunda replied.

Suddenly Arati came out with a solution, why don't I become the idol for the goddess Kali. I am a girl, so I can easily act as goddess Kali and once the worship is over I will again become what I am, this way no one will know about this and the purpose will also be solved, Arati suggested her brothers. Both Mukunda and Sundar was amazed with such a brilliant idea and finally it was decided that on Saturday evening Arati will be goddess Kali and after the worship she will become herself again.

SATURDAY

In the afternoon of Saturday the three assembled in the place to complete their plan of worshiping and Arati wore the Sharee on her frock and became the idol of Goddess Kali. She stood on the platform she made, but this time as an idol and

Mukunda became the main priest whereas Sundar his helper. They had collected flowers and cheap sweets from the home earlier on that day. The puja begun with Mukunda's chanting of mantras of without any meaning. Actually he did not know any mantra so he kept chanting whatever came in his mind just copying the tone of the main priest of the village as he had heard. Arati was standing still as she was the idol, so was not allowed to move. Sundar was following the directions of Mukunda. After some time the worship was done and the Prasad was given by the main priest to all including the goddess also, who was actually being worshipped.

Now everything is completed and we must return home, Mukunda said to Sundar and Arati.

Brother you are missing one thing, it is not yet completed, Arati uttered to Mukunda. Last but not the least step of worshipping as the idol should be immersed in to the water as per the process, she added. Mukunda and Sundar looked at each other as it was a valid point. The two brothers put Arati as an idol on their shoulders and walked towards the pond to immerse the idol. While reaching the shore of the pond Sundar and Mukunda started taking seven rounds as they have seen their seniors to perform the ritual of taking seven rounds while immersing any idol.

What the hell are you naughty guys doing here, a sudden female voice shocked the three. It was the elderly maid of the house Durga, who was washing kitchen utensils some distance away from the place where Mukunda and Sundar was taking rounds keeping Arati on their shoulder. She left the utensils there and hurriedly approached them. She could not resist herself to ask the same.

Arati like a knowledgeable person replied seating on the shoulders of her brothers, get out of here, you know I am Goddess Kali now, I have been worshiped and now they will immerse me in to the water. She added, either you get out of here or I will curse you. Don't dare to be cursed by the goddess Kali.

Durga was shocked for a moment and in the next she, in the highest possible voice started shouting and rebuking all the three, the priest, his right hand and finally the Goddess too. Scared Mukunda tried to make Durga understand that their intension was good but Durga was in no mood to listen to him. Sundar was standing speechless and Arati was almost in the verge of crying. Listening Durga's loud voice Arati's mother and other women from the house came out and found Mukunda, Sundar and Arati standing by the pond and Durga scolding at them. Automatically Durga's expression became more dramatic in describing what she has seen and what would have happened if she would not have resisted the kids from doing what they were intended to do. It did not take much of time for the kids and especially for Mukunda to face the enquiries and the final threat that every naughty boy has to listen for the maximum time – wait and let your father return home today.

In the evening Mukunda, Sundar and Arati became the most obedient and attentive students with open books in front of them but actually their entire concentration was on the door. Sundar's father and uncle returned home late in the evening and got to know about everything in the tea table itself. Finally the call came for the three from the adjacent room and all the musketeers entered the room with heads down.

I would like to know what happened today, Brijendra asked his son Mukunda.

With the hardly audible voice Mukunda depicted what they have done in details but intentionally skipped his stealing of a sharee from the store.

Brijendra and his youngest brother Atanu, who was again the father of Arati, just burst in to laughter. Do you two idiots know that you boys have almost killed your sister, Brijendra asked to his two sons. Mukunda and Sundar did not say anything and then with permission left the room.

They were amazed and thankful to the goddess Kali that they were released without any punishment.

A PRESTIGE MATTER ...

Both of you, Satyendra asked two of his younger brother to grab their attention and said, your friend Ranen is waiting for you in the lawn, he informed them.

It was a Sunday morning, Mukunda and Sundar was seating on the mattress with their books, opened in front of them. The boys was pretending to be very serious about their studies, but actually how attentive they were was a million dollar question. They have been expecting the arrival of their friend from the morning and was quite informed about the reason for his visit. They looked at each other, jumped up and ran out of the room. In few minutes Mukunda and Sundar was standing in front of their father, Brijendra with their common friend Ranen.

Brijendra by that time has almost lost all his businesses and was going through a tough time. The robbery in his house had cost him a lot. He was anyhow running a rice shop, in which even he was facing tremendous crunch of fund. Once from an affluent businessman in the area, currently he has become a person with not as much of income as would be enough to support at least all the needs of his family. He was seating in his drawing room with his breakfast and was occupied with some business related jobs. He seemed to be extremely attentive towards the piece of paper that he was holding in his hand.

Father, Ranen is here, he wants to ask your permission, Mukunda uttered to his father in a timid and low voice. Ranen and Sundar were standing behind him.

What happened Ranen, anything special, Brijendra raised his face from the paper and asked with his as usual hefty voice.

Yes uncle, actually my father has sent me to invite Mukunda and Sundar, like every year in the Lakshmi Puja at hour home, Ranen replied almost mumbling.

Hmm, great, which day is the occasion going to take place? Brijendra asked the little boy again without raising his eyes this time from the documents he was surveying.

Ranen looked at his friends and then replied, coming Thursday uncle and they are invited for the *Prasad* and *Khichdi Bhog* in the evening.

Okay, they will obviously be there, Brijendra replied with a smile on his face. He continued, and what about your studies, everything going perfect. This time he asked the boy looking directly in the eyes of Ranen.

Yes uncle, everything's okay, Sundar also helps me in mathematics, Ranen answered cheerfully.

Sundar helps you? Really? Is he knowledgeable enough to help other? Brijendra looked at his son, who was standing silently behind his elder brother and friend. He nodded his head and said, hmm, then it's okay, you may go now, Brijendra again immersed in to the documents in front of him.

When the boys left the room, Brijendra raised his eyes again and his eyes followed his son Sundar. Hallucinations occupied his minds. He kept the paper aside and started judging this son of his. The boy lost his mother so early in life that he perhaps could hardly remind her face. The boy is so shy and introvert that Brijendra has hardly heard him talking to anybody, even with his elder brothers. On top of all the god cursed him with such a terrible typhoid and that too at this early stage of life. But still the boy does not complain or lose his heart. Sometimes Brijendra could not understand whether the boy is the feeblest amongst all his sons or the strongest one. He is a mysterious character, at least for Brijendra. But one thing he knows that the boy has received two things from his mother, firstly the determination and secondly the face. He looks almost similar to his mother, same dreamy eyes, same brownie hair, identical glowing and fare skin, just like same. But at the same time Brijendra knows that the boy's determination to anything and the characteristic of standing tall for a cause is tremendous. Again, alike Bimala, as if the boy is a smaller version of his mother from the innermost core of his mind. Brijendra turned his face to the painted image of his first wife Bimala, hanging from the wall. He stared for a while and then again immersed in to the papers he was busy with.

In Bengal some Bengalis arrange for Lakshmi puja in their home in the last week of the month of August or in the first week of September, which is generally arranged in a flamboyant manner. The family that organizes the event generally invites their neighbors, friends, relatives and also greet them with special type of recipes of rice called "*Khichdi Bhog*". Though sweets and other food items are also used to be an inseparable part of the menu but the main attraction relies on the Khichdi bhog. This special food item use to be so rich and heavy in nature that it is really tough for someone to eat a lot of this. But at the same time it is so tasty that you would never like to stop.

Ranen was not only a classmate but at the same time a good friend of Sundar and was from a well to do family background. He used to come from a nearby village. The only son of his parent after his four elder sisters, the boy automatically was a bit over pampered and indulged by whole of the family. But that did not impose any negative characteristics or snobbish persona on his mentality or behavior. Ranen was a very open minded boy with always a smile on his face. The only problem for Ranen was that he was very much afraid of Mathematics and always used to depend on Sundar's help on this subject. Sundar also liked to help Ranen for his friendly behavior and open minded attitude. So for that reason Ranen used to come to Sundar's place frequently and spend time on discussing mathematics, basically getting guidance and help from Sundar. Mukunda, though was not a classmate but as he also was from the same age group so eventually became a friend of Ranen. Sundar and Mukunda also used to visit Ranen's house and were common faces to his parents. Ranen used to invite these two brothers in all the events in his home. Ranen's mother had a great expertise in cocking various kinds of recipes. She was a masterpiece in cooking many uncommon items and sometimes many common items in such an uncommon way that actually made it tastier than the same item prepared in the conventional way. Sundar for his love for food and gentleman's style of eating was a very beloved one to her.

One of such event was the Lakshmi puja, worship of the goddess Lakshmi, which used to be arranged by Ranen's family every year. And Ranen always used to invite all of his school friends and classmates in that. Except Sundar and Mukunda the others were Kedar, Sitesh and some other boys from the school. Out of those in the main team except Kedar all the others were from a moderate or low income family, whereas Kedar was from one of the most affluent families in the area and that actually developed a feeling of superiority complex in his inner mind. Though he never expressed that superiority feelings to any one directly and was just like any other boy at that age but the only problem with him was he always used to create an environment of challenge even in those things of lowest priority or negligible importance. Above all he always wanted to win in such stupid challenges. Loss in any challenge to anyone used to create a typical psychological sense in him, which used to trigger him more to make another challenge at the earliest possible and to win that any way. Many a time this attitude created problems for himself also but in this regard he was incorrigible.

It is almost a rule in more or less every family in India that when the kids return from their school, the first thing they have to face is a meal. And the rule of the game is that you have to eat that, whether you like it or not hardly matters.

Though for Sundar and Mukunda that obligation was negligibly existed but for many their other friends it was there. On the other contrary to their friends, Sundar and Mukunda used to just keep the school bags at home and get out in the village without any compulsion. But that day was different. After getting back from school they did not go to play. They knew that to get the pass to go to Ranen's house in the evening they had to show a tremendous studiousness towards their studies. The boys had to create a sense that they have read for hours and have completed all their tasks, so now are eligible to be permitted for getting the pass for going to their friend's house for enjoying the Lakshmi Puja event. After carrying the show for two to three hours they approached their father for the valuable pass, who had just returned from his business. After a short investigation and as the boys reminded him about his permission given to Ranen just before a couple of days, the permission was granted and they were legitimate to go.

Don't be too late there, and you must return home at the earliest, the final order was issued by Brijendra to his two sons. Nearly at seven in the evening the brothers arrived at the pre scheduled venue of meeting and found all others have already reached and waiting for them. So all of them started for their destination of the day and reached by next half an hour or so.

Hey I am so happy that all of you have reached, great. Please come with me inside the house, Ranen was waiting at the gate for his friends and lead them inside the house where the puja was actually being organized. Ma, all my friends have come, he introduced his friends to his mother.

The lady was busy in managing all the requirements for the puja. She turned back and found some the friends of her only son were standing behind her. I am so happy to see you all here, enjoy yourselves and ask anything you need either to me or Ranen or any other, Ranen's mother welcomed the friends of her son heartily.

You don't worry Ma, I will take care of them, Ranen's eldest sister, who was helping her mother in arrangements intervened and she personally took the responsibility to serve the Prasad to the gang of boys. The amount of Prasad distributed by Ranen's eldest sister for each of the boys was no less than a heavy tiffin consisting mainly of different kinds of fruits and sweets. After completing the Prasad Ranen took his friends to his room to spend some time until the main attraction of the show arrives, the Khichdi Bhog and the Mixed-Vegetable.

So this is your room, Mukunda asked Ranen. Ranen just nodded. Sundar approached the wide and open window and stared outside. Who lives in that house? He asked his friend Ranen showing the house just neighboring.

It is Ankur da's house, Ranen replied. He added, you know Ankur da right, our senior in the school.

Sundar thought for a while and nodded his head. The house is nice, he replied.

Ranen, all of you come downstairs, the Bhog is ready, the boys were gossiping on different things when Ranen was called by his mother to bring his friends in the specially decorated banqueting area where the dining was actually arranged for all the invited people. Let's go for the bhog, its ready, Ranen said to his friends and all the boys moved for the same.

At that time there was no chair table concept in the rural places and people used to seat on the ground on cushions for eating. So the boys let themselves sat in a single row on the ground on cushion. The Khichdi Bhog was served and the boys started eating. They were gossiping, laughing and enjoying the foods to the fullest when Kedar did what he has always been expected to. I can challenge anybody on eating Khichdi, I bet no one can defeat me in this, he threw a challenge to all his companions.

So finally you are on your track right? You are again challenging? Don't you remember that you were defeated just two days back in the challenge you threw in the school, Sitesh mocked him.

You keep your mouth shut or dare to accept the challenge, that was something else and this is separate, Kedar stubbornly replied to Sitesh.

Sitesh shook his head and avoided Kedar. He did not accept but Sundar did. Okay, I do accept, but what is on the table, he asked Kedar in front of all.

The looser will buy a pen for the winner next day at school in the tiffin time, Kedar was excited and replied with utter promptness.

Now the bet was sealed, there was no option for Sundar to be unsuccessful in winning the bet as the price of a pen was beyond his capability to arrange and he has already accepted that challenge so he was bound by his own words and the race began. Ranen's mother and his elder sister was serving and the challenge also excited them and as well as the others present in the hall. The two young boys were given same amount every time they finished off their plates and Sitesh was given the responsibility of counting the number of times each of the competitors were served with an audible voice. Finally the competition attracted all others in the hall and took nearly one hour unless Kedar surrendered. Sundar was declared winner. Will you mind to announce that you are going to buy a pen for the winner next day at school in front of all, Sitesh asked Kedar with a sarcastic smile on his lips. Kedar promised. Unfortunately, this is the second time in last three days you lost a challenge, Sitesh teased Kedar again by salting his wounds.

Ranen, we should leave now, Mukunda uttered to Ranen after the *Khichdi Bhog.* Otherwise we will be too late and you know father will rebuke us for the delay, added. Ranen acknowledged and after informing Ranen's parents and elder sisters the boys finally started walking back to their respective homes. The speed automatically declined for the boys compared to their speed when they started in the evening. It took nearly an hour for the group when they reached the main market place of the area. All the way till here Sitesh and others, except Sundar were making fun of Kedar and teasing him on his challenging everyone every time in everything. From here they had to take separate paths to their respective homes, so they decided to seat for a while before getting separated for the night. I am very thirsty guys and badly need some water, Mukunda said to others and get in to a sweet shop of a family friend for a glass of water. Water is perhaps in the top of the list of those things, thirst for which is always better understood when someone else asks for it. Especially in a group the thirst spreads like an epidemic. So as usual one by one all the boys started feeling the thirst and queued after Mukunda.

Where all of you boys are coming from, so late in the evening, the shopkeeper Ratan uncle asked Mukunda?

We all went to one of our friend's house to attend the Lakshmi puja there, Mukunda replied. We have been walking for long and we all are thirsty, may we have some water uncle, he added.

Surely, is this something you need to ask? The waterskin is there, Ratan pointed his figure towards the corner where the waterskin was kept with a stainless still glass on top of it.

Mukunda moved forward and automatically the other boys made a queue behind him. When all the boys were waiting in a queue behind Mukunda, Kedar found that just made hot Rasgullas were being taken to the showcase from the inner room behind the shop usually where the sweets are prepared. Uncle are these Rasgullas just prepared, he asked the shopkeeper.

Yes son, these are just coming out of the stove, Ratan replied with a smile on his face. Would you like to have one, the old man asked in reply with a smile?

Then what Kedar said was unpredictable to everyone present. Kedar suddenly left the queue and turned towards all the boys who were standing in the queue to satisfy their thirst for water. He then announced, if anyone from the group could eat one kg of Rasgullas including the sweet juice and that too nonstop right now then I will pay the price for the same, but if he fails then he will have to pay the price.

Are you an insane or something else? Sitesh got irritated of this ridiculous challenge and asked Kedar. Everyone was annoyed but Kedar was stubborn. It was more than limit, Sundar was also irritated but he finally decide to stop this nonsense of challenging once and for all. Okay Kedar, I accept the challenge but the bet is not the price of the Rasgullas but also one more thing.

What the hell are you doing Sundar, Sitesh asked his friend quite loudly. Why are you accepting this nonsense?

I know what I am doing, Sundar turned his face to Sitesh and replied. His cool sight was enough to pacify the excitement in Sitesh. Tell me what else in on the bet, Kedar asked Sundar excitedly.

If I win you will pay the price as well as stop this nonsense of challenging for ever, are you ready, Sundar asked Kedar. Kedar thought for a while and finally replied, okay.

Kedar ordered one kg of Rasgullas to Ratan and it get served at the earliest possible. In a small wooden table Sundar and Kedar was seating facing each other. An earthen pot was kept on the table containing the Rasgullas. The other boys stood surrounding the table. Sundar started one by one, without any interval. Initially it was easier but slowly it was getting more and more tough. He understood that he need to slow the speed down so started chewing slowly and breathing in between. The trick worked and it became a bit easier for him to manage. As per the challenge he was not allowed to drink water in between, which made the situation toughest. All the others including Ratan uncle was looking at Sundar. He had understood that Sundar was not feeling very comfortable. The old man intervened, son this challenge does not worth so much that you risk your health, Ratan uttered to Sundar. No one will have to pay anything, he added. But Sundar carried on without looking or giving any concern to anyone or anything else other than the sweets. Finally completing the Rasgullas he lifted the earthen container and drank the juice in one shot. Then he placed the earthen pot down on the table. His exhaustion was well visible on his face.

It was unexpected to Kedar, he was actually more than shocked. Either you stop this nonsense of challenging or just don't be with us from now onwards, Sitesh came to him and with a calm but determined voice told Kedar. Kedar did not reply and paid the bill. Ratan uncle asked Sundar if he is facing any issue. Sundar replied that it is ok. Finally they came out of the shop and took their respective way back to home.

Mukunda and Sundar reached their home nearly at half past nine and found that all the family members have just started their dinner. Go freshen up and come join us in the dinner, we have just started, Brijendra told his sons. Now it was a terribly hard-hitting situation for both of them but for Sundar it was nightmare.

None of them had the courage to directly say what they have done that evening so the two boys stared at each other and silently let themselves sat for the dinner. The dinner was served, Mukunda was more afraid of Sundar than of himself and was closely watching his brother with tremendous scare as well as curiosity. Sundar first took one small amount of rice and put it in his mouth. It was quite impossible for him, but he actually waiting for his father to finish off his dinner and leave the place so that he can stop and silently leave too. So he was chewing the small amount for long time to kill time. But Mukunda failed to understand the plan his brother had in his mind and started getting anxious of Sundar's health. Sundar took much more than usual time to finish the first amount and took another small amount. Now it was beyond the capacity of Mukunda to bear with such a bizarre situation.

Stop eating or you will die, your stomach will surely burst, Mukunda just screeched out quite audibly forgetting completely that many other members were also present there including the person they were most afraid off, their father.

His words dropped like a bomb shell in that small kitchen. Everyone was shocked except Sundar, who was seating with his eyes fixed on the plate in front of him. He was perhaps trying to understand what the consequences waiting for him in very close future. Everyone present in the room looked at Mukunda. Who will die and what for, Brijendra with utmost surprise asked him. His deep weighty voice was more than enough to run a chill in the spine of both Mukunda and Sundar.

The game was over. Mukunda had no other way but to express what they have done that evening and said everything in details from the Prasad to Khichdi Bhog to finally the Rasgullas episode. Everyone looked at Sundar but he was seating speechless with his eyes fixed on the ground and was mentally preparing for the next consequences of punishments. Brijendra turned at Sundar and asked, is what Mukunda told right?

Sundar did not say anything just nodded his head. Suddenly Brijendra started laughing loudly and directed Sundar to leave the plate and get up. Sundar could not believe his own eyes and ears. He silently stood up and was yet to move out of the kitchen when Brijendra called his name again. Sundar turned without raising his eyes from the ground. You don't need to do something to prove your heroism like this again, Brijendra said his son. Brijendra paused for a moment and then added, but I must appreciate your spirit. You may go now.

Sundar did not reply and left the kitchen silently.

STAY WELL …

SOMETIMES IN EARLY 1900s

Mr. Bhattacharya, personally I strongly oppose what you say on women's education.

The tall, well-built and learned man announced his views categorically and overwhelmingly in the presence of many elderly *Samajpatis* like Shirshendu Bhattacharya, the eldest and most widely respected amongst them all in the village. His deep and loud voice shattered all seating there. He did not stop there and continued, I, Daipayan Mukherjee, not merely think rather believe from the core of my heart and through the lights of the education that I have earned, that without educating the women in the society, the society itself can't be educated or be developed. I have been and will always be a supporter of the views and thoughts of Shree Ishwar Chandra Vidyasagar regarding this. The man paused for a moment and stared at those who were seating in front of them. Except Shirshendu Bhattacharya, all other were whispering at each other's ear, only Shirshendu was staring straight in the eyes of the passionate speaker. Daipayan continued, I don't feel any complexities in sending my daughters to school and I do promise that I will, whether you like it or not is entirely your choice and I am no way interested about knowing that. Daipayan completed and stared at Shirshendu Bhattacharya for his reply.

Suddenly the whisper stops and a pin drop silence prevailed. No one has ever thought even in his most ferocious dream that some could challenge Shirshendu Bhattacharya and that too in front of the entire village committee. Daipayan, today has crossed all the limits. All the eyes present there were moving from one face to the other, both silent and perhaps looking at nothing other than each other's eyes.

Shirshendu Bhattacharya first broke the silence. The man stood up and remarked, hmm, so Daipayan you have settled your mind to upheaval against the rules and regulations given by our holy scriptures, Shirshendu asked the young man standing in front of him. He added, and you expect we will not resist you from committing such nuisance.

For the first time a slight smile played its strings in Daipayan's lips. He replied to the question with the same on his eyes, firstly as per my knowledge and studies none of our ancient holy scriptures forbid us to educate the women, otherwise we did not have hrishikas like Lopamudra, Raomasa, Agnirasa, Apala, the list is too long to be depicted. The details of them are depicted in the divine Vedas. If you think I am saying something wrong then I would request you to arrange a debate session anytime as per your convenience in front of all the people in the village. You can even invite anyone from anywhere who you think would be a man knowledgeable enough for such debate. Secondly if there is any such forbiddance for women's education in our religion or Holy Scriptures, then why do we, the mighty men of the society worship a Devi, Saraswati as the goddess of education? Why not any Dev? Daipayan paused for some moments. The people seating there started looking at each other. They were not courageous enough to counter the young man as they know Daipayan is a very knowledgeable person and don't say anything which he is not extremely sure about. I think I have told what I have come here to tell you all. I am going to send my daughter to school from tomorrow and now I must leave as I have to set out for my workplace, Daipayan completed. No one uttered anything or tried to stop him and he left the place as confidently as he came here fifteen minutes before.

Daipayan Mukherjee, Sundar's maternal grandfather was a very educated person. He was a high ranking Government officer under the British rule in India in a famous ship yard in eastern part of the nation. He had a very happy family consisting of himself, his wife and four daughters. He was a man of very gorgeous personality and also an attractive appearance. At that period of time, i.e. more than hundred years back from now, he was so in favor of women education that he disregarded all the prejudicial rules and regulations present at that time in the society encumbered upon the common men by the so called "*Samajpatis*". Daipayan disregarded all such prejudicial rules and admitted all his four daughters in the school. He also disregarded the societal rule of child marriage for girls and educated his daughters up to a certain level and only then arranged their marriage when they reached their youth. All his four son in laws were educated and from reputed, established and well to do families.

AFTER SOME YEARS

Sundar's mother, Bimala was the youngest of the four daughters of Daipayan Mukherjee and almost fourteen years younger than the eldest, Avantika. When the eldest sister got married Bimala was a child of four or five year old. Avantika was married to Partha Sarathi Chatterjee from the neighboring village, a professor of Mathematics in the local college. He was a very educated man and a good person by nature. Partha Sarathi always used to be engaged with his studies and had a personal library also in his house. As the life moved on Avantika and Partha Sarathi became parents of two sons. The elder one was named Manu, who eventually became very beloved to his three maternal aunties. As it is always the birth right of the first child of any family, Manu was vividly pampered by all of them. He actually lived his childhood in the house of his maternal grandfather until the other three daughters of his maternal grandfather got married and originally was always over pampered by rest three younger sisters of his mother. This kind of over caring made Manu a very dependent kind of person. He never needed to ask for anything of his needs as every time someone or other of his three aunties were ready to take care of all his requirements and that too sometimes even before he needed it. This kind of extra sensitive support made the boy a very emotional kind of personality. Manu grew up and became a very jovial but at the same time much disciplined boy. He was a good student from his boyhood itself and at the same time he was highly interested in games and sports, especially in gymnastics and body building. The more he grew up the more he became beloved to people both from within the family and also outside. In the while all his three maternal aunties got married one after another. The last of his companions, i.e. Bimala, when got married and went to her husband's house Manu became cruelly alone in the house of his maternal grandfather. At that point of time his maternal grandfather and grandmother had become aged and it was not possible for them to take care of a boy properly and Manu also lost his interests in that house as there was no one to company him.

One day Avantika and Partha Sarathi came to Daipayan's house. Father both of you and Ma have become aged and alone here, I think you should live with us now, Avantika said to her father while discussing various other family related issues. I have discussed with my husband and he is also of the same thought, she added.

How far this house is from yours, don't worry about us, Daipayan replied with a smile. He continued, better you take Manu with you as I have many times witnessed that he feels very lonely here. To be here with two aged person will make him even lonelier, which is absolutely not desirable. There at your house, I think he will get a companion in his brother.

But I think he should be here to take care of you, Avantika replied. At the minimum he would be helpful to contact us in any emergency situation.

No, absolutely not, Daipayan replied. If any such thing happens to any of us or even both, then that will be our fate. But for that I will never ever suggest to make my beloved grandson to live a lonely life. He continued, Avantika we have lived our lives happily and now it's our duty as well as responsibility to help the new generation to live their lives on their own terms and conditions. You know, he is a very emotionally sensitive boy and gets hurt very easily. That is not all, he is very introvert and shy type of character who does not share any feelings of pain with anybody. Please be very careful and sensitive about him. Take him with you and give him more adoration and care than he is used to. Avantika and Partha did not say anything, just nodded in affirmation.

Within a few days Manu came to live with his parents. He was actually not very keen to relocate but Daipayan made him understand that what he is doing is the best for Manu. How far your father's house is from this one, he asked his grandson. You could anytime come here on your will. When finally Manu left the house, his eyes were moist.

Father, may I talk to you now, Manu asked for permission to his father. Partha Sarathi was reading the newspaper in the morning at his drawing room when he found his elder son Manu standing at the door and staring at him.

Yes, surely, he replied. Folding the newspaper and keeping the same on the table beside he turned towards his son and asked, tell me what you need to talk about, he added with a smiling face to encourage his introvert son to share his mind.

May I join the Akhara in the neighboring village, Manu uttered with a slow and soft voice. He continued, there they train boys in wrestling and gymnastics. I am interested.

Why not son? This is absolutely appreciable, Partha Sarathi appraised the interest of his son. I know the trainer personally and will talk to him about you today itself, Partha Sarathi replied to his son.

Thank you father, Manu replied and left the room.

From next day Manu became a dedicated member of the club and his father always encouraged him as he had a natural inclination towards those activities. In due course Manu built up a great physic.

Choto Mausi (youngest aunty), are you there?

Bimala was preparing the lunch when she heard the voice. The voice was extremely well-known to her. It is Manu. Saroj, please take this, Manu has come, she put all her work to Sarojini and almost ran to the door to welcome her beloved nephew. Manu used to visit the house of his youngest aunty, i.e. Sundar's paternal house frequently as it was one or hardly one and a half hours journey from his own house. Daipayan and his wife has passed away in between years. Both of them accepted their last journey peacefully. Sundar was a child then of around two years of age.

When Bimala finally found Manu, he was standing with Sundar on his hands. Sundar was more interested to open the wrap of the chocolate he was gifted by his Manu da. So, how are you doing, Bimala asked Manu. And what about your parents and brother, she added. And you have again bought these chocolate for this naughty boy. She then pointed her eyes to her own son and said, you will eventually lose all your teeth very soon. Sundar did not even bother and concentrated on the chocolate he was gifted.

All are okay, Manu replied to his aunty. I am going to uncle's shop, and taking Sundar with me, he turned to move.

You just have arrived, get freshen up, eat something and then go, Bimala suggested but until then Manu has crossed the main gate.

Manu was very affectionate to Sundar. He loved the kid very much. Whenever he was here, he used to carry Sundar on his shoulders and roam here and there around the place. There was a small stream of four to five feet wide, made for watering the farming fields in the village. Manu always used to cross that cannel jumping from one side to the opposite and that too carrying Sundar on his arms. Sundar used to be so happy about that and always insisted him to do the same over and over again. That day also Manu headed towards the cannel and jumped cross it with Sundar. Sundar as usual requested his brother to do the same again. Okay, I will but you have to promise that you will not say this to anyone, Manu smilingly asked the kid knowing that Sundar would not be able to resist himself but sharing this joy of his with his mother.

Even after his repeated suggestion of not sharing this to anybody Sundar always use to tell that to his mother after returning home. In addition, the kid use to describe how strong and powerful Manu da is as if it was his own achievement and Bimala use to rebuke Manu with a passive indulgence. Manu use to take his young brother to the nearby market and bought him biscuits of one Anna (a very old form of paisa, which obsolete today), which for Sundar was more precious than anything and everything on this planet at that time and age.

Pranam uncle, Manu came forward to touch Brijendra's feet as per the ritual and in reply Brijendra bless him with good wishes and fortune. Brijendra has just come from his shop when he found Manu playing with Sundar. So, young man how are you doing and what about your parents, I hope everything is alright he asked Manu in reply.

Yes uncle, everything is absolutely okay, Manu replied. Tea and snacks were served to both of them in a while. It seems you are doing well with your physical exercises, Brijendra commented to Manu with a smiling gesture while sipping the cup of tea. Yes, and I can defeat you in arm wrestling, Manu replied with so much of enthusiasm and confidence. Really, then let us have a duel, Brijendra open heartedly accepted. You seat here and watch me winning the duel, Manu placed Sundar on the bed from his lap and the two started. In between Satyendra, Mukunda and Narendra has circled the table in highest curiosity to witness the duel they could not even dream of. Sundar and all his elder brothers have become spectators. Though Brijendra was a tough fighter and the duel lasts for quite long but Manu finally managed to seal the same with a winning smile. I told you I will defeat you, he loudly appraised himself.

I would have been less happy if the opposite had happened, Brijendra replied and praised Manu. I am proud of you my son.

For Sundar and his brothers it was something implausible. How could anyone in this universe defeat their father? The man all the brothers were most terrified about is defeated by Manu da in arm wrestling. That one scene truly speaking made the image of Manu da in Sundar's mind as the bravest and most powerful person ever on earth. He wished, one day he would become a man like him, he wished, one day he would jump cross the cannel, he wished, one day he would defeat others in arm wrestling, he wished, one day he would have one Anna for purchasing biscuits from the village market and above all he wished, one day he would become like his Manu da.

But as the wise people always says, "*good time never lasts for long*", and that became the hardest fact in the life of Sundar and his brothers very soon. Sundar's mother passed away while giving birth of her youngest son, mainly due to excessive weakness and bleeding. After the death of his maternal aunty, who was more a friend than a guardian, Manu da's visit to Sundar's house became a seldom incident. Finally when Brijendra married for the next time, eventually then Manu totally stopped coming to that place, once a second home for him. It was no less than a heart break for Sundar.

Sundar please come with me, Manu da has come to meet you. Sundar saw his eldest brother Satyendra calling him loudly from a distance. Sundar was flying kites with friends in the small area adjacent to the canal. Nearly after three years from the day Sundar had met Manu da last time. For a moment Sundar could not believe his ears and in next he started running towards home handing his kite and other things to another boy who was accompanying him in flying kites.

When Sundar entered the house he found Manu da seating in the drawing room. He was wearing a short length white dhoti and another same kind of cloth for covering upper portion of his muscular body, a traditional dress as per the Hindu customs for the death of someone from the family, especially parents. It was clear form his appearance that he has not combed his hairs for some days now. His eyes were showing the tremendous tiredness he was going through. Sundar stopped at the door. Come here, I have brought biscuits for you, Manu gestured with his palm to call Sundar. Sundar came forward slowly. His mind was full of dilemma as he has never seen his hero so calm and pacified. Manu da gave a packet of biscuit to his beloved brother with a pale smile on his lips.

Why are you wearing cloths like this, Sundar asked his cousin brother?

Because I have become as unfortunate as you guys, I have also lost my mother Sundar, Manu replied. His eyes were moist. I have come to invite you for the final day of her last rights. Uncle said it would not be possible for him to take all you brothers with him on that but still I will request him to at least take you with him on that day, he added.

Manu stayed for one or two hours and when he was leaving he raised Sundar on his hands, there were drops in his eyes. In a broken voice he told Sundar two words – "stay well". That scene Sundar would never forget till his last breath. His hero, his superman was crying, an unbelievable phenomenon for Sundar.

Sundar could not attend Manu da's request as Brijendra was going through a bad time in his business, which he failed to overcome ever again, so he alone attended and did not take any one with him.

Avantika's death created a massive loneliness in Manu's life, which in turn extended the distance between him and his home. Partha Sarathi was busy with his own works, studies, college and social involvements. For Manu the Akhara became the only place where he started searching for ways to get out of that vast loneliness. Rest of the time he used to roam here and there aimlessly. A boy who had always been over pampered by people surrounding him and have never had to take care of his own was now left alone to take care of his self. Someone or other was always behind him there to ask him, rather force him for taking foods and fulfill other necessities as and when required. But now in this cruel loneliness he started missing out those things, there was no one with him at the toughest stage of his life. Sometimes he used to forget his breakfast or lunch even. Time did not stop, and in such a way Manu da spent four to five years of his deserted life. He abandoned life and life in turn abandoned him.

Manu, please take the medicine, the old servant said to Manu.

Manu was lying on the bed in his room. I don't like it, he replied without opening his eyes.

I know son, nobody likes medicine, but it is necessary now, the elderly man replied. Once you get back to as you were then nobody will request you for medicine, but for now please don't say No son, the man keep on requesting the young boy. Manu opened his eyes, pull his body on his elbow and silently obeyed the elderly man's request. He actually never learnt to disobey, rather was more comfortable in obeying elders.

More exercise and less food and lesser rest had started taking its toll from Manu. The man who once did not know what illness is, has now started falling ill every now and then. His father consulted with various doctors and physicians but the phenomenon did not change and after suffering for quite a long time it was diagnosed as Tuberculosis. A disease at that period of time in India hardly used to be considered as irredeemable.

A BOY OF 17 YEARS NOW

Sundar, now a boy of 17 years of age, had just returned after providing tuitions to his students. In this long interval of time there was hardly any chance when Sundar met his Manu da. As the two closely attached families have become alien to each other after the two bridges, Avantika and Bimala broke down. But Sundar has lived his dream of becoming a strong man like his hero as well as influencer, Manu da. Even he has defeated the terrible typhoid in achieving his dream. He has reminded those golden days of his life with Manu da every now and then and hoped that one day when he will really come up with a physic like his hero then he will go to visit him. He has dreamt of defeating his Manu da in arm wrestling one day.

It was almost 9:30 in the morning and Sundar was getting ready for his school when the doorbell rang. He opened the door and was surprised. It was Fanindra, Manu's younger brother waiting at the door. So lucky the day is for me, almost after eight years I am seeing you brother, Sundar greeted his cousin brother. Please come in, he added. Fanindra followed his cousin brother in to the house. Sundar guided him to the drawing room where his father was seating. You meet him and I will be back in five minutes, Sundar uttered to Fanindra and left the room.

When Sundar came back he found Fanindra was talking to his father. Sundar you don't need to go to school today, Brijendra told his son. Go with Fanindra, Manu has called you, he wants to meet you, he added.

Surely father, but why have not he come, is he okay, Sundar asked Fanindra.

Nothing as such, he is just busy with other things and so has sent me, Fanindra answered to Sundar with a pale smile.

You get freshen up and take your lunch before you set out, Brijendra advised Fanindra.

Fanindra and Sundar started their journey after lunch. Sundar was highly enthusiast as he was going to see his hero, his superman and that too after so long a period. How he is now, is he still practicing in the Akhara, is there something about his marriage, so many questions Sundar asked his cousin brother on the journey. Fanindra did not answer even a single question directly. The only answer Sundar received was, what the hurry is, you will get all your answer very soon, once you are there. That one and a half hour was too long for Sundar to wait for the answers of his curious questions but he had not have any other choice but to wait.

Partha Sarathi opened the door when Sundar and Fanindra reached their house. Sundar and Fanindra was waiting outside. Pranam uncle, Sundar touched Partha's feet as per the ritual and in reply he was bless with good wishes. Where is Manu da, Sundar asked his uncle?

Go upstairs, he is waiting for you in his room, second in the right side, Partha Sarathi directed the young boy to go to Manu da's room. Sundar almost galloped the steps, ran to the door and in next moment he was there standing wordless at the door of the room. What the hell he is watching at? Manu da was lying on a bed and an old servant was seating by his side with a hand fan made of palm leaf. But, is that my hero who I saw for the last time eight years back. A person so tinny that the only difference between him and a skeleton is just the human skin, which he retain and the skeleton does not. There were deep dark circles underneath his eyes, he was coughing whenever he was trying to talk. Sundar suddenly just lost himself.

The old man seating by Manu da's head said something in his ear and help him turn towards the door. So now the strong man needs the helping hand of an old one to take a turn. Ohhh God, how could you do this to yourself? The words come automatically came out of Sundar's mouth.

Manu da called Sundar near to him by waving his hand. He could not even uttered anything. It was looking like he could hardly wave his hand even. When Sundar came near to him there was a pale smile in his face. As if the man was acquiring all his strengths to smile. Manu was trying to tell Sundar something but it was so mute that Sundar had to take his ears close to his mouth.

Sundar I am so happy that you have come to see me in my last time. Look your Manu da has become so feeble that he can't even seat, he uttered to Sundar. He started coughing again vigorously.

Manu da please don't talk any more, Sundar requested his brother. We will talk for hours once you get well, he added. Manu sipped some water from the glass the old servant was holding in his hand. He turned at Sundar and smiled. I know what I am suffering from and what the future of it and that too very close, so let me talk, Manu said to Sundar. He continued, Sundar do you recall those days when I used to come to your house and go for jumping that cannel?

I still cherish those days, you too still remind that, Sundar asked. He started moving his fingers in Manu's hairs to comfort him as much as possible or might be comforting himself, Sundar des not know the answer. Those are the only happy moments I had in my life to recall brother, and nothing else, Manu replied. His eyes become moist.

The two stayed there for nearly an hour until the elderly servant came to inform that the doctor has come for routine checkup. Okay, Manu da, I should go now, Sundar said to his brother. I will keep on coming until you get well, he added. Manu smiled and replied, Brother there will be no meeting any more ever after this. He paused for moments as if he is gathering all his energy and strength to complete his word. He continued, at least on this earth there will be no more meeting. "Stay well" brother, he completed with a pale but deep smile on his lips.

Sundar was watching his Hero, his Superman being defeated by the misfortunes of life. He could not watch this anymore, and almost ran out of the room in the adjacent balcony. In moist eyes when he looked at the horizon, the dusk was falling upon his world.

OPEN THE DOOR …

SOME TIME IN EARLY 1930s

Bimala was at her late teen age when she was married to Brijendra, a young, dynamic and hardworking man at his mid-twenties. He was at that time struggling to establish his newly formed business on a relatively stronger base and also to make the same flourish. Brijendra had two younger brothers, Shantanu and Atanu. At the same time as the eldest amongst all the three brothers, he also had to take the responsibilities of other family affairs. His father Kali Charan was a sagacious kind of person and used to be totally standoffish from any family or financial responsibilities, which compelled his eldest son to take up all those even before Brijendra was an adult. He hardly had any leisure time to spend at home.

When Bimala came to her new home, she found a friend and a younger brother in Atanu, Brijendra's youngest brother. Atanu at that time was a boy of eleven years of age. His eldest brother was no less than a father figure to him and he used to respect him as much as he was afraid of him. Atanu was a very introvert kind of boy who had no so called friends. He found a motherly elder sister in Bimala to whom he can talk his mind without any fear. In a very few days the two became best friends. As the time passed by Atanu grew up. Contrary to Shantanu, Atanu was not very much interested in studies, rather he used to help his elder brother in his business as and when ordered, otherwise he used to help Bimala in the kitchen.

I think you have done with your studies and basically seating idle at home, which is totally worthless, Brijendra uttered to his brother Atanu on the dining table at lunch. You must learn to take responsibilities now. Brijendra continued, I have decided that from tomorrow you will help me in the business in a much serious way than what you have been doing for last few years, he completed. His deep and loud voice, moreover the dictating tone was enough to run a chill in Atanu's spine. Atanu helplessly looked at his last resort, his sister-in-law. His eyes were clearly seeking for rescue from such a situation.

What does he know about business? And moreover I think he is not yet mature enough also for such heavy jobs, Bimala while serving foods to the three brothers uttered to her husband. I think he needs some more days to get accustomed with the business works and also to learn the way he is learning under your guidance. After all Atanu is anyway helping you in business, she added but with a feeble voice.

Brijendra raised his eyes from the plate and looked straight at his wife for some moments and then said, I was even younger when I took up the responsibilities of the entire family and what he is doing now is not helping in business rather helping himself to earn his pocket money. He continued, actually what you said is absolutely perfect, he now will have to learn how to help in a business. Brijendra paused for a moment and then looking at his brother completed, right from tomorrow morning and I don't want any excuses this time. No one dared to say anything else, Atanu's fate was sealed.

You will take care of the stock and at the end of every day you will report me the stock status, Brijendra directed his brother. Atanu's training had started from morning. He nodded and get back to his place. Remember one thing very carefully, the stock physically must not mismatch with the transaction books, before living the place Brijendra gave his final order.

Time passed by and within some months Atanu learnt to manage the stock, talking to the suppliers, handling customers and more importantly working the full day in the business without being bored off. Brijendra also noticed the improvement in Atanu and now he could rely on his youngest brother regarding business needs. As Brijendra concentrated on new ventures of businesses, the responsibilities of the existing one became mainly on Atanu.

Brijendra involved Atanu more in the business with greater responsibilities but till Atanu was so afraid of his elder brother that for anything he needed, he used to request Bimala to talk to Brijendra. She was the only person to whom he could freely share his mind and thoughts and also his wishes. One such day in the evening when Bimala was working in the kitchen Atanu came and started helping her. Is it possible for a single person to manage such hectic jobs every day and that too four times daily, while helping he started talking as if he talking to himself. Dada knows that I am occupied by the business responsibilities, he should have thought of at least one person who could help you here in the household jobs. He needs someone like me to help him but why does not he understand that you too need someone to help you? He turned to Bimala and added, this is almost unbearable for anyone to take this huge burden alone and that too every day, this time he mentioned Bimala. She was silently listening to Atanu while working in the kitchen and without giving any importance or reply to any of Atanu's questions. Noticing no response from Bimala, Atanu continued with more thrust, there should be at least another person who could help you as I am helping dada in the business. He has always been like that only, will dictate but never understands what others need. It was clear to Bimala what actually Atanu was trying to mean but could not say the same directly. Bimala did not respond but she has got what she will have to do on this and how. Finding no response even after such a great and desperate attempt Atanu left the kitchen almost with the highest level of disappointment. A magnanimous smile played on Bimala's lips watching Atanu leaving the kitchen.

Brijendra and Atanu was waiting at their dining room for Bimala to arrange their dinner. Brijendra was getting a bit restless as the delay was unusual. Bimala generally keeps everything absolutely organized and make nobody wait at the dining table for food but today Brijendra has been waiting for last fifteen minutes. Any problem in the kitchen, he finally could not resist himself from asking the question to his wife who was there inside the kitchen.

Brijendra's question was not even completed in full when Bimala entered the room. She kept the utensils and pots quietly on the ground in front of her husband and started serving him and Atanu. Atanu was seating speechlessly keeping eyes fixed on the plate in front of him.

It is becoming impossible for me to manage the children in one hand and the kitchen in other, I need someone who could at the least help me in some of the household jobs, Bimala in a slow and low but complaining tone said to her husband. It was the third day from the kitchen episode when Atanu initiated the point to his sister-in-law. The glow in Atanu's face was evident enough to say that he was silent but happy. He was not even aware of his success and for last two days was planning for some new ideas. But he got the shock when after listening his wife Brijendra replied, okay then from the next day I will arrange for a handmaiden to help you in your daily activities in the kitchen.

Atanu's face was visibly darkened, he lost the hope but Bimala did not left the field and replied, and who will pay that maiden? Do you know how costly they have become nowadays? And more over that maid will not take care of everything as her own family and will only work when and what I will direct. I need someone who will not only help me but at the same time will be my companion.

For Brijendra it was now the limit. Is there any other option, he asked to her wife. Bimala was just waiting for this moment and probably someone else was even more.

Why don't arrange for Atanu's marriage? I will get a company as well as she would be the best person to help me and also will be a member of the family, Bimala suggested. She continued, Atanu is now working in the business and also earning so what the harm if he gets married.

Brijendra stopped eating midway, looked at Bimala and replied with a surprise in his voice, what, marriage of this "good for nothing" guy, who is not even mature enough to take care of himself. He continued, he will take responsibility of a girl, and you ask me to believe that.

Don't take it otherwise, when we were married you were even younger than what he is today, and you also did not have an elder brother to guide you, this time Bimala replied diplomatically. She took the same path Brijendra use to take when he talks about Atanu, citing example from his own life. Brijendra did not answer to this and he kept silence. Nobody extended the discussion any more but the decision was taken.

The next day Sundar's father informed all his confidants that he has decided for the marriage of his brother at the earliest possible time and he is in search of a girl from an educated and cultured family. It did not take more than a few moths Sarojini came to her new home as Atanu's wife.

Sarojini was a girl of fourteen years when she got married with Atanu. Her ancestral house was in a nearby village and they were one of the most respected family of that area. Her father, a teacher in the primary school of the village was a very decent and educated person and her two elder brothers were also just like her father, learned, decent and soft-spoken. After getting married with Atanu, here in her in-laws house Bimala became a friend, philosopher and guide of Sarojini in her new life. Sarojini used to call Bimala "Didi". Bimala in turn found a beloved younger sister in Saroj, the name by which Bimala used to call Sarojini. The two young ladies became so friendly and dependent on each other that women from neighboring families in the village used to call them no less than two sisters from same mother. Within a few days Sarojini became so dependable that Bimala handed over many of her responsibilities related to family to Sarojini and Saroj happily accepted all of those and used to carry out each and every of those responsibilities so accurately and completely that as if she had been doing these for years. Even Sarojini used to take care of Bimala's children and Bimala was free of any tension regarding that. When in one instance a lady from a neighboring family asked Bimala, how could you be so sure that Sarojini will be taking proper care to your children? She added, I am not saying anything against her intension but she is not yet mature enough.

Bimala laughed at that words and replied looking at Saroj, she is even more capable of taking care of all the children in the family than me. I can even die peacefully without any tension about my children, unless Saroj is there.

Time passed by, Bimala and Sarojini became more close, dependent and beloved to each other. Sarojini became mother of her first son, Noni just three months before Bimala gave birth to Sundar, her forth son and fifth child. That was the period of time which I consider as the golden time of my life, Sarojini used to say everybody all along. Unfortunately golden times are always use to be short and that was also true for Sarojini. Bimala passed away after two and a half years of Sundar's birth.

Promise me Saroj, from this very moment you will take care of my children as you have been doing till date and will never let them feel that they don't have their mother, in the death bed Bimala said to her most trusted friend and follower, Saroj. That was the last lines Bimala spoke to her and took oath from her on that.

Didi, I take a vow in the name of the Almighty that till my last breadth I will take care of all our children as my own and will never ever let them feel that they don't have their mother, Sarojini promised with flood of tears in her eyes. Right then Sundar entered the room and found his mom lying on the floor on a straw mattress and his father seating on the floor by the left side of his mom. Many other people have gathered in the room. His youngest uncle Atanu and aunty Sarojini were also seating there amongst others. There were tears in their eyes. Old handmaiden Sarala took Sundar near his mom and sat him down on as close as possible to his mom's head. Bimala was not capable of saying anything anymore, she was just looking at Sundar with wink less eyes. Suddenly a drop of tear flowed out of her eyes.

Why are you crying mom? Who has rebuked you? Good kids don't cry, Sundar tried to wipe the drop of the salty water with his small palms while telling all those that his mom use to say to console him when he cries. Bimala did not answer, she wanted to say her son so many things but had lost her voice. She wanted to adore him, taking Sundar in her arms but she did not have the strength to fulfill her wish, she was still looking at Sundar. Sarojini came forward and gave a small glass filled with water in Sundar's hand and guided him to pour some slowly in the mouth of his mother. Sundar looked at his aunty first and then turned his eyes towards his mother. Then he followed what his aunty guided him to. Suddenly Sarojini broke out in to tears holding Sundar in her hands. Suddenly all broke out in to tears and the priest closed the eyes of Sundar's mother who was lying in front. Is mom sleeping? Sundar asked to himself. He could not understand why mom did not open her eyes. Perhaps she is sleeping.

GUILTY TO SELF

Time never waits for anything or anyone. After the unfortunate death of Bimala the time was tough but life did not stop. Days changed to weeks, weeks changed to months and months to years. The kids grew up and now after fourteen years of Bimala's death Sundar and Noni was studying in the high school. Sundar always used to ask about his mother to Atanu and Sarojini and both of them used to be so happy to share each and every bits and pieces of their time they spent with Bimala and their experiences of love and affection they received from her. They always used to describe that time as the golden time of their lives which they will never forget. In one such instance while preparing the dinner in the kitchen Sarojini was depicting about Bimala to Sundar. Even after so many years I still could not believe that Didi is no more with us, Bimala said in conversing with Sundar. She continued, I still imagine in one fine morning didi will come back and call me by the name she gave to me, "Saroj". Sarojini was trying say something more but perhaps lacked the words to properly depict her feelings. If this really happens what you will do, Sundar without thinking about anything asked spontaneously to his aunty just out of childish curiosity.

Sarojini was clogged by the sudden question for a while. She turned at the young boy and stared for some moments before saying anything. As if she was searching for words in within her mind. And then after some moments she uttered, I have never thought about it that way, but truly speaking I don't not know what I will do, Sarojini replied with a very serious expression in her face. She again paused for some moments and continued, you know son, if nevertheless what you just said come true, perhaps I will be the happiest person on earth.

Ma, is Sundar here? Suddenly Noni entered the kitchen searching for his brother-cum-friend and the discussion was stopped. Hey Sundar come with me, I have to show you something great, Noni uttered to Sundar and almost dragged him out of the room with tremendous enthusiasm. Though Noni was showing him something he has made but Sundar's mind was not there. He anyhow managed Noni and got out of there. His mind was downright occupied with more than a few disturbing questions and was probing for their answers. Is it possible that after so long a period of someone's death a person still believe that the dead person could come back? Is aunty actually loved and still love my Ma so much even after so many days? Sundar was thinking laying on his bed that night. Everyone in that room was sleeping peacefully except him. She must be telling so just to appease me, Sundar finalized but not fully. Everything you must test before you decide whether that is true or not, Sundar told the lines he had been taught in the school by the science teacher to him.

"See in your own eyes and then only have faith in", this typical answer instigated a tremendous idea in Sundar's mind and he decided that he will examine himself that how aunty rally reacts if his mother comes in front of her. He planned within his mind that for the same he will need a white sharee. This is quite a mandatory thought at that age that all the dead souls of women use to wear white sharees and speak in a nasal voice. Now the question is from where would I manage a white sharee and that too without being noticed by anyone? He asked himself and found the answer also. Two days back Parbati aunt's mother, had come to her daughter's house. She is a widow and use to wear white sharee, if I could manage one from her for a night and in the next morning return the same back in its place then there is hardly any chance that she will be able to notice, Sundar said to himself. And as he provides private tuition to Shibnath and Manu, Parbati aunt's children, so it will not be a very difficult task for him, he confirmed.

Sometimes people carry on their ideas without thinking twice that what the consequences and effects would be of their deeds on other people. Sundar at that age with his curious as well as immature mind and adventurist nature did the same without given a second thought about how much his amateur activity could affect the beliefs and faiths of those people whom he is going to make a test with.

Next day evening while returning from Parbati aunt's house after giving tuition to Shibnath and Manu, Sundar, without being noticed by anybody, took a white sharee from the room where Parbati aunt's mother was staying. After returning home he silently kept that sharee in a corner of the lawn in such a way that nobody could notice that.

After dinner Sundar went to bed with his brothers but he did not sleep and waited for other to sleep. Nearly after half an hour or so he woke up, being confirmed about that except him all others in the room are in deep sleep. He woke up from his bed silently and came in front of the next room where his father was sleeping. After being cent percent sure that no one is awake in the house, he came outside and went to the place where he had hid the sharee. Taking the sharee in his hand he came to the other part of the house where his uncle Atanu was living with his family.

Very intensely he observed the area to be sure that no one is awake there to watch him too. After being confirmed, he ascended to the sunset of a window of the room where Atanu and Sarojini used to stay. Standing on the sunset he first wore the white sharee and fall a part of the same in such a way that people inside the room could see that. Now the second part, he then changing his normal voice in to a nasal feminine one called his aunty – Saroj. He intentionally used the name by which his mother Bimala used to call Sarojini. He called but no one answered. Somewhere in his mind he was also afraid of what he was doing, so he paused for some moments and scrutinized the surrounding again. After some time he again called his aunty – Saroj, wake up, see I have come. This time reply came from the room – who? Who is calling me? The reply trembled Sundar from inside but now there was no looking back at this position. He continued. Again in the same nasal feminine voice he replied – it's me Saroj, your didi. Won't you open the door for me? I have returned Saroj. Sundar was intended to scare his aunty but he never thought that while doing this the scene will change in such a drastic way.

Hey, wake up, didi has returned, Sarojini started calling her husband Atanu. Come with me, didi is waiting outside, we need to open the door. Atanu had also heard the call but he was thinking he is hallucinating in his sleep but now getting the same response from wife, he became sure of it and woke up from his bed. Boudi, just wait, we are coming, Atanu's voice was widely audible to Sundar form where he was hiding. Now he was in trouble. By then he had understood that his venture of scaring his aunty in the name of his mother has gone in vain and now his uncle and aunty is coming to open the door.

He was sure that if they found him here playing with their sentiments and that too in the name of their beloved Didi then it would certainly become a nightmare for him. Now the only way left to him was to escape. He thought for some moments and looked around him to get a possible way out. If he tries to get down from the sunset he will be caught so he can't do that. So he had no other option but to ascending on the roof and wait until his uncle and aunty return back to their room after searching the lawn. He did the same but the hue and cry was already created. Hearing the same Sundar's father and step mother have also arrived on the place. One of the neighbor Abhay uncle has also arrived with his wife and a gossip by this time has been started about what has happened and Atanu was describing the entire scene to the small gathering. Sundar has understood that within a few minutes all the children will also wake up and arrive this place and the only missing person will be none other than himself. This thought ran a chill down Sundar's spine and the scene was more than enough to victimize the victimizer itself.

So he first put the sharee off and then silently scrolled to the other side of the roof and from there used the drainage pipe to get down to the back side of the house. From there he ran to the main gate in the opposite side of the building. He then climbed the main gate of the house and get in to their part of the house. He looked around to see anybody is looking at him or not and silently joined the gathering from behind.

He heard Atanu and Sarojini depicting the incident to others present there. They are cent percent sure that it was Bimala. They have even seen Bimala but unfortunately they delayed to open the door as they were sleeping and she did not wait. Sundar witnessed tears in the eyes of his aunty as she was cursing herself as main culprit because the delay in opening the gate cost her to lose her didi for the second time. She was cursing herself to the level that she is so ill fated that she missed the opportunity to get her didi back. This whipped in the inner mind of Sundar. He had understood that his childish activity have wounded these people emotionally at the core of their heart. He was feeling sorry but he too was so scared that he could not convince himself to confess to them. He promised to himself that he will never ever commit such foolish thing again.

By the next morning probably there was no one in the village who did not hear about what happened last night. Many of them, especially the senior people even suggested Brijendra about some measures that should be taken in such a condition when someone's soul is trying to come back. As the time passed by the feeling also faded but three people could never forget the day Atanu, Sarojini and Sundar himself.

NOT THE LEAST

"I have fulfilled all the responsibilities you gave me from that most unfortunate day of my life to till date. Now all of our children are mature, married and established. They are living happily with their own family and our grandchildren. Had not yet the time arrived for me to meet you again?"

Sarojini kept her promise she once made to her didi throughout her life. Even at her late-eighties, many have witnessed her complaining to an old black and white photograph of her didi hanging from the wall of her room. All have seen tears in her eyes whenever she used to talk about her didi, Bimala.

THE MAN WITH BIGGEST HEART ...

Hey Sundar, searching for books?

On that day Sundar went to the local library, one of his favorite places, to return the old book he got issued last week and at the same time to get another one to be issued for this time. He was searching for books and wandering around the dusty racks when he heard someone calling him from behind. Sundar turned and surprisingly found Surya da was standing behind the book's rack behind him. Sundar nodded smilingly in reply.

Surya was nearly eight to ten years older than Sundar and originally a batch mate of Sundar's eldest brother Satyendra. Surya was perhaps not only from the richest family of the village but at the same time his maternal grandfather was the most respected amongst all in the vicinity. Surya, a soft spoken good looking man with very fare complexion, nearly six feet tall, well maintained stylish hairs, generally with unshaved whiskers and last but not the least always with a smiling face, was a well-known and impressive personality in the area and more specifically in the young group. He was a man with a great amount of social involvements and at the same time tremendous emotional attributes in within. Surya used to live in his maternal grandfather's house with his mother, who became a widow at a very young age. After the death of his husband she came to her father's house back with her only son Surya, a child that time. Surya's grandfather was actually the Jamindar of the village and he had no son. So his grandson was his only successor. Surya used to be profoundly pampered by his grandfather but his mother was an esteemed and authoritarian lady. She always kept a critical watching eye on her son and his deeds. Due to her such attitude and personality she was widely respected not by her son only but the entire village also. Surya was even afraid of his mother more than anything. She also had a kind heart and helping personality for needy people of the area.

Do you come here daily, Surya asked Sundar.

Not exactly but once or twice a week, Sundar answered.

What kind of book you like to read, I mean novel or fiction or detective stories or ghost stories, Surya continued.

Anything interesting, precise and short answer came from Sundar.

Have you read any piece of Sharat Chandra Chatterjee, Surya continued?

Not all. One or two I have, Sundar replied fixing his eyes on the rack for the book he was searching.

Have you read "Pather dabi" yet? The next question came to Sundar from the opposite side.

Yes, but very few other such book is available here, Sundar replied and turned towards Surya. Sundar continued, actually I am searching for "Gora", I have heard that is a great piece of Rabindranath Tagore. Could you tell me in which of these racks that will be available or the book is not available at all here. I asked the librarian but he could not tell me.

I don't think that will be available here, or may be available but in which rack it is placed is out of my knowledge or even wildest of imagination, Surya replied and smiled pointing at the rusty dusty racks.

Have you read "Gora", Sundar asked?

Yeah, some years back, Surya replied joyfully. He continued, it's really a great piece of literature and I think everybody should read that book at least once. Would you like to read "Gora"? He asked.

Yes but the book is not available here, Sundar replied. A bit of frustration was visible on his face. Surya came forward, placed his right hand on Sundar's shoulder and said smilingly, don't worry, this is not the only library on this planet. He continued, tomorrow I will go to Town Library as I go there every Tuesday and Friday, if you wish you can come with me in the afternoon nearly at 5 PM, and I am sure you will find that there.

Sundar raise his eyes with full of hope and replied, surely I will come but where would I wait for you? And one more thing I must say, I don't have bicycle.

You don't have to worry about all these, come to my home at 5 PM and we both will go in my bicycle, Surya replied. Surya suddenly looked at his wrist watch and his expression said he must be late for something. Okay, Sundar I have to go now, eventually Surya left the place, almost ran for his bicycle parked outside the main entrance of the library.

THE JOURNEY BEGUN

Oh, you are really punctual comrade, Surya uttered to Sundar who came to his house right at the scheduled time in the afternoon the next day.

You asked me to come at 5 in the afternoon, Sundar replied with a calm but deep voice.

Yah I remember, just wait for five minutes as I am not yet ready, Surya replied and moved to the adjacent room. He came back in much less than the time he asked Sundar to wait. Let's go, I am ready, he said to Sundar and while leaving told to his mother, Ma I am going out and will be late, don't wait for me in the dinner table. No one replied.

They started in Surya's bicycle. For sometimes they rode through the main road and then left and took a village path. Surya was driving the cycle. The two reached the town library within ten to fifteen minutes. You wanted "Gora" right, Surya asked Sundar and guided him in to the library. The way Surya was greeted and well come by the librarian made it apparent to Sundar that Surya is a very well-known and appreciated member of the house. Shankar da this is my brother, he need "Gora" of Rabindranath Thakur, can you please tell me in which rack the book is, Surya asked the librarian in one stretch.

Wait, let me check the register, the middle aged man replied and opened a sizable register that was lying on his table. Yes got it, third rack, most possibly second row, the man replied looking at Surya. You stay here, let me get it for you, Surya suggested Sundar and moved towards the rack. What is your name, the librarian asked Sundar. Sundar replied. If you really love to read books then I would suggest you to make your own membership card, it won't cost you much, the librarian told to Sundar. Yes, I will in a short while, Sundar said.

Surya has already returned. Shankar da, I have to leave now, I have to attend a meeting, Surya uttered. Next time we will have chat and tea together, okay, he added and set to leave. Sundar followed him. Be aware Surya the time and situations are not good, while getting out he heard the librarian saying. So where do I drop you, Surya asked Sundar cycling back from the library. He added, I have to meet someone, either I can leave you where you want or I can take you with me but the only problem is, it might be late to return home. I am free and don't have any issue to be with you, Sundar replied. Then be with me, Surya said and continued cycling.

Shortly after some time Surya left the main road and took another village path. That was hardly any road, very narrow and filled with potholes of various shapes, sizes and depths. They kept changing such narrow roads from one to another and drove for quite a sometime. Finally when they stopped they were standing in front of a small mud house. It was already quite dark all around. Come with me, Surya da parked his bicycle and asked Sundar to follow him. The door of the house was locked from inside. He knocked the door and someone asked from inside, who is that?

It's me, Surya, Surya replied. The door opened and they entered in to the room. It was a small room without a single piece of furniture, only an oil lamp was trying beyond its capacity to create as much light as it could generate to help people seating there to recognize each other's face. Surya entered first and then called Sundar, who followed him with hesitations and thousands of thoughts in his young but curious mind. Three or four persons who were already present there looked in to Sundar's face and the person who opened the door and still standing first opened his mouth – who is this boy Surya?

Ohhh sorry Anil da, I forgot to introduce him. His name is Sundar, he is my brother, Surya replied smilingly and casually. Sundar first got to know at least the name of one person in the room except his companion. He looked at the person, a man nearly at the same age of Surya da, very thin and with normal height, uncombed bushy hair and unshaved beard. The man was wearing a trouser and a shirt. As par my knowledge you don't have any brother, right Surya, the man calm and quietly uttered.

Yah, he is not my own brother but nothing less than that, rather more, Surya replied with confident. He added, He is a very nice boy and from my village. I know him and his family for years. Absolutely no problem, don't worry, he completed. It was extremely doubtful for Sundar to understand how he could create any problem to these people whom he doesn't even know properly. Not even their names, except the one whom Surya da called by the name Anil. The next question came from another man in the room, is he a member of the party Surya? Then turning to Sundar he asked, by the way, how old are you boy? Though the question was partially to Surya da and partially to Sundar but before the later could say anything the former answered, no not yet a member but will become very soon. He did not talked about the second question, intentionally or not nobody knows.

Okay take your seat, the man then asked the two and eventually Surya and Sundar sat on the ground. In the meantime the third man asked Sundar, which class are you in boy? Class Ten, Sundar answered. He was feeling thirsty when he was answering the question. First time in his life he felt that sometimes answering the simplest question becomes the toughest job. The people were gazing in to each other's eyes, Surya da even got shy. After a while the eldest member of the room who was seating in the corner of the room and till then have not even looked at Sundar and actually was concentrating on a piece of paper and undoubtedly was reading something with extreme attention now raised his face for the first time. He distributed one piece of the paper to each one present there in the room except Sundar and with a tremendous profound but slow voice said, read this carefully and ask me any question, if there is any hindrance in understanding. Surya da replied to that man – let me introduce my brother first to you Binoy da.

The man quietly turned his eyes at Surya da and replied, thank you Surya but I can do that on my own brother, you please focus on the pamphlet and try to understand the directions given by the party. Everyone including Surya da started following his instruction gently and without any more argument. Now the man turned his attention towards Sundar with gentle smile in his face and said, so you are in class ten, that means you are a boy of sixteen or hardly seventeen years. Am I correct? Sundar nodded his head without saying anything. The man continued, by the way my name is Binoy and I am the senior most here in this group, all here are my students. Now tell me one thing would not your parents be anxious about where you are at this time of evening?

No, no one will be anxious about me, Sundar replied upright.

Binoy da nodded his head and then said, I can understand that your father might be busy with his jobs but what about your mother? She must be very anxious. Sundar did not answer the question and kept his eyes on the ground. The question came again but in another form, so you don't care about your mother? This time answer was evident, so he looked at the man directly in to his eyes and replied, I don't even remind her face, I can just remind her eyes last time when she was looking at me lying on the death bed. I was two and a half year old then and was seating beside her head when she passed away.

Everyone present in the room suddenly got a blow and looked at Sundar but the questioner himself was perhaps in the most awkward position. Binoy da was feeling uneasy. There was a pin drop silence in the room all of a while. Finally Binoy da broke the silence and changed the topic, do you know who we are? What are we doing here? What exactly we do? What do you know about us? Sundar replied in a cool but strong voice, I don't know anything about you or what you do or what exactly you are doing here in this room, what I have understood is that you are friends of Surya da. He continued, as much as I have heard about you people while coming here with Surya da that you are good people who wants to do something good for the poor and needy. Powerful and rich people don't like you so you are carrying out your mission very secretly and all of you are highly devoted towards your mission. That is all what I know.

First time those present in the room, except Surya made a loud sound as they laughed. Binoy da after the laugh again asked Sundar, do you know even the police and administration of the state is in search of ours and if they could catch us, then certainly they will love to throw us in the jail and will try their best to break us to get information about others in the team? Don't you afraid of police?

I have never faced police, so how can I be afraid of something I have never faced, Sundar replied. The men laughed again and appraised the answer. For next half an hour Binoy da told many things about their political and social ideologies and thoughts. Everyone in the room listened very carefully to it. Some questioned were asked by one or two and he answered each of those questions with endurance. Finally when the meeting completed it was nearly 8 or 8:30. A bunch of that pamphlet were distributed to each of the men in that room except Sundar and obviously Binoy da, as he was distributing. They came out of the room and Anil da locked the room from outside. Now when they were yet to leave Binoy da asked, Surya take your brother in our next meeting if he wishes to come. And yes of course take care of him, he added. Surya da nodded with a winner's attitude and replied, surely Binoy da, I will.

When they came back home it was nearly 9:30 PM.

LIFE WAS NEVER THE SAME ANYMORE

Now Surya da and Sundar has become close friends. They have started attending meetings regularly and also even started visiting faraway places to attend plentiful of such meetings. Surya da had another job of taking care of the farm that belonged to his grandfather. The farm was really enormous in size. As his grandfather became older and there was no other male in the family so automatically it became his responsibility and he used to do that very willfully. Especially when he needed some pocket money. As per Sundar the main reason of his willful involvement to this duty was something else. He actually used to sell a part of the produce from the field itself to earn some money and used that money to sponsor some other members of the party who were from poor or not-so-affluent families. He used to help some of party events also from that earning. He was a man who never thought of making properties or earning money more than required to live a normal life. Surya da never even thought of savings. He was one of the most pampered boy Sundar had ever seen. He was never asked any questions by the elders of his family. He was so beloved that on that period of time he used to use things for his personal care, which were even impossible to think about boys like Sundar and all but he never felt any pride for that or never detached himself from others. If anyone asked for anything from him, he never even used to think twice before giving that thing to that asking person without any hesitation in mind. He was a separate breed altogether.

Sundar, come outside, I have a good news as well as a bad news too to share with you, Sundar heard Surya da's voice. Sundar was reading in the room that was for all the brothers in his ancestral house.

Just wait, I am coming, Sundar replied and came out in hurry to meet the man waiting for him. What happened to you, so early in the morning, Sundar asked him anxiously. He added, everything is alright. One thing is right and one is wrong, Surya da replied smilingly.

Please stop creating illusions and tell me what the issue, Sundar asked directly this time.

The good news is due to my good result I have got a government job, Surya da replied smilingly. But there is also a bad news, he added. And what is that, Sundar asked. I am not going to join that, Surya da replied with the same smile.

Have you gone crazy or what, Sundar asked the man standing in front of him.

No, I am absolutely okay, both physically and psychologically, Surya da replied. He continued, see, what I have already been possessing by the grace of my ancestors is more than enough for a man to live an affluent and happy life, now if I stick on the job then I will be doing wrong to may be another person who needs the job much more than I do. And you know what our ideology says, a man should not possess more wealth than he needed.

You must be crazy man, do hell with all this and join the job, Sundar insisted.

No brother, you can leave everything else for your ideology but can't leave your ideology for anything, Surya da said. He added, okay, then see you in the afternoon, bye for now. He turned back and in minutes was out of sight.

Sundar did not try to make Surya da understand as he knew that could be next to impossible. Surya has become the friend, philosopher and guide to Sundar, whom Sundar actually loved and respected from the core of his heart.

AND THE POLICE ...

IN LAST FEW YEARS

Life has changed a lot for Sundar. After the ill-fated death of his mother at a nascent age there was absolutely no one to take care of him. He grew up in a home environment where the things he received in abundance were negligence, humiliation and harshness. Sarojini was the only person who used to take care of Sundar and his elder brothers but that also did not last for long. Brijendra got married for the second time but unfortunately his second wife who was too young to be married. Eventually she could not bear with the pressure of marriage life for long and passed away within a couple of years. Brijendra then got married again for the third and last time. The tight bond that existed between the two brothers – Brijendra and Atanu, was deteriorated and the two family separated from each other. Though they used to stay in the same house but an invisible boundary was mounted and for Sarojini it became almost impossible to cross the boundary to take care of the children of her beloved Didi as that would be treated as snooping in to someone else's family matter. But still she did not lost her courage and hope. She used to jump in to save the children her beloved didi had left behind from various atrocities and sometimes even used to become harsh on people who tried to resist her from accomplishing her responsibilities. But except those instances the overall condition was hard-hitting enough to either break a child from inside or to make him the toughest one.

So at the end of the day life became a rough and tough terrain for the boy and in every step he found no one to adore or at the minimum extend a helping hand towards him. This is the way life started teaching Sundar about what in reality life is. This no-one's-beloved, no-one-to-be-think-about feeling injected a typical sense in the mind of the boy. Perhaps that is the reason, the more he grew up the more fearless he became. It is said that the Almighty never takes everything away from you and for Sundar he left three women, who were no less than mother-figure to him, Sarojini, Parbati and Kanonbala.

Kanonbala was actually the widow of the youngest brother of Sundar's Grandfather. She did not have any child and used to live in a distant village. Emptiness of her own life propelled her towards Brijendra's family. Once in every two to three months she used to come and stay with the family for one or two weeks. She loved Sundar very much and Sundar got an oasis in the deserted life in his Grandma.

A SUDDEN CHANGE

Time was passing through without any significant incident unless one day suddenly one incident quaked not the village only but all the villages in the vicinity. It was the time when Sundar had just joined his graduation in the local college in the night section and at the same time working in the railway locomotive. One such eventless day when Sundar was going to the station in the morning to catch the train for his workplace he found some local shopkeepers were discussing something very excitedly. What happened uncle, so early in the morning you people have gathered here on the road, he asked one of those people.

The man he asked the question turned to him with a tremendous surprise in his eyes and said, don't you know what happened last night? His expression was clearly saying his surprise on the ignorance of the young boy about the incident he was mentioning to. Sundar sensed something unusual and came closer to know what actually had happened and said, no I have no update about anything. The man looked at the surrounding and in a whispering voice said, last night in Natunpara village some dacoits had attacked the house of the Roy family and snatched away everything forcefully. The man continued with more fright in his eyes and voice, most furious part is that the dacoits were carrying fire weapons and while their operation they shot the head of the family Shankar Prasad Roy down to death as he tried to resist those dacoits.

Roy family was quite wealthy in the village and was also very well known to the people of the area. More over at that period of time it was next to something unbelievable that dacoits in a village carrying fire weapons. Their desperation also created a huge sense of insecurity in the minds of the people. It created a severe panic in the minds of the people of the neighboring villages also. Everyone was scared about their own family and life. Have the police caught any of those vandals yet, Sundar asked to the man. In reply he slowly moved his head with a typical facial gesture showing a negative answer. Sundar did not say anything and moved forward to his workplace but his mind was disturbed.

A tremendous and abrupt change was thrown on the area. The main market which used to be open till late evening started closing down as early as possible. The people at home becoming highly frightened if anyone makes a delay from the scheduled time to come back. The entire locality and its people were terrified. Police started discussing with the elderly and veteran people to accumulate a group of young boys to work as volunteers in every village, which will serve as a night guard. Many discussion took place but except a handful no one was ready to allow their boys to serve as volunteers and that too as night guard.

I think we must stand and join the night guard, Surya said to the others present there. He looked at Sundar who was concentrating more in eating the puffed rise mixed with masala from the paper packet in his hand than what Surya da was saying. Sundar, what do you think about that, this time the question was direct. Sundar actually had missed it first time so he raised his eyes from the paper packet, looked at Surya da and asked, about what? With visible irritation Surya repeated the question again. Before Sundar could have said anything Patru replied, I am ready to join, I am not afraid of any dacoits or whatever it is.

Great, so you have got the bravest man on this planet as your company, Sundar replied to Surya da and again concentrated on the puffed rise.

Sundar don't make fun of it, are you ready to come or not, Surya da asked with irritation in his voice.

Sundar looked at Surya and said, actually it depends on many things, like how much and how prompt support we will be getting from the police on daily basis, just one aspect from a list of many. He threw the paper packet after finishing the puffed rise and continued, you know, I don't want to be the goat for the sacred offering. First discuss all these with the local police officers, get their assurance in black and white and then only I will join, not before that, he completed. Okay, we then could go to the police station to discuss all that tomorrow, Surya replied. Tomorrow in the evening, after I return from office, Sundar informed. Surya nodded his head in support.

Next day in the evening Surya, Sundar and Patru went to meet Ramendra Ghosh, in-charge of the local police station to discuss about the matter. After a long discussion they were motivated enough and informed that they are ready to work as volunteers for the night guard. But this time result was unexpected as Ramendra babu did not agree to them. I know all of you three boys well due to your involvements in various social and volunteering activities but this time I must say that three is too less a number to be significant in such a situation and I can't take risk of your lives. He continued, moreover unfortunately you are the only people who are ready to volunteer but even if I overlook the number, still one group in one village only will serve no purpose. We expect at least a team of ten volunteers for each village so that it carries a substantial weightage, he added.

Could we then start the night guard in our village on our own, Surya asked the officer? Ramendra babu thought for some moments and then replied, it would not be possible for me to allow three young boys to start the night guard party on their own. He continued, you know the situation is so tensed around the place that if anything wrong takes place to you then the entire responsibility will be on my shoulder. That will be too much of risk to be taken, so I would not permit you to start any such activity at least right now, he completed. Surya tried to say something but the officer waved him off.

Finally the trio returned to their last resort, the club, with no hope in their mind. Patru asked unanimously, what will happen if we start without police permission. Sundar replied, The-Bravest-Man-on-Earth, the police is patrolling the area at night and if they see us roaming around the village at night they might misunderstand us with the dacoits and that could create a hell lot of problems for us. Patru looked at his friend and nodded. Finally after discussing on many such option no way came out and it was decided that once the situation become normal again they will revisit for the police permission and until then they have to be cautious.

Sundar, grandma has come and waiting for you, Satyendra informed his brother once he enters the house. Sundar come here, see what I have brought for you, the elderly woman asked Sundar by a hand gesture and at the same time gestured him to seat beside her on the mattress. She drizzled her hand in to her bag and bring out a book, handed it over to her grandson she smiled and said, you love to read so I have bought this for you. Sundar smiled in regards and asked, so how are you doing.

I am fine, don't be worried about me, I have lived my life, she replied. Tell me one thing Sundar, I got to know there was a massive plunder here in a village some days back, she asked. Kanonbala was also aware of the situation but she did not seem to be very much worried or scared about it. Yes, two days back there happened an incident of loot and murder in a nearby village, Sundar replied. He added, why, you are afraid of that.

With a smile on her lips she replied, what would I be afraid of? I have nothing to lose at this age and I had already lived my life to the fullest possible. So I am not even very much worried about dying in the hand of a doctor or a dacoit or anything else. Both the young and the old laughed together.

It was summer and Sundar unconditionally arranges his bedding on the roof top at night. After the incident he keeps a sturdy bamboo stick by his side which he had prepared recently on his own. Kanonbala decided that this time she will also sleep on the roof top as in such a scorching summer that will be much more comfortable than being boiled overnight in the room. She called Sundar after dinner and said, make another arrangement besides yours on the rooftop for me. She continued, I am not going to get boiled in the room for the night, it is far better over there than here. Sundar's step mother initially was not ready to allow that but then considering the scarcity of space in the house she became liberal on that and accepted the suggestion. Kanonbala then directed Sundar to make that arrangement permanent for her until she is here in this house. So from that day, after dinner Sundar had one more job to arrange an additional bedding on the roof top for his grandma.

Perhaps it was either the third or the fourth day from the arrangement started. Sundar and his grandma was sleeping on the rooftop. Almost in the midnight, a sudden furious sound destroying the silence compelled everyone in the locality to wake up. Sundar and his grandma also woke up and was seating on their bedding when again another same harsh sound penetrated the peace of the night. It was more than enough to let Sundar seat idle. He jumped up with the bamboo stick lying beside his bed and moved towards to staircase. Where are you going Sundar, grandma asked him worriedly? Come downstairs closing the door, Sundar replied on the go and did not bother to stop or look behind. On the same move he added, I am going to see what is happening. The voice of the elderly lady was even audible when Sundar was already on the road. She was screaming at the highest volume she could to stop her adored grandson from chasing the sound.

Coming down on the road the first name came in to Sundar's mind is Patru. Patru that day was sleeping in the club room so he would be the easiest to wake up, if not already. Sundar did not give any second thought and started running towards the club. It was hardly five hundred meter from his house, so within a few minutes he reached there. Patru was also wide-awake and form the window he was watching the roads when he saw Sundar running towards the club room. You must have heard the sounds, Sundar asked Patru reaching in front of the window. Yes, surely, Patru replied affirmatively. He added, the sound was coming from side of the railway bridge on the river, he pointed his finger to mention the area where he suspected the sound was coming from. Would it be safe to go there, he asked Sundar in reply. Sundar did not reply to that question, called him to follow and started moving towards Surya da's house which was on the way to the railway bridge from the club. When Sundar and Patru reached there, they found Surya was already out of his house holding a same kind of bamboo stick in his hand. The sound came from that side, before Sundar could have asked anything Surya informed the same as Patru about the direction of the origin of the sound. The three just wait for a moment and without expensing any words between them together moved towards the suspected location to chase.

While running Sundar said to the other two, before chasing anyone we will observe the situation first. The other two nodded their head in affirmation. It took nearly five minutes for them to reach the place. Form a distance they found nearly four or five men were standing in front of a car. They slowed their speed down and silently came closer to those men and took help of the bushes beside the road to hide themselves in a low land. From behind the bush they carefully noticed that there are exactly five men but due to darkness no one was identifiable and was just looking like standing shadows. Two of them were smoking but in that timid light of their cigarettes it was impossible to recognize their faces.

Hiding behind the bushes they planned their chase. Surya whispered, those two who are smoking must be the leader of the gang and only they would be carrying guns. Sundar replied, I also think the same. He added, let I and you hunt for those two leaders. He paused for a moment and then continued, Patru, you from the other side will chase any one of the other three who will come first within your range. Surya replied, okay I will count up to three and on three we will move together at once. Perfect, Sundar replied. As planned they suddenly came out of the bushes and were just on the way to hunt the men when what happened was no way expected by the three boys. Light from powerful electric torches were thrown on their face which actually made them blind for some moments and at the same time a very known voice called them by name and asked to stop. The three were already stopped and after adjusting their visions they became capable of seeing when the car ignites its engine with a gurgling sound and put its headlights on. They found Ramendra babu coming out of the car. And out of those five people standing outside they easily identified two from the local police station but the fourth and the fifth person was unknown to them. Who are these boys Ramendra babu, it seems you know them well, one of them asked.

Sir, they are local boys, I know them, Ramendra babu answered with high regards to that man. He added, these boys are involved in many social activities in the locality, brave and educated. Ramendra babu turned towards Sundar, Surya and Patru, who were in quite confusion about what is going on in front of them. Ramendra babu then said to the boys pointing to those two men, they are very senior district level officers and have come here to judge the situation of the locality after that unfortunate case. The trio standing silently looked at each other.

The man who just before sometimes has asked Ramendra regarding the boys came forward and asked, what are your names young men. Surya answered on behalf of them all. The man again asked, can you tell me one thing, what instigated you boys to chase us. Surya again spoke first, the sounds were something like gun firing and we thought there might be some problem as it happened some days back, so we chased the sound if we could do something. The officer then asked them with a smile on his lips, pointing towards their bamboo sticks, what is that "something" you guys could have done with these sticks if we had actually been a gang of dacoits with guns. Sundar replied coolly looking at the man, sir that "something" is at least better than nothing. The officer nodded his head in appreciation and then asked, who of you first decided to chase. He, Surya pointed his finger to Sundar and depicted what happened from start to end in brief. The officer turned his eyes at Sundar and asked, have not your parents restricted you. Sundar on the same cool note replied, there is no one to be worried about or restrict me at the house I live. "At the house I live", the officer uttered the phrase as he was quite surprised by this line. He asked, do you live in any hostel or boy's mess. Before Sundar could have said anything Patru replied, Sir actually he, pointing towards Sundar, had lost his mother in the childhood and some years back from now he has lost his father too. I am sorry boy, the officer said to Sundar and did not ask any more question. It's alright sir, Sundar uttered in a low voice, this time there was no stubbornness in his voice.

Surya came forwards to use this opportunity and proposed the officer, Sir we are actually planning to start a night guard party in our village after what happened in Natunpara. The man turned to Surya and appreciated his idea and said that would be really good. Surya continued, but sir if the local police helps us with the basic necessary equipment like torch and other things then it will be extremely supportive for us. The officer accepted that proposal positively and directed Ramendra babu to call a meeting with the local people next day and announce the same and also facilitate these boys so that they could start their voluntary night guard service in their village. Then he looked at Sundar, placed his hand on the boy's shoulder and said, don't to be so fearless because there might be no one at home to restrict you but you must restrict yourself sometimes. He added, and being cautious is not cowardice rather it is quality every brave man needs to learn. He continued, life teaches us everything which we need but for teaching us it takes the way just opposite to the way we are used to. Generally, first we get the lesson and then to prove that we have got the lesson exactly and properly we use to appear for an examination. But life does it just the opposite way, it first throw us in an examination and then from that it teaches us the lesson it wants to. As the great people said everything in the universe has two sides – one good side and another bad side, the good side of such tough way of teaching is that once you successfully pass the examination then you will probably never forget the lesson unless you want to forget what you have learnt, otherwise if you fail the same at least you will become sure about one of the many options that would not lead you to the success. He patted on Sundar's shoulder and get in to the car.

May I ask you something sir, Sundar asked for permission to the officer for asking a question? The officer smilingly replied, sure, go ahead.

How did you people recognize that we were there behind the bush, he asked the officer. This time all the men laughed together loud and the officer with a smile in his face replied, we are in the police services and we are taught to be alert as well as skeptic in any point of time, be it on duty or otherwise, and that is what I have just taught you, being cautious is not cowardice rather it is quality every brave man needs to learn.

Eventually the jeep started moving, leaving the boys behind with a valuable lesson and experience.

DONATION ...

Maiti babu, I came to know from my neighbor that the local police has called a meeting today in the afternoon at 4 PM in police station, the middle aged man who asked the question was Nimai Haldar.

Nimai was a very feeble minded and not so well to do at his life. On the contrary the man who he stopped to ask the question, Atindra Maiti was from an established background, both economically as well as socially. Though Atindra was not the eldest among his brothers but he was the head of all the six brothers. The Maiti family was one of the most well to do and established people in the vicinity. They had a joint family of six brothers and used to live in the most majestic house in the area. They had high earning from not only many types of businesses but at the same time they also had acres of farming lands. From farming also they used to earn quite well. Out of the six brother the eldest Sadananda Maiti was a calm, soft-spoken and polite type of personality and was to be of hardly any importance within the family or among the brothers. Atindra, the second in line was just opposite of his elder brother in all respect. He was a man of tremendous authoritative attitude and at the same time perhaps with the most skeptic mind about each and every thing. He was in fact the head of the family and the decision taker on behalf of the family. All the others used to follow Atindra for any decision. Atindra was a man of tremendous distrustful and suspicious mind. He never used to accept anything with an open mind and used to sniff something wrong in almost everything. He was going to his work in the morning when Nimai stopped him to find an answer to his query.

Hmm, they came to my office yesterday, as well as also visited the other important and respected persons of the society. It was written in the invitation letter they have given that they need to discuss something very important with us, so have requested us to come to the police station today in the afternoon, Atindra replied in his exclusive authoritative posture. That answer was not what Nimai expected, so he asked to satisfy his mind, any idea dada, what they actually want to discuss with you. This was something irritating for the man questioned. How would I know unless I talk to them? Atindra replied with a visible irritation. Nimai with a flattering smile nodded his head and supported the answer, obviously, my question was itself foolish. Atindra waved him off and moved ahead.

That day in the afternoon when Atindra entered the police station it was almost filled with the people who have been called for. Within a few moments the officer-in-charge Ramendra babu came and announced, thank you all for coming here gentlemen. He cleared his throat and continued, as you all are aware that a heinous crime has taken place very recently and to restrict any such crime in future we propose a plan to you all. After discussing with the young boys of various villages we have decided to make a night guard volunteer for each village taken ten boys in a group for each day. We will provide the basic amenities like torch, sticks etcetera and would request you all to promote and support this idea at your respective villages. You all, as the respected people of your area if come forward for the cause then we are sure that this idea will definitely be effective enough to stop such crimes to happen in future. He finished and gazed at the people seating.

The first man stood up was Surya. I....we support this idea and would like to start to volunteer as night guard of our village from tomorrow.

May I know how some young boys will resist dacoits with fire weapon, with sticks and torches, Atindra asked the question to the police officer. Ramendra babu smilingly replied, they will not resist Atindra babu, they will blow the alarm so that we and all the villagers get informed. He added, the rest will be done by us only. The meeting after such small question answer session completed.

Succeeding that meeting another informal meeting was arranged within the village next day with people from each family to finalize the cooperation from each family so that there could be a ten member team for each night. After a long discussion and debate Surya proposed, from each family one male member will volunteer for one night out of seven in a week as a night guard. Some of the people agreed but maximum did not. Then finally it was decided that those family from where there will be no direct cooperation will donate a minimum amount on monthly basis to the night guard party so that they could make an arrangement for some basic refreshments like tea and coffee for themselves. Many of the people who were present agreed on that except one or two. Out of those one or two families the strongest opposition came from Atindra Maiti. He never accepted anything with an open mind, so this idea of night guard party first and the option of donation next received a high opposition from Atindra. He directly announced in front of everyone, I and none of the member of my family feels any necessity of this night guard party and if really dacoits come then those people in the party will be the first to disappear. Atindra's declaration with his arrogant attitude created a mess in the meeting. Those people who were not quite ongoing with this idea but were hesitating to gather enough courage to declare their opposition openly in front of others got the strength to take the same path with loud voice. And above all those who were in dilemma to support it or not started saying that when no one is supporting then it's better to drop the idea before substantial investment is done. So finally the stage came where the number of supporters for the night guard party became too less to start it but suddenly Surya stood up and declared, whatever you intelligent veterans think I don't care, but I will start it from tomorrow and will carry this on even if there is no one to support me. Sundar stood up next and said, I am with you. Patru and some other members of the club stood up one by one and supported Surya. The scene at the end became such that the seniors and the young people got divided in to two separate paths facing one another.

Why you can't come for three days a week, Surya's irritation was visible from the way he asked Biju. A meeting was called in the club to finalize who will volunteer for which days of a week. Every member was asked to volunteer for three nights per week but that seemed not possible for many which irritated Surya. Biju replied, two nights per week and that is maximum I could do, either you take it or leave it. Surya was in the verge of losing his temper with this rough attitude shown to him but Sundar hold him back. After a long planning within all the members it was settled that Surya, Sundar and Patru will volunteer for every night and the other boys will join them as per their availability, maximum up to two nights per week. For Sundar there was no one to be worried about whether he sleeps in the house or in the club or anywhere on this planet. For Patru due to scarcity of space in his home it was better to sleep in the club room than in the home and for Surya it had become a matter of prestige. So from that day the first ever voluntary night guard service was introduced in the village with seven people – the three musketeers and four other boys.

AFTER SOME MONTHS

It was running quite successfully for months of summer with the three constant and other adjustable club members who used to join rotationally and from the bare minimum amount that was being donated by those handful number of people of the village who supported this job. After the summer the more the monsoon appeared the number of volunteers decreased dramatically. People started providing various excuses for not attending on their scheduled day. Eventually the winter came with more excuses and nearly zero attendance for the voluntary service and lastly it became permanently a three member team. On the other hand those people who were supporting and donating for the cause also started skipping their monthly donation with the reason that when there are only three people in the team so it is actually worthless to invest on this and more significantly it is better now to stop this as no one in the village is eager for the service.

One night in such a situation Surya, Sundar and Patru was roaming around the village when Surya first said to Sundar and Patru with a frustrated mind, I have decided to stop this as there is no one to support the noble cause and on top of that due to my decision you two are being burdened to spend sleepless nights just to keep my promise. Sundar was silent and concentrating on the cigarette he was smoking. Patru with utter exasperation replied, Surya da you know the blunt people will only understand the necessity of this if and only if an actual problem takes place and any of the house get robbed. Surya turned his eyes to Patru and smilingly replied, then let us stop this unless that happens and let us wait for the day when the people themselves will request us to reinitiate. He added, what do you say Sundar.

Hmm, I was thinking something else, Sundar replied. While passing the cigarette to Surya he asked, why can't the same happen tomorrow or day after? Surya and Patru both were a bit shocked. Patru asked him, what do you actually mean by that?

Sundar took a long gasp and explained, look around you, how many windows are open in the houses? He paused and answered his own question, zero. Friends this is winter and everybody is sleeping in their home closing all the doors and especially the windows, right. Certainly but what purpose would it solve, Surya replied. Yes I am coming to thins brother, be patient, Sundar replied smilingly and continued, so even if they have to wake up suddenly at midnight they will need at least five minutes to settle down and open the windows to watch what is going on the street. Surya replied, that is ok but how will that help us. Sundar started again, now first we will appear as robber and any how we will have to make a hue and cry in the middle of a night. After that we will run from that place and take the circular path of our village to reach the same spot but this time whistling and shouting that there are robbers. He continued, next day we will call a meeting in the club and declare that for only three boys it is extremely dangerous to carry out the night guard service in such a terrible situation and we are withdrawing. And you know what will happen then.

Surya thought for a minute and replied, your plan is not bad but how would we make such a hue and cry that will force more or less the entire village to wake up at midnight. Sundar replied, that is the only point to be discussed and planned.

Patru was till then listening to the discussion, now he said, Surya da if we charge a bomb on Maiti's house as Atindra was the leader of the opposition. Both Surya and Sundar laughed and asked, do you really know what you are talking about. Surya added, do you know how to make a bomb and more specifically what are the ingredients needed? This time with such a sarcasm Patru got offended and replied, look guys in my maternal uncle's house I not only have seen people making small crackers those are used in ceremonies but I myself also have made one or two with my cousins, as that is their business. He continued, so I know what the ingredients are and how to make crackers.

Surya asked, what will happen with small crackers? As you said those are only used in ceremonies and not by the dacoits my boy.

If we could make a sizable version of the same then it could generate a sound loud enough to scare all the villagers and make a hue and cry especially in the middle of a placid winter night when everyone is peacefully sleeping under their blanket, Patru replied. Sundar and Surya gazed at each other as what Patru was saying had a solid point. Sundar asked, where the ingredients will come from. Patru excitedly replied, in that case tomorrow I shall go to my maternal uncle's house and arrange for the things needed.

Finally after a long discussion and planning it was decided that next day Patru is going to his maternal uncle's home and will come back within two to three days with all the ingredients required for making three big size crackers and at the same time the knowledge of how to actually make those crackers.

Patru took two more days from the scheduled day of his return to come back. It was early evening of Sunday, so he was sure that both Sundar and Surya da will be in the club. He directly came to the club from the railway station. He got them there but two or three other members were also present so he called Surya da and Sundar outside. Surya da asked about his delay but he smilingly replied that he will tell him afterwards then showed the bag in his hand and boastfully said that all have been arranged. The three planned to meet again at night and before going to home Patru hid the bag behind the banyan tree near the club such a way that no one could locate it.

At night when the three boys reassembled, the excitement was beyond imagination. Let me show you the things, Patru went behind the tree where he has kept the bag. He then very carefully placed it on the ground and opened it. The things that came out changed the excitement in to sheer tension – three jumbo sized crackers which could easily be called as crude bombs. Surya da and Sundar looked at each other first and then at Patru, whose face was glowing with pride of success. They were somehow scared. Surya da first asked, Patru what are these? Have you gone crazy? You are planning to charge these bombs in the village? Patru replied, these are just to create enough sound. Sundar interjected, what do you mean by enough sound, so much so that not the people of this village but the surrounding villages also wake up at the middle of the night? Patru with a serious face then touched the paining nerves of the other two, look either we will use it tonight or from tomorrow there will be no night guard service, choice is yours. He continued, I have done my job and now it's your turn to decide what to be done with these?

It was more than required to agree Surya and Sundar to carry on. They waited for some hours within the club room and nearly at 2 AM they came in front of the Maiti's house with their face covered by their shawl. There was small garden in between the boundary wall and the main gate. They carefully watched the surroundings first and found none. As decided earlier Surya threw the first cracker on the main gate but nothing happened. Surya and Sundar looked at Patru with dilemma. Patru did not say anything. He steadily came forward and threw the one he had in his hand with the maximum force he could employ. And this time it was successful. The cracker burst with such a tremendous powerful sound that it was enough to wake the entire village up on the toe. The three suddenly got stopped for a moment and then the only word came out of Surya's mouth was "run". They took the pre-decided circular path. Sundar asked, what to be done with this one in my hand? Patru replied, throw it anywhere you want. Sundar said, then why not on the Chakraborty's wall. Surya replied, go ahead. While crossing the house of Prakash Chakraborty, who was a flatterer of Atindra Maiti, Sundar threw the last one and that also burst creating the same amount of sound like the earlier one. Then while running the three started blowing their whistles and shouting "dacoits have raided the village".

Within two to three minutes when they returned back in front of the Maiti's house they found the door till closed and people from inside were shouting for help. Some other people of the neighboring houses who were looking from their windows got some strength seeing the three boys there and came out. Slowly some other people also gathered there and started gossiping about who has seen what. They came up with different kinds of imaginary scenarios which as per them they have seen by their own eyes. Everyone tried to be more knowledgeable than the previous one. The discussions created a kind of comedy scene over there for the three Guards-cum-Dacoits.

The police also arrived within some minutes and scrutinized Maiti's house and found that the main door was severely damaged. After a long discussion a general meeting was called in the club ground and all the people who have witnessed were called to describe in details what they have seen.

Next morning in meeting, the first persons who were called to share what they have seen were Surya, Sundar and Patru. You were on the streets last night, what have you seen, Ramendra babu asked them.

Sundar told, sir we were on the other side of the village and rushed to the area following the sound and found seven or eight people standing in front of the house. He continued, those people ran away seeing us coming and blowing whistles. Perhaps they have thought we are police men. What happened next? Ramendra babu enquired. Surya replied this time, sir we tried to follow but did not dare as we were badly outnumbered. He added, and sir we also have decided that from tonight we will not carry on this "night guard" any more, we are only three people and if such thing happens again then it might be highly risky for us.

It was a master stroke as all the scared people including Atindra Maiti also came in to a requesting mood and in a sugar coated tone said, I personally appreciate the three boys and their courage. He continued, they have actually saved my home and family from a great danger. I request them to carry on the great service for the society and I promise in front of all the villagers that I will be the first to contribute for this service. Finally the villagers decided to support the voluntary night guard service as planned earlier. You three come to my office in the afternoon to record your versions, at the end the police officer Ramendra babu asked the three boys to come with him to the police station in the afternoon.

The three boys were standing in front of the table of Ramendra babu when he asked the first question, where you boys have managed the bombs from. Surya tried to bypass the query, how do we know sir that where the dacoits have bought the bombs from. Ramendra babu with a smile replied, Surya I am in the police service for long and never seen dacoits using bombs without shrapnel and just to create sound. At the same time the one that did not burst and was lying in the garden is with me now. I have checked that, and it is nothing but a sizable cracker.

He added, I have carefully scrutinized both the areas where the two bomb were thrown and had not found sign of even a single shrapnel. The boys were caught and had no point to present in front of the experienced officer to defend what they have done, so they just stood tightlipped looking at the ground. Suddenly Ramendra babu laughed out loudly and said, I must say you boys are very smart and actually given the best possible medicine to those people who were opposing the good idea just to avoid a small cooperation. He then added, but at the same time I warn you not to do such adventure again as that might create problem for you guys also.

The Ghost ...

"Ghosts catches the small boys and girls if they don't abide by the elder's suggestions or obey their words. They live in the tree top and come down to catch those disobedient naughty kids".

There will hardly be any boy or girl in the villages of India who have not heard this lines from the elders of the family and especially when they don't want to eat or don't want to seat with their books in the evening. Whether they read or not at that age is not so important but what imperative is that especially provides their mother a slice of time to complete her house-hold jobs with lesser worries about the kids who are always on edge to do something ill-disciplined. The elders always use to show the kids the dark arrears outside the home and more specifically big trees adjacent to the house to tell them those lines to make the kids' seat without doing something disturbing or wrong. Truly speaking at that age it is generally use to be a horrible experience. In the morning or day time when the same kids use to look at those trees with an incisive eyes and frightened mind to find out any symbol of ghosts, the don't. But those breed of more curious kids when ask the same to the elders they generally reply that, *Ghosts don't stay there in the day time, they only come after the sun sets and wait there looking for small kids like you, who don't abide by their seniors' word.* This actually gives birth of more anxiety about ghosts and also helps to developed many more questions in those young minds. The same kids even sometimes carry that uncanny feelings after they grow up. But the question remains same – do ghosts really exist?

The membership for all have not yet been collected properly and this is third week of the month, may I know Patru what's the issue, Surya da asked Patru. It is almost midnight and there was hardly any person in the village who was awake except Surya, Sundar and Patru. The three musketeers were seating in the extended portion of the old temple in the village. Surya was scrutinizing the membership register to find out how many members have already paid their monthly membership and how many have not yet.

What would I do? Patru replied, and continued, I ask for the membership to all almost every day but they always come up with some or other excuses. Yes I know, but anyway we have to collect it by next two to three days, Surya replied and closed the book. Are you sleeping, he asked Sundar, who was lying on the other part of the place in closed eyes. No, waiting for the rain to stop, Sundar replied without changing any stance. Yah, this is so boring, Patru added.

The three were carrying out their duty of night guards in the village and adjacent areas. Every member was bound to work as a night guard for at least once in a week but maximum of the boys from the well to do families except Surya used to avoid the duty. They were ready to pay an extra amount as membership for quitting the job. That actually was helpful for boys like those, who had no one in the family to restrict them to join the night guard team. Those boys who joined willingly had used that as a chance to spend times with friend in the club, playing cards or carom or stealing mangoes or coconut or whatever to enjoy. Generally Sundar, Surya and Patru – these three were regular members. Surya willfully and the rest two had no one to resist or pay for them.

It was the month of July and the monsoon was in its full swing. It was raining continuously for more than an hour. Electricity was a distant dream to villages at that point of time. The three got bored with cards and was seating idle. As it was raining, so there was no way to roam around the village also and the three guards actually were fighting an uneven battle with the suicide squad of mosquitos which were even ready to sacrifice their own lives to suck blood from the three human being. Rather they were guarding themselves from the attacks of the mighty mosquitos. Patru followed Sundar and laid himself down on the floor and then Surya followed the same path.

Hey guys let us have a walk, the rain has stopped, perhaps they were feeling a bit drowsy too when Patru first noticed that the rain has stopped. He called his companions to inform and wake them up. He added, otherwise tomorrow itself we are going to be submitted in the hospital due to malaria. Both Surya and Sundar woke up and noticed that Patru is correct, the rain has actually stopped. The sky above was totally free of clouds and probably it was a full moon or very close to that as the environment was full of fascinating moon light. A moist wind was blowing just how it happens after a long rain. There was no sound except some frogs, who were expressing their bitterness in loud voice as their homes are flooded and some unknown insects were also informing that they are still not asleep. So the boys happily decided go out for a walk in the village road. At the least the walk will help to get out of the sheer boredom and drowsiness. The three got out of the place. So which way should we start from Surya da, Patru asked.

I think it will be better to go up to the main road and return, Surya answered.

Why, do you expect the tea stall is till open to serve you a hot cup of tea in this romantic weather, Sundar mocked him?

Then you suggest, Patru asked.

Why we don't take the basic direction towards the DPR ground, Sundar suggested.

And Mr. Think tank what you are expecting to get there, this time Surya da returned the tease.

At least we will have the opportunity to have a smoke which we can't have here or anywhere in the way suggested by you, Sundar replied. He is right Surya da, the point was valid and well accepted by Patru.

Okay, majority wins, then let us move, Surya accepted.

DPR ground or the way it was named was the largest ground in the village and vicinity. The name originally came from the name of David Provincial Railway. The old day's DPR line was through beside the ground. Some part of the railway track were still visible and in the opposite side of the field there was standing a big old two storied building. Once the building used to be a big office when the British raj was present in the country and the Provincial Railway was at its pick of magnificence. But when the raj ended the provincial railway also breathed its last. So there left no one to take care of the once glorious building and in subsequent time it faced the same fate of any abandoned building in India. The costly doors and windows made of tick wood were the first things that vanished, then the ornaments of the building got looted by the people and it was left with some partly broken big old walls and roof and none the less a staircase without its railings. Slowly people started feeling scary to visit that area after the sunset due to its appearance, and as it always happens in such cases, automatically stories came up about uncanny experiences. Though nobody has ever witnessed anything in his own eyes but they always have heard from or about someone who is a very close person of one of his very close friend or relative who has experienced that typical things or sometimes have seen ghosts in that building. Some even was a bit more knowledgeable about all these and have been knowing someone who has even seen British Ghost in that building. So when the number of such stories increased, automatically visitors to that area decreased.

I don't have cigarette with me, Patru said.

That is expected and we know this well, Surya da replied. You don't have to be tensed, he added. I have cigarettes but not enough for the entire night, hardly three or four, he completed and stared at Sundar. Out all the three only Surya used to carry cigarette packet as only he was financially capable to afford that.

I have a packet of bidi with me, Sundar replied.

Okay then, Surya replied with an expression of satisfaction clearly visible on his face. Sundar, Patru and Surya da used to go to the ground to smoke as there were hardly any chance of being caught by any elder person from the village. So they were walking towards the DPR ground. In the name of night guard they were carrying two handmade bamboo sticks, a whistle and one torch light, which were provided from the local police station. Let me blow the whistle for once or twice, so that the village people should know that even in such a night we are awake in their defense, Patru said and started blowing the whistle.

Stop this man, you are just night guard of a tiny village and not the brave soldiers, who Re standing in the border with the risk of their life to save the nation, Surya da said Patru. You don't need to make everyone feel that you are awake. Sundar smiled, did not say anything.

They were walking in a leisurely mood and it took them ten to fifteen minutes to reach the DPR ground. Hardly the boys had reached the ground, suddenly the rain started again. Though it was not heavy but well enough to compel them to run for a shelter. The boys had no place to hide themselves except that nearly destroyed building. They took shelter under a portion adjacent to the staircase. Surya ignited one cigarette and another he offered to Sundar. Surya da are you going to attend the meeting tomorrow, Sundar asked Surya.

Perhaps not. I have some other important engagements, but still if I could manage those by the afternoon then I will be with you, Surya replied. Otherwise inform Binoy da on my behalf that I will meet him day after tomorrow at his place, he completed. What you people do in these meetings, Patru asked a common question for both the other boys. Sundar did not reply but Surya did. We discuss various political issues that are affecting our society and country adversely. Why you are asking this, you said once that you are not interested in politics, Surya asked.

I am not even now, just out of curiosity, Patru answered. They were busy discussing about the issues of their everyday life. Even busier in fighting the battle with another bunch of mosquitos who actually got a great dinner all of a sudden and attacked the three with full attention and offence from every possible side and in every possible area of their body open to them. Mosquitos are same in all the parts of the globe. You could never satisfy them. They finished the cigarettes in sometime but due to rain it was not possible to get out of there so they waited. It took quite some time for the rain to become milder and the boys decided to move out. Though it was not as clear as before the second phase of the rain but it was not even very dark also. Sometimes the lightening on the sky were making the surrounding very clear for just few moments and then darker for the next few. The three boys rose up and just were to start moving out of that place when Patru suddenly turned back and stopped. Sundar and Surya da did not notice that Patru was looking to something. Suddenly he said out loudly, who is there?

Sundar and Surya was busy with some other discussion so they had not noticed anything but when they heard Patru shouting at someone and that too in that kind of a deserted place, which is hardly visited by anybody and on top of that in the middle of a rainy night, they stared at each other and turned back to Patru. Patru was still looking at that direction. What happened? Whom have you seen there, Surya da asked Patru?

I could not recognize but someone has crossed from this side to that, Patru replied. He indicated from his left to his right side. Are you sure you have seen someone traversed from this to that side? Sundar asked Patru with a milder voice so that if someone is hiding behind the wall then their conversation should not be audible to him, otherwise he would be alert. Perhaps Patru understood the untold reason of Sundar's whispering. He replied the same but just by nodding his head in an affirmative posture. His eyes were fixed at that half broken wall, as per Patru behind which that person was hiding. The three boys gazed at each other and just by hand gesture planned to check the back side of the wall. From one side Surya da will cover and from the other Sundar. Patru will wait to help either one of the two as and when required. They actually were highly excited about catching a thief red handed. Sundar and Surya da each took a bamboo stick in hand and simultaneously jumped in to the back side of the wall. But there was no one. They looked around but there was no sign of any human presence. They came back to their previous position with a doubt in mind.

Sundar was yet to ask Patru whether he has confidently seen someone or not but that was not needed any more. This time it was Sundar who saw a shadow traversed just in the direction opposite to what Patru said. This time from right to left side. He could not helped to but to instinctively ask quite loudly the same question Patru asked, who is there?

Surya da and Patru followed Sundar's eye sight but before they could have seen something the shadow disappeared. The boys looked at each other. All of them again visited the opposite side of the wall, but this time together. They were shocked as there was nothing or none. The same thing happened for one or two more times. It was quite a long time that the boys were there and had searched more or less all the walls and corners but found nothing. The place of excitements in their mind were being captured by a sense of doubt, rather an uncanny feeling probably when they saw the same phenomenon for the last time and the ultimate word came from Patru, Ghost.

Nobody knew which was there in that word, but what they experienced, that single word just cemented the three boys. They got as closer as possible to each other. The three young men with two sticks in hand abruptly felt as the weakest people in the universe. They became so weak psychologically that they actually started looking at each other only and not to any other direction. All the three young people who were so brave and exited just before some moments or so about catching a thief, suddenly became so feeble minded that they even did not had the strength to get out of that building. Surya da first spoke out, Sundar, Patru let us get out of this cursed place.

The other two also were wanting to do something same. They started walking back foot together but their eyes were fixed at that walls. Suddenly while back tracking Patru skidded. Though he did not fall on the ground by holding Sundar's hand but the torch light which he was holding in his hand till then threw a beam of light towards the first floor of the building. The light fall on a corner of the staircase. By instinct all of their eyes followed the light and the three boys just got speechless for some seconds and then they laughed perhaps the loudest ever in their life.

It was a family of monkeys who had taken shelter in that "Haunted House" as the rain disturbed their normal life by moistening their usual home in the trees and compelled them to live that night in there. So when a group of their successors entered in to their temporary shelter they probably got disturbed for the second time and started watching the men without making any noise. While watching one or two of those monkeys perhaps had crossed from one side to the opposite. In the mild moon light the boys actually saw the shadows of those monkeys' on the ground and when after following those shadows and searching every nooks and corners of the building they failed to find anything they lost their logical sense and thought it as – Ghost.

Finally laughing for some time the three came out of the house. The rain had stopped. They fired three bidis and started walking back to the old temple, where they started their journey that night.

Thank you Patru, Sundar broke the silence first.

Why, Patru asked.

If you would not have slipped all three of us from tomorrow morning would have started believing in Ghost, Sundar replied.

It proved another thing also, this time Surya commented. He continued, though we do not believe in ghost but some way or other we have not even disbelieved the same from the core of our heart otherwise the thought would never had come to our mind.

Exactly, Sundar replied in a short way and paused for some moments. Perhaps this incident has made one thing very clear that we should always believe in those things which you see under full light, otherwise you can get totally opposite impression of something you have seen in mild or no light, Sundar completed.

It was nearly the time of the dawn when the boys returned to the place they started from.

EVERYBODY THINK SO ...

WHERE IT STARTED

Enough is enough kaka, why would I go with that man whom I don't even know by his name, Sujata asked her beloved uncle Atanu. Her irritation and rage was quite visible on her face. She continued, you requested me to follow all the ritual, I did. You asked me to recite all the hymns, well I did that too. You told me I am getting married, I affirmed. Now you are telling I will have to leave my own house and go with that man, and you contemplate I will abide by that too? Then you are wrong, I am not going anywhere, and that is final, she completed and let herself sat on the floor. Everyone standing there were utterly shocked. Except some handful, everyone present there knew Sujata almost from the very first day of her life. They knew the cheerful, always helping, broad minded girl is straight forward and speaking-the-truth-on-your-face type but they had never seen such stubbornness in her behavior. They were surprised.

This is the rule of the society my princes, once a girl gets married she has to go with her husband, Atanu replied in a lengthy way. It was really tough for him also to live in a house where Sujata is not present. He uttered to his beloved princes in a very placid and adorable voice. Other senior ladies of the family and the neighborhood including Sarojini came forward to agree Sujata. They also tried on their own ways to make her understand the very basic rule of marriage for a girl is to live with her husband. They even had to cite example of their own to manage the situation. After listening to all of them, Sujata finally settled the deal, well I would only go with that person if kaka comes with me. Atanu looked at his elder brother Brijendra who was actually standing at the door of the room. The bridegroom and his companions were waiting so there was no other option but to agree with Sujata's demand. Brijendra directed Atanu to get ready at the earliest to accompany the newly married couple, Sujata and Gopal.

Sujata was the first daughter of Brijendra and Bimala, eldest amongst the brothers and sisters of Sundar, next to her was Satyendra, Narendra, Mukunda then Sundar and finally Anil. Anil was the last child after giving birth to whom Sundar's mother passed away. Sujata was a very straightforward kind of character and as a first child she was pampered a bit more than others in the family. She never used to hinder herself from telling loudly anything she felt right and justified even in front of anyone, whoever he is, and for this nature the senior people from the neighborhood also loved her very much. Even Brijendra also used to be afraid of his own eldest child. She was nearly fourteen years elder than Sundar and typically was no less than a motherly figure for him throughout.

Sujata was married at the age of fifteen years of age. The next day after the marriage when the girl is sent to her in-law's house became a never forgotten piece of incident in the family. Atanu was given the responsibility of guiding and accompanying the newly married couple to the bridegroom's home. He arranged a bull cart for carrying the couple to the nearest railway station and other team members were to walk. He was planning and managing everything as Brijendra gave the responsibilities to him.

Now the situation changed and he was to be ready to accompany the couple up to the destination, so he went inside to get ready for the sudden travel.

A PARRALEL PLANNING

What are you doing there, Narendra asked his elder brother Satyendra. Why you are seating in the grass hamper, he added surprisingly.

At the time of Sujata's marriage Satyendra was a boy of nearly eight years and Narendra at his fifth. While roaming around Narendra found his elder brother seating, rather hiding himself under the bull cart that was arranged to carry the couple to the railway station. Satyendra was actually seating in the hidden hamper underneath the cart to hold the thin-cut grasses for the bulls. Unfortunately now he is caught red handed and had no other option but to take his brother in confident to succeed in his plan. He silently came out of that place putting his finger on his lips directing Narendra to shut his mouth. Don't you shout you idiot, I have a plan, Satyendra whispered to his brother. He continued, uncle is going in a tour and he will not allow us to be with him, so that is why I have planned to hide myself until the railway station after which he will have to take me with him. Satyendra looked at his brother.

Then why only you, I will also go, Narendra replied.

Okay, but don't talk, Satyendra directed his brother. They tried to seat in that hidden hamper but that was not spacious enough to accommodate the two. We can't hide here, otherwise both of us will be caught, Satyendra said to his brother.

Then I will tell uncle that you are hiding here with the intension of being with him, Narendra threatened in reply. Now it was a terrible situation for Satyendra. He was seeing his chance is slipping out of his hand, which can't be allowed. As the wise men say, critical situation makes a man intelligent. Okay then, first I am going and then when the cart will return for taking the other people then you will exactly do as what I am doing now, Satyendra uttered to his brother. Narendra seeing something is better than nothing had to agree to the proposal. But his waiting came to a never ending one as the cart never returned to take him.

So finally the team started the journey from Sujata's parental home to her in-law's house, only after including Atanu and obviously Satyendra, but unknowingly. Now when the people reached the station and the newly married couple came out of the cart, Satyendra also came out of the hidden place. What the hell are you doing here, Atanu's embarrassment was quite visible and he asked his nephew out of absolute exasperation. And that too in such a condition, he added. The boy replied with stubbornness, I will also go to the tour with didi. Atanu's embarrassment was absolutely logical because of three reasons – firstly, the station was far away from home so Satyendra could not be sent home back alone without any senior guiding him, secondly the train schedule was so that it was not possible for him to take Satyendra back to home and come over again within that stipulated period of time and thirdly seeing her younger brother, suddenly and unexpectedly, Sujata also requested her uncle to take Satyendra with her, which created an emotional environment. The bridegroom and his family members also suggested Atanu to take the boy with them.

So Atanu decided to take Satyendra with him and directed the cart owner to inform about the situation back at home and tell them not to worry about the boy. Satyendra came in such a condition that if he is to be taken then new cloths should be purchased for him. That actually became another lottery for the boy and he was given new cloths by his uncle and became a part of the team in the journey.

THE LIFE BEGINS

It was almost afternoon when the bridal party finally reached Sujata's in-law's house. It was a remote village in the adjacent district, which was a journey of nearly four to five hours out of which three hours by train and then again bull cart and finally a walk of fifteen to twenty minutes.

Don't get in, first of all the arti should be done and then both of you and my son, will have to complete required rituals and then only you will enter the house, a middle aged lady said all these to Sujata and her husband Gopal in a very authoritative voice. Her appearance was clearly depicting her a widow, a white sharee and very simple golden bangle was all what she was wearing. She is my mother, Gopal said to his newly married wife standing by him in a timid and whispering voice. The lady had already gathered some ladies from the neighborhood to carry those rituals. She will not take part in to these as she is a widow. Those ladies started directing the couple to follow certain procedures for those rituals. Some of them were also cutting jokes on Gopal, who did not even dare reply to any of them. Gopal's mother was following and giving instructions to those ladies. It took almost an hour or so for the rituals to be completed. You will have to wait for seven more minutes there only as my Guru Ji had said that the perfect time of entering the house will start on exactly five minutes to six o'clock, she spoke again. Sujata noticed while saying the word "Guru Ji" Gopal's mother folded her hands and touched her forehead with both of her palms touching each other, to show her respect for that "Guru Ji". Everyone had no other choice but to wait there unless she announces, yes you may enter now.

In next two days the house which was full of relatives and visitors became free from them all and the festive mood was over. Sujata found her new family consisted of three members in total, she herself, her husband and her mother-in-law. She came to know that her mother-in-law became widow at a very young age with her only son and only light of hope for life, which made her love and affection for her son Gopal more than blind. Though she possess high prejudices about many things but it was very much a natural kind of behavior especially at that period of time in the society and especially in a distant rural area. Sujata's husband Gopal was a very calm, gentle, soft spoken and introvert kind of person. He was a man who probably never contradicted or argued with anybody throughout his life on any issue even if he was on the right side, just the polar opposite of the nature of his wife, who if feels that she is correct on any issue, could even contradict the Almighty and that too loudly.

Now I have to get back to workplace, it was the tenth day of Sujata's marriage when Gopal said to her. He added, day after tomorrow I have planned to leave. Sujata was combing her long hairs after dinner seating in their private room. Where you stay there, she asked. We have a men's hostel there, Gopal replied. Why you don't take both myself and your mother with you then, Sujata asked. I can't take you two women in a men's hostel, Gopal replied. He continued, and I need some time to make the necessary arrangements to take you there. He paused for a moment and continued, Ma will never leave this house as this is related to my father's sentiment for her. That is why I come here once or twice a month to take care of her. As much as possible after managing my job. Gopal completed with an elongated breath which showed his discomfort. Okay, no problem, you first arrange a proper house there and then I will talk to Ma regarding this, Sujata said smilingly to her husband. The man she refused to come along with just ten days before, had fallen in love now.

Keeping his wife and Ma at his native place Gopal finally left on the scheduled day for his workplace.

When Gopal returned next time at his place after a month he was surprised. His wife's straightforward nature has already become well-known to the neighbors within this short period of time after from their marriage. The more he heard about her nature and open heartedness from his mother and the neighbors, the more he actually loved her. To him it seemed to be an immature behavior and a kind of childish nature to be adored. Gopal noticed Sujata is actually the only person in the family who use to keep everyone lively.

The time passed by and the frequency of Gopal's visit at his native place became more frequent than it used to be before his marriage. After spending a year or so of such life Gopal managed to rent a house near to the location of his work place. He informed everything in a letter to his mother. Sujata read that to her mother-in-law, Ma your son has said both of us to pack everything that we think essential and he is coming here next week to take us with him there, Sujata said to her mother-in-law. The lady smiled back and replied, I have almost completed my life, better you go and enjoy your part of life. She paused for a moment and then added, I won't leave this house unless I am forced to leave by the death.

Why not, Sujata asked in a loud voice as she always does. How I would manage everything on my own, that too in an unknown place, she added. You will have to be with us, she completed.

Okay, then I will send Adhirath with you, he will help you there, the lady replied adorably.

Ohhh, so you are equalizing yourself with Adhirath now, Sujata's disagreement was clearly visible?

I know you are right but he is an old attendant and actually had been taking care of Gopal from his childhood, he is a good man the lady smiled back and replied.

Have I ever said he is not a good man or he had not done his duty to your son ever, Sujata asked.

I know but as I have already said to Gopal many times, I won't leave my house, that is final and don't request or argue with me for that, the lady replied. The chapter was closed.

LIFE CHANGED….

Sujata looked back from the village path, her mother-in-law is still standing in the gate and staring at them leaving. Some other women were accompanying her but she was alone, cruelly alone. Sujata felt a cry bubbling in her throat for the old lady and the loneliness yet to haunt her down from now. Gopal tried his best, first he tried to agree his mother by requesting and then he argued and finally shouted for the first time in his life. Sujata has never witnessed Gopal shouting but Gopal failed to agree his mother to be with them at their new house in his workplace. Finally he took only his wife with him and before leaving thousand times he repeated to his mother to take care of herself. I will come as frequent as I can to see you, he lastly told his mother before leaving. Don't be worried, I will be fine, the lady replied smilingly. And now they are leaving their house.

New place, new home, new people, new environment, new responsibilities and that too as a lead female character of the family and especially the master of the kitchen at the age of sixteen years made Sujata much more than just happy. Adhirath was also sent to stay with them by her mother-in-law to help Sujata in household works and her husband Gopal in shopping and all.

Tell me what the items to be purchased today, Gopal asked his wife while sipping the first cup of tea of the day in the morning fixing his eyes on the newspaper opened in front of him. Every alternate day in the morning before going to office Gopal used to ask Sujata for the list of the things required for kitchen as he is going to the market. First you leave the paper and concentrate then only I will say, Sujata replied. She added, every day you forget one thing or the other. Gopal raised his face and smilingly replied, okay tell me now. As usually Sujata uttered a long list, consisting almost everything possible, may be out of which many are already there in the kitchen in ample quantity. Gopal was well-known about this and finally directed Adhirath silently to make a proper list. This was actually an open secret to both of them but at the same time they used to enjoy that. After returning from market while arranging things in the kitchen Sujata will ask Gopal for those items that she mentioned but Gopal has forgotten to bring and Gopal will ask for absolution in return for his forgetful nature with an artificial pale face to his wife and at the same time will promise that next time he will surely bring all those items and will never forget anything in future.

Life was literally at the apex of happiness but suddenly one news stormed Sujata. It was Sunday, Gopal was leisurely seating in the balcony of his house with his morning tea and the newspaper when someone knocked at the door. Adhirath was not there in the house and Sujata was occupied in the kitchen so Gopal came to open the door. Uncle, you, so early in the morning, everything's okay, Gopal was shocked to see Atanu standing in front of him. His blackened face, uncombed hair, unshaved beards and tired appearance created a doubt in Gopal's mind. Where is Sujata, Atanu timidly asked Gopal. She is in the kitchen, Gopal replied. While talking to each other Gopal has guided Atanu in the house. He pulled a chair and offered the elderly to comfort himself. Atanu sat himself down and uttered, call Sujata. Sujata was by now approaching there, she had already heard the voice of her uncle.

Uncle you are here, you can't imagine so happy I am, Sujata said to Atanu and suddenly stopped looking at the man seating in front of her. Come, my princes, seat here, Atanu pulled another chair and passed it to Sujata. She did not cared and asked, what has happened to you, why you are looking in such a terrible condition. Atanu first directed her to seat and then finally said what he has traversed so long a distance to say, Boudi is no more with us, your mother is no more with us. It took some moments for Sujata to actually understand what she was listening. Gopal, shocked and shattered was standing like a statue. Atanu's eyes were moist. Sujata screamed at the top of her voice. She looked at her husband without any expression and then covered her face with her palms she cried. She cried for long holding the hands of her most trusted friend, philosopher and guide, her uncle. Gopal was standing still, as if he has lost the words to console his wife. Sujata wanted to come to her parental house to see her brothers but she could not because of her own pregnancy.

Yes Sujata was pregnant and the couple was expecting to receive their first gift of love soon.

.... ONCE AND FOR EVER

I have decided to send you back to village, there is no one to help or guide you in such a condition here, Gopal one day told his wife. At the least there you would get the guidance and suggestions from not only my mother but the other senior women in the village also, he added. Sujata's pregnancy has reached its middle stage and Gopal was worried about her wife.

I do also think the same, but you will have to come once in every alternative week, Sujata replied. Sujata supported the decision and decided to return back to her in-law's house as her own mother was no more so there was no question of returning to her parental house. Next week Gopal returned to his village with his wife and said his mother that Sujata will be here unless she becomes fit enough for household jobs. Gopal's mother was also very happy with the news as she was going to be grandmother. After keeping her back in the village house Gopal went back to his work place with Adhirath, who will take care of the household unless Sujata get back to her responsibilities. Everything was just picture perfect.

In due time Sujata gave birth of her first child – a son. Gopal, his mother, other relatives, neighbors, everyone was so happy. Tomorrow I will go to Guru Ji's ashram early in the morning to prepare the Kundali of my grandson, Gopal's mother said to her son one day. She continued, you stay here and take care of the arrangements for the social rituals for the baby. Don't go alone, it's quite a distant place, take Adhirath with you, Gopal suggested his mother. But she refused by saying, I don't need any attendant to go to Guru Ji's ashram, he will better be here to help you in the arrangements. Gopal knew very well that once his mother has finalized something in her mind then there is hardly any power on earth which could change her decision, so he replied, as you wish then.

Are you alright Ma, Gopal noticed that and asked her. When in the evening Gopal's mother returned from the ashram she was looking tired and exhausted. The devastation was visible and her behavior was restless. She just nodded but then asked, did not say anything? Let me call the doctor, you are not looking well, Gopal said. He was turning towards the door when his mother called him, don't need to call anyone, just ask Adhirath to give me a glass of water and leave me alone for sometimes. Gopal did not call Adhirath rather himself took the water for his mother. He placed the glass on the table and left the room. Just before leaving he turned and said, if you feel any problem just give me a call, I am there in the adjacent room, and then he left the room. At night Gopal came to call his mother for dinner but she declined and replied that she is not feeling any hunger and will skip the dinner. Her voice and attitude was such that Gopal did not dare to repeat his request and silently left.

Gopal arranged everything as demanded by his mother and required for the purpose of the program. As per the local priest's verdict the ceremony was scheduled after two weeks. Gopal's leave was over and he had to get back to his job, so next morning he left, informing that he will return two days before the function. Perhaps that was the decision which affected not only his own but also smashed his wife's life.

Sujata noticed that the behavior of her mother-in-law has changed a lot after returning from the ashram. The woman who was so happy to be with the baby for all the time has started avoiding both Sujata and her son. Somehow she even was so frustrated that she started abusing Sujata in her every deeds. Just before some days the baby, who used to be the heart throb for the elderly lady has become the fiercest enemy of her. Finally what she did is the ugliest activity the humankind probably could ever think of. It was the dawn of day, four days before the ceremonial day, Sujata was sleeping in deep after managing her son for the last night as the kid was crying. The prejudiced lady took the child off his mother and silently went to the adjacent cannel trenched by the farmers for supplying water to their fields and threw the little life in to the water. Some people who were guarding their fields at night saw that and when they understood what has happened, one of them jumped in the cannel to save the life but when that man took the baby out of the water it was too late. The ultimate damage was done. Life had stopped before it could have begun properly.

The other men standing there chased Gopal's mother for her deed and what she replied was more than shocking, "the kid is cursed and will become the cause of my son's death and that too will happen within a year, so I did not have any choice but to kill him". When people chased how she has come to know all these bogus things, she replied, my Guru Ji has prepared his Kundali and that is written there. She did not say anything more….in her life….forever.

The news spread like wildfire in the village and the vicinity. When the breathless body of her son, wrapped in wet cloths, was taken to Sujata and she came to know from the other women from the village what actually has happened she tried but failed to cry. She just screamed once with all of her might and fainted.

After two days when Gopal came to celebrate the ritual and social function for his first child he was driven to offer the kid his last right. He tried to ask many things to his mother but could not. He could not bear the presence of that lady for long. He found his wife shattered. Her eyes were dull and vacant. She did not even look at her husband. When Gopal came out of his room he found one of his elderly neighbor was waiting for him. Yes, uncle, any problem, Gopal asked that old man.

Try to make Sujata cry, at least once, otherwise you will lose her too, the man said those words only and left the place.

TIME PASSES BUT SOME MOMENTS DON'T

Gopal did not spend any more days in the village. The very next day he left the village with his wife for his workplace. His mother did not come out of her room to send them off, Gopal from the outside of the closed door of the room just said, Ma we are going. No answer came.

Gopal changed his life a lot and started spending more and more time at home with his wife. He also started trying to engage Sujata in household works but failed. Sujata was changed. She did not speak for months with anybody not even with her husband. Gopal tried many times to make her cry but she did not even cry for once. Gopal finally tried to make her cry by remembering her about the child, if our boy would have lived, he would have become a boy of four months today, Gopal tried the worst possible way to make a mother cry. He was helpless, he was actually doing so out of sheer desperation. He had already lost his first son but he was not ready to lose his beloved wife. Sujata did not even bother to look at Gopal. She stood up and left the place silently.

Why don't you consult with some physicians, Chittaranjan, Gopal's colleague suggested him. I am not saying she has lost his mind or something like that but I found that might work, he added so that Gopal don't take his words offensive or otherwise. As suggested by some neighbors also Gopal started consulting with physicians. Many doctors were consulted but no change was visible. Sujata had become a living dead. Without finding any other means finally Gopal took her to her parental house one day. Sujata entered the house almost after four long years, but there was absolutely no excitement in her eyes. Once the girl who used to energies the entire locality had become a speechless stone sculpture. Sarojini and Uma came forward and hold Sujata, but there was no visible change in her expression. All the family members were standing still and watching her steps. She slowly entered the room where her mother used to live. Sundar, a boy of three years or so at that time seating on the bed. Nobody knows what happened to Sujata seeing Sundar. She came to her younger brother, grabbed him tightly in her hand and first time after months she screamed and finally she cried.

She stayed in her paternal house for some months and engaged herself only to take care of her brother Sundar. She refused to get involved in any other thing and the elders in the family totally gave her the freehand to spend her times with the boy.

In due course of time Gopal again took Sujata back with him. Though she was not out of that shock totally but at least she had started conversing, though too less, with people around her. But one symptom became prominent in her, sometimes suddenly she used to loss her mind and started behaving like a mentally unbalanced person. That phenomenon used to stay for one or two days and again she used to become a normal person slowly. But within that period of time she behaved like a child. This was going to be a lifelong occurrence for her.

People suggested Gopal to have their second child so that Sujata's mind will be diverted from the shock. Time passed by, she gave birth of her second child – a girl, and then two more boys but the scenario did not change.

Years passed by, in the meantime Gopal's mother passed away.

DO YOU TOO THINK SO?

Sundar has grown up and he use to visit his elder sister's house frequently as for him Sujata was no less than a mother figure and for Sujata Sundar was more a son than a younger brother.

Sundar there is a letter for you, Mukunda handed over an envelope to his brother who has just returned from his many involvements. Sundar took the envelope and found it was from his brother-in-law, Gopal. In some short and simple lines he has requested him to come to his house. He has also mentioned that Sujata is facing that psychological problem very frequently now a days but she is not ready to go to any doctor for consultation. She is becoming very annoyed whenever anyone is requesting her for consulting with doctor regarding her problem. Gopal has also mentioned that as she loves Sundar very much and generally abide by all the requests he makes to his sister so if he could come and manage to take her to the doctor. It was more a call of duty than affection, Sundar thought for some moments and planned to go next day. When he reached Gopal's house it was afternoon. Before meeting his sister to get a glimpse of the current condition he went to Gopal's office.

You are here in my office, Gopal was surprised seeing Sundar at his office first.

Before I meet her I need to know in details the current situation, Sundar replied. Gopal took him to his office canteen and ordered for two cups of tea and described the present issues of Sujata's annoyance over doctors in details. After discussion Sundar moved to his sister's house.

Adhirath opened the door. He was surprised too seeing Sundar at the gate. It is really good to see you here, at the most in such a situation, the elderly man uttered to Sundar. Where didi is now, Sundar asked in reply. Adhirath pointed towards a room closed and locked from outside. Sundar first reached to the children of his sister and adored them, then he moved forward to meet his sister.

Sujata was kept in a room locked from outside. Sundar opened the door and entered in. Sujata was seating on her bed and looking outside through the window by the side. Seeing her brother Sujata got so happy. Hey Sundar, its great satisfaction to see you here, she said in joyful mood. Come seat here, she pull a chair for Sundar. She asked so many questions about so many people from her village. The brother and sister kept on chatting until dinner and no one disturbed. In the dinner table she personally served food to all and especially to Sundar. There was absolutely no psychological instability visible in her.

Tomorrow I have to meet someone in a place almost an hour's journey from here, so please call me early in the morning, after dinner Sundar told his sister.

You know for so many days I have not gone out to any place, Sujata replied in a mournful face. They always keep me closed in the room, she added. Gopal silently was watching the conversation between the brother and the sister.

Why don't you come with me tomorrow then, Sundar asked her? I will return in the evening so there is absolutely no problem, he added. Sujata became ready instantly with full of her mind. Before finally going to bed Sundar said Gopal that he will go with his sister in the first bus and directed Gopal to take the next bus so that didi don't suspect anything.

In the morning they started as planned. Sundar and Sujata took the first bus. The place where they had to go for meeting the doctor was nearly an hour's distance. The name of the place was "Kundugram" and the place was famous for a specialty hospital for the psychological patients.

Now when the bus was yet to reach that place Sujata asked her brother, Sundar you do also think like others that I am mentally disturbed, right? And that is why you are taking me to the hospital and where is my husband? He must have planned all this and that is why you visited my house all of a sudden. Right? He must also be coming next to us?

Sundar was actually shocked. He never anticipated such a simple yet the toughest question will be asked to him in such a straight forward way. He had no answer for that question. He started mumbling and searching for the best possible excuse that he could present but found nothing. Seeing her brother in such a terrible situation Sujata herself came in to salvage and told Sundar, look brother, I am no way mentally disturbed or a psychological patient but the problem is that I still could not forgive myself for what happened to myself years before. You won't believe I still remind his face. Even that night before falling asleep he was so happy, he was laughing and touching my face with his two small and soft palms. I can't forget. I still hallucinate he is asking me – why did you sleep so deeply ma that someone took me off from you and you did not even wake up? You were not there when I was helplessly searching for you to save me. I was losing my breath and you were sleeping peacefully Ma. She completed and stared at her brother.

Sundar was speechless, he became standstill and was looking at his sister without even blinking.

Sujata continued, if he would have lived then he would been almost at your age by now. He would have become a friend of yours. You know I can't sleep, he comes in my dream and ask me questions. I am disturbed by the life itself, I just can't bear with this anymore. Can you please tell me what should I do?

There was no answer Sundar had for the question. They were seating in the bus stand itself. The next bus arrived and Gopal get down from the bus. He found his wife and Sundar in the bus stand which actually surprised him. As per the plan they should have been in the hospital. He slowly approached the brother and sister, Sujata was staring at the farming lands beside the road. Sundar stood up seeing Gopal approaching. Gopal asked – you two are here? Is the hospital closed for today?

She does not need any treatment, she is absolutely alright, Sundar replied

What you mean, Gopal asked.

She had not yet forgotten the darkest day of her life and probably yours too, Sundar replied. He continued, I don't know she will ever be able to or not. No doctor, no treatment, no medicine and perhaps not even the Almighty could do anything better to her. Medical science is not yet that developed that it could wipe the face of a child out of the mind of his mother.

What I would do now Sundar, Gopal asked.

Repent for whatever had been done to her and to you too, Sundar replied. Though you have also felt the pain but still at the end of the day you should be the last man standing by her throughout the life, he continued. Nothing else you could even do.

In the meantime they have not noticed that Sujata had approached to them and was listening to their conversation. She came to her bother and said, you have grown up. You have started behaving like a mature man. Then she turned to Gopal with a whitish face and told her husband, let's go home, I will try not to disturb you anymore. My kids are alone in the house and they also need their Ma, to be with them.

WHERE WOULD I GO ...

Gopal da two cups of tea for us, Sundar placed the order for himself and Sunirmal to the owner-cum-cook-cum-waiter, rather all-in-one of the college canteen. Hey Ranen what are you doing here man, your classes are over at least two hours back, Sundar looked back and followed the eye of the caller and his companion, Sunirmal and found Ranen seating in the corner table. Ranen looked at Sunirmal and Sundar and ask them to join him with a turn down smile which was typically not Ranen as he always used to be very cheerful type of personality. Both Sundar and Sunirmal sensed that something must be disturbing Ranen and looked at each other in confusion. They approached and sat themselves facing Ranen on the same table. Sunirmal could not resist himself from asking, what happened man, you are looking very much worried about something.

I believe that there is no Mathematics in Bengali honors, Sundar joked. He added, then what you are tensed for.

Ranen with a dimmed smile replied, this is Man-metics and much complicated than Mathematics.

Sunirmal intervened, if anything serious, I mean if we could come in to help. In between Gopal da served the tea. Over the tea the discussion proceeded.

I hope you still remind Ranen, the boy from the well to do family of a nearby village. A very nice boy who was classmate of Sundar and used to depend on him for helps on Mathematics. These days both Sundar and Ranen was in their college days. Ranen was in Bengali honors in the local college where Sundar was doing his graduation in accountancy. So they were not classmate but batch mate now. Ranen was under the influence of modern thinking like Sundar and many other similarly educated young people of that time. They were part of that generation that was challenging the age old formal procedures and social regulations that had been running through the society from the time unknown and ruining the life of people living in that society to the maximum possible as well. Those regulations were no less than the heaviest burden the people living in that society had to carry not only throughout their life but even after that also.

While Sundar and Sunirmal started sipping their cups Ranen asked unanimously, you know Ankur da from our village, our neighbor, living in the house adjacent to ours. He continued, how a man's character could change so drastically and that too within just five years, I can't even imagine. Sundar, do you remind I told you when he got a great job in a big organization after completing his graduation from this college itself, just some years back. Sundar nodded his head in affirmation. Ranen started again, after one year of getting the job he got married with a girl named Anamika from Sonarpur village. Ranen again asked Sundar, you must know Sonarpur.

Yes I do, I have visited that village in several occasions, Sundar replied. Sunirmal turned towards Sundar and asked, where is Sonarpur? A village hardly five kilometer from Ranen's house, Sundar replied.

Exactly, Ranen confirmed and continued. You know Ankur da and Anamika used to be so happy in their married life. They were just the perfect match. After two years they got their first son Amlan. They were so happy but I don't know what happened from the last one year that there is always problems in that family. From my room I can see Ankur da treating Anamika just like a street dog if not worse. The same Ankur da who used to love his wife so much, using slangs for her and you don't believe sometimes I from the window of my room have even witnessed him whipping his wife so roughly that you can't even imagine. From the same place I have also seen Anamika weeping, seating in the corner of the backyard of the house so that no one can see her tears. An agony mixed with anger and annoyance was clearly visible in Ranen's eyes.

What is the reason behind Ankur's such bizarre behavior? Sunirmal asked.

I don't know, Ranen replied.

Sunirmal asked again, what the other members of the family doing? He added, are they supporting such activities of their son being tightlipped?

Ranen replied, I have never seen them opposing and I believe when they are not opposing the deeds of their son then they must be supporting it, otherwise they could have opposed Ankur. He continued, I have never heard them talking to Ankur on this matter or even trying to stop him when he misbehaves with his wife.

Sundar was listening silently till now and finally he asked Ranen, why Anamika has not asked her own father or any other family members to intervene when no one from her in-laws is supporting her.

Ranen replied, I had tried to know that by sending my youngest sister to Ankur's house to talk on this with Anamika before some days. Anamika had replied that she would not disturb other people's lives for herself and also added that she knows no one from her own family will be able to help her.

The cups were empty and cigarettes were burnt to the stub but none of the boys had anything to say for some time. Finally Sunirmal said to both Sundar and Ranen, look guys, if you think we should and could help that stranded lady then the first job will be to know the reason behind the change in Ankur's behavior. He continued, then only with evidences we could inform the situation to Anamika's family and if no solution comes up then we could approach the senior people of the village to take care of the case and discuss the same with Ankur and his parents. Ranen and Sundar gazed at each other, thought for a while and finally decided that the plan is acceptable and the three boys decided to go ahead with the idea.

Spying – that is what it should be called, became the prime job for the boys from the very next day. They started gathering details about Ankur from various sources as much possible for them to reach. They started asking questions as many as possible, direct and indirect, to Ankur's friends and batch mates. But unfortunately even after continuing this for some days the amount of information they were able to gather was no more than some basic details about Ankur. The only thing amongst all they came to know was common from all the sources and that is Ankur in recent days has started avoiding his friends and mates. The most amazing thing shared by all the sources was that everybody suspected there might be some problem in Ankur's life, more specifically in his family life and everyone actually pointed their figures towards his wife directly or indirectly for the changes in Ankur's behavior. Stunningly, maximum of those people said that they don't even know Ankur's wife when they were asked why they think Anamika is the reason behind the change in Ankur's behavior. Finally more or less everyone without any knowledge or proof provided, decided that there might be something wrong in the character of Anamika, otherwise a nice boy like Ankur would never have changed so much.

End of everything the venture was becoming more frustrating for the boys as after deploying the best effort they could not find anything up to their suspicion.

One day while returning home from a personal job Sundar found Ankur travelling in the same train. He was returning from his office. Sundar intentionally followed him and get in to the same compartment but maintaining a safe distance so that he is not spotted but could keep watching Ankur's move. Suddenly Ankur left the train at Panchagram. That was unlikely as it was not the nearest or usual station to Ankur's home. Sundar did not think twice and followed him. Ankur walked through the road beside the station and entered in to a house. Sundar spotted a tea stall just opposite of the house, entered in to the stall and ordered for a tea. There was no customer except Sundar. Sundar used that opportunity and started gossiping with the owner of the stall. Uncle can you tell me when is the next train, Sundar initiated gossiping with the shopkeeper. The shopkeeper replied with the exact time and asked where Sundar would go. While gossiping with the tea stall owner Sundar started asking many indirect questions on the locality and the people. His intension was to know about the house and the occupants of the house where Ankur has entered. Finally he found what they have been searching for last few days. In this house Ankur lives with a woman and in the neighborhood he had told people that they are newly married and had rented this house to access his office in Kolkata, which is easier from here than from his house in the village. Sundar silently waited in the tea shop ordering tea with always an eye fixed on the door. It was nearly ten o'clock at night when Ankur got out of the house and started walking towards the railway station. Ankur did not notice that Sundar was following him. He waited for the last train to return to his house.

Next day in the college Sundar asked Sunirmal to come with him and visited the canteen in search of Ranen. Ranen was not there. After asking one or two classmates of Ranen they found that Ranen has not come to college today. I need to meet him anyway, Sundar told Sunirmal. Is there anything serious, Sunirmal asked? Yes, I going to Ranen's home, Sundar replied, I would request you too to come with me.

Ranen was seating in his study table when the two entered in his room. What a pleasant surprise, please come, Ranen welcomed his friends. Sundar said, Ranen yesterday I have witnessed something very serious about Ankur and I need to share that with you two. Ranen and Sunirmal gazed at each other. Sundar stared at them and started depicting his experience of spying on Ankur.

I doubted something like that, Ranen said. His utter anger was apparent form his expression.

What's next? Are we then going to Anamika's paternal house to discuss these with them, asked Sunirmal. Sundar replied, that is the first thing we must do. Ranen nodded his head supporting the decision and unanimously it was decided that they are going.

THE HEAVIEST BURDEN TO CARRY

The very next day the three boys started for Sonarpur in the morning. Do you know the exact address of the house, Sundar asked Ranen. Ranen replied he does not. No one of them knew the paternal house of Anamika so after reaching the village they had to ask people to locate it, which took some time for them to find it out. It was an old house with an even older boundary wall. The main door was closed from inside. The boys looked at each other before knocking the door and finally Sunirmal came forward and knocked on the door. After some tensed minutes a middle aged man opened the door. Whom do you want, the man skeptically asked the unknown boys. Are you Mr. Gourango Das, Sunirmal asked the man? The man with a suspicious look nodded his head. We are from Ankur's village, Ranen came forward this time and said the man. The name did its job and the boys were welcomed in. Sundar watched it was a typical average village house with three to four rooms in one row with a common porch. The middle aged man introduced himself as Anamika's eldest brother. Two more men and three women came out of those rooms as Gourango started calling them. The boys again had to introduce themselves in front of the other family members. It was quite a sizable family of Anamika's three brothers, their wives and kids. They welcomed the boys when they came to know that the boys are from the village of Anamika's in-law's house. They were offered seats and served water with enthusiasm.

The scenario suddenly changed when Ranen described everything he has witnessed and then after what he and his friends have found out. Gourango babu we think, you, the elder brothers of Anamika should at least talk to Ankur and his family regarding this, Ranen said the man. He continued, and if the situation does not change then you must contact the administration to take your sister back here. The three elder brothers and their respective wives started gazing at each other.

Ranen concluded with, I and my friends will support you in doing this and if required we would also talk to the elders of the village on this.

Initially they stared at each other for some time and then one of them replied, what you say is absolutely right, but the problem is each one of us have the responsibilities of our own family and as you can see that none of us is as affluent as we can take the additional responsibilities of Anamika and her son. The man paused for a moment and continued, on top of that this house has only four rooms out of which in three we live with our family and the fourth is used for various other purposes so where Anamika and her son will stay even if we take them back here. Finally in philosophical mood the man concluded, everyone has issues in his or her home or in life and it is always his or her own responsibility to try and solve those issues.

What kind of brothers these idiots are, at least I can't understand, Sunirmal's disgust was clearly coming out of his voice. His irritation was changed to anger. He continued pointing to Ranen, we have the no other option but to discuss this with the seniors of your village. Ranen nodded his head and replied, I also feel the same, every afternoon all the elderly people of the village meet at the Kali Temple and that will be the best place to discuss with them on this. He stared at Sundar and waited for his concern silently. Sundar has not uttered even a single word after coming out of the house. His face was telling that many emotions were fighting with each other or may be with himself within him. He did not notice Ranen and Sunirmal was waiting for his reply. What do you say Sundar, finally Ranen asked directly for his concern.

Sundar raised his face and looked at both of the boys, he paused for a moment and then said, being very truthful I have a strong doubt whether the senior people will even support us.

Why are you saying so, asked Sunirmal? Sundar looked at him and said, Sunirmal when those who had seen the woman from her birth, who had grown up with her, who had shared every moments of grief and happiness with her, are not even ready to discuss the matter then how could you expect those people who does not even know the lady properly will stand up against this, especially when they are the people who have been supporting each and every such thing from the core of their soul? How could you think that those people who think a women is a property of a man would ever stand against this? I am doubtful.

Then why we are fighting for the cause when we do also not know the lady, Ranen asked. Do you know why, Sundar uttered, because we are not too old to be selfish in the name of "family responsibilities" or "social integrity", and on the other hand not even too young to follow the dictates of those selfish people as duty bound.

Finally they decided to approach those seniors right that day in the afternoon. Sundar and Sunirmal did not return to their respective home and came to Ranen's house to spend rest of the hours before meeting the seniors. At nearly five in the evening they reached the place where the seniors of the village use to meet every day and discuss various issues mostly related to how the new generation is taking the society towards destruction by not disregarding the age old rules and regulations. Approximately ten to twelve people were there. Ranen first approached those people and ask permission to say something. Sundar and Sunirmal waited by the side but did not speak as per the plan as they are unknown to those people and also not inhabitants of that village. With permission Ranen described everything from the very first day of his witnessing the phenomenon to Sundar's founding of Ankur's extra marital relationship to finally their meeting with Anamika's brothers and at the end asked for the decision from the seniors. The environment was changed and all of the people were staring at each other and actually everyone was waiting for someone else to speak first.

The three young and enthusiasts have already gathered a clear idea from the facial expression of the people that they are perhaps the last people standing to the cause of the lady. Still they nurtured their last hope. Everyone was in a dilemma about what to say and where to start from.

The oldest in the group Mr. Roy made the first comment pointing to Ranen, look son this is typically an internal family issue and I am in a dilemma that whether we as outsider should enter in to this or not. He added, son you are too young to understand the complexities of a man's life. Another person from the group said, on top of that the lady has asked for help neither from you nor from us, so I believe our intervention will be treated as unsolicited one. As if all the others were waiting for this and now everyone started giving valuable insights on such issues which finally in the line that a boy like Ankur can't do this without any provocation or solid reason. Some of them even did not bother to raise question on Anamika's behavior and nevertheless even on her character.

Ranen tried beyond his best to make them understand that this is not what they are thinking and this kind of violence within a family should not be allowed, rather must be opposed unitedly, but he failed. Then one of those people crossed all the lines by asking Ranen, tell us one thing Ranen, what is your intension of taking so much of interest in someone else's wife. Ranen would have lost his mind if Sundar have not controlled him by holding his hand and pulled him back from there.

Whatever happens I don't care but I have decided that tomorrow is Sunday and Ankur will be at home, I will personally go to Ankur's house to talk to him, Ranen said to his friends returning to his home after the meeting with the seniors. Sundar and Sunirmal looked at each other, Sundar said, not you but we will go to talk to Ankur.

It was almost ten o'clock in the morning when Ranen with Sundar and Sunirmal knocked the door of Ankur's house. Anamika opened the door. Ranen asked, is Ankur da at home. A voice came from inside the house for Anamika, enquiring who is at the door. Anamika replied, it is Ranen and his two friends. The same voice asked Anamika to let them come inside. Entering the room they found Ankur was reading newspaper seating on a chair. He looked at the boys and asked Ranen, what happened Ranen? Ranen did not wait and directly came to the point of what he has seen and what Sundar has witnessed, he directly asked Ankur what he says on this. Ankur's face was blood red in anger but at the same time he was not in a position to show the same as his extra marital relationship was known to these boys. He just replied with a stiff face and burning eyes, Ranen it is my personal life and I will not tolerate any unwanted intervention in it.

Ranen with the same kind of attitude replied, sorry to say Ankur da but when your neighbor is disturbed by your behavior then it crosses the boundary of so called "Personal Life" and inevitably becomes a public affair.

Ankur became furious and challenged Ranen, you can do whatever you like to. I do not care what you think or do. He added, at the same time you are free to do anything but I will carry on my own way of life.

This time Ranen lost the control on his anger and almost shouted in reply, if your behavior disturbs my life anymore then you will come to know what I could do and how far I could go to destroy your "own way of life".

The situation suddenly changed and both the men stopped speaking when they found Anamika entering the room. She coolly came and ask Ranen and his friends, leave the house. Ranen was shocked, he said, we are fighting for your causes. Anamika with the same cool voice replied, what do you think Ranen, I am living with this man for every moments and I do not know what you boys are talking about. A pin drop silence followed her words. She herself broke the same, I know everything, even though I exactly do not know the details of that other woman but I know it long back that there is another woman in Ankur's life. She continued perhaps with the melancholiest smile and depicted all the proofs that she had encountered on this and still kept her lips tight. Ranen, Sundar and Sunirmal was shocked knowing everything but Ankur was probably shocked at the highest possible. Sunirmal could not resist himself from asking, sister how you are standing with all these and why till date you had not informed the police or the law as this is a crime.

Anamika looked at Sunirmal for a moment and then asked the toughest question, if I would have done this and left this man and his house, could you tell me where and to whom would I have gone to? She continued, where would I go if the society, which I am a part of asks questions on my character just because I am a woman who is willingly or has to unwillingly living alone without her husband under certain unavoidable circumstances? Where would I go if the people and family where I was born and spent nearly one third portion of my life start thinking me as an unasked for burden of relationship on them? Where would I go if the same people for whom I have smilingly sacrificed all my rights as a child just because I am a girl, repudiate to share just a corner of their house for me because once I was married to one person who disagree to take my responsibilities anymore now? Where would I go if the man I relied upon and shared all my belongings including my soul and moments of every emotion, suddenly not only start behaving like an alien with me but start treating me no better than an unwanted street dog which has entered in to his house? Where would I go brothers?

She paused for some moments, tried to control the drops that were irresistible. She failed and wiped her eyes with the corner of the sharee she was wearing. Every other living body in that room was simply shattered. She continued to depict not her case only but for all those women in the society who are at the same juncture where she was standing. As a girl unless I got married I was living in my father's house. After I got married I had to leave that house in which every single dust was adorable to me and was sent to live with some unknown people in an unknown environment in a new house. I was taught to love this unknown house and I followed that instruction in each and every step from the core of my heart. It was my husband's house. When my father passed away that house became my brothers' house where I used to visit once or twice every year with my husband. Days will pass by and I will become an old lady. My husband one day will pass away and his house will become my son's house. I spent more than half a century in different houses but never had the chance to live in "My House". Now in my last days I will be thinking which one was my house?

Again she paused and wiped her tears. Ankur was trying to say something but Anamika stopped him with waving her hand and continued with a broken voice and destroyed soul, from the day I was born I was the responsibility of my father, my identity was "daughter of someone". After my father my identity becomes "sister of someone". Once I got married my identity becomes "wife of someone" and finally one day my identity will become "mother of someone". I spent quite a long life just with different identities "something of someone". Out of all these where was "I" in my identity as a woman? Simply nowhere. So finally I lived a life in which I had no place to go on my own will. I lived in different buildings, loved and took care all of them probably much more than other members who were also sharing those buildings, but not even a single of those was my house. I lived a life without an identity of my own. Have I lived a life of a human being or just a robot which can laugh, cry and reproduce and that too on someone else's will?

She finally stopped with tears in her eyes, looking at Ankur. She was broken from inside and so the three young boys. Ankur was standing with his head down. She took a minute to control her emotions and thanked the three boys, you know Ranen every girl will be proud of having brothers like you boys, but I request you to leave me alone with my sufferings. She added, I have no place to go, no one to call. You boys leave this place and request you not to come here again.

Ranen, Sundar and Sunirmal had nothing to say and turned to leave the house when Anamika called them back. They turned around, Anamika with a smile requested them, please make a promise to your sister that you boys would never be the cause of another Anamika. The three boys were speechless and left the house.

These were the questions that made Sundar and his modern and progressive thinking friends simply flabbergasted. The lady who demanded answers for these questions was not a very experienced, highly educated or high society woman, rather she was no other than any woman from the rural India. A lady who was married perhaps even before she could have completed her teenage.

You know Ranen, while walking down the village path Sundar said, we should be ashamed of the double standard of feeling proud to call our nation as "Motherland", whereas on the other hand in personal life actually feel proud to be "*Baap ka Beta*".

No Water for you ...

Sundar, this is no less than a third degree torture man, Surya replied keeping his eyes closed. He was lying on the bed and was in no mood to wake up as early as 9 o'clock in the morning.

It is already 9, are you waking up or should I go alone, Sundar asked in reply. There was absolutely no room to carry on the leisurely sleep, so Surya had to wake up. With an irritated face he left the bad and said while moving towards the wash room, you are pathetically punctual man. He added, I don't understand you are a human or machine. Sundar ignored and concentrated on accumulating the necessary papers from Surya's desk and drawers, which will be needed in today's meeting.

It was the time when Sundar had become a full time member of a political party. To be specific not only a member rather a dedicated member. Almost every day Surya and he had been attending party meetings and working hard on the party agenda. They had to travel to the remotest villages of the districts and also outside to meet people there, discuss the party agendas and inspiring them to support and help the party to strengthen its base. As he was a good organizer and that was known to the party leaders so sometimes he even had to attend more than one such meetings and that too in remotest villages of distant locations. In a normal day to attend such meeting he and his fellows used to cycle for nearly forty to fifty kilometers and on top of that generally two persons in one bicycle as in those days bicycle used to be a rare and quite valuable and costly possession and it was not affordable for everyone to have his own bicycle. Normally they used to start in the morning closely at nine to ten and used return sometimes in the evening or at night. Now if somebody asks Sundar to name three important things in his life then he probably would answer – Party, Party & Party.

The day was started just like any other day in Sundar's life. As usual he woke up with the dawn and after completing his daily physical work out in the club he came back to his parental house, taking his bath in the river in his way back. Got prepared and went out for Surya da's house. Surya was not yet ready then, which is actually the daily matter. Surya used to wake up a bit late in the morning compared to his friend and every day Sundar had to wait for him for some time. In the meantime Sundar used to gather and accumulate all necessary things for that day's journey and other activities.

Surya became ready in next forty to forty five minutes. They took their food together in Surya's house, which again was another common thing in their daily life and finally they started their journey in Surya's bicycle. Surya asked, so, what is today's plan?

Sundar replied while paddling, firstly we have to go to Durganagar to meet Debotosh and hand him over the pamphlets we were given that day by Anil da. Debotosh will have to spread those to the people by today, otherwise it could be tough for him to arrange people for the next big rally. Durganagar was a journey of nearly Thirteen to Fourteen kilometers from where the duo had started.

Surya uttered, yah, Debo is working really hard. The boy is doing well. Already he has established a good public relation in the village. He is no doubt a valuable member. What next?

Sundar continued, next we have to go to Debipur to attend the meeting.

Surya replied with surprise, from Durganagar to Debipur, another fifteen kilometers and that too in this scorching summer. Ok, then?

Sundar added, then from there to Naldanga to meet Anil da and collect something. Naba informed me last night that Anil da has directed us to meet him there. He has to deliver something very important to us.

Surya mocked Sundar, what is that "Something" for which we will have to cycle for one more mile?

Sundar replied, we will come to know about that only when we will meet him at Naldanga. He added, you know Anil da much more than me, have you ever seen him to disclose anything unless it is extremely needed?

Surya replied with a long breath, yah man. He is a separate breed altogether. Sundar smiled and continued cycling.

While this conversation they reached near the only higher secondary school of the area. Sundar stopped and parked the bicycle under a tree and both of them waited for Naresh, another friend and fellow of the duo and was working as a temporary teacher of Mathematics in the school. Naresh was a good student and was from a lower mediocre family. His father was a clerk in a government office and a very placid and introvert type of person. He used to live in his ancestral house with his wife and three sons – Naresh and his two younger brother. Naresh got involved in politics a few months back when he was seating idle after completing his graduation in Mathematics from the local college. He was a soft spoken and a person who likes to speak less and listen more. Basically an ideal good boy kind of character and exactly the same reputation he had to the people.

After waiting a while they saw Naresh coming towards them in his second hand bicycle, which he had purchased from a local repairing shop just after getting the temporary job. After reaching the place he parked his vehicle and apologized to the two, sorry for the delay guys.

Surya asked, it is alright, but why are you late? Any problem?

Naresh made a cheeky sound and replied, one teacher is absent today and I had to take his classes also. As you know till you are in a temporary job you have to abide by all the orders from the higher authority, be it logical or otherwise hardly matters.

Sundar intervened, I think we should start now, it will take at minimum one hour to reach Durganagar. He added, Debotosh would be waiting for us and it is also risky to stand in public with so many party pamphlets. Right?

Surya promptly supported, yah, sure. Let us start. Naresh followed him.

They started towards Durganagar. It was nearly eleven in the morning under the scorching temperature of the summer. In one bicycle Sundar was carrying Surya and Naresh was on his own. They were discussing about so many things relating to upcoming meetings, works and responsibilities and also about so many other things. The road to Durganagar was through farming fields, so actually there was no big trees or villages in between and there was no chance for the travelers to avoid the mighty sun in that summer. It took more than one and a half hours for them to reach Durganagar as they had to halt for two or three times in their journey due to tiredness and fatigue. While reaching there, they did not found Debotosh at the place where he was scheduled to wait for them. They got down from their bicycles and looked around but Debotosh was not in their vicinity.

Naresh asked, Surya da, are you sure that he has mentioned this place?

Surya da replied while looking around, yes, Debo always use to wait here for us, whenever we come to Durganagar. Perhaps he has gone somewhere. He paused for a moment and added, don't worry he will come surely.

Sundar suggested, let's go to Tara da's Tea stall, Debo might also be there.

Surya accepted the suggestion, better. Let's move.

Naresh was there for the first time, so many things were unknown to him, he enquired, who is Tara da?

Sundar answered, a local person, he runs a small tea shop here in the village.

Naresh was surprised, tea stall that too in this small and remote village. He continued, how does he make his life with this earning?

This time Surya replied with a pale smile on his lips, once he was a farmer, he had some farming land of his own also. He added, in last draught he had to lend some money from the local money lender and the local money lender took the opportunity of his illiteracy and cheat him. Surya paused for a moment, ignited a cigarette and continued, cheat him just with one extra "zero" and the farmer became a beggar.

What do you mean, Naresh could not understand Surya and asked in reply.

With the same smile Surya answered, one extra "zero" and rupees 50 became 500. So easy to befool the poor of this country.

Naresh was eagerly listening to Surya, he asked, then.

Surya smiled back and continued, then what? Tara da had to hand over his land to that cheat and now he is running a tea shop here to support his family of four members. He himself, his wife and two children. He added, be with us and you will get to meet so many people like Tara da in the villages of this "Sonar Bangla". Either nobody knows the reality or they don't want to face it.

In the meantime they had reached near the tea stall and found Debotosh seating there. Looking at them, Debotosh stood up and welcomed them with a smile, so guys, ultimately you have reached. He continued, I thought you people have evaporated in the scorching summer. He looked at Naresh as he was seeing Naresh for the first time. Sundar introduced each other. Once the introduction was over they ordered for tea and let themselves sat on the wooden bench of the shop. Debotosh started, I thought you guys are not coming today. I waited for nearly an hour and then came here. He continued, actually I was a bit tensed because today is the last day to distribute those pamphlets. By the way have you taken those? Where are those pamphlets?

Sundar handed over those pamphlets to Debotosh, who quickly placed those in his bag and asked, total one hundred right?

Sundar replied, no, only fifty I have managed for you. He added, rest fifty we have to give to Alok. He was also running out of pamphlets. I have been directed to give the other fifty to him.

Debotosh replied with a visible discontent on his face, ok but not ok. He took a long breath and added, how would I manage with fifty only? I asked for one hundred and fifty, then they said that is too much and they could provide one hundred only and now they have sent even half of that. Now what would I tell those people who are waiting for these?

Sundar replied, I understand your situation brother, I also told them the same thing but could not manage more than these. May be next time I hope they will listen to us.

By this time Tara da served tea to all the four. By that time Naresh noticed that a small girl was helping the shopkeeper. She was hardly eight or nine years old. He asked Surya da, who is this girl?

Surya replied, she is the younger daughter of Tara da. Previously his elder daughter used to help him in this shop. Surya turned towards Tara da and asked, by the way where your elder daughter is. Is she not here today? Surya added, has she gone somewhere?

Tara da, with a smile in his face replied, don't worry, by the grace of the God everything is ok. Actually I have told her not to come in the shop as she is going to get married next month.

Surya da asked, to whom? What does your would be son-in-law do?

Tara da replied with the same smile, you know him, Raju from this village itself.

Naresh asked Surya da in low voice, how old is the girl?

Surya da replied while sipping his cup of tea, almost thirteen or fourteen years. He turned to Naresh and said, don't go by age, in a well to do family a girl of her age is a sweet heart and in a starving family the same girl becomes a burden for the others. He paused for a moment and added, this is our society. A rotten, terribly unhealthy and disgusting society that need the harshest medicine to get well from all such maladies.

In the intervening time they had completed the tea and discussion. Surya paid for the tea and leaving Debotosh there the trio started for their next destination. Debipur, was another journey of nearly fifteen kilometers. What is the exact time now Surya da, Sundar asked? Surya looking at his wrist watch replied, it is showing the least possible number it could. The mighty sun was at its crowning glory and likely in a mood to burn everything down to ashes on this planet. The journey became more heinous than the previous one. They had to take more time to cover the distance. Sundar and Surya da exchanged driver's seat for two or three time as they were in the same bicycle. Naresh was alone so he had no choice but to go on cycling. They had to take more frequent breaks this time and rest for sometimes to start again. Finally it took more than two hours for them to cross that fifteen kilometers and finally when they reached Debipur the watch was showing ten past three.

The meeting was already started. Those who were seating looked at the new entrants and had an initial welcome. There were some new and unknown faces, very young, conceivably at their late teens or early twenties.

The seniors were elaborating the party agendas and what changes the society needs to the juniors and semi-seniors. They were describing on how to bring those changes which are genuinely necessary for the well balancing of rights for all. They were giving them brief of what they should do and what they should not. How to spread their views and thoughts amongst the people and how to make them understand the need of the hour, so on and so forth.

Subhashish, a senior member who was giving the speech suddenly stopped and asked, Surya and Sundar both of you are old fellows and also veterans, why don't you share your ideas and the ways you are working on ground on that. He continued by addressing the gathering, friends meet Surya and Sundar, they are veterans in our ideologies and both of them have immensely contributed to grow us with their hard work and selfless devotion for doing something better for the society. He added by inviting the duo, I would request them to share the experiences of the hurdles they have faced and how they have overcame those in their way of achieving the goal. First Surya and then Sundar had to take the dais and shared their experiences with the audience. After that the new faces got introduced by respective seniors to the others. Naresh also got introduced to those present there. Finally the meeting came to an end nearly after an hour. The trio stood up to leave. The seniors there requested them to wait for sometimes as they have also arranged tea for everyone present but Sundar said, we have to go to Naldanga from here as we have another important job there to be accomplished. He added, after that we will have to return to our village, which is almost ten kilometers from Naldanga, so some other day we will be part of this tea party.

They started for Naldanga and reached within next ten minutes. They found Habu, a young member was waiting for them in the scheduled place. Where is Anil da, Surya asked Habu? Habu replied, Anil da is not here, he had to attend some other important meeting so he had left. He added, but he had given these to me to get these delivered to you. Habu pointed to a sealed packet and a small letter he was holding in his hand. Sundar took that packet and the letter. The letter was for him and Surya da. He opened the same. It had just two lines –

"Dear Friend, please collect the packet and you will get to know what to be done in another such letter placed inside. I wanted to meet you guys but had to leave for some urgent work. May be next time. Yours Anil da".

They did not spend any more time there and after thanking Habu started for returning home as after such a long cycling and that too in such a sweltering summer they were actually starving.

They hardly had crossed one or two kilometers and was crossing a small village when suddenly Naresh stopped cycling. Before the other two could have understood anything he fall on the ground all of a sudden. Sundar and Surya stopped and hurriedly came to Naresh but he was totally senseless. They called Naresh but he did not reply. Surya suggested, water. Sundar, he needs water.

They looked around and found a hut nearby. An elderly person from the hut was looking at them from a small window. Sundar drew Surya da's attention towards that hut and said, you be with Naresh here, I am going to that hut. They must have water, he completed and rushed to that hut. The man was still on the window when Sundar reached the hut. He told the man, uncle our friend had fainted due to this extreme heat. He added, as we have been cycling for long. He paused and requested, we need some water for him. Would you please give a glass of water?

And the reply he received he never ever forgot. The man intensely looked at his face and replied, you are the party boys, right? Get out of here right away.

It took some moments for Sundar to understand what exactly the man said. He anyhow checked his irritation and requested again, ok uncle we will get out of here once our friend comes back in sense, but please give some water for him. He continued, otherwise it might turn in to fatal condition for him.

The Man with the same expression replied, I told you once, no water for you guys, and suddenly closed the window on the face of Sundar.

It took five seconds for Sundar to understand. He returned to Surya. Naresh was still lying senseless on the ground. Surya looked at Sundar with a hope of water but found nothing in his hand. He asked, where is the water you went to bring?

Sundar replied, No Water for you … party boys.

Surya perhaps did not understand and before he could say anything Sundar ran to the other direction, to a small dirty pond. He took his shirt off and put it in the water of that pond to soak the same and took it to Surya.

Surya da squeezed that soaked shirt over the face of Naresh for sometimes and slowly Naresh opened his eyes. He was back in his sense. It took two to three minutes for him to become normal. The three boys waited there for some time under a tree and then again started their journey to home. This time Surya was cycling alone and Sundar was carrying Naresh in his bicycle.

Sundar was speechless after the incident. Surya sensing that asked Sundar, what happened? Why are you so shy?

Sundar replied, whom are we working for? These poor people of the society, who does not even consider us as human being and not ready to give a glass of water and that too in such a terrific situation where a boy could even die?

Surya with a pale smile on his lips replied, the problem is not that they don't know we are fighting for them rather they know it very well. He paused and then continued, the original problem is two folded my friend, firstly they can't believe that anybody could fight for their cause selflessly because nobody had ever did that, so they have doubt in their mind about us and it is very obvious. Secondly it is our fault that those, for whom we are working don't even know us. He again stopped and asked Sundar, tell me one thing, does not it prove that we need to throw more efforts to make them understand the truth, the reality.

Sundar did not reply, but he remembered that day for ever.

THE PROCESSION ...

What is the plan for this year's puja, Mr. Secretary? Surya asked Sundar while entering the club room.

Sundar was concentrating on the donation and collection list from the previous year in the club. Sundar missed what Surya asked as he was more involved in the task in hand. Are you telling me something, he raised his face and asked Surya staring at him?

Mr. Secretary would you mind to share the plan for this year's puja with me, Surya mocked with a funny face. Stop joking and look at the list, Sundar replied, we have missed to collect donations from so many people who promised to give after the puja last year. He added, otherwise we would not have suffered so badly.

Patru and some other boys entered the club. So, I think there is some important discussion going on, right, he commented while taking his seat.

Sundar turned and looked at all the boys present there in the room pointedly from one to the other and said, it is good to see you all here. He added, as all of you know that we hardly have one month and some days left to complete the arrangement for the puja, but unfortunately till now we don't have any specific and well-organized plan for this year. He paused for a moment and continued, I was looking at the collection list from the previous year and found so many donations uncollected just because we forgot to approach the donors who asked us to visit them after the puja. If this year also it remains the same, then I must say it will not be tough only but the toughest for us to carry on.

Raja, another member who came with Patru asked, what the plan is for this year. He added, I have heard they are planning something fabulous this year, he pointed towards the only other club of the area. Patru supported Raja, yes I have also heard something like that. He added, what we are going to do, I mean to say do we have a plan.

Sundar replied, yes we do, but before coming to that I need to have all of your promise that you will put all your effort on that. He added, if you guys are ready, then only I would share my idea, otherwise you suggest what to be done. He completed and stared at all present there.

A BRIEF BACKGROUND

A small tiny river, named "Pritha" is flowing by the northern side of the small village. The river is the main source of water for the villagers and for the teens and the young boys it is much more than that. As this is where they get chance of spending times in various cheerful activities in the name of bathing. Sundar and his friends were no exception, from their boyhood to their teen age, he and his friends have spent quite a large portion of their everyday time in Pritha's water. They just not only used to bath but used to swim for long or play water games and so on.

In the opposite bank of the river there is another village named "Natunpara", where actually used to live the well to do families of the entire area. They were mainly the business people as the main market of the many surrounding villages was also adjacent to that village. The importance of Pritha to the villagers of Natun Para was no less than that of the villagers in this side. For them also this was the mail source of water. The boys from that village also used to come to the river for the purpose same as the boys from this side. Due to the differences in social and pecuniary status a typical mindset was created between these two groups of lads. A typically They-are-not-like-us kind of feeling was developed in the young minds of the boys from both the sides. From such feelings and mindsets a competitive environment was created. This typical competitive sense used to be prominent in every filed, from the bathing at river to football match, from schools report card to organizing different events in the village, almost in each and everything possible. So any time anyone of the two parties gets a chance, they used to pull the other one's leg.

There are only two clubs in surrounding twenty or twenty five villages in and around the area – one is in this side of Pritha, which though is basically a club of the boys from the economically scrawny families but is the oldest in the vicinity. So boys from the adjacent rural communities of the same condition were members of the club, and automatically the number of members was reasonably higher than the number of members in the other club, which was situated in Natunpara at the reverse bank of the river and was basically ran by those boys from the affluent families of that area. As the economic condition and flourishing of any such organizations or clubs used to be directly proportional to the financial state of its members so automatically the club in the other village is in a much better condition than that of the one in this side of Pritha. But as every coin has two faces and generally everything has at least one positive side so for the club in this side had one highly positive feature – manpower.

From many decades the worship of goddess Saraswati is used to be organized with full coloration in the month of January or February in the villages and in the surrounding area. This is the principal festival that is organized by every club and with their best possible capacity and every one of them wishes to become the winner of the Best Prize which they will cherish with pride until the next year. Generally the festival is for two days but here it stays for four days and in the last day a procession is held with the idol of the Goddess Saraswati with lightings, band party etc. Music is played from the loud speakers with the maximum volume limit it could achieve. So undoubtedly it is the grandest event in the locality.

For that period of the year every member of each of the clubs probably stretches himself beyond the best of his capacity to support his club. Every parent rebukes and shouts on the mischiefs and time spent by their children in organizing this event leaving their studies but somewhere in their inner mind they also support their children taking part in the organizing the events and their activities. They cherish their own time and what they used to do for the same purpose. End of the day they also ask who is going to do what? Where the idol is coming from? Who is the artist? Will all get completed within time? And so many such questions which they could not control themselves to ask and automatically show their interests too on that.

BACK TO THIS DAYS

It was the time when after rigorous physical workout of four to five years Sundar had built a well-structured body and also had started becoming a well-known face in and around the area due to his social and political engagements. He is also a regular and prominent member of the club in his village and had developed a support base for him in the mind of the people and especially in the youth for his fearless activities and selfless services. This year the post of Puja Secretary has also become his responsibility like the last year. He was looking at the various things necessary for arranging the event and was fully occupied with all that possibilities and hurdles. As like in this side of the river the other side also was engaged in their arrangement in full enthusiasm. Last year they came second, so this year it has become a matter of prestige for them to be the best as they all had to bear with the boastful teasing and mocking eyes for the last one year from their rivals. If this year they could not deliver something extraordinary and fabulous then another such long year of insult will follow.

It was the month of January that year and both the clubs in the opposite bank of river Pritha was busy in the arrangement for the worship of Goddess Saraswati. As Sundar was given the responsibility of the Puja Secretory that year, so it was his responsibility to arrange everything in such a way that there will be appraisals from all, be it a direct or indirect stakeholder or a general visitor.

In the opposite side Shyama Charan Dey, the old foe Shyama was carrying the responsibility that year. Shyama was from a rich family and had a good physic but a bit short heighted and with dark complexion. As he used to sponsor a good pie of the expenditures for the arrangements so automatically he got some flatterers always surrounding him and chanting praises for him. Now both the clubs were trying their best to hide their own plans and to sneak in to the plans of the rival club. That year the club in this side of the Pritha planned to bring lights from Chandannagore for the first time in the area, so automatically it raised the eyebrows of the reverse side's. They planned to hire a small truck for the procession, which itself is going to be something arranged for the first time in the area for the purpose of procession, because till the last year the idols and the lights were basically carried by man pulled vans. But Shyama and his associates succeeded to hide their plans from their rivals.

In the competition there was no prize for the Second Runner up and the only prize was offered on the quality and innovativeness of the procession arranged. So both the clubs were keen to present something new as well as enchanting in front of the jury to be the contender for the only prize.

I have thought that this year we will hire the lightings for the procession from Chandannagore, Sundar declared in the meeting. He added, but before you response I would like to mention one thing very honestly that hiring lighting from there will cost quite a lot. He continued, we will have to concentrate on collection of donations as well as we will also have to put good amount of efforts on our own to save some costs of transportation and carrying things from there to here. Do you all agree?

Great plan no doubt, we are ready, Surya replied with an appreciation.

Surya da I know you are but I want this from each and every one personally and not from you on their behalf, Sundar stared at Surya and uttered placidly. Patru, Raja and all others present their supported and promised to be there with whatever they could.

Sundar then announced, Okay then I am contacting with the vendor and I would suggest Surya da and any one of either Patru or Gour be with me when I will go there. He added, Gour, it will be better if you come with us as you have a better understanding in this matter than any of us present here. Gour nodded his head.

Finally everything was arranged properly and the day of worship came. All was good, absolutely no issues were there. Though the people from this side tried even beyond their best to found out about the plans and programs of the opposite side but they failed.

On the second day of the event Ramendra babu from the local administration came to visit the event in the club of Sundar's village with his family. After visiting the puja he came across Surya and Sundar, who were busy in various internal arrangements. Surya approached Ramendra babu and asked, so how do you find the arrangement. Ramendra babu replied, very beautiful. He paused for a moment and then asked, have you taken permission for the procession? Surya was a bit surprised as the same is usually taken on the third day. Though taking permission about the procession from the local authority basically was a kind of formality but used to be followed without any omission.

He replied, we generally apply for the permission on the third day, so tomorrow any of us will go to submit the application as we always do. He continued, why, is there any change of rule this year?

No young man, Ramendra babu replied with a smiling face, nothing of this sort, the other club has come to submit the application today itself that is why I ask you also. He was turning to leave when he suddenly turned back and said, by the way are you also going to hold the puja for five days?

Surya replied in astound, no sir, we will hold it as usual for four days, but why are you asking this question.

Hmm, then why they have asked the permission for the procession on the fifth day, Ramendra babu uttered to himself more than he replied to Surya.

Surya did not ask any more question and send off the visitor. He then promptly get back to Sundar, who was busy in directing some younger boys to arrange something in the ground properly. Surya called Sundar in a corner and shared which he has just heard from Ramendra babu. Sundar's eyes were narrowed. There were so many questions stimulating in his mind but he just said, Surya da call everyone of the organizing team in the club room.

Many discussion happened and many possibilities were presented but nobody could find out the real cause of deviation from the normal rule by the opposite club and finally it was decided that they will go by their plan and without any deviation.

On the scheduled date of procession, that is the fourth day, Sundar with the members of club started their procession from their village in the evening with all their arrangements and especially those lights they have hired from Chandannagore. The theme was to show the thirteen events that are celebrated by the Bengalis in a year – "Baro Mas a Tero Parbon", meaning thirteen celebration in twelve months. In the first man pulled van there was a welcome message and the name of the club was written by colorful chains of small bulbs and in next thirteen vans those thirteen lights and in the last van the idol was placed with full flamboyance. After all the vans there was the last van carrying the music system with gramophone records and a microphone, which was generally used for various kinds of announcements for the viewers to let them inform about the theme and all. The procession started in the evening and took almost three to four hours to complete the entire path – from the village to the railway station and from there to Natunpara, crossing the road bridge over the river Pritha and from there back to the village. It was a tremendous hit as the people of the area for the first time viewed that kind of gorgeous lights depicting very common things of their lives in a very uncommon way. But no prize or ranking was announced as the other club was scheduled to show their arrangements in the next day. So the administration announced that the result of the competition will be declared on the next evening.

After the entire day's work the next day in the evening Sundar was setting to go to the club for some recreation. He was on his way when Dhruba, a junior boy from the village came to him more or less flying on his bicycle. He was breathing so intensely that he could not talk for some time. Sundar asked him, what happen to you? Why are you running so hurried? Any problem?

Dhruba replied, Sundar da they are announcing that they will kick us on our face.

Sundar failing to understand what Dhruba was meaning asked, who is saying what? Who is announcing and what for they are announcing such nonsense?

Dhruba replied, boys from the Natunpara club have hired a truck and they are announcing over loud speaker that they will kick us on our face.

Actually the long day made Sundar a bit abstracted about the event of the last day. Suddenly it sparked in his mind and he asked Dhruba to be more confirmed, tell me in details what happened?

Dhruba depicted the entire scene without even breathing what he had just witnessed before coming to the club, I was coming from the market and saw that they have started their procession. I stood by the road to watch. They have hired a truck and over from the top of the truck playing a song in loudspeaker – *we will kick on their face* – and just after that someone in the loudspeaker asking the members – on whose face? And the members are shouting "on their face" and pointing their finger on this direction, I mean in the direction of our village and club.

The scenario got clear to Sundar. That means this is the insolent behavior of the other club to insult them. It actually made him a bit angry with those people. He asked Dhruba, give me your bicycle and go to our club and inform Surya da or anyone from our batch present there. Tell them I have gone to see what is happening.

Sundar did not wait and Dhruba ran to the club. There in the club Surya da and some other members were busy playing carom and cards. Dhruba shouted for Surya da and depicted the entire thing from the procession to his telling the same to Sundar da and Sundar da's move.

Surya da actually got a bit irritated over Dhruba, could not you wait for coming to the club and telling this? You don't know what you have done. Then he perhaps uttered to himself, I know Sundar, he must have gone to chase them alone. Then Surya said unanimously all who were present in the club, come with me, and then started running towards the market. Before leaving the place he turned towards Dhruba and directed Dhruba to inform the same to as many members as possible at the earliest and tell them all that Surya da has asked them to come to the market.

When Sundar reached out the procession it was just on the bridge over the river. He found that Dhruba was right, from a jumbo size loudspeaker placed on the truck a song is being played with the same words as Dhruba said and seating on the roof of the driver's cabin someone with a microphone in his hand asking the same question and pointing his finger towards their village and every member shouting in support of that person. It did not take any time to recognize the person on the roof top – it was Shyama. The scene just made him almost crazy and he forgot the circumstances. Sundar simply came in front of the truck and placed his bicycle on the road in a crossed manner so that if the truck moves forward it will collide with the bicycle. The driver instantly pressed the break and the sudden stoppage made the procession imbalanced for a moment. The song was stopped and Shyama was also surprised. After the first instance he found that Sundar was standing in front of the truck placing his bicycle in such a way that it is actually impossible for the driver to move forward by passing him. He shouted to Sundar, want to commit suicide?

Sundar replied, no, you black goat if you have the guts then come down from the roof and say what are you saying standing here in front of me. He added looking at the boys who were shouting in support of Shyama, if you are men and not eunuch then come and chase me one by one and I will let all of you see who will kick on whose face.

As I have already told Shyama was of dark complexion and people used to pull his legs by telling him "black goat". So Sundar's words made a terrible situation for Shyama. Though they were more in numbers but no one from his fellows dared to chase Sundar. The entire thing became a chaos. In the meantime Surya da and other guys from the club reached the place. So as the exited conversation between the groups increased the tension also increased. Finally the local administration had to intervene. They tried to come both the group down to a normal state. After the things became semi-normal Sundar told the administrative people pointing to Shyama that, they can carry out their procession but they have to stop playing the song and they have to say sorry for their insulting acts to us.

The demands were logical so the administration asked Shyama and his fellows to stop playing the song and to apologize for whatever they have done. Finally boys of this side came back to club and the others carried their procession on, though the way they tried to create hype was demolished.

Sundar had you lost your mind or what, Surya asked Sundar while seating in the club. He added, have you ever thought what could have happened if had they all chased you together?

Sundar looked at Surya and replied, you are telling me this? You, who have always taught others that don't think how much support you have behind you when you stand against the wrong, because if you are righteous and fighting against anything wrong then there might be hundreds against you but they are weaker than you alone.

You must be crazy man, Surya replied smilingly.

Women ...

Hey Sundar wait. I need to talk to you son, Atanu asked his nephew, I need your help.

Sundar was going out somewhere when he found his uncle calling him from behind. He turned back and approached Atanu, yes uncle tell me, is there any problem. Noni was also standing by his father. There facial expression though was not tensed, rather happy still Sundar asked again, what happened Noni, any issue.

Atanu smilingly replied, no problem son, there is a good news. He continued, as you know your sister Arati has grown up to the age of marriage, so we, means I and your aunty, were trying to find a good match for her. He paused for a moment and then added, we have finalized on one prospective boy. Sundar was listening carefully, he looked at Noni and then again back to his uncle. Atanu started again, he knows you well and I think you also know him.

What is his name and where does he live, Sundar asked. He added, I mean how he knows me, in that case I believe he is from a nearby locality.

This time Noni replied, his name is Gautam, you know the boy. He continued, he lives in Jotepur, with his mother. Sundar steadily recognize the boy and replied, yah but, he turned to Atanu and said, I believe we could have waited some more days so that Arati could have become more prepared for a married life. He paused and choose his words carefully as discussions on an issue like this kind is generally of highly sensitive nature, I mean to say, this could be done after one more year. He completed and looked at Atanu.

Atanu before replying also waited as he knows what Sundar is telling is not totally wrong but he also has his constraints, I understand your concern for your sister Sundar but as you know my financial situation, he paused and added managing a smile on his face, and at the end, today or after an year hardly matters when you know we have to do it.

Sundar understood what his uncle wants to say and replied, alright uncle, when you and aunty have finalized then it must be the best for Arati, I have no doubt on this. Just let me know when and for what you need me and I promise that I will be there with you.

Atanu placed his hand on Sundar's head on a blessing posture and said, I knew it, you will be there. He left the place leaving the two young boys to carry on the discussion.

The name of the boy was Gautam Mukherjee, the only son of his mother, Sumitra, who lost her husband at the early stage of her life and singlehandedly brought her only son Gautam up to this stage of his life. Gautam was working in a nearby jute processing unit and used to live with his mother in his ancestral house at Jotepur. He was almost six to seven years elder than Sundar. As both was from the same locality so was known to each other. Gautam might not be a very well to do kind of person but used to earn enough to maintain a balanced and standard life. So on an average he was a good option as a son-in-law. Finally Arati's life reached the day when she will has to leave behind all her bonding she had nurtured for so long in her father's house and to move forward to make the second phase of sacrifices that she had been taught to as a wife she would be making. Atanu and Sarojini paid a dowry as much as was possible for them to the bridegroom. The more they had to squeeze themselves for arranging the dowry the more they used their parental emotions that whatever they are doing they are doing it for their only daughter. They kept this part almost hidden both from Sundar and Noni as the two young boys with modern mindset were deadly against the age old and disgusting system of Dowry. Atanu knew that if Sundar any way comes to know about this then he will surely be the first and most active one to stand against this. Atanu was well aware of his nephew's stubborn mentality against all such things which Sundar use to call, "Long tending rotten societal systems that are pulling the entire society down to the worst".

On that day, Arati's eyes were flooding with tears as she was leaving for her in-law's house leaving all her sweet memories of childhood behind. Sarojini was also feeling the pain but at the same time trying her best to console her daughter. She was trying to resist her eyes from becoming moist, but that was beyond her capacity to hold her emotion back from bursting. After meeting Sarojini and other female members Arati came to meet two of her childhood companions, Sundar and Noni, who were standing at a corner. To manage the situation Sundar said to his cousin sister, either you stop crying and smile otherwise I promise that I will surely make you the idol of Goddess Kali. He paused and added, and this time there will be no Durga mausi to protect you. The words in fact succeeded to bring a smile, though pale, on Arati's lips.

At the initial phase life was as good as normally expected by a girl like Arati. She was quite happy with her new life. Gautam was working harder than before to make the ends meets properly and Arati was perhaps harder than her husband to help him achieve his target. They got their first son within two years of their marriage. Gautam's hard work got noticed by the higher management and he was promoted to the next level. This good news made Arati probably more proud than her husband but she was totally unaware of the evil that was waiting to enter in her life holding the hand of this good news. For the first few months everything was as usual but slowly the increment in earning injected arrogance in Gautam's character. The man who used to be a polite and well behaved person gradually became a discourteous as well as boastful one. It was day by day becoming tough for Arati to find the man she married just some years back. The arrogance and conceit on the other hand introduced the most fatal thing in Gautam's life, he got addicted to alcohol. Within a very short period of time the man who always used to be the least possible spendthrift and more pragmatic regarding expenditures suddenly became too much extravagant. His extravagant expenditures started creating hindrances for Arati to run her household affairs smoothly, whereas Gautam's expectations rose higher because as per him as he was earning more so naturally he was pouring more money to the family. Arati was stretching herself almost beyond limitation to make her husband happy, which on the other hand started taking its toll on her health. The most unfortunate part was Sumitra who was witnessing the faults of her own son but overlooking it. Sometimes even she was accusing Arati for the same.

In such a situation the only light of hope for any girl is used to be her mother to whom she could at least share her feelings of agonies. Though the financial condition of Sarojini's own family was not so good but still she used to help her only beloved daughter with the maximum possible for her. The mother and daughter kept this situation hidden from all other members of the family, including Atanu.

Time passed by on its own speed, leaving behind three long years. In the meantime Arati became mother of her second son. Gautam became more addicted to alcohol and automatically the conditions of the household deteriorated to the maximum possible. It became unbearable for Arati when Gautam started demanding for more financial benefits from his father-in-law's house. Arati tried her best to humbly make her husband understand that it is extremely impossible for her father to pour more aid to her family as he also has other members of his own family to be taken care. This reply was treated as arrogance by Gautam and resulted initially with verbal abuses but took hardly some times to turn in to physical assault. Astonishingly Sumitra was silent and did not say anything, rather her silence actually taken as a support by her son for those condemnable activities he was doing. Arati in the beginning did not disclose this to anybody and kept these tortures secret even from her mother. But when Gautam crossed all the limits and one day injured Arati in a serious manner then she had no other way but to disclose her agonies to her mother. Sarojini was shocked but did not lose her patient and decided to talk directly to her son-in-law as well as his mother. On the next day she approached Gautam's house and said to Sumitra, didi is that what I gave you my only daughter for. Sumitra tried to bypass the question by saying, I do understand what has happen to Gautam but I believe that was just an accidental case. She added, as you know my son is not that arrogant. May be he on any instinct has over reacted.

Sarojini turned to Gautam, who was standing with his eyes fixed on the ground and head down. She asked, what you would like to say about this Gautam. Gautam did not answer and left the room. Sarojini had no other choice but to talk to Sumitra, didi you do know that Arati's father is not also going through an affluent time. She continued, I have tried to stand by my daughter saving the maximum possible for me from my household till date. I have never let her father know all these, but is it you say we married our girl with you son for. Sumitra also chose to be silent on this matter and Sarojini had to leave the house without any answer or assurance keeping her only beloved daughter there.

For sometimes it got stopped but started again within a few days. Sarojini this time talked to her husband for the first time about what Arati has been bearing with for months. Atanu was almost shattered and the next day in the morning he personally came to his daughter's house to talk to his son-in-law. Gautam was arrogant this time with Atanu and abused him without even respecting his relation with fatherly figure at the minimum. Atanu came back being tremendously insulted with a broken heart. Sarojini was waiting for his return with anxiety and when she got to know what her husband has faced, she broke down in to tears.

THE SECRET LICKED

Atanu and Sarojini did not notice that Noni was present in the next room while they were discussing about Arati and all that has happened to her and if there is something that could be done from their side to help their daughter. Noni minutely listened to every details but did not react.

Sundar, Noni called him, I have something to share with you.

In the evening Noni got the chance to meet Sundar when the later returned home. From his expression it was clear that there is something serious. What happened, any problem, Sundar asked his cousin. Noni thought for some moments before he starts depicting all he has listened his parents discussing about their sister. Sundar was taken aback by what he was hearing. He did not speak for some moments and was actually visualizing the scenario that his sister is going through. He raised his face and asked Noni, where is uncle and aunty now. They are at home, but they don't know that I have listened to their discussions and moreover shared that with you, Noni replied. Sundar did not ask any more question and directly headed towards Atanu's home. Noni followed his cousin.

Sundar with Noni approached Atanu and Sarojini. Atanu welcomed Sundar with a smile and said, come Sundar, seat here, we are just preparing tea. He added, will you take a cup. I would like to talk to Gautam regarding what he has done to Arati, Sundar directly came to the point. Atanu first looked at Sarojini then his son Noni, who was standing beside Sundar and then his eyes anchored at Sundar. He mumbled to say, look son sometimes these kind of misunderstanding happens in married life, we the seniors of the family will surely manage it. Sundar's cool and expressionless eyes were fixed on him. He stopped for a moments and added, I know what you boys are feeling worried for but don't lose your heart, everything will be alright.

Atanu was not willing to permit them as his thought was that the young boys might mess the situation more but Sarojini this time opposed her husband and reacted, why you are holding them back when they are willing to stand by their sister. She continued, don't you think that they are almost in the same age group, she paused, looked at Sundar and added, I believe they might change the mindset of Gautam. She continued, above all Arati is affectionate sister of both Sundar and Noni so what the problem if they try once. Initially Atanu opposed the idea but could not hold his position for long and finally permitted the two boys to at least talk to Gautam once on this but at the same time forewarned them not to lose their patient whatever the result may become. Sundar was silent till now and then he said to his uncle, I promise that we will not do anything losing our tolerance.

Sundar after getting out the room informed Noni, tomorrow we will go to meet Arati and at the same time talk to Gautam. Noni nodded.

Next day Sundar and Noni approached Gautam's house early in the evening. After meeting Arati they had to wait for some times until Gautam came back from his work place. They met Gautam to discuss on the issue. Sundar called Gautam and said, though uncle and aunty have not said me anything but I came to know from both Noni and Arati that there are some problems going on between you.

Actually I am sorry for what ever have happened, Gautam replied, I promise these will not be repeated.

This time Gautam did not misbehaved as he was a bit scared. He knew Noni as a hotheaded person and regarding Sundar he was scared of his reputation in the locality as a person who always stand for the right cause and used to be supported by the people, especially by the young batch.

I will hope that we will not have to come here for the same reason again, Sundar said and turned to Sumitra. He did not say anything to her but his eyes said many things to that lady. Neither Sundar nor Noni behaved arrogantly with Gautam but they clearly made their point to him that next time they should not get any complaints from their sister on this issue. Sumitra and Arati was witnessing the entire scenario standing in the same room but keeping their mouth shut. Before leaving Sundar approached Sumitra and said, you are senior to me and I should not try to teach you anything. He paused and arranged his words carefully, I have lost my mother early in my childhood so I could not learn it from my mother but have always been told by the seniors that all the children are equal to the mother and what I feel is that my sister should not be anyway less to you than your son. He then moved out of the room and Noni followed him.

Nearly for next one month everything was absolutely alright and there was no problem in Arati's family life unless one day when Sundar found his nephew Govinda, the eldest son of Arati, waiting in a queue outside the free medicine counter of the local health center. It was a scorching summer day and Sundar, Prasenjit and Surya was returning from a party meeting. He was a bit shocked seeing a boy of hardly five or six years waiting for medicine that too alone. He stopped his bicycle, came to Govinda and asked him what happened? Govinda was happy to see his maternal uncle and replied, mother has sent me to collect the medicines written on this paper. The small boy then show a piece of paper to Sundar. It was a medical prescription issued by the doctor of the same health center dated back to three days. The prescription was in the name of Arati. Sundar asked Govinda, what has happened to your mother. Govinda replied, some days back father thrashed my mother with a bamboo stick and that had damaged her head. He continued, mother's skull was damaged and she was severely bleeding. He added, generally mom herself comes to collect the medicine but today she is suffering from high fever so she requested me to get the medicines from the health center. Sundar's jawbones were already tight and the last question Sundar asked, where your grandmother was when your father thrashed your mom. Govinda replied, she was in there itself. Sundar took the paper from Govinda and told him to wait under the tree and himself stood in the queue.

Surya knew about the unrest that was going on in Arati's married life. After listening the detailed about the current situation from the little boy he came to Sundar and asked, what you are going to do. Sundar calmly replied, now I will collect the medicines and deliver that to Arati. He added, you and Prasenjit should not wait here in this heat for me as I think this will take some time. Its better you go home, I will see you in the evening at club. Surya did not reply to Sundar and came back to Prasenjit and told him, I will wait here with Sundar. He added, you go to Sundar's house right now and inform Noni that I have called him to meet me at the earliest in the Jotepur crossing. Tell him personally so that no one else get to know about this. Prasenjit was yet to ask something but before he could have asked Surya said, don't waste time, go now.

It took twenty minutes for Sundar to collect the medicines. He came to Govinda, took him in his bicycle and moved towards Arati's house. He asked Surya da about Prasenjit and Surya da replied, Prasenjit has gone for an urgent job. In next five minutes when Sundar with Govinda and Surya da reached Jotepur crossing they found Prasenjit and Noni already waiting there for them. Noni was shocked seeing Govinda with Sundar and Surya da. He asked Sundar, where have you found Govinda? What is he doing at this time? Sundar said Noni what he has listened from Govinda. Within few minutes they approached Arati's house but before entering Sundar stopped Surya da and Prasenjit. He requested, Surya da and Prasenjit both of you please wait outside as your presence could give Gautam a chance to make the affair public, which I don't want to offer that rascal. Surya and Prasenjit nodded and stood by the gate.

Sumitra's face literally faded seeing Sundar and Noni with her grandson. Sundar entered in to the house and found Arati lying on the floor with high fever and a bandage on her forehead. He gave the medicines to her. Arati too was not ready for such a situation. Sundar returned to Sumitra and placidly asked, where is Gautam? Before Sumitra could have answered, Gautam entered the room and saw Sundar and Noni there, which was more than enough to freeze him. Sundar was looking at him with a coolest possible eyesight. Gautam had just started mumbling to ask for sorry and will never happen again kind of words when a tight slap stopped him before saying anything more. For next five minutes the scene worsened. Sundar was literally hammering Gautam with the strongest blows. Sumitra was shouting at the highest of her voice and crying for her son and requesting Arati to stop her brother. Noni, who was famous for losing patient even trying to stop Sundar. Last but not the least, Gautam more or less became a sandbag for a boxer. Listening the hue and cry Surya da and Prasenjit also entered the house and seeing the scene tried to hold Sundar. Sundar was unstoppable, as if he has got a gigantic power which is no way stoppable by any normal person.

Finally when everyone failed Arati came and hold the hand of his brother and said, he is my husband, please don't smash him. Sundar stopped. Arati's eyes were moist but due to her love for Gautam or her brother's affection for her, nobody knows. Sundar looked at Arati and found a tremendous pain in her face. He lifted Gautam from the ground holding the collar of his shirt. He was tremendously injured and was not even well enough to stand on his own.

Turning Gautam towards Arati Sundar barked at him, look at the woman you scoundrel and thank her for stopping me otherwise I would have killed you mercilessly. He continued, you have been torturing her for so long but she never let you down and gave her everything for you and your family. I am just letting you go for her and for the final time. You know the tragedy with the Indian society and more specifically with the men like you is that what you are taught you don't believe, what you believe you don't follow, what you follow you don't act and finally what you act is no way taught by your age old culture. Unfortunately this is mainly true for the men in the society who always try to prove themselves greater than their counter part by frequently sidestepping their will and mainly depending on their strength. On the other hand the women in the society probably the greatest enemy of themselves. Sundar turned at Sumitra and continued, from the day a girl child starts to understand her surroundings and the society at large, she is being taught by everyone in the family including her mother too that one day she will be going to someone else's house after marriage so she must learn to cooperate. In the name of cooperation they are actually forced to sacrifice their every right and even the smallest thing of love. That starts with the glass of milk or the better portion of the meal which she sacrifices for her brother. Then she had to sacrifice for her dream of education even if she is much more efficient than the male counterpart of the family. After getting married she sacrifices her every small wishes even for her husband and finally at her old age the same series runs again and again for her sons. Women are not only taught to sacrifice their rights and lives rather are taught to accept the humiliation imposed on them by their male counterpart without any reason.

He again turned to Gautam and continued, you worship various goddesses like Devi Durga, Devi Kali, Devi Lakshmi or Devi Saraswati as the symbol of power, strength and wisdom but you don't believe in women empowerment and strengthening. Our age old religious teaching had always suggested that except your wife all other women should be believed as your mother or sister but that is not followed. Finally we like to follow the western culture but we don't like to act like them regarding the freedom for women in taking decision for themselves. So at the end of the day a typical situation exists in the family in a micro view and in the society in a macro level. He paused for some moments, inhaled and continued, the second thing is the problem women faces from the other women in the family. A mother feels proud of his son-in-law when she sees that the boy is taking care of her daughter but on the other hand become the bitter most critic when her son does the same for her daughter-in-law. A tremendous psychological thinking, I don't know how and when started, but still exists in the minds of the women that her own daughter should not feel the agonies she had faced in her life but her daughter-in-law must sacrifices all those she had made in her life and sometimes even more. Finally the humiliation in the most acute form that a girl needs to face in her life is Dowry. The amount both in kinds and coins that needs to be paid by the family of a girl to the family of the boy whom she is going to accept as her life partner. Her respect and reputation in her new home depends entirely on that amount – the more the amount the more the respect. Even after that, many a times the demands from you people extends with time to such a limit that the girl left with no other option to kill herself.

Sundar looked at Gautam and said, Gautam, you as from the young batch I expected will deny to be a blind follower of the age old beliefs that had been hampering the development and forward movement of the society from time unknown. We should challenge such rotten ideologies. But in your case please be informed and informed well that this was your last chance. Remind, next time you commit any nonsense to my sister then you are dead. Nobody on earth would be able to resist me from torn you in to pieces, Sundar completed. Then he turned towards Arati and stared for some moments before he left the house.

No more complaint ever came from Arati again after that day.

DEATH CAN'T STOP LIFE ...

Mahim da, one cup for me....

Sundar ordered a cup of tea while letting himself sat on the bench made of bamboo sticks in front of the tea stall adjacent to the railway platform. He is returning from his workplace, the railway locomotive where he has joined as a porter some days back. Today there is no meeting and also there is no college. Due to a holiday the local college where he is pursuing his graduation in Accountancy in the evening batch is closed. Day before yesterday Parbati aunty has gone to her paternal house with uncle and their children and will come back only after three more days so there is not even the duty of attending his students as Sundar teaches them as their private tutor. So this is an absolutely free evening and the only place to go is the club which he plans to head for after the tea.

There it is, Mahim placed the earthen cup filled with hot tea on the bench. He returned to his desk and asked, Sundar may I request you one thing. Surely, why you are hesitating so much, Sundar replied. No, actually I need some help, Mahim said, only if you could manage that, there is no issue if it creates any problem for you. Sundar stared at the man in front of him and said, Mahim da enough of formalities, now tell me what you want to say. Mahim smiled back, you know Biren, my son. Sundar nodded and then replied, of course I do, by the way what he is planning for after his school final. He added, his result was literally awesome. Yes, that is where I need some help, Mahim replied. He is planning to continue his studies and that too in science, which will coast something more than my capacity. He continued, I do also support his intension, though I have managed a large part of that but I am failing short of some amount, which if you could lend me. He did not pause to complete, I will return you as early as I could manage. Hope as well as helplessness, the two emotions that were simultaneously being depicted from his eyes.

Sundar raised his eyes from the earthen cup and replied, why are you being so hesitant about this? No problem, you come to our club next Sunday in the evening when all the members will be there. In between I will discuss the same with them and every one of us if could donate a portion of the total then the problem will easily be solved. He paused and added, and in that case you will not have to repay the debt. Mahim smiled with respect and respite in his eyes for the young man seating in front of him and said, thank you brother, I will certainly be there on Sunday. Sundar smiled back and said, nothing to thank me Mahim da, I do also know how it feels when you have the zeal to continue your studies but no means to support it. Mahim left the shop with a bucket in his hand to fetch some water requesting Sundar to watch in his absence.

Sundar had already finished the tea and seating with a cigarette in between his fore and middle finger, he lost in thinking about the current state of his own life.

How a boy studying in standard eight had to start earning to support his education as well as to satisfy his family. A student of standard eight suddenly became a private tutor teaching kids of primary school. The scene suddenly came and created a bitter feeling in his mind when he was insulted at that age for not earning and taking his foods from the house. In his mind he thanked Parbati aunty for giving him the opportunity at that time when it was the toughest job for him to carry his self-respect and his zeal for education together. Now he has become railway locomotive porter and again that to support his graduate education in Accountancy and family responsibilities. His mind went back to the day when he joined the political movement, how from that day gradually his involvement with politics has become so much that today it is a part of his life. How the home had become a place just to sleep at night. Sometimes that one and only purpose even is fulfilled either in the club room or in any other place as per the requirements and availabilities. He was visualizing everything in his mind as if he is watching a movie of his own life in the theatre of his mind, accompanied by his soul only. Sundar laughs at himself thinking about the way the days are being spent. For him the day starts at the earliest possible in the morning, then he used to spend some time in practicing his physical exercise, the only thing which he is truly addicted with. Then bathing in the river and after that going to provide private tuition, where he used to teach all four children of Parbati aunty. From there directly going for his work in the locomotive. Working there for the whole day, from ten to five and then attending the classes in the evening college. If there is any party meeting or event then the classes become the second priority. Finally returning to the village club nearly completing the evening. After spending the only slice of a day's time there to get some light discussions, games or at least refreshments for the mind. After that, nothing is fixed, sometimes going to the ancestral house otherwise used to sleep either in the club room or in Surya da's house. There is absolutely none at home to think about my return or situation, Sundar smiles on his own. So I am also is kind of a man free from any such concern about anyone in this universe. This was the normal and casual path the life had taken for me and I also am no way disturbed about this.

Would you like to have another cup of tea, Mahim intruded in to Sundar's thought? Sundar was so immersed in his thoughts that he has not noticed Mahim's return. He raised his head and replied, No, may be some other time, he paid the bill for the tea and added, I have to go to the club. He left the shop and started walking towards his village.

Sundar was on his way to his village when he found Surya da and Patru was coming from opposite direction. Surya da stopped his bicycle approaching to Sundar. Sundar watched at Surya da's face, he was looking terribly anxious about something. He found the same in Patru also, very serious. He asked Surya da, what happened? Where are you two going so hurriedly and that too in such an odd time?

Surya replied, we were coming to you only.

Sundar asked, why? Any issue?

Surya thought for a moment as if he was arranging the words to be uttered, a bad news for us. Suresh came to my home just before an hour or so. He informed that Nitin has suddenly passed away in an accident.

The sudden news shocked Sundar from the core. Nitin....why........ I mean how?

Surya depicted, as per Suresh, Nitin was returning from his farming land when it happened. He pause for some moments and continued, though all the farmers from the village generally returns together but today Nitin was delayed as he has to fill the land with water, so he had to work for a bit longer and it happened when he was returning home. Actually it was dark then and he failed to notice the snake on the muddy road and stepped on to it and got bitten. As no one was there so he only got noticed nearly after two hours when his wife went out in search for him and found him lying dead on the road.

Sundar asked, what happened after that, how Suresh came to know all these.

Surya could not say anything. His eyes have turned red in anger. Sundar looked at Patru who then said, no one in the village was ready to touch the dead body as he is from the lower cast. Finally his wife with the help of Suresh took the body to his house. A slang came out of Surya's lips for those so called upper cast people who had implemented that snobbish cast system in the society.

Sundar asked, Surya da have you visited Nitin's house yet?

Surya replied, not yet, we are actually waiting for you to come as otherwise there was no way to inform you. He added, and as Suresh is already there, it would need at least three more people to carry the body to the burning ghat.

Sundar didi not look at anything and said while moving his bicycle, let go. We are already late.

They started cycling towards Nitin's house. It was no less than a half an hour cycling distance. All of the three were silent, rather thunderstruck.

Reminiscences from old days started filling in to Sundar's mind......Nitin, A poor man from a remote village. He was from the lowest strata as per the cast system of the society. An illiterate person who as per the so called societal structure of casts used to earn his living by clearing dirt from the houses of the upper caste people of the society for generations and that too for a measurable amount of income. But Nitin was a hardworking man so except that he in other times used to work either on the small farming land he had or as a daily labor in others' farms. He was a very soft spoken and shy type of person who was totally aloof from all the unnecessary and disturbing things of the rural society and unambiguously restrained himself from discussing anything negative about anyone in and around. He never indulged himself in any controversial or provocative discussion, which is very common especially in the rural society.

Sundar can still remind every moment of the incident that built the bond of brotherhood between him and Nitin. That one incident totally changed Nitin's life. Suddenly that soft spoken and shy type of person became a loud and hard spoken man. A man who was so introvert all of a sudden became so rebellious and gallant that those who used to scare him in many things started being scared of him. That one incident changed a man from his core.

The passages took Sundar back to a day of October three years back from today. Generally every year Nitin used to work for overtime in the previous one or two months before October to earn some more bucks to save some so that he can arrange for some new cloths and other things for his family and especially for his two children in the Durga Puja. As this is the main festival for all the Bengalis in a year so like everyone Nitin also used to try his best to arrange for new clothes, shoes and other things for his family and friends, mainly foods and sweets for that time and enjoy those five days of the year the most he could, forgetting all the hardships of life he had faced in the last year and might also be facing in the coming one. Nitin was more than happy that day as he had earned a bit more than his expectations and so while returning home after his long day of work in the afternoon he was in a great mood. He was crossing the market, when he suddenly recalled that his children that year had asked for new pair of shoes which turned his way towards the market. He purchased two pairs of shoes from a shop for his two kids and indulged himself also with a pair of new slipper. His happiness made him absent minded about the fact that in the way to home from the market area he will have to cross the place where all the Samajpatis used to gather in the afternoon to discuss all their concerns about the degrading values of the society and respect for them. He also forgot that as a member of the lowest strata of the rotten and disgusting cast based system he does not have the right to wear a shoe in front of those who are from the upper most strata of the same system, mainly Brahmins and additionally those who are the Samajpatis either due to their cast or due to their strong economic conditions.

So when Nitin was crossing that place wearing his slipper suddenly Kalicharan babu, one of the senior most from the group noticed that and called him, hey Nitin, come here once. Nitin failed to understand the reason of calling him and without thinking any negativity he approached to Kalicharan babu. Kalicharan suddenly stood up and tightly slapped Nitin on his face. Nitin was so shocked that he could not even realized for what he had been slapped and in a timid voice he asked, what have I done wrong sir? All the others were watching and enjoying the scene.

"What have I done wrong sir?" Kalicharan mocked him asking the same question looking at the other people seating there. Then he turned towards Nitin and said, you illiterate scoundrel, you are passing by the Samajpatis wearing shoes and asking what wrong have you done? Finally he ordered Nitin, take your shoes off and take it in your hand and get out of there. Nitin was so humiliated that he would have cried if two young boys had not came in to his support.

Sundar and Surya was returning from a distant village after attending a party meeting when they witnessed the whole episode standing opposite side of the road. It happened so uncertainly that they could not reach before the poor man was slapped without any reason for so. But after listening to the order Kalicharan gave, they finally could not restrain themselves from entering in to what was going on. Surya first intervened and said, Kalicharan uncle forgive him once. Let him go now and he will not do it again. Then he turned to Nitin and requested, say sorry and go from there.

This solution was not acceptable to Sundar, he was stubborn and asked, Surya da tell me one thing, why would the man say sorry? He added, when he has purchased the shoe on his own hard earned money then who the hell these people are to decide whether the man would wear it or not? Or where the man should and should not wear his shoes? Though the questions were for Surya but those actually for those Samajpatis, so automatically Kalicharan and his companions became angry with this young stubborn boy. Kalicharan asked Sundar, who the hell you are to teach us lessons about what to permit and what not to? We are the people who finalize the rules and regulations to be followed to maintain the divine order in the society.

Sundar turned towards Kalicharan and said with a teasing smile on his lips, Permit! Who are you to permit the man whether he will wear his shoes or not? Have you paid for his shoes or you are given the responsibility by the government of the country to look after who is wearing what and where? It was a direct insult for Kalicharan which fueled him to the uttermost of his anger. He almost barked at Sundar, do you know whom you are talking to? Do you know what I can do with you and this man you are standing in support for?

Sundar step forward, nearly at a hand's distance from the barking man and with coolest but most determined voice replied looking directly at the eyes of Kalicharan, as per my understanding this man is not your slave and you are not his master, so you don't have any right to dictate him anything. He added in the same pace, secondly you do not feed him if he starves for a day. Thirdly unless I am talking something legal and logical I just give a damn to care who you are. He paused and then completed, and finally I would like to see what you can do to me but, don't forget any of your drastic step will compel me to forget your seniority of age, which might be fatal for you.

Surya tried to say something to manage the situation but Sundar stopped him with a hand gesture without even looking at him. Kalicharan was shivering in anger and addressed his companions, will you guys do nothing and watch this boy abuses me in front of you? Though the people seating there were senior to Sundar and Surya but two or three were young enough to take the call. They stood up and came forward. Seeing them standing up Sundar understood that the situation might get confrontational. He suddenly looked around and snatched the bamboo stick from Nitin's hand, which he was carrying with him. At the same time with the other hand he pulled Nitin behind him. Surya though was not prepared for such a state of affairs but now he had nothing but to support Sundar at whatever the situation demands. Nitin from the beginning was silently watching the two young guys whose names were not even known to him but who had been fighting for his cause and that too with the most powerful people of the rural society who are impregnable. All of a sudden the situation instigated him also to come forward and stand by the unknown duo who were fighting his cause. Sundar looked by the side of his eye that Nitin also has come forward to fight for the rights he deserves.

Sundar first opened his mouth holding the stick in an offensive posture, don't blame us if you find yourselves in the hospital soon or may be worse. This man will be responsible for whatever happens to you people. He pointed his finger to Kalicharan. That direct threat was enough to push those braves back. One of them came to Kalicharan and told him, uncle this is not the right time, we will see to it when the proper time will come. Kalicharan was also not ready for such a thrust so he also back tracked. Situation was under control. Sundar, still holding the stick in his hand looked at Nitin and told him, let us accompany you to your home. Before leaving he looked at Kalicharan and his fellows and announced unanimously, if anything wrong happens to this man or his family, remind that I will not let anyone of you go freely and that's a promise. You will repent for your deeds for rest of your life.

From that very day Nitin was totally changed. He had understood clearly the theory of survival of the fittest. Slowly he became a friendly person and down the line a close one to both Sundar and Surya da, who used to visit his village very often for various political and social activities.

Sundar, I think we have almost reached Nitin's house. Sundar's thought broke off by Surya's voice. They had reached near Nitin's home, from here the path is so narrow and muddy and slippery that cycling is not possible. Rest of the way they have to walk through the mud. They parked their cycles and started moving towards the mud hut from where a dim ray of light was trying its best to prove its existence in the dark night. Looking them coming towards the hut, Suresh who was standing outside and waiting for them, came forward. Surya asked him, where is Nitin? He corrected himself, I mean Nitin's body. Suresh did not reply, he show the hut by pointing his finger towards that. Sundar asked, where are the other villagers? Suresh mocked Sundar with a smile of disgust in his face, other villagers? Brother no one is ready to take the sin of carrying the dead body of a "Methor" and secondly whoever will do so will have to borne the expenditures for the cremation of the same also. He added, now you tell me who will take so much of pain and that too for such a poor man? No one had anything to say. They were just shattered. Surya first spoke out, let's go in. All the four boys moved towards Nitin's home, first Surya and then the other followed him.

The door was open, first Suresh entered the room, then Surya, then Patru and Sundar entered last. Entering there what they witnessed was horrible, a small oil lamp was trying its best to fight the darkness, Nitin's body was faded and lying on the ground over a straw mattress and his wife was seating near his head holding their two children beside her. The elder one was crying and the younger one was not even old enough to understand what has happened to his father and why his elder sister is crying? He was actually looking at the four unknown guys who have just entered their room. Nitin's wife was seating like a statuette. There was absolutely no expression on her face.

Looking the situation for a while the four guys came out of the room and Surya asked, Suresh we need bamboo sticks, he continued, from where to arrange those sticks to frame the carrying bed for the dead body to the burning ghat. Suresh answered, I have managed only one bamboo and that too from the neighboring village, he added, the only bamboo tree in this village is possessed by the upper cast and they are not ready to give their resources for a "Methor". He stared at the other three people standing and said, I believe we have to manage with the single stick by fastening the body with the stick for carrying.

Each of them looked at each other and silently sealed on the decision Suresh has given.

They entered the room again and holding together carried Nitin's lifeless body outside, then started fastening the body with the single bamboo stick. When everything was done Sundar and Suresh approached to Nitin's wife for her permission and Sundar said, sister it's time to take him. She was looking at the dead body of her husband with a blankness in her eyes, holding her two children, one in her hand and the younger on her lap. Suresh for formality again asked her permission to take her husband's body, she did not say anything. Suresh and Sundar was just turning back when she for the first time asked something, Could you tell me one thing? The boys turned at her when she asked the question that Sundar would never forget throughout his life. She asked with a slow but deep voice, could you tell me one thing, how and what would I feed these two little lives now? There was not a single drop of tears in those eyes that were staring at nowhere in particular, but everywhere in and around her. Perhaps a helpless and worried mother was heavier on a mournful and tormented wife who has just lost her husband. The question was probably the toughest to answer for even the wisest man on earth at that point of life. No one present there had any answer for the question, they just brought their eyes down to their feet.

While carrying the mortal remains of Nitin to its final destination for his last rights, unless the hut became invisible before crossing the last diversion of the village road, Sundar looked back for the last time and found that a mother preparing for the fiercest battle that was yet to start just after a few hours from now when the young kids will say, Mother, we are hungry.

THE DEVIL ...

Putting the empty cup on the table Surya uttered to Sundar while igniting his cigarette, you know people say it is toughest if not impossible to understand a woman, but I strongly disagree.

Sundar was seating across the table and was more interested in the cup of tea and the paper he was immersed in to. They were seating at Surya's house and just before some minutes they were served tea and some snacks by the handmaiden. Sundar has also been informed by Surya's mother that tonight he will have his dinner here. It was monsoon and also raining outside so they had nowhere to go. He and Surya while waiting as usually got involved in their own job. Sundar raised his eyes from the paper he was concentrating on and stared at Surya, are you telling me something, he asked. Surya after taking a long puff and throwing the condensed white smoke out of his mouth and nostrils repeated what he had just said before a moment or two. What do you say, I am right or not, he added with his previous lines.

Sundar placed the paper on the table and paused for some moments, he carefully arranged his words and replied, I think on the topic you have chosen, I possess a knowledge even worse than of a greenhorn and at the same time what is haunting me right now, much more than this topic is the hell of the pile of necessary works that are lying in front of both of us. He pointed his eyes to the papers lying on the table and continued, I believe you do also know that tomorrow morning we will need these to be handed over to Anil da in the meeting and that to mention without fail as he has conveyed. He stopped and stretched his hand to ask for the counter of the cigarette Surya was smoking.

Still, tell me one thing, which you find more complex women or the life itself? Surya asked. Sundar looked straight at Surya's eyes and replied, I don't have any knowledge about the first one but regarding life what I feel, it is the best teacher, but it teaches us in the toughest possible way and when it punishes us for our mistake, the punishment used to be so that you would never forget. He continued, I personally was not very much follower of this theory in the childhood but the more I matured, I found that this is absolutely true and true for even the smallest mistake you make in your life. Just when at a certain age we start thinking that we have seen enough of life and have earned a great experience, it suddenly opens a new page and shows us in the most unexpected way what we have never witnessed before. This teaching goes on until we breadth for the last time.

Surya transferred the cigarette to Sundar narrowing his eyes expressing his frustration with this statement and said, you know Sundar I have never seen a man as unromantic as you are on this planet. He paused and added, probably will never encounter such another in my life.

Thank you for the complement and now see this, Sundar pointed his finger on a portion of the page he kept on the table and continued, in the area of our jurisdiction only in this point we are lagging behind others. I think we will be asked question on this tomorrow, so we must prepare a suitable answer for that.

Surya took the sheet in his hand and after a look on that he replied staring at Sundar, but in all other areas we have achieved the best.

Yes I know but the problem is if you rank top in all but one subjects and fail to secure the minimum marks required to pass in that single one then you are no better than a failed student, right? Sundar added, so we must have a suitable answer to present before we meet Anil da tomorrow.

Hmm, by the way when at tomorrow we have the meeting, Surya asked, and where. We will have to reach Bishrambag by ten o'clock in the morning, Sundar replied. Oh god, I have done a terrible mistake, Surya replied. What, Sundar asked. Sorry man, tomorrow you will have to attend the meeting alone, I have another important work to be completed, Surya replied. What, what could on earth be more important than this meeting, Sundar was surprised, you know who all are coming and this is the platform perfect for raising all the points we have been discussing for so long. How you could say that you have something more important. Surya closed his eyes and chose his words before saying, I request you please spare me for tomorrow, and please don't ask me right now what that important job which is more important than this meeting to me. Sundar stared for quite some moments at Surya's eyes and replied, for tomorrow's meeting, well I will manage but I would request you to be more cautious on whatever you are going to do tomorrow as I sense there is something unusual because this is the first time ever you asked me not to ask you something.

The chat did not last far as the handmaiden intrude and informed that the dinner has been served.

Next day Sundar was sleeping in his ancestral house in the evening. Generally he does not sleep at this time but today was a bit different day as he had to go to a Bishrambag, a village almost thirty kilometer from his place to attend the meeting. He started early in the morning but while going there it started raining and he in between nowhere, had no shelter to wait for so got totally soaked in the rain. The entire day he had to bear with that drenched cloths which in turn took its toll and caused a mild fever for Sundar. So when he came back to home he was suffering from an unbearable headache and at the same instance due to that fever he was so tired that could not indulge himself to go elsewhere or engage in anything else but laying down for rest and fell asleep in moments.

Dada, Surya da is asking for you, suddenly he sensed that someone was calling him. Opening his eyes he found one of his younger brothers standing in front of him. What happened, Sundar asked in a slow and tired voice? His brother repeated what he just has said to Sundar and asked, should I tell him that you are not well and sleeping. No it's okay, you go, he dismissed the boy who was standing in front of him.

Sundar looked at the wall clock, it is half past seven in the evening. He thought that Surya da might have come to know the reason of Sundar's absence in the club room or would like to get the details of what happened in the meeting. He came out of his house and found that the rain has stopped and the sky was clear enough compared to the previous days. Surya da and Tarun was waiting for him under the coconut tree nearly at a distance of thirty to forty feet from the house but they were visible, may not be clearly but fair enough to notice and recognize them specifically. Sundar approached closer to them slowly and asked in a smiling face, Surya da is anything special that you both are waiting for me. Surya da and Tarun both were a bit surprised seeing Sundar in such a drowsy condition and Surya asked, were you sleeping at this time. Sundar told them in details about the long day he has spent and also informed that he was actually suffering a mild fever. Let me see, Surya placed his palm on Sundar's forehead to sense the temperature and found it might not be too high but surely more than normal. A shadow of tension appeared on his face which Sundar realized and thought that Surya da might be worried about his health. To pacify Surya he said, do not worry about this, from tomorrow itself I will be absolutely ok. Surya da was quite but this time Tarun uttered to Sundar, actually we have come to you for a help that is required tonight. It was more than enough to make it clear that there is something serious. Sundar asked Surya da, what happened? Any problem?

Surya da did not say anything but just nodded his head, his eyes were on his feet. Sundar asked again, Surya da tell me in details what happened. Surya said, Bijan uncle had passed away in the evening at the local health center and now there is no one to take his mortal remains from the health center to the cremation ghat.

Sundar was a bit shocked. He knew Bijan uncle for long as a very kind hearted and helpful person who has actually helped a lot of people throughout his life. The man used to live in a neighboring village, and above all was a good person. He was a very successful person as a business man. He started his life from poverty and worked day and night for establishing his business. Currently he is one of the well-established persons in the area but he never forgot those though days he spent in poverty and the man always remained a person down to earth. Though he did not have his own child but during the course of his life he has taken care of his nephews just like his own children. He brought them up, educated them and in recent past handed over his business also to them. He and his wife now a days used to spend their time mainly in religious and spiritual activities. They used to help the poor families in the neighborhoods by giving them necessary things like blankets in the winter, tarpaulins in the monsoon and even earthen tiles and bamboos to repair their mud houses as and when needed. Bijan uncle never forgot his early days of poverty and always used to help the poor people in their needs and today such a man is lying dead in the local health center just like an orphan and there is no one to take his mortal remains to his home for once so that his wife can see him for the final time and there is nobody to arrange for his last rights. Sundar asked Surya da and Tarun, what his nephews are doing? Where are they? Where are those people whom he helped all over his life?

Tarun replied, for his nephews, they have already received what they wanted for and now they don't have any compassion or duty or even responsibility left for the old man and his widow. He paused for a moment and added, and those poor people whom he helped, probably have not yet been informed about this.

Surya da was listening to Tarun silently, now he added, Patru is there in the health center and completing the necessary formalities, he continued, but only three men i.e. myself, Tarun and Patru will not be enough for carrying the body back to Bijan uncle's home first and then to the cremation ghat. He added, and that is why we have come to call you but now it seems in such a physical situation this will not be recommended for you to be with us. I suggest you to take rest and don't be worried, I will manage someone else from somewhere.

Sundar did not answer Surya and requested them, wait here for a minute. He returned to his home and came back within earliest possible time being ready to be with the duo. Surya tried to restrain Sundar but failed. Finally the three boys started for the Health center. When they reached the place they found Patru waiting eagerly outside the health center for them. Patru informed them, I have completed all the formalities and the authority had permitted to take the body of Bijan uncle for his last rights. Now they had to arrange for bamboos and ropes to make a structure for carrying the body. You don't need to go with us and just take rest here, Surya said Sundar and then asked Tarun and Patru, you two come with me. Sundar waited in the health center and the three went to search and arrange the required materials. It took some time for them to arrange and make the structure and when they finally started for Bijan uncle's house it was nearly half past nine. In a rural place that too in the night of a monsoon it was nearly the midnight. They reached Bijan uncle's home in next half an hour and found that his widow was waiting at the gate with another aged lady who actually was the handmaiden of the house. Those two ladies silently completed all the necessary religious rituals without even crying, as if they were turned to stones. Just after completion when Surya da approached the elderly widow for the permission of taking the dead body of her companion of more than five decades, her eyes became wet and she closed her wrinkled eyes and slowly nodded, just two droplets made their path through her chins from her eyes.

It was quite a long distance from that village to the cremation ghat and usually a walk for nearly an hour but that day it took more than two hours firstly due to the illness of one of the four, their speed was slower than usual and secondly rain started in between and they had to stop for nearly half an hour on the way. When they reached the cremation ghat at the bank of the river Ganga, it was a bit more than midnight. The cremation ghat was a very uncanny kind of places with no lights except the fire of the burning pyres here and there in the area and no locality in the surroundings or even nearby. The only audible sounds are either the sound of lamentation of those people who were cremating their near and dear one or the crackling sound of logs, including bones and fleshes of the mortal remains of human remains are being burnt in the fire. Except those who have carried a dead body to cremate there use to be no other human existence except the "*Chandal*" who used to earn his living by helping people in making the pyres and burning the dead bodies they have carried with them here. The person generally used to be fully drunk due to the nature of his work and the workplace, otherwise the job he performs is hardly possible for any man in his normal sense.

Today, when the boys reached the burning ghat they found Kalua, the Chandal, a non-Bengali person and originally from Bihar, was doing something in his small cabin made of bamboo and palm leaves. He was a well-known person to all these boys and the vice e versa due to their frequent visits to the cremation ghat. Kalua was actually preparing his bed of straw mattresses to go for a sleep in the extension area of his one room house. He halted his preparation seeing those boys putting down the dead body off their shoulders. He came out to them and asked, what happened Surya babu? Won't you people have a holiday even in such a terrible night? Then his eyes fall on Sundar and he smilingly continued, hey Sundar babu you are also in the company. He was totally drunk and a deep alcoholic smell was coming from his existence. Surya smiled at him and replied, what to be done Kalua? We don't have allowed ourselves any leave or holiday. Kalua laughed loudly and replied, today you are the third group here, he added, one in the morning and the second one was completed just before half an hours from now. He paused and pointed his eyes to drag the attention of the boys to a pyre, which has almost been burnt down to ashes and said, look the iron bars where the pyre was arranged are still red. I thought there will be no more for today and was planning to go to bed when watched you people coming. He completed and started laughing, showing his typical yellow teethes.

Tarun joked, so we are the unlucky third, everyone laughed out lauder. Then he advised Sundar as he was suffering from fever, you seat beside the body and don't need to work any hard. He then suggested, Surya da you, we three will be enough to arrange the logs from the shop. The shop which sells logs are at a 5 minutes' walking distance from that place. Surya supported Tarun and said, absolutely perfect plan, then he turned at Sundar and said, you better seat beside the dead body for guarding that from animals searching for dinner. At the same time he requested, Kalua start your part of the job, i.e. to prepare the place where the body will be placed for its final destination. Okay then, I am waiting here, Sundar accepted the decision and sat beside the dead body and Kalua went to prepare the place as the soil was totally wet so he had to manage a heavy task on that rainy night.

Sundar could not remind for how long he was seating beside the body, he was probably feeling a bit drowsy when suddenly he felt something moved at a snail's pace nearly two or three meters by his side. First thing came in to his mind is, he might be dreaming. He checked his consciousness, no he is totally aware, he can see Kalua preparing the cremation spot. The iron bars where the last dead body was cremated are still in a mild red condition. Then he asked himself, is he hallucinating in high fever? No, he answered himself, because still he can sense a nearly inaudible sound of crawling in a close proximity. He can feel a very slow movement in his proximity, may not be very close to him but not too far away from him as well. Is it any reptile, snake.... with the idea that snakes are the most common creatures possible in monsoon in such a situation because when the rain water enters their holes in the ground they become refugees from their homes and start searching for a safer place and becomes very much vindictive. With the thought suddenly his nerves got stimulated and he took up a small wood stick lying near him. It was so dark that nothing was visible so he silently and without moving started to follow the slight sound of crawling. Within a few minutes he noticed that the sound was moving from his proximity towards the spot where the last dead body was cremated but with frequent but short halts. After a while when that element reached near that place towards the spot it was moving to, Sundar saw just a shadow like body in the dimmed light of the iron bars. A body moving with four legs but mainly crawling with its chest, it was moving slowly and with extreme cautiousness. Every now and then it was getting stopped and moving his head to sense if there is anything which could hurt it. It was actually looking very similar to a lizard without its tail but much bigger than any normal lizard found in the locality in shape and size.

Sundar's eyes were following that shadow without blinking. Slowly it moved to the bars and started sniffing the ground and scratching the ground with one of its front legs. From the gesture Sundar sensed that it was picking something out from there and putting that to its mouth probably. It was perhaps eating something from there. He stood up, holding the stick tightly in his hand and started moving towards that element as silently as possible fixing his eyes on that creature without blinking. He reached a near proximity of the element and suddenly he got so shocked that he was not even able to believe his own eyes. It was not a snake or lizard or anything, it was a probably a human or may be something very close to call a human.

Yes probably, his face was depicting many emotions at a time – there were doubt, agony, uncertainly, hesitance and so many things that could not be described by words. He almost lost his balance and was trying to control himself when all of a sudden Kalua shouted from the spot where he was preparing the ground for the cremation, nearly ten meters from the place where Sundar was standing, don't thrash that Sundar babu, get out of there, it's a devil.

It was impossible for Sundar to move, he was actually feeling like his legs have been buried in the ground, but hearing that shout the element or human or devil or whatever it is turned his head towards Sundar, stared at him and frantically disappeared in the dark. All within a couple of seconds. Sundar was still standing speechless with the stick holding in his hand when Kalua approached him. Kalua's touch bring Sundar back to a normal stage of mind. Kalua uttered to him, Sundar babu thank you for not thrashing the Devil, otherwise it could have killed you. He continued, it's so dangerous that it could kill a man even from a long distance. You are so lucky that it did not kill you. Nothing was impregnating Sundar's sense, he was stoned.

Sundar did not reply to Kalua. He knew that he could not make a man like Kalua understand that it was nothing like devil or so, it was perhaps a human being who was actually searching for burnt fleshes to satisfy his hunger irrespective of the nature of the fleshes of a human or something else. Though he could never understand the cause for what that human became a cannibal but that scene he witnessed was something for which the word unbelievable is even too insufficient.

HOMEWORK ...

It is better to eat your own wastes than eating a free meal and being a burden to the family, a lady barked on a boy in the lunch table.

All the members of the family was seating around and some of them even started staring at the boy from the corner of their eyes. The plate containing the lunch in front of the boy even started laughing and taunting his survival in such a manner as if the plate is echoing the words just said by the lady. The words are echoing all across the kitchen room, everything in the room, the walls, the doors, the windows, the utensils, the reflection of his own face in the glass of water placed by the plate, everything was laughing and teasing the boy. He can't hear anything except the cruel and insulting sounds. He wants to cry, he wants to call his own mother but he could not do that either as she had passed away long before. His voice has been chocked in within his throat itself. His vocal cords are vibrating to such a terrible limit that it may anytime tore apart but could not make any sound. His eyes have dried down as any desert and instead of tears a flow of blood may come out at any point of time.

Sundar opens his eyes almost scared, he was perspiring and still he can feel the micro sized drops spread across his face. There was absolutely no sense of drowsiness in his face though he was sleeping, rather the expression could easily be termed as sufferings. He looked out of the window in his right side. Though some rays of light are trying to cut through the dark night and trying their best to show the blueness of the sky but they will have to fight the battle with the darkness for some more time to achieve their goal. He got up from the mattress and fetch a glass of water from the waterskin kept in the corner of the room and poured himself with the same. There is absolutely nothing to do so he returned to the mattress and lied down again. He knows for next half an hour he will have to lay without any sleep but with closed eyes and wait for the morning. Lying on the mattress Sundar started thinking of the day he just dreamt of. A day that could never be wiped out of his mind.

The day when he was first humiliated in the lunch table for not earning and living life as a burden on the family, Sundar was a boy of fourteen years, studying in standard eight and had just recovered from a deadly and quite long suffering from typhoid. There was no one who had a hope of his survival from the typhoid but by the grace of the Almighty he survived and that too only depending on the liquid medicine served from the government hospital for free. His physical condition at that time was so that he was even not capable of standing on his feet for half an hour at a stretch. In such a condition one day at the lunch table he was told those mighty words, "It is better to eat your own wastes than eating a free meal and being a burden to the family". Today it is irrelevant who uttered that to him on that day, though Sundar could and would never forget that face and more over the relationship between them, perhaps one of the most sacred and respected one in a boy's life as per our culture and tradition. That day he could not eat and promised to himself that at the earliest possible time he will pay more than the bills he makes on the family. The emotional relations left with only professionalism form there on. He turned to a paying guest from a member of the family.

This time who came to his aid was Parbati aunty. She at that point was having a family of four children, two sons and two daughters. Parbati aunty got to know the details from Durga, the common maid of the two families. She was shocked and ordered Durga, you go right now and inform Sundar to meet me at the earliest. Sundar, when came to meet Parbati aunty, she did not expressed anything about her knowledge of what Sundar had to bear with that day just before some hours. She just said, Sundar you know I am very worried about the education of my eldest son Shibnath and searching for a private tutor for him who can take care of his studies. She paused and showed a mock concentration on her household jobs that she were doing. As if after managing that she added, if you could take the responsibility then I would be very happy and satisfied. I have also talked to your uncle about this and he has also agreed with the idea. For Sundar it was probably the best thing he could have thought about so there was no point of denying and he happily replied, okay aunty I will start coming from tomorrow morning. Parbati did not ask for anything from Sundar and she herself also fixed quite a good monthly remuneration for Sundar for the job. And from the next day Sundar joined his first job as a private tutor to Shibnath.

Sundar was quite serious about Shibnath's study and Shibnath also loved and respected his teacher just like his own elder brother. Time passed by, Shibnath grew up and so his younger brother Mantu and two sisters Rekha and Rakhi. Shibnath was very serious about his studies and so was his teacher. Both of their seriousness and dedication started bringing good results for Shibnath in all the examinations. Parbati was happy that her choice was not wrong. With time Mantu and the two sisters, Rekha and Rakhi all became students of Sundar. Both Shibnath and Mantu was serious about their studies but for the two girls Rekha and Rakhi it was more favorable to spend time in the kitchen cooking, soothing or helping their mother than to in the studies. Though the girls were very gentle and polite in nature and used to respect Sundar no less than their elder brothers but whenever it comes to studies they were probably the most inattentive and casual kind of students on earth. Sundar also used to adore those two little girls just like his own little sisters but on the other hand used to be very much angry for their casual approach towards studies. He used to hide his affection for the two and posed as a tough teacher. Sometimes even he used to blame his Parbati aunty for allowing her daughters in to kitchen and also report to Janardan uncle that his daughters are extremely inattentive and casual about their studies and if this continues then they have no chance of passing the final examination and also there is no point of spending money every month for the education of those two girls. It was the time when Shibnath and Mantu both had passed the final board examination and Shibnath was studying in the final year of his graduation in literature with Bengali as an honors subject and Mantu in the same college was studying in the first year of graduation in pass course. Rekha was preparing for her final year school board exam and the youngest of them Rakhi was in her standard eight.

Sundar now is also working in the railways after completing his M.Com. This is a respected and also well-paid job compared to that one he was doing in the locomotive. At the same time he is highly occupied by his political activism though nowadays due to his government job he is facing many hindrances and legal barriers for political involvements but still he is carrying out both. Moreover he is still teaching Rekha and Rakhi as a private tutor, managing time from his busy every day schedule. Actually Rakhi and Rekha is the only students he is teaching now and for him they were much more than just students rather he used to feel the responsibility for the two as his own younger sisters.

Every day he use to start his session early in the morning and continues for nearly three hours before going to his office. As Rekha is now at her final year of school and preparing for the board examination so Sundar is emphasizing more on her than Rakhi who has two more years to the final examination. To force Rekha to concentrate on her preparation Sundar has started giving as much home task as he was certain would be no way possible for Rekha to complete in one day but with an aspiration that even if she could complete three forth of the task given to her then also it will be more than sufficient and for doing so she will have to spend maximum of her time on studies rather than spending time either in the kitchen with her mother or roaming around here and there in the village.

But that trick also has not worked successfully as Sundar while checking the home works, he had given to Rekha, found himself wrong about what he anticipated about his student. Seventy percent was too far from what Rekha has worked on her home task. She has worked on hardly ten to twenty percent of the home task and that too in such a negligence and casual approach that her exercise books for home tasks became such that it has more writings in red color written by her teacher than by her in blue. After that Sundar has also tried other possible ways to make her understand about the toughness and seriousness of the board examination. He tried to scare her regarding a bad result and the consequences if she does not come up with a better result. He also tried to make it clear that with a good result how many options she would have for further higher studies. Sundar has cited the example of her own eldest brother Shibnath who is now concentrating on the preparation of his graduation as well as job related examinations. When he was telling all this to Rekha, she with her eyes down on her feet was pretending to be very serious and listening to all those very seriously. But now after this it became clear to Sundar that when he is out of her sight, Rekha simply forgets everything and continues with the same casual approach. As a teacher it was a tough situation for Sundar because his student was not willing to understand his words and also is not being interested in studies.

One day being disgusted Sundar asked Rekha, Go and ask both of your parents to come here and also tell them that I have categorically asked both of them to come. He added, also call Shibnath. In next ten minutes both Janardan and Parbati came to meet the private tutor of their children. What happened Sundar, Parbati aunty asked? Sundar raising his face handed over the exercise book to her and said, aunty if Rekha decides to be so casual then I think you guys need to be more serious about her. He paused and continued, otherwise there will hardly be any hope of her passing the board exam successfully. He completed and looked at them. After checking the script Parbati replied, believe me Sundar I am tired of saying this girl to study but she hardly listens to me. She added, and your uncle used to be in the office, so this girl has got a freehand of doing anything and everything except her studies. In between Shibnath has entered the room. Sundar thought for some moments and uttered to Shibnath, I am giving you the responsibility of taking care of Rekha especially when I and your father is in the office. He added, I would like to direct you to compelling your sister to complete all the home tasks I have given and would give every day. Shibnath nodded.

This arrangements did not even worked for more than a week. On the third day Shibnath came to Sundar and reported, Sundar da Rekha does not listen to me or follow my instructions and for me it is impossible to spend time on such unfruitful activities and that to in the final year of my own graduation. He paused and added, you know I am working for both my graduate level exam and also continuing my preparations for the job related studies. He selected his words carefully to complete, I am really sorry Sundar da, and it would have been possible if she would have at least the interest.

Hmm, I expected you with this realization even before, Sundar replied, okay I will have to find out some other way to handle this girl.

After that day Sundar became a teacher tougher than he had ever been to any of his students. Actually it became a challenging issue for him that whatever happens he will make Rekha study and pass the examination with honorable marks. Parbati aunty and Jagannath uncle both were in favor of Sundar and was also sure that whatever Sundar is doing, he is doing for the betterment of their inattentive daughter who to Sundar is no less than his own younger sister. Sundar started to punish his student for each and every negligence more than that of her mistakes. He used to make her stand for her negligence and mistakes, on one leg for quite a long time holding her own ears by herself. Sundar aimed to mainly shame Rekha in front of her younger sister so that she starts studying. This worked for some days with positive results but slowly Rekha became habituated to such punishments and shames and in recent days Sundar has noticed that the same results have started coming out again.

THE PRESENT DAY

Sundar woke up from the mattress as the sky started becoming brighter. He knew that his day has started. Firstly he will have to go to attend the gym then from there he will come back after taking his bath in the river. Then after getting ready he will go to teach his students and from there his workplace. So huge pile of works and that to be managed within a period which is much less than adequate.

Sundar reached Parbati aunt's house almost at 7 in the morning. He found none of his students present in the room where he seats. Aunty, Sundar asked, where is the two girls? Are they still sleeping? Before Parbati could have speak Rekha's voice appeared, Dada we are here, coming in two minutes. Sundar let himself sat on the mattress on the floor. In next five minutes the girls appeared with a cup of tea and biscuits for their teacher. Sundar while sipping the cup started checking Rekha's homework and it was literally no less than frustrating for any teacher.

The uncountable numbers of mistakes done due to complete casualness and utter negligence actually made Sundar probably angrier than anything but he controlled himself. Anyhow managing his annoyance he said, this morning not going to teach you people, rather I would like to talk to Rekha about some serious matters.

With the coolest possible mind he asked, Rekha why you are not pouring your attention in to your studies.

Rekha replied with the same approach of looking down to the ground, to be very truthful Sundar da I don't like to study.

Sundar paused for a moment and arranged his words, don't you see Shibnath and Mantu? When in the same house two of your elder brothers are so attentive towards their education then why you are losing that zeal within your mind?

Seeing Rekha not speaking Sundar repeated his question. Now slowly Rekha replied in a mild voice, I am separate entity and my brothers are separate and they might like to study but I don't get any interest on this.

Sundar finally asked the last question he found proper to motivate his student, when your father is working so hard for day and night for the betterment of you people and on the other hand your mother is also trying her best to support you then why are you not at the least respecting their hard work and support by providing them the minimum that they are expecting from you. And they are not asking you to do something for them rather they are asking you to do something that will benefit you in future. He continued, you know you are no less than my own sister to me, even I always use to be worried about your negligence and fickle mindedness. He paused and added, could not you concentrate a bit more on your studies to get a good result, at least for this year when you are going to face the final board examination. Could not you work a bit harder to stand along with the expectations of so many people who love and adore you?

The reply that came was beyond the limit of the tolerance for Sundar as Rekha replied, tell me one thing, have I told my father to work day and night, have I told my mother to cook for me in any situation and Sundar da I am quite capable of doing everything I need.

The rude and mindless answer made Sundar furious. He stood up and also stood Rekha up by holding her hand and started dragging her out of the room. Standing in the courtyard of the house he almost shouted to call Parbati and Janardan. Both of them came out of their rooms, Shibnath and Mantu also came out of their room and Rakhi was standing behind her elder sister like a statue. None of them had ever witnessed such angry and shouting Sundar.

Sundar looking directly to Janardan said what Rekha had just answered him and without any pause announced, today she must know the value of parents and their support. Today I will let her feel the agony of those who are not blessed by these and are compelled to fight in every step of life to survive, keeping their self-respect undamaged. Then he turned towards Rekha, who was almost in the verge of crying and said, if you were not a girl then today I would have slapped any of my student for the first time in my life as a teacher.

He mindlessly looked around the place where he was standing and suddenly started dragging Rekha towards the lavatory outside the house. While moving towards that direction Sundar ordered Rakhi, go and bring all the books and exercise books of you sister from the room. Rakhi was taken aback and actually was in a dumbstruck condition. Before she could have understood Sundar said, can't you listen what I just said? She did not hesitate to get back to the room and returned within few seconds with all that she was ordered to bring. Sundar nearly threw Rekha inside the small lavatory putting all her books and exercise books in her hand and locked the door from outside. He turned back and asked Shibnath for a lock and key. Shibnath brought the thing he has been ordered for like a hypnotized person. Sundar locked the door and kept the key in his pocket and announced, the door will only be opened when I will return from office. Then he turned to the lavatory where he has locked the girl and said, if I found that the tasks are not done then I promise that you will have to spend the night in there also.

Every one present was spellbound. Sundar did not look at anyone and just left that place and went to the station for his train to office without taking his food which he used to take in his aunt's house every day.

Sundar spent the entire day with a disturbed mind and could not even concentrate on his works. He had a political meeting scheduled in the evening but he cancelled that either and from his office came straight to his aunt's house. Entering the house he first noticed that the door which he locked up in the morning and found that in the same condition as he left it in the morning. He called his Parbati aunty and asked with a low voice, what is she doing? Have any of you called her in between? Has she taken lunch?

Parbati aunty shook her head and replied, I tried to talk to her once or twice but she has not responded.

Sundar nodded his head and moved towards the jail where he has locked Rekha for the entire day. Every member of the house gathered in the lawn when Sundar unlocked the door of the lavatory. He found Rekha was still wiping her eyes. He called her to come out of there and took her to the lawn where Parbati aunty and Janardan uncle was standing spellbound with their other children. Rekha was standing with her eyes fixed on the ground when Sundar told her to look up. He continued that to him Rekha is no less than his own sister and he could even forgive her if she neglects her studies but he will never forgive if she any way disregards the sacrifices her parents are doing for the betterment of her. He added, you must also remind that only a person could understand the value of parents who has lost them, just like myself. He then pointed his finger to Parbati aunty and said Rekha, if this noble lady would not have stood by my side one day then today perhaps I would not have been living a life I am living. So don't ever disregard those people who cares for you not because of their duty but because of love and affection. This was enough to wet the eyes of the people standing there. Rekha promised that she will never talk like she did in the morning.

Finally the best part was Rekha really became serious about her studies and she passed her final board exam with quite a good result but neither Sundar nor Rekha, not even any of the other people who were present their that day could ever forget the incident.

Position ...

Mahim da Akhilesh will come to your shop for me, tell him to meet me tomorrow in the morning when I will go to office. Tell him that I will bring all the papers he needed.

Sundar informed the tea shop owner in the railway station. He is returning from his workplace and was almost running. He continued, tell him I am going to attend an important meeting at Natunpara, if he wishes, he can come there also to meet me. Mahim was listening to Sundar letting all his jobs halted, he asked in reply, where in Natunpara? Sundar answered finally before leaving the place, he knows where to come, and you just tell him that I am in Natunpara and that will be enough for him to understand. Sundar left he place almost on the trot as he was already late for the meeting. While cycling towards Natunpara he was cursing himself for the last cup of tea he indulged himself for with his colleagues in the office and that cost him to miss the previous train he planned for to take. And finally he had to wait one and a half hours for the next one. Pathetic, simply pathetic, he uttered to himself.

When Sundar reached the place the meeting was in the verge of completion. He apologized to the people seating there for his late arrival and took a seat beside Anil da, who actually called him and pointed the place to him to seat. The meeting gets completed by next half an hour and while coming out of the place Anil da said, don't be tensed, there was nothing extremely important that you have missed and the other details that you need to know will be conveyed to you by Surya. He looked at Surya who was walking besides. Surya nodded his head in affirmation.

After Anil da left Sundar and Surya started returning to their village. So, what happened in today's meeting, Sundar asked Surya who was cycling by his side.

Nothing new man, all those old talks about how to do what and all, Surya replied. He continued, you know all these much better than even those who were distributing the free "Gyan". Sundar smiled back as he has understood that Surya is not in his original mood. He is someway or other is in a disturbed mind.

While entering the village Sundar said, Okay Surya da, today I am not coming to club and I need to get back to home now. Why, is it too late to go to club, Surya asked surprisingly and continued, I believe there are people there till now. Sundar replied, not that, actually tomorrow in the morning before going to office I will have to handover some important documents to Akhilesh. He added, he will be waiting for me in the station and I will have to prepare all those by the night itself. Surya replied with a long haul, Okay then, good bye, then he added, I must say one thing that you are really a dedicated one for the party.

The two boys smiled and took the respective path to their respective destination.

When Sundar finally get his jobs done, it has crossed the midnight boundary long back. Get some sleep man, tomorrow you will have to catch the train at 9:50 AM, he uttered to himself. He flattened his mattress on the floor and let himself lay down. It did not take more than some minutes and he lost his consciousness.

The 9:50 AM train is one of the most important trains because of three reasons, firstly it is the last train for the daily office goers from the area as the next train is just after two long hours so if you fail to avail this particular train then it perhaps is better to apply for a leave for the day than to go to office. Secondly for the college and university students, this is the train with most suitable timing and finally the local milk men who goes to the city to sell their daily produces use this train and used to return in the late evening train after spending the day in the city collecting the previous day's dues. All the three kind of passengers are generally quite good in numbers and have their separate groups and each of those groups typically avail specific compartments also. They generally avail the same compartment daily and surprisingly even the same place of that specific compartment for their daily journey. Each of them generally enjoy the journey in groups and pass the time by playing cards and gossiping within. These kind of groups sometimes become very helpful for the irregular or seasonal passengers as they are always in a good numbers and somewhere in their mind a sense gets developed that as they are regular passengers so they have more rights and responsibilities than the irregular or seasonal passengers, but at the same time this "more rights" feeling creates problems also. They somehow assume that the irregular or seasonal passengers must always listen to their advices or should I say directions as because they are daily passengers and have that "more rights". This is the way it is going on for how many years or may be decades no one knows and probably the same way it will go on forever.

It was just like another day for Sundar. In the morning he woke up early and after completing his daily work out practices and tuition class he was ready for going to his work. His ancestral house was at a walking distance from the railway station, so he generally starts two to three minutes before the scheduled time of the train. But that day he had to go to the station a bit earlier to deliver some documents, which he has prepared last night for Akhilesh, one of his co-worker in the party. As Akhilesh in turn will have to hand over the same to another party worker who will wait for him in front of the factory where he works which is by the river Ganga, and finally the same papers will be distributed to the factory workers. So he started a bit earlier and reached the station fifteen minutes before his normal time of reaching station every day. Akhilesh was waiting for him outside the station in Mahim's tea stall as per the schedule. Sundar delivered the papers to Akhilesh, who then swiftly put those in his bag. Akhilesh ordered for two cups of tea for himself and Sundar. After the tea Akhilesh went out for his next assignment and Sundar moved towards the platform.

Like every other day Sundar let himself sat on the bench under the specific tree where he use to seat. Everything was as usual unless a hue and cry attracted his attention towards a place hardly fifty feet away from the wooden bench which he was seating on. He noticed that some people have surrounded three men, one elderly man and two young boys and are shouting not only in a very offensive gesticulation but with offensive language also, as if they are so angry that any point in time they can even pursue those three people with physical assault. On the other hand the elderly man out of those three people was trying to say something but neither he was allowed to speak nor any one from the shouting men was ready to listen to him and the two boys were just trying to get out of that situation. Their facial expression was saying their state of mind which could only be termed as terrified. Other passengers awaiting the train were staring at that cacophony from distance but none was making any effort to stop that or at least listen to that man who was trying to say something. There was even not a single person who was interested to rescue the elderly man and the two young boys from that violent group.

What are they shouting for, anything serious, Sundar asked one of the co-passenger who came after him and was seating by him on the bench. I don't know, may be pickpockets, the man answered casually. Pickpockets, they are not looking so, Sundar uttered in his mind and with a curiosity to know what exactly has happened walked to that place. He easily identified Sanatan Ghosh, the leader of those people who were shouting. Sanatan Ghosh, a man almost at his early fifty was a very rich person from a village in the nearby. He not only had the largest dairy but also had many sources of income which actually created a sense of superiority and an arrogant attitude in him. The elderly man with two young boys was speaking in a broken Bengali, it seemed from his tone that he was not a local fellow and what all he was trying to ask those arrogant group was what wrong had he said? The two young boys were saying unanimously in a mild voice, we don't need anything, just let us go. But no one was listening to them. They were trying to pull the elderly man out of the chaos but the way they were surrounded by the group, it was tough unless the group let them pass out.

Out of the same curiosity Sundar slowly enter in to the group by replacing one or two from the outer circle and asked one of those shouting people what happened? Why are you shouting on the elderly man?

The man whom Sundar asked stared at Sundar and replied, those three idiots have ruined one of our tub full of milk, and added, now who will pay for that. Sundar then slowly moved towards the elderly man bypassing the man he had just asked about the matter and some others of his group. He gently knocked the elderly man and when the man turned to him he asked the elderly man, have you or any of you really ruined their tub of milk. Finding someone asking something with a moderate attitude the elderly man also got some chance to say what he was trying for quite a long time. He looked at Sundar and he said, yes it is true that unfortunately one of my young sons has dropped his towel in the pot but that was really unintentional. He added, we did not have any intension to do any harm to them. His eyes and expression was clearly saying that the man is not lying.

When the man was talking to Sundar, Sanatan came forward and almost barked at the man, I do not want to know it was intentional or unintentional, he paused and continued, but as the jar of milk has been dirtied so you will have to pay the price for the same, otherwise I know very well how to claim our dues. Though Sanatan showed an authoritative and rough attitude but he was speaking legal so Sundar had no point to counter. He looked at the elderly man and asked whether he could pay the price? The man replied, yes, I am ready to pay the price and I was trying to say the same thing from the very beginning but there was hardly anyone who was eager to listen to us. The man paid the price to Sanatan without any hindrance and then he asked Sanatan, when I have paid the price for the milk then the milk belongs to me and you should give it to me.

Sanatan denied with an insulting smile and said, you must consider yourself and about your companions fortunate that you all are fortunate enough that your wrong doing is being waved off and now if you do not leave the place right away and demand for the milk then it will surely cause you people to be landed in the hospital. The elderly man was brave enough and did not set back, he asked Sanatan, I have bought the milk and now the milk should belongs to me. Sanatan lost his mind and was just in the way of thrashing the man when Sundar instinctively caught his hand and asked looking directly at Sanatan's eyes, what the wrong the man is saying? He added, he has paid for the milk and now it should be handed over to him only. It is no way your property now.

Sanatan was a bit shocked as he never expected that a boy as young as his son's age could hold his hand publically and that too asking questions to him. His entire rage fall on Sundar and with voice loud and rough enough to be called as a shout he asked Sundar, do you know whose hand you are holding?

Sundar with a placid voice replied, I don't need to know whose hand I am holding as far as I am not doing anything wrong. Sanatan tried to free his hand with a shudder but failed. He then tried with all the force he could employ but understood that the boy is a tough nut to crack. Sundar till now was holding Sanatan's hand with the most placid expression any man could hold at such a juncture of any incident like this one. Now with same calm voice he asked, are you done or would like to try for some times more? Sanatan was shocked, his group members were also shocked by the coolest arrogance and answer but that was for a moment. The next moment some of them started pushing Sundar but could not free their leader from the grip of the unknown boy.

Sanatan pointed his eye to those who were with him and said, at least thirty to forty people are there with me and you should keep that in mind. He added to show his authority, otherwise in my one order you will be crushed and thrown out of the station just like a street dog.

It was much more than what was required to ignite the anger in Sundar. Son I don't need the milk, suddenly the elderly man intervene and said to Sundar, you leave that man. He added, you are alone and heavily outnumbered. But what the simple man failed to understand that the issue is not the milk any more, rather it has become a matter of tussle between righteousness and wrong. In the meantime the number of people who were silent viewers have also increased and from there some men who were well known to the area came forward and one of them, an elderly man came forward and asked Sanatan to give the milk to the man and at the same time asked Sundar to leave Sanatan's hand. Sanatan sensed that influential people are opposing him so he did not lengthen the tussle and obeyed the decision. Sundar's job was done so he also obeyed the decision and left Sanatan free. But Sanatan's last words mentioning "street dog" were still burning his soul. This is not the time and the issue is not over, he uttered to himself and maintained the calm for that moment.

Meanwhile the train arrived and everyone except Sundar board the train. Sundar cancelled his job for the day and from the station directly came to Surya's house.

What are you doing here at this time, Surya was astonished seeing Sundar in such an unexpected time. Have you not attended your office today, is there any urgent meeting, Surya added. Sundar found Surya da was preparing to go somewhere so he just bypassed the question and asked, where you are going. Surya replied that he had three meeting that day. Sundar asked to join and was more than welcomed by Surya. The duo set out as per the schedule.

They spent the entire day by roaming from one place to another as per the meetings scheduled by Surya. Visited many villages and party workers, attended the three meetings and distributed documents and pamphlets among the party members. Surya noticed that Sundar was typically shy during the course of the day, which is exactly the opposite of his nature. Finally Surya could not resist himself to ask, Sundar I have been watching you from the morning and today you are typically shy, is there any problem? He added, this is exactly the opposite of you. If I could help you, you can tell me.

Sundar with a smile replied, everything is as it is and nothing special has happened. You don't worry, you will be the first person I will share my problem with. Surya smiled in return and nodded.

They stopped at the tea shop just outside the main market of their area but on the main road where they always used to stop for tea. Some other boys of their age and locality were already there enjoying their time. It was late evening and surprisingly after the first round of tea, Sundar ordered for the second cup of tea. In the complete course of time Surya noticed that Sundar was curiously looking at the road as if he is waiting for someone but Surya did not ask any question as he knew his friend very closely and was confident that Sundar will only share his mind when he will decide to share otherwise it is impossible for anyone to force him to share something or even cross the mighty walls that he has built around his inner mind. Those walls are impregnable.

The second cup was not even finished when the body language of Sundar changed snappishly. Suddenly his eyes became narrowed, he kept the unfinished cup aside on the bench they were seating and nonchalantly walked to the middle of the road. Surya and all other boys noticed that he had stopped two cyclist on the middle of the road by holding the handles of their bicycle and one of them has actually fallen on the ground losing his balance and the other one has somehow managed to balance and standing on the road. Surya sensed something must have happened. He said all the boys, come with me, there must be something wrong. All the other boys followed their caller to the spot. Surya identified the man standing on the road as Sanatan Ghosh, then he stared at Sundar and asked, what happened?

Sundar's feeling was clear from his facial expression. He did not reply to Surya rather asked Sanatan, so, now you thrash and throw me like a street dog as you said in the morning. He added, I hope you have not yet forgotten, or should I remind you the way I think fit for you. The second man who had fallen on the ground is now standing by Sanatan and in a very low voice requesting for something to Sundar, who did not even bother to look at the man. His eyes were fixed on Sanatan.

Sanatan had understood that his morning misbehave is taking its toll. Surya intervene and asked Sanatan, what is the issue? Sanatan as if was waiting for the moment and he suddenly with a very low and wretched voice and in folded hands replied, actually I have unfortunately committed a mistake in the morning, he added, I am ready to ask for the forgiveness for the same. Surya and all the other boys looked at Sundar and Sundar depicted what actually happened in the morning and with an angry, rough and determined attitude told Sanatan, now I will show you what is called thrashing someone like a street dog. The other boys in the group were actually enjoying Sanatan's humiliation as they all knew him and his attitude. They in their inner mind were actually wanted and so encouraging Sundar to thrash Sanatan.

Surya was the only person who understood that the situation will go beyond control if not stopped right at that moment. He turned at them and almost barked on them to stop fuelling Sundar's anger. The boys though unwillingly but had to stop. He suddenly ordered Sanatan with a rough attitude and loud voice, your offence could only be forgiven if you ask for mercy to him, pointing at Sundar, and that too seating on your knees with your hands folded. Sanatan was as if just waiting for something like this. He promptly sat on his knee and with folded hands ask for mercy to Sundar and also promised that he will never ever repeat such mistake. Sundar understood that Surya da had in fact managed the situation from becoming worse so he also with an authoritative attitude said Sanatan, go home and always remind this day before doing any misbehave to anyone. He paused for moments and then added, keep in mind that it hardly takes any time to get the position changed.

Sanatan and his fellow just disappeared from there as quick as it was possible for them. The boys returned to the tea shop. Sundar ordered another round of tea.

Surya looked at Sundar with a smile in his face and said, I smelled something has happened seeing your shyness but this is really much more than something.

PROVE IT ...

I think we should go for formal registration of our club, Surya said to his other two companions seating in the tea shop.

In the morning of a chilling winter Patru and Suren was more interested in the cup of tea and the newspaper than anything else and more precisely any such complicated issues line registration of the club and the legalities of the same and all. Just before some minutes ago almost a serious situation was created between the two regarding who will read the front page first. Somehow Surya has managed the situation and now Suren was reading the front page with a pride of winning and Patru has to satisfy himself with the page containing the news of sports and games. Nobody actually showed any interest to what Surya has just told to them anonymously and that was enough to irritate the speaker. I am saying something important to you people, so this is time Surya with a louder voice repeated that he is telling something important. Or should I torn the papers apart to get a slice of your valuable time, he completed staring to the two. It was good enough to attract attention of both the concentrating readers. They simply stared at each other and folded the respective part of the newspaper at their possession and kept that aside.

Which club you are talking about? Patru raised his face and asked gazing at Surya. Surya with a bitter mood asked in reply, how many clubs do we have? He paused for moments and continued, the registration is extremely important and if that is done properly then no one even in future also will have the right to dislodge the club from the place it is standing now or the members from the club. But who will try to displace the club or us from there, Patru asked with surprise. Surya shook his head and replied, I know what you are saying is okay but on top of everything we must have a legal document in support of our being there and moreover the same will help us establish our claims in future.

Suren now intervened and said, Surya da I think before finalizing anything we must call a general meeting among all the members and only then we can decide if majority votes for this plan. Surya turned at Suren with an irritated face and replied in a rebuking tone, who are those mighty members? When necessity arises, there are only five to six people and in case of decision taking fifty will come to basically create hurdles. He paused and arranged his words and said, today evening in the club I will talk to Sundar, Biswa and Gopal and finalize this. It was clear to Suren and Patru that somehow Surya da is serious in this matter so they did not oppose, rather agreed that they will also be there in the evening. The discussion was over for that time.

The day was too long to complete for Surya. In fact he was eagerly waiting to discuss the matter with Sundar, his closest companion and strongest support. He knew that Sundar has gone to his office and will be available only when he will return in the evening, so Surya had no other option but to wait until the evening. He has talked to Gopal in between and agreed him on the matter and now he has to agree Sundar and Biswa, for both of them he will have to wait some more hours. He finally decided to spend the time by attending some political meetings in nearby villages to make himself busy. As it always happen to everybody that you can join a meeting at any time on your choice but generally get rid of it when others let you go. When Surya finally returned to his village it was already evening and found all other including Sundar and Biswa waiting for him in the club. By the way the place they call 'Club" is basically an elevated 8 feet by 8 feet platform under the banyan tree made by bamboo and covered with straw for the protection from rain mainly. Surya first placed his bicycle beside the platform and joined the people.

Patru informed me that you have something very important to discuss with us regarding the formal registration of the club, Sundar asked while smoking the cigarette. Before saying anything or coming to the point Surya gestured to Sundar asking him to pass the cigarette. Sundar passed the same and after one or two puff when he found that everyone is looking at him with utmost curiosity, he replied with highest level of energy he could gather in his voice, I have decided that the formal registration of our club is the most important thing we should concentrate on right now. And for your information about that I have already talked to one of my maternal uncle who is a lawyer. He paused for a moment and continued, my uncle has assured to help us about the registration and also have informed me that we just need to give the address and a committee details of the club and rest will be done by him and his associates. Surya continued, in a specific venue, which my uncle will inform us in due course beforehand, the committee members will only have to be physically present in the judiciary for the final enrollment process. And most importantly he will not charge anything from us except the registration fee and the stamp fee, which we will have to manage.

Biswa asked, only that stamp and registration charge or there are some other costs to be taken care off. Surya replied that he has also discussed the same with his uncle and he has told that is not very high and he will also manage the same so that they will have to pay the least possible amount. Everyone happily supported the proposal except Sundar. Surya knew that Sundar will be the person who will enquire the most before going in to it, but once he is satisfied he will be the man to fight for the cause even more than any other, including Surya himself. Seeing him seating silent Surya asked his consent, so what do you say Sundar? Should not we grab the opportunity? Sundar shook his head and said, Surya da everything seems to be okay and a committee could be formed any time, even now itself if required, but the question is what about the address of the club? He continued, if I am not wrong then this temporary makeshift platform made of bamboo and straw is even less than the least that could be cited as an address. He patted on the platform they all were seating. It was a valid point that made everyone silent on this matter. Sundar continued, a proper room is the minimum criterion for an address to be mentioned in any legal affair, he paused and added, but it will incur a cost and now the main concern should be the room. Again for building a room we will need resources and the question comes here is where from and how the amount would be arranged.

After that the discussion continued for long and many plans came from each and every one but nothing got finalized.

DOWN THE LINE TWO DAYS

Boys, good news for all of us....

Surya's happiness of achieving something very valuable was visible on his face as well as from his body language. He almost threw his bicycle and jumped on the makeshift bamboo platform to take his seat. What happened? What makes you jumping like a frog, Biswa asked in irritation and interest both. Irritation as Surya while taking his seat almost leaped on Biswas lap which has injured him a little, but that is negligible. Interested because from the last day they discussed about the room and all, they seem to have failed to find out even a single option which could materialize their dream. And certainly now Surya has come up with a solution and that too so happily that means he has got something which would or at least could solve their problem.

Surya took a cigarette out from his pocket and ignite it first. After a long haul and throwing a good chunk of thick white smoke stared at the other people who were eagerly looking at him.

I have got a person who has agreed to sponsor the room for the club, Surya da announced. It was todays after the last meeting in the same place on this topic Surya has come up with a sponsor, everyone present was amazed. They looked at him with all the curiosities about who the person is. Surya with a wide smile on his face continued, I have talked to Avinandan Mukherjee and Mr. Mukherjee has agreed to sponsor the club room. We won't have to spend a penny from our pocket.

Avinandan Mukherjee was from a well to do family from the locality and also a local political leader with an ambitious mind and cunning nature. He had tried his luck in the local body election many times but never succeeded. This time also he is trying his luck in the local body election which is going to happen in next three to four months.

Surya da have you thought, why a calculative man like Avinandan would sponsor our cause? Patru asked. Surya never expected that question in such a straight and direct fashion, he answered with mumbling tone, actually Avinandan has offered me, rather us a deal. And what that great deal is all about, this time Sundar intervened. Surya arranged his words before commenting and then after a few moments he said, the deal is Avinandan will sponsor the room and in return in the coming local body election we will support and promote him. This is not that bad a deal, means it's a win for both of us, Surya completed but this time his expression was not that jovial as it was just some minutes before.

For some moments nobody talked and everyone was looking at each other. Sundar first opened his mind, so we are going to support a greedy politically ambitious cunning person just to have a room which we would call our club, right. He added, Surya da, I don't know what other present here would say but I am sorry to say that my ideology and personal feelings does not support this decision. Biswa was as if waiting for someone to speak against the proposal and he got what he was waiting for from Sundar. Surya da, I also don't think this is the best way to have what we need, spontaneously he supported Sundar. Suren also expressed his incredulity on this proposal. Now all the members were looking at Surya for his remarks. Surya was silently listening to all and now when his turn came he with a strong voice supported the boys but at the same time he asked, but tell me one thing, do we have any other feasible option to achieve the ultimate target, a club room.

First of all, let us have a proper costing of the work in details and then only we could try to develop a strategy for the same, Sundar replied. This time he is serious and Surya could well understand from the tone as he is the man who knows Sundar the most amongst all seating there. Patru intervened and said, I believe we must contact Kashinath, the only member of the club who is a mason by profession and he could easily provide an estimation of expenditures. Everyone supported that and Suren was sent to call Kashinath from his house which is just a walking distance from the place.

Suren came back with Kashinath within few minutes. Kashinath was a bit surprised of such an emergency call and that was clear from his facial expression. Sundar understood that and to normalize the situation he asked Kashinath, why you don't come here whenever you get free time. He added, this will keep your mind fresh from the daily hazards you have to face in your work life. We all do that. Kashinath smiled in return and nodded. Sundar came to the point then and said, actually we are planning to build a room for the club and we need to know what it would cost to build such a standard size room. Kashinath thought for a while and what he told was too much for the boys to accumulate. The situation was tensed and the team started asking detailed questions on how the cost could be reduced. Kashinath got involved into it and started providing details like approximately how many bricks will be needed, what should the least amount of cement be invested, so on and so forth. After a long brainstorming session it was finalized that bricks could be managed on request from the local bricks fields as a donation as all the owners of the bricks fields are local and well known to someone or the other. All other thing could also be arranged within affordable cost but the main problem is arranging cements as that is a costly item and no one is going to donate that for free. Suddenly Kashinath came with an incredible solution. He proposed, why we don't use fine mud from the riverbed and mix that with adhesive in place of cement as it was used in the constructions of earlier days and for the roof I propose corrugated tin plate which again is cheaper. He continued, yes that will increase the labor cost a bit, but all the labors are from the village itself and that cost is almost negligible compared to the cost of buying cements from the market.

From the glowing eyes it was clear that the idea has touched the perfect string in everyone's mind. Surya said, then the only things we have to manage are Kashinath's wage and transportation cost. He added, now transportation will be done by the club members by themselves so that is done. Now everyone looked at Kashinath to know what he will charge for the job. Kashinath promised that he will only take the lowest possible wage.

Next day onwards the boys started their venture to accumulate resources by meeting several people, requesting them and agreeing them to donate. Some donated, some rejected and some other asked them to come after some days. As Sundar and Biswa had to go to their respective job everyday so Patru and Suren accepted the responsibility of carrying bricks and other necessary things to the ground where the proposed room has been planned for. Kashinath used to visit once in the afternoon to watch the progress and one day he suggested that the work could be started with the already accumulated resources. Surya suggested that next day a small religious ritual will be performed and then the work will start.

As per the plan next day a priest was called and a small puja was arranged before starting the work. Bless this room so that it stays for years, suddenly Biswa asked the priest. The priest with a smile of satisfaction suggested the boys to ask the same from the God.

Believe me my friends, the same one room structure is still standing with all of its might on the same place till date and without even a single change or modification made in the following decades, except some ornamental beautifications.

The masonry work raised the eyebrows of the people of the locality. They were in dilemma that where the boys arranging the resources from and who is paying the cost. It had already decided amongst the members that no one will speak or discuss anything to anybody regarding the work and so no information was available to the people to satisfy their curiosity which actually made them more curious and also skeptic about the project. Kashinath involved his brother as a helper in his job so that it could pace the work faster. Sundar and Surya was more involved in exploring their personal relations with various people in various places to accumulate resources and Patru and Suren was actually helping and monitoring the day to day work. Biswa was more involved in planning and directing Kashinath and his brother in their work.

Avinandan was astonished probably the most out of all. He employed all his sources to find out the sponsor behind the curtain but even after many desperate attempts he failed to find out anything. The more the structure was taking its shape, the more impatient he was becoming. Finally he took a drastic step one day. He gathered some seniors from the village and instigated them to protest and close the work. He asked them about the ownership of the land and also conveyed that such a room where the young boys could do anything within the walls and being unnoticed, would become a threat to the peacefulness of the village. He also suggested that as the seniors of the village they must stop the work right away. It did not take long for a seasoned politician like him to get appreciation from his listeners. He was happy that half of the job is done and now the rest half is to be done. He announced that if we need to do something then why to wait, Avinandan was in no mood to delay the venture. He leaded those group of senior people to the place where Kashinath and his brother was working and Patru and Suren helping them.

Reaching the spot Avinandan requested Radha Raman Gangully, the most senior in the group, Radha da you are the most senior among us and I request you to lead us as your experience and honor will be the best to counter these hooligans. Radha Raman shook his head in affirmation and came forward to face the boys. Are you the owner of the land, the old man chased Suren directly. Suren could not understand the question clearly and stared at Patru who was again at the same dilemma. Radha Raman continued, first go and bring the legal paper and then start the building. He did not stop there and added, by the way who has permitted you to build a structure here and who is your leader, Surya or Sundar? Where are they?

Suren and Patru tried to calm the old men down but Avinandan did not allow them to do so and intervened, do you know, if I complain to the law and administration, you boys will be arrested straight way and spend the rest of your life in jail. He rebuked Kashinath and his brother too for working here. Finally they forcefully stopped the work and ordered the boys to leave that place.

Who is Avinandan to direct us whether we should build the room or not? Is he the owner of the land? Sundar asked to no one but to everyone present in the tea stall adjacent to the railway station. Surya with Kashinath Suren and Patru was waiting in the railway station for Sundar and Biswa to return from their jobs. Suren described in details what happened today and it was clear from his voice that he is afraid of the situation. Okay, tomorrow I will talk to Avinandan, Surya tried to neutralize Sundar's mood understanding what is going in his mind, but failed. No, the work will resume from tomorrow and I will be present there, Sundar stared back and replied. Surya was just expecting something like this and he knows Sundar much more than others. He could expect which direction the situation is turning to. He tried his best with the last option in hand almost knowingly that there is hardly any chance that the option will work. But you have your office, Surya said. Sundar stared at Surya and with the most determined and coolest possible voice replied, I am taking a leave and that is final, I will be there tomorrow from morning. He then stared at Kashinath and said, both you and your brother must be there at work at the earliest. Kashinath looked at Surya. Surya silently gestured him to uphold to what Sundar has just said. I too will be there tomorrow, Biswa announced at the last.

Kashinath and his brother was involved in their job and Patru and Suren was helping them. Seating on the bamboo platform Sundar was actually preparing himself for the confrontation that will arise soon. Surya and Biswa was accompanying him. Suddenly Sundar saw Bappa, a teenaged boy from the same village was passing by the place. Bappa come here once, Sundar called the boy and once the boy approached, he asked, can you do me a favor? The boy nodded happily. Sundar continued, then please go to Avinandan uncle's house and tell him that the masonry work has again been started in the field. All others were staring at Sundar. Once Bappa left the place he looked at Surya and asked for a smoke. Have you lost your mind, Surya asked Sundar while handing him over what he has just asked for. When we will have to face something sooner or later, then why not right away, Sundar said in return.

They had to wait for nearly an hour after Bappa left the place when they noticed Avinandan was coming towards them and Patru and Suren both confirmed that this time with more people than yesterday.

I warned you to stop this nonsense and you guys are carrying it till now, Avinandan barked on Kashinath and his brother. Kashinath replied that he has been ordered to carry out the work by the boys of the club and started at Surya and Sundar. Both of them had already jumped off the bamboo platform and was moving towards Avinandan.

So you are the leaders, Avinandan this time chased the young duo.

What is your problem? A direct question from Sundar that mumbled his chaser for a while. In the mean while an old person from the team following Avinandan remarked that this is an issue to be discussed in the village with the senior people.

Sundar came forward and with proper respect, addressed the old man as uncle and informed pointing at Avinandan, uncle this is the person who some days ago wanted to sponsor this club room. He added, would you senior people ask this man why he is opposing something today which he was even ready to sponsor from his own pocket just before two to three weeks.

Avinandan found all the eyes were following him. I thought earlier that this will be beneficial to the villagers, Avinandan replied.

And what happened or you witnessed within this three weeks that changed your mind on this and from beneficial it became harmful for the village and its people? Sundar was questioning a man doubly aged than him. Senior people who were with Avinandan started discussing in within and different opinions were coming out from various corner of the gathering behind Avinandan. Seeing the situation skipping from his hand Avinandan asked Sundar almost shouting, are you the owner of the land?

No, but are you the owner of the land? Sundar replied. He continued, if "no" then who are you to stop us? Are you the law and order? Administration? Court of law? What you are? You are nothing but a three times defeated "locally world famous" leader.

The last line made everyone smile except one who was actually burning from the core of his existence, Avinandan. He left the place but before leaving his eyes said clearly that he will not let this boys go very easily on this.

And do remember one thing now onwards, don't ever try to establish wrong over righteousness, Sundar said, you will always find me in front of you then and I promise that would be something you would curse yourself for rest of your life.

No one after that day intervened the work and within next three weeks two rooms stood up there. Actually the number of bricks collected from various sources was much more than required for the planned room, so the boys decided to build another room where they planned to run a free tuition center for the students from the poor families of the locality. Surya finally achieved his goal of registering the club. The free coaching center was also became popular in the locality. The boys started contributing in the coaching center in their free times. For next one month everything ran as picture perfect but suddenly one day the situation changed. The local body election was announced and on that day in the afternoon a rally was scheduled in that area by the ruling party which was to be leaded by a very famous leader Mr. Agnishwar Majumdar. Agnishwar was a very senior and popular leader with various social involvements and also a Member of Parliament. The village was under his constituency and from there Avinandan was fighting the election under the same political banner.

That was a Sunday and the boys were gathered in the club when a person from the local police station arrived at the door of the club. Who is Surya and Sundar, he asked anonymously. Surya and Sundar came out of the room and

Surya said, I am Surya and he is Sundar, pointing his finger to Sundar who was standing by him. You two have been summoned to the local police station, the man announced. When we would have to be present, asked Sundar. Right now, come with me, the man uttered and turned back to move. The boys looked at each other and then with a dilemma in mind the duo followed the man.

Though initially they were dazed but the reason became clear when they were told by the officer in charge in the police station that a report has been launched against carrying out illegal and unsocial activities in the club. They are being directed to close the club rooms unless they could arrange a legal order on opening the same. Surya tried to negate all the allegations his best but that yielded no result. Sundar was standing silently and just before leaving the place he asked about only one thing, who had launched the complaint? It was expected, Avinandan Mukherjee. Both of them searched for Avinandan to talk on the matter but did not manage to trace his whereabouts as he was busy on the arrangements for the rally.

In the evening when all the boys were seating on their old place Dhruba certainly brought the most awaited news. He has seen Avinandan inviting Mr. Agnishwar Majumdar and other leaders to his home and they are going to have an internal meeting there. The news just sparked the boys and all of them moved for Avinandan's house.

Agnishwar Majumdar was seating in the main position and all others surrounding him when the boys entered the room. So Agnishwar babu you and your party is selecting this liar, fraud, corrupted, greedy and power monger as the candidate with a hope of winning? Sundar directly throw his words to Agnishwar pointing his figure to Avinandan. It was more than enough for Avinandan and his followers to raise their voices with an aggressive attitude. Biswa came forward this time and said Avinandan directly, for your information we are in no mood to show our muscle power but if you and you followers insist us then we will not even bother to give you guys a good taste of that too. The situation was a mess with both the groups pushing each other when Mr. Agnishwar spoke out, stop this nonsense I said, a voice with dignity and authority. Everyone restrained them from going any further.

May I know who you boys are and what have instigated you to blame our choice of candidature in this election? In fact doing that you have raised a question mark on our party and its intelligence too. It was second time the man spoke and this time looking at Sundar directly. Surya came forward and introduced himself first. He then depicted the entire occurrence from the very first day of his discussion with Avinandan to the present time when they are standing in the house of the same man.

Sensing the situation Avinandan said to Agnishwar, don't believe them sir, they are lying relentlessly.

Sundar replied, Okay, let us all move out of here and ask the people of the village if we are lying or if they had ever noticed any of us doing anything wrong in those room. He added, if Avinandan could prove his words we promise we will break those rooms down to dust by tomorrow but if he fails to prove I promise, I will torn him in to pieces.

Should we go Avinandan? Agnishwar asked directly looking at his candidate but received no answer. Avinandan was standing with his head down. Everything was clear to the seasoned politician. Just go to the police station and dismiss the complaint you have lodged unlawfully against these young boys, he ordered Avinandan. Then he turned towards the boys and continued, I admire your courage and honesty, but don't be so short tempered young boys. He added, I assure you, there will be no problem in future regarding this and even after that if there is any issue on this regards then directly come to my office. I promise you my cooperation.

They boys came out of the house with the widest possible smile on their faces. They have own both the battles with their own accord.

Be cool boy …

Which train for today Sundar?

The elderly man who asked Sundar the question was an office colleague, named Suvendu Haldar. A very senior person in the office and a dignified man. He was coming downstairs when he saw Sundar crossing the stairs two at a time. Noticing Suvendu, Sundar stopped and approached him. Don't know yet, going to check the roster and collect the chart from the office, Sundar replied smilingly. He asked then, and yours is. The same as usual Guwahati express, the elderly man replied. He continued, at this age it's very tough to match up with different schedule, you know. This is time for you people to do all that. I have almost scheduled the last few years that I will have here until retirement. Sundar smiled back and replied, not bad, I will remind your policy, may be after some thirty plus odd years. Both of them laughed simultaneously and took their respective ways to their next hop.

It was sometime at the middle of 1960s and Sundar had been working in the railways for last four to five years. Initially he was in the sorting section. At that time railway did not have todays' computerized ticketing system and tickets for each station from each station used to get printed in dimmed yellow soft board type thick papers. After getting printed all the tickets of a section used to get accumulated in the head office of the section and then it was the duty of the people of the Sorting Department to sort out those jumbled up tickets in to a predefined manner and after that those tickets were distributed to the counters of the specific stations of that section. After working some days there in the Sorting department Sundar was shifted to the Checking department and currently he is working in the checking department but for the long distance trains, more specifically mail and express trains. Though he was in a government job but have not left his political identity as well as involvement yet. But he was not carrying out those activities openly as it was not permitted for any government employee to be a part of any political establishment.

Sundar entered his office at the second floor. Chowdhury da give me the roster please, he asked the man responsible for maintain the roster in the office and currently seating across the large sized wooden table just in front of the entrance gate of the room. The man was concentrating on the newspaper and pushed the roster towards the seeker without even staring. Sundar after signing at his respective cell pushed the roster back to the man and asked, which train for me today. This time the man has to keep the newspaper aside to fetch another register from his desk and a seer irritation appears on his face as of doing such a great hard job. He checked for the register and replied, Howrah to Delhi express, 8:15 PM, platform 5.

Okay, and thank you for sharing this immensely valuable information, Sundar teased to irritate Chowdhury a little more and was successful as after turning back and getting out of the room he could still listen the man almost barking at him. Sundar then entered the next room and collected all the official papers, charts and documents that will be needed for his work of the day. He will have the responsibility of carrying his part of the duty from Howrah to Mughal Sarai, a very important station in between Howrah and Delhi where the section of the railway changes and the duty of the checking staffs from Howrah are to be handed over to their counterpart of that section.

The train was scheduled to leave Howrah in the evening at 8:15 and Sundar knows that he will have to work for long hours in the train so will not get chance to have his dinner until midnight. He thought to have some food before the duty is formally started. Chakraborty da I am going for my dinner and will be back on time, Sundar informed the leader of his team, the CIT (Chief Inspector of Tickets) for that day and went for food.

After having his food when he came back to the station the train was already placed and all the passengers had boarded in the train. As per the Indian culture the relatives, friends and family members of probably each of the passengers were there in heavy numbers to see off their beloved. There was not even a single window in the platform side which was free from those relatives and friends. Everyone who is not going to travel was busy asking the traveler for buying something for him or if there is a child then something for the child at least. The railway hawkers were shouting to advertise their saleable items in full swing and creating a huge hue and cry. Some people who arrived on the platform a bit late were still searching for the seat they have reserved and also creating disturbances for those who have already settled themselves in the train.

Sundar looked at the big clock fixed on the platform and hanging from its roof in the station. It was showing 8 o'clock, so there are still fifteen minutes left before the train will leave the station and will start its journey towards the destination and so will Sundar. He came in front of the Railway Mail Service boggy and decided to have a smoke, as on those days smoking was not banned in anywhere including Government offices or public places like it is now. He spotted a space free from all hustle bustle just in to the opposite corner of the platform and started his smoke when two of his colleagues of that day's journey, Mr. Sil and Mr. Sengupta came approached him.

Hey Sundar need your help man, Sengupta said.

Regarding what, Sundar asked back.

Sil is not feeling well today, Sengupta pointed to his companion and continued, so if you could help him by checking the two coaches under his jurisdiction. Which are the coaches, Sundar asked? Sengupta replied, those are just adjacent to the coaches under your jurisdiction. Okay, no issue I will do that, Sundar replied and looking at Sil said, give me the charts for your coach and you go and take a seat. But what happened to you, he asked Sil.

Don't know man, Sil replied, just from the evening, after I came office I started feeling drowsy and now I feel perhaps there is a fever too. He added, though not high but still feeling very week and not well. He handed over the charts to Sundar and went towards the RMS boggy to seat with ease.

Sil, Sengupta and Sundar were at the same age and good office friends who used to help one another from time to time in various issues, so Sundar did not hesitate to accept the added responsibility and suggested Sil to go to the RMS and take rest. He assured that Sil does not need to have any anxiety as he will complete the additional job with full care. Sil thanked him and went to the RMS coach to take rest. Sengupta and Sundar stood there unless the signal changed from red to yellow and the train whistled to announce the commencement of its journey and at the same time to inform those people, who were there in within the coaches of the train to see off their beloved, that the time has come for them to get down. In next one or two minutes from each of the door of all the coaches more people came out than stayed inside and the train also started moving with slow pace. Sundar and Sengupta boarded the train and Sengupta went for the coaches under his jurisdiction through the vestibules in the train and Sundar waited for ten to fifteen minutes to let the passengers finally settle down before he start to ask for and check for the tickets of the passengers.

Sundar spent almost twenty minutes standing in the door of one of the Air Conditioned compartments which was under his jurisdiction and then started his job. He had decided to check the two Air Conditioned compartments first as there used to be no local regular passengers, especially those returning from their offices. Generally local people try to avail the express trains for their return journey to home due to some reasons, firstly these trains will not stop at all the stations like the local suburban Electric Motion Unit coaches so the journey which used to be of more than an hour decreases to a forty minutes or even less and that too without any break, secondly as the train does not stop at each and every stations so the crowd also use to be much lesser than the same in the suburban trains which make the journey more comfortable and lucrative. Those regular people generally travel in the sleeper coaches sharing the seats with the person who have reserved the same for his long journey and normally a single sleeper seat is shared by four to five people including the owner and with the only consideration for the owner is by leaving the window seat for him. On the other hand, the owners of those reserved seats generally bear with this unauthorized access to their reserved property because of mainly two reasons, firstly they are usually tremendously outnumbered by those regular people and also not as united as those people and secondly the owners know that they have to bear with this only for an hour or so at the maximum so they generally don't react on this.

Finally Sundar started his duty after the period of time which he allowed for himself to wait outside in the pavement of the first Air-conditioned coach under his jurisdiction. The train was moving in a slow gear and there was absolute zero rush in the passengers. No hawker was allowed in the high priority air conditioned coach, which in those days was generally availed by the VIPs or by the high ranking government officials whose journeys used to be sponsored by the departments or by the resourceful people who had abundance of money to spend on such costly tickets. With a short and rapid gaze Sundar found all the passengers had already settled themselves in their respective seats and enjoying their journey either with the co-passengers or companions or family members. It took nearly half an hour for Sundar to complete the checking of tickets and reservations for the entire coach. Everything was completely alright. After checking the last person in the coach he was just moving towards the vestibule that leads to the second coach when he found the most senior person as well as the leader of their team for that day, the Chief Inspector of Tickets (CIT), Mr. Chakraborty was coming from the opposite side. He had also already noticed Sundar. Chakraborty approached Sundar and asked him whether he will be able to take care of the two additional coaches of Sil or he would need any help. Sundar replied, I have already talked to Sil and I have confirmed him that I will do it. He added, Chakraborty da you don't need to be worried about that and I don't need any help. And also suggested him to go to his coach and assured him that after completing the duty he will come to submit a report to him within Asansol, a nearly four hours journey from Howrah. With the assurance from Sundar, Chakraborty da was happy and replied with a smile, okay, by the way when I have to travel back the entire coach then let me be with you when you check the second air conditioned coach. He paused and added, after that I will move to the coaches under my jurisdiction. It was nice and both of them agreed and they entered the second coach.

The duo had almost completed examining the tickets for half of the coach when they first noticed an unnatural behavior in one of the coup they were yet to move in to. In that coup of four seats seven people were seating. Three middle aged gentlemen with valid reservations and tickets. Those two who were in the upper births were seating in their respective births but the third passenger in one of the lower birth was sharing his seat with two other young guys. And in the fourth seat there were two more young men seating. Sundar asked for the ticket to one of the young man from the group and the man handed him over one ticket.

The young batch was approximately at the age group of late twenties or early thirties and were seating with a single ticket. Sundar checked the ticket and found the age of the owner of the ticket mentioned is forty eight. It was a dubious situation. The person in whose name the ticket was booked is Mr. Laxman Chatterjee. Sundar asked the man, who is Mr. Laxman Chatterjee?

The man replied, dada has gone to washroom and will be back soon.

Sundar asked the people, so the ticket belongs to none of you. One from the group replied with a neglecting attitude and without looking at the questioner, yes none of us is the owner and the owner of the ticket is our elder brother and he has gone to the washroom and will be coming soon.

Then where are your tickets, the next question Sundar asked to the same man. The same man in the same attitude like earlier replied, we don't have tickets and we will get down at Gopalpur. In the mean while this arguments had attracted attention of the co-passengers of the adjacent seats and they were leaning to know what is happening. Sundar was not just irritated rather a bit humiliated and feeling tempted about the way the man was speaking. Chakraborty da interfered in to and asked the people, do you know gentlemen that this is a crime to travel without ticket in a train and that too in an air-conditioned compartment. The people just looked at the man and started laughing in such a manner that was more than humiliating. It was enough, but Sundar checked his temper and with a calm voice asked them, you guys are not allowed to occupy seats here and better you stand up and get out of the compartment. He added, and you would also have to pay the fine for the illegal job you have committed. That was even beyond the expectation for those people also and the man who was talking till then stood up and chase Sundar. He suddenly grabbed the collar of the shirt of Sundar and with a scary voice asked, do you know who we are and whom we are escorting?

Sundar with a sudden move grabbed the man's neck in his hand and in such a way that it could anytime be broken with a firm round. Locking the man's neck in his hand Sundar asked that man, I do not need to know who the hell you are or the man you are escorting, but I alone could be enough to through you and your boys out of this running train, which I believe would not be very healthy option for you. The other three were initially taken aback with such sudden change in the situation but it took moments for them to respond and they came in to an offensive position. One wrong move from any of you will leave your friend dead with a broken neck, Sundar coolly said towards the three.

All of a sudden a strong but cool voice came from behind Sundar, Ashoke, stop it and get aside. That was enough for the three to set back. Sundar felt that the man who was within his hand had also became cool. A middle aged man came in front of Sundar and asked the first of the four to leave the collar of Sundar. The man who was arguing with Sundar with so much of attitude just obeyed the order just like the best boy in a class obeys the teacher. Now the man looked at Sundar and with a smile and in a requesting mode said pointing to the boys, I am sorry for the mischiefs done by those boys and I am also ready to pay the fine for the four. He paused for a moment and then added, may I request you if you could leave the neck of the boy. Sundar left the neck of the man he was holding. May I know what the fine I need to pay is, the man again ask. This time Chakraborty intervened again and informed the amount. The middle aged man without any more argument paid the fine. The train in the meantime had arrived Gopalpur and the four people slipped out of the coach without even a single word.

Sundar came back to his duty when the middle aged man approached him again and asked him and Chakraborty, would both of you mind to come to my seat for some time. Sundar replied, sorry but I have to complete the checking for the rest of the passengers and nonetheless I am already delayed. The man with a thin smile replied, young man it would not be too late for you, and firmly added to the two, come join me for a while. Chakraborty da followed him and gestured Sundar also to follow. The three sat in the seat and the man first started the talk by asking Sundar, what is your name and where you are form. Sundar answered both the questions and asked the same to the man but he intentionally did not notice the question and again asked Sundar, it seems you have a great physic but don't you think you took a great risk of chasing four men together? He added, there should always be a difference between courage and inviting dangers. Sundar did not answer the question directly rather he by passed by saying, they were wrong and were doing something illegal and punishable, he paused and arranged his words, what I did was my job and also responsibility not only as a government servant but at the same time as a citizen. The man again smiled and nodded his head. Then he asked Sundar again, do you know what would have happened if I would not have come in the right time? It seemed to Sundar that there was a pinch of threat in the question for him and a boastfulness for the man himself. That sense generated a stubbornness in him and Sundar replied, then I think I would have thrown all four of them out of the train. This answer raised the eye borrow of the man and he laughed loudly, looked at Chakraborty and told him, I think you are his senior, he is a great boy but a bit hot headed. Take care of him.

Sundar was looking silently at the man. Then the man looked back to Sundar and with an appreciating smile patted on his shoulder and said, I appreciate your courage and that is what I expect from a young blood but be cool boy at least for the sake of God don't be so courageous that makes even people like us to think.

Sundar replied with a confident voice, sorry but I believe in myself more than anything else.

The man was stunned but he managed himself and replied, then for the sake of your parents. At least you have duties and responsibilities for them.

Sundar with the same cool voice replied, both of them had passed away long back. I was nothing more than a child then.

Everyone in the coup was silent. After a while the man told Sundar again, I am going to Delhi and will be back after twelve days. Please come to my house once, I would like to have a chat with a boy like you.

Sundar smiled and said, I asked you sometimes now, your name and place but you have not yet answered, so how do I know where to come and whom to meet?

The man this time laughed louder and replied that, ok, my name is Laxman Chatterjee and I am the Member of Parliament from Jagatpur, not a distant place from your village, right? So when are you coming?

It was the time when there was only one political party ruling almost all the states in Indian soil and was also in the central power with thumping majority. In West Bengal also the same party was in a strong hold and having many MLAs and MPs. One of those leaders and also an MP was Mr. Laxman Chatterjee, who once used to be a local goon who became a leader by the support of his group involved in many illegal activities and also the affluence he had earned through those means. Then he got the election ticket and became an MP subsequently due to his muscle power and no opponent in his area. Though that person was not a gentle man as per the definition and there were ample amount of criminal cases against him in various jurisdictions but at the same time he was kind of a Robin-Hood-type-of-character in his locality and constituency due to his engagements with the poor and needy people of the area and his helpings towards the poor which actually helped him to make his stature like that.

Everyone in the coach was astonished. Sundar was also shocked thinking that till then he was arguing with an honorable Member of Parliament, but he managed his expression and replied, Okay I will try to come as quick as possible after twelve days.

The train was reaching its next stop, Bardhhaman junction, Sundar and Chakraborty stood up as they had to complete their job of checking the coach wishing the man a good night.

After getting out of there Chakraborty asked Sundar, so when will you go to meet the MP.

Sundar looked at him with a smiling eye and replied, hopefully never.

The Cyclists ...

Dada we need your suggestion regarding an issue, Sundar stopped and turned back in astonishment as the voice was too familiar to him but he could expect his brother at this place and time the least.

Sundar had just arrived in the station from his office when Anil, his younger brother approached him with three other of his friends, Rishi, Sumanta and Dhruba. He was a bit shocked seeing all those boys in the railway station and that too waiting for him. Sundar asked in return, what happened, is there anything serious at home or in the village. Before Anil would have told anything, his friend and a close aid of Sundar, Dhruba answered, don't worry Sundar da, nothing serious anywhere, we actually have come to seek your suggestion and help regarding a tour we are planning for.

Sundar initially thought that they might be asking help on railway reservation or may be some financial contribution as generally had happened in the past in various cases. Hmm, would you guys like tea, Sundar asked the boys and moved towards the tea shop as it is his regular practice to have a cup of tea after returning from office in Mahim's tea stall. The boys nodded happily and followed Sundar to the stall.

So, what kind of help and suggestion you guys actually need, Sundar asked the boys while let himself seat on the bench outside the stall and at the same time ordered tea for all of them. All the four young boys were hesitating a bit and this time also Dhruba took the responsibility to depict their detailed plan of tour to Sundar.

He started in such a humble tone that if Sundar rejects they will drop the plan and said, actually Sundar da we are planning a bicycle tour to Murshidabad, and clarifies their plan more precisely by adding, planning means if you think we are capable of doing that only. Sundar was a bit taken aback but did not respond right away. He estimated in within his mind that the place Murshidabad will be at a distance of approximately two hundred kilometers from their village and with upward and downward journey, it will become almost four hundred kilometers. Travelling this long distance and that too on bicycle will not only be tough rather bone breaking. In the meantime the tea was served.

After a sip, Sundar raised his face and asked the four, do you know how far the place is. Almost all of them replied simultaneously the same distance that Sundar has calculated just in his mind. The answer he received from them and in such a details that convinced him that at least the boys have done their research very thoroughly before approaching to him for suggestion. Then Sundar asked, now tell me, what kind of suggestion you are seeking for from me.

Anil replied, we want you to be with us as a guide and team leader as this is our first bicycle tour, he paused for a moment and stared at his companions and continued, we are not confident enough to go without any senior. Sundar replied, to complete the tour it will need at least six to seven days and this will really be tough for me to manage leave for so many days. The boys were stubborn and kept on demanding which finally convinced Sundar to promise them that he will talk to his boss in the office next day and try for permission. Sundar was also bore out of his routine life of office, politics and club so he also got excited and mentally involved in this venture but did not express that and told the boys that he will talk to his boss next day regarding leave and then only he could assure them.

Shankar da I need a six days leave, this is highly critical, next day Sundar approached his boss Shankar Chatterjee in the lunch time. Shankar was seating in his table with loads of files. He raised his face and asked, six days would be too long. Is there any problem. Sundar thought for a moment and replied, not any problem but family requirement, you know. Okay, Shankar da replied and asked him, is there any specific reason. Sundar replied, yes, actually I will have to take my younger brothers to a short tour to Murshidabad. He intentionally did not disclosed that it is a bicycle tour. After thinking for some moments Shankar da granted him the leave and asked for the dates in which he is going to be absent. Sundar thought for a while and planned it from next Monday to Saturday to include both the Sundays before and after. Okay then, Shankar replied and added, apply formally by today. The leave was granted and Sundar was very happy. He completed rest of his works for the day and with a blooming mind took the return train for his home.

He found all the boys eagerly waiting for his return in the railway station itself. He told them, the good news is that I have managed a leave for next six days and moved to the nearest tea stall to plan the details of the tour. He suggested them, you guys write down a list of all the necessary things to be gathered which will be needed on the way. He continued, check the conditions of your bicycles and complete any necessary patch works if needed in next two three days so that we can start the journey as early as possible in the coming Sunday morning. Finally he asked them, now you people come with me to the local police station to request the officer-in-charge for granting us a letter depicting our journey so that we could request for shelter in the police stations for the nights on our journey.

Sumanta asked, we would rest in the police station. His voice clearly showed his panic. Sundar turned to him and assured, that is a safer place than any other places and I believe we don't have enough resources to manage a lodge or hotel for all. He paused and said, by the way in many places where we will have to spend the night do not even have any such hotel or lodge accommodation too. Sumanta nodded his head but the doubt in his mind was not clear.

The officer in charge was well known to Sundar and willingly wrote an authorization letter for them. Sundar kept that letter carefully with him and asked the boys to complete the jobs he had given them and at the same time gave them some money which they will need for the same.

THE JOURNEY STARTS

Sunday morning at 8 AM the boys and Sundar gathered at the predefined point in front of the local school where the journey will start from. Sundar first asked the boys regarding the arrangements and personally checked everything. Everything was perfectly arranged. The details of the arrangement said that the boys had really worked hard. The weather was also good and Sundar finally described the plan for today's journey to the boys. He depicted, today we will cover nearly 68 KM from this place to Nabadweep. He continued, today we will be covering places like Jirat, Guptipara, Kalna and Dhatrigram. I have planned that we will have our lunch at Kalna which is almost at a distance of 52 KM and if we can proceed as per the plan then we will reach Nabadweep late in the afternoon or early in the evening. He continued, as you all know that Nabadweep is a famous place and have many historical attractions to visit so tomorrow i.e. on Monday we will visit all those places and will stay at Nabadweep only. Day after we will start again. Sundar stopped and finally asked, any question. Everyone present shook their head. Sundar finally asked, if anyone of you have any doubt then I will say, we can cancel the tour right now, he added, but if you realize and say about the same in the mid-way then that will be a great problem to deal with. Everyone stared at the speaker and confirmed that they don't have any doubt in their mind regarding their capacity or the tour itself. Okay, let us then start, Sundar declared and the team paddled to their tour.

All these discussions and conversations took almost an hour to be completed and when finally the group started their journey for their next destination Nabadweep, it was showing 9 AM in the watch. Initially the energy level of the members were so high that Anil, Sumanta and Rishi started competing with one another as if they were in cycling race. This childish behavior took its toll and gifted fatigue in return to those over enthusiasts very soon. Just after cycling in that hurried manner, after crossing five to six kilometers the three boys became so exhausted that Sundar had to stop for the first time in the journey in a road side tea stall. After a tea break Sundar called them all and said, this is first and final warning to you all that there would be no racing from now onwards and the team will move together in a constant speed, he paused and added, our next stop will be at Guptipara only for another tea break.

The journey was becoming more exhausting with time as the sun was rising higher and the temperature too. They had to cycle nearly 20 KM to reach Jirat, a small place in between the place they started from and Guptipara. The team took nearly two and a half hours and reach Jirat nearly at 12:30 PM. Sumanta was feeling very tired and exhausted and so was Anil but none of them could accumulate the courage to convey their tiredness to Sundar. Sundar, Rishi and Dhruba again was showing no interest to break their journey at Jirat and were cycling as steadily as they started. To attract Sundar's attention on a short break Anil asked his elder brother, dada what is the distance from here to Guptipara? Sundar coolly replied, as per my calculation I think we have to travel nearly 20 KM more to reach Guptipara. Anil asked again, and how far is Kalna from there. In the same calm manner Sundar replied, from there Kalna is another 9 KM, he added, there we have planned to take our lunch.

The news that Guptipara was another 20 KM from Jirat and moreover in the calm and quite way of audacity Sundar replied to his brother that neither Anil nor Sumanta could gather mental strength enough to request for an additional stop over at Jirat. In the meantime they had covered nearly couple of kilometers from Jirat and both Anil and Sumanta became too tired to paddle continually anymore and out of sheer fatigue suddenly Sumanta first and then Anil stopped cycling under a big tree beside the road. Dhruba was cycling by their side and he was surprised seeing the two stopped, he asked, what happened to you, he added, we don't have any break planned here. Anil replied, it is impossible for me and I think for Sumanta also to keep on cycling anymore unless we get a short break. Sundar and Rishi had also stopped. After listening to Anil, Sundar looked at his watch and it was nearly 1:30 PM. Sundar asked a local man coming from opposite side, excuse me, can you please tell me what is the distance from here to Guptipara. The man thought for a moment and replied, I think you people have to travel nearly 15 KM more to reach Guptipara from here. Sundar thanked the man and calculated in brief, in that case they have to travel nearly 23 KM to Kalna and then another 26 KM to Nabadweep, so in total nearly 50 KM as per the plan by end of today. It seemed hard-hitting for those boys, especially for Anil and Sumanta but Sundar did not disclose anything and waited there.

The people waited there for nearly fifteen minutes and then they again started paddling. This time Sundar announced, be very much clear that we have to reach Guptipara by next one and a half hours and there they will have their lunch. He added, in between if anybody needs anymore rest then the tour is cancelled and I am going to return to home. The last line was more than enough to create a serious environment. Anil and Sumanta was feeling the heat more than their tiredness. Though it was tough and bone breaking for them but they kept on cycling and the team stopped nowhere in between and finally when they reached Guptipara the clock has just crossed the 3 PM mark.

They stopped in a road side hotel for their lunch and Sundar directed, please be informed that no one of us will be allowed to have heavy food, he paused and added, also no Rice because that will make us all feeling heavy-eyed. So we have only chapatti and vegetable. It took almost one hour to complete their lunch and when the team again sat on their bicycle it was 4 PM. It was conveyed to everybody that the next stop will be at Kalna for a tea and tiffin break and they have to cover this 23 KM stretch by next two and a half hours. The journey was terrible and they reached Kalna nearly at 7 PM with a five minutes stopover in between, which Sundar had to allow witnessing the condition of the boys. After an extended tea break of half an hour the team moved for their next and final destination for the day's journey, Nabadweep. Nabadweep was another 26 KM from Kalna. After a long and strenuous day this last 26 KM took more than three hours with several short breaks in between and when they reached Nabadweep it was nearly 11 PM.

Sundar from a road side hotel bought some chapatti and vegetable again for the team and after asking a local person from the same shop headed towards the local police station. The police station was nearby so the team reached there in five minutes. Sundar showed the application and authorization signed by the officer-in-charge he managed from the police station of his own area. They were well accepted and a corner of the room was allotted to them for the night. They took their dinner and arranged their own beddings, so nothing else was needed. Before going to bed Sundar said to the team, tomorrow we will visit the places in Nabadweep and we will have to start early to avoid rush. He added, we should be aiming to start as much as 8 in the morning. All the members nodded, willingly or not, is a question unanswered. They reached their bed and the extreme tiredness was much more than required for the boys to fall asleep by next two minutes, if not lesser.

Though the boys planned to start at 8 AM for the Nabadweep city tour but could not make it before 10 AM due to extreme fatigue of yesterday's journey. Almost everyone except Sundar and Dhruba was feeling muscle pain and more achingly pain in their back. Enquiring from the police station they found three main places of interest in Nabadweep, Golden Gouranga Temple, Sri Chaitanya Saraswat Math and Dwadas Lord Shiva Temple.

Before starting today's journey Sundar briefed the team, today we have a planning of visiting the famous places in Nabadweep and then move forward to Krishnanagar. He stopped and added, as you all know that Krishnanagar is a famous place due to its royal palace and temple. So after visiting Krishnanagar we will move forward to Muragacha and will stay there for the night. From Nabadweep to Krishnanagar we will have to cover a stretch of 20 KM and Muragacha is another 17 KM from Krishnanagar. Finally he stared at all the faces intensely and asked, are you ready for the same, think before you say yes. Every one of the team nodded to express their readiness and so the journey started.

All the places were nearby as Nabadweep is not a very vast town and they completed their visit within next two hours. Their energy levels were enhanced by their achievement of the first success of visiting places in Nabadweep. All the discussions were in and around those places and what they have seen. They started for Krishnanagar and planned to reach by next two hours and have their lunch there. It was a hot and humid day and the nature started taking its toll on the adventurists. Finally the team reached Krishnanagar at 2:30 PM with couple of short breaks in between.

Since long Krishnanagar is a famous place for its glorious past and mainly due to the most famous king Maharaja Krishna Chandra and one of his close aid Gopal. The most interesting and attractive thing for the boys was the Palace of the mighty King which was not very far also as per a local man to whom they asked about how to reach there. In next half an hour the team reached the

Singha-Duar – the main gate of the palace. All of them became shocked and speechless. They have heard so many stories of the glorious past of the city and the king from their grand generations like any other child in Bengal. Once the city was so wealthy that even the Nawab of Murshidabad was jealous of that but today the boys are actually standing in front of a ruin of a great architecture of the past. The king and kingship have gone and there was no one to take care of the enormous building and its artifacts. It should have been the duty of the government but they have lovingly forgotten their responsibilities. Some people are living with their families in some micro sections of that endless palace but many other portions have been destroyed due to no maintenance. Some portions are still standing tall but symptoms of destruction in near future is very much visible. Once there used to exist a great boundary wall which now is vanished except some pillars those are trying beyond their capability to stand and prove their mighty past.

Everyone was so shocked that there was no discussion on anything. They roam around the destruction and ruins for some time and finally decided to move forward to their next destination Debogram. The team decided to take lunch first as they have to travel a long distance to reach Debogram.

First lunch at a road side hotel and then a rest for 15 minutes, finally the team started its journey to Debogram at 4 PM. Very soon the speed slowed down to lower than average and the journey turned in to more a tedious and exhausting job than a thrilling adventure. Sundar was used to such long distance cycling as because of his social and political involvements, many times he had to travel to faraway villages on cycle and that too carrying Surya da along with himself. Dhruba and Rishi was also stretching themselves to the maximum possible limit and there was no doubt that in this first cycling tour of their life they were performing more than expected. The other two members, Anil and Sumanta was getting exhausted very frequently and the entire team was getting stacked for them. Finally when they reached Debogram the hands of the clock has crossed the 11:30 PM mark. They already had there dinner in between at a place called Muragacha, so they headed straight towards the local police station to request to allow them to stay there for the night.

Debogram was a small place, not more than a village and the police station was even smaller. Only one standard sized room with old walls and a three side open balcony. The officer allowed them to use one corner of that open balcony if they could. With no other option the boys arranged their makeshift beds there for the night and after such a bone breaking, day long journey it did not take any more time to became unconscious about the rest of the world. But unfortunately that did not last long. The night at Debogram police station became a nightmare due to ruthless attack from all possible sides by probably the most disturbing and deadly enemy of sleep, mosquitos.

I personally wish the mosquitos around the world must establish a union or organization like "*World Mosquito Federation*" or something like that and issue a universal ID card against a monthly, quarterly or yearly agreement of blood to be donated by human being and seeing that card no other mosquito will attack him anymore, Rishi woke up in the middle of the night and uttered either to himself or the other members or the mosquitos.

Every other member was feeling the same pain so everyone woke up and sat on their respective beds. The fatigue was more painful than the mosquitos. So after cursing those mosquitos for the maximum possible and making some clapping sounds for those failure attempts to kill as many as possible of them the boys laid down one by one. Finally the boys had to spend the night with cent percent fatigue and zero percent rest and on top of that a long journey of 60 KM was awaiting for them next day.

Next morning the boys did not wake up as they had not slept for the night so there was no question of waking up. They got prepared with all their bags and baggage by as early as 6 in the morning. When the group entered the nearby tea shop, the owner was just preparing his stove for the day. Sundar depicted other the plan of the day, as per the plan we have to reach Berhampur by the end of today from Debogram. He added, as per my planning, after every 10 KM we will take a break for thirty minutes and will have our lunch at Debkunda which is approximately in the middle of the journey. The boys nodded more in cumbersome than enthusiasm. Each of them consumed three cups of tea to push their energy level to the highest possible and the team started from Debogram at 8 AM.

Sundar da stop, get back, Sundar and Rishi was approximately 10 meter in front of the other three when they heard Dhruba calling them to stop. Firstly a sleepless night, secondly cycling nearly 140 KM in last two days and finally a hot and humid day jointly took its tax from the enthusiast boys just before entering Debkunda. Sumanta had fallen on the road from his cycle and had lost his sense. Sundar and Rishi returned in hurry. The boys lifted and lied Sumanta under a tree beside the road. Dhruba and Sundar went in search of water and the other two boys sat by their senseless companion. Within few minutes Sundar and Rishi returned with water in an earthen pot and found Sumanta had already regained his sense but still lying. His eyes were blood red and also had a high fever. Sundar was carrying some basic medicines with him including some for fever also expecting something like this could anytime happen. Would it be possible for you to cycle anymore, Sundar asked Sumanta. The boy did not speak, just shook his head to indicate his incapability.

Sundar sensing the criticality of the situation said, as Sumanta is not capable of cycling any more so I will carry him in my cycle. He paused for a moments and thought before he said, Dhruba could you manage to drive your cycle and manage Sumanta's with another hand at a time. Dhruba nodded and the journey resumed.

They reached Debkunda in next half an hour and entered in to a road side hotel for lunch. It was discussed that they will not return from so close to their destination and for rest of the journey Sundar, Dhruba and Rishi will carry Sumanta in rotation and any of the other two will manage two bicycles. Anil was exempted from any of this responsibilities. After lunch they took a long rest and waited for the sun to climb down and started again in the afternoon. Frequent breaks and lowest speed caused a long delay in reaching Berhampur. The team reached Berhampur nearly 11 PM.

They already had their dinner at Saragachi, so the team directly headed towards the police station. Berhampur is quite a big town and so was the police station. After getting permission from the officer-in-charge to spend the night there Sundar asked the officer, can we have a doctor for one of our teammate. He added pointing to Sumanta, he has been suffering in high fever and also got senseless some hours before. The officer looked at Sumanta and replied, yes certainly, just let me check with the doctor in the local government hospital. He then dialed a number from in his office telephone and talked to a person for some minutes. After keeping the phone down to its receiver he asked one of his junior and ordered, go to the doctor's quarter and take him here with you, he added, take my jeep.

The doctor, an elderly person, arrived in few minutes. He checked Sumanta and assured that there is no serious issue. Whatever has happened to him is due to the fatigue and excessive physical pressure. He then looked at the officer and said, when your man will drop me in my quarter I will give them some medicines for the boy. The doctor then encouraged the group and left.

Murshidabad is just 20 KM from here so before going to bed Sundar, Rishi and Dhruba decided that they start in the morning at 9 AM and also listed the visiting places. Regarding Sumanta the plan will remain same, the three will carry him one by one.

Murshidabad is one of the oldest town in Bengal and to be specific even much older than Calcutta, which itself is more than 300 years old. There are numerous famous places and museums in the city which are not only old but at the same time great examples of Indian architecture and engineering marvels.

Next day they started as per the plan. Sumanta was much better than yesterday because of the rest and obviously the medicines provided by the doctor. Though he tried to establish that he could but he was not allowed to cycle by other members of the team. Though he tried to convince that he could but it was Sundar's strict order that he would not be allowed to cycle. Sumanta had no other option but to obey the order.

Their first place of visit was The Hazarduari Palace, or the palace with a thousand doors. This palacc was built in 1837 for thc Nawab Najim Humaun Jah, descendent of Mir Zafar. It has thousand doors (among which only 900 are real) and 114 rooms and 8 galleries. Parallel to the north face of the Hazarduari Palace, stands the Nizamat Imambara, built in 1847 AD. After spending an hour or so and with a splendid experience they started for the next place in their list Nasipur Palace. This imposing structure was built by Nawab Murshid Quli Khan in 1723-24. It took half an hour to reach the place. It was no less beautiful and marvelous than the earlier one. The building was enormous in size but even the smallest pieces of the art works were exactly the same in shape and size. Every single piece is so symmetrical that it seems to be made by machines and not by human but originally when the building was developed there was no such machine. The boys roamed around place for some hours and then proceed to their next destination which is Katgola Palace, the palace garden of Raja Dhanpat Singh Dugar and Lakshmipat Singh Dugar and their famous Adinath Temple were built in 1873, by Harreck Chand. The walls of this temple are also intricately designed. A typically Jain style of ornamentation lends a unique beauty to this Jain temple. It is about half a km South-East of Mahimapur. Though some of its glory has been lost, it still remains a major tourist attraction, chiefly because of the beautiful temple with an admirable work of stucco. They also visited many other extremely valuable and extraordinary things like Jahankosha Canon & Khosh Bagh Garden.

After a full day excursion they returned to Berhampur by the evening with mesmerizing experiences. The officer in charge was waiting for them to listen their experiences and also he was worried about Sumanta's health. He was happy seeing the boys, more specifically Sumanta in a much better condition than last night and invited them to his quarter for dinner where the bachelor stays alone. It was more than expected for the boys to have home cooked foods and that to in the official quarter of a police officer. After dinner they talked for some time and described their tour from the beginning. Finally the officer asked the most vital question, so what is your plan for returning home, cycling back or would you avail the train. He added, I personally would not recommend you cycling back so long and more importantly with one member in a bad health condition. Sumanta supported the same and said, it is not possible for me to travel back the same way.

Now the question aroused that Sumanta could not be sent alone via train and one has to be with him. Anil was perhaps waiting for the chance and promptly replied, I am also unable to make the return journey by cycling as some dangerous and painful burning scars have already appeared in my back and those are really paining. He added, if you guys don't believe than I could even show the same. All started laughing and finally it was decided that Anil and Sumanta will return by train from Berhampur and the rest will return the same way they came here.

The next day was Thursday and as per plan Anil and Sumanta took the early morning train from Berhampur and the rest three after thanking the police officer, started cycling back to their village. This time they explicitly avoided to stay at Debogram police station as they already had a great experience of spending a night with mosquitos. They planned to return by Saturday but it took one more day for them and they reached their village on Sunday. First the three approached to the police station to thank the officer-in-charge and let him inform about their safe return and then they returned to their respective homes.

It is widely accepted that from the time unknown the youth had always been interested in challenging. Sometimes they had challenged the society, sometimes the monarchy, sometimes an established government or its policies, sometimes the age old social beliefs and customs, sometimes even more drastically the Mother Nature. If they have found nothing to challenge then many a times they have challenged themselves to test how far and how much they could stretch themselves and bear the pain of challenging. Undoubtedly some of them had lost the challenges and some had won but collectively all had earned great experiences out of these challenges.

HOW COULD YOU ...

While handing over a white envelope Satyendra said to Sundar, Suprakash has given it for you.

In that evening Suprakash, a boy from neighborhood came to meet Sundar in his house. Unfortunately Sundar was not present and he only got to know from his elder brother Satyendra when he handed Sundar over an envelope at his return. Only this one, Sundar asked his elder brother. He added, or there are others too. Satyendra shook his head to confirm that for today this is the only one. Sundar took that in his hand and looked at the same without any importance as this is kind of an everyday phenomenon as letters from various engagements including political and social use to come. It was already too late for dinner so he thought to have his dinner first and all the other things then after.

After dinner Sundar opened the envelope. A small piece of paper with some lines written on it,

Dear brother Sundar,

When you are reading this, I am far away from you. I never interacted with any of my students as much as I have with you. I still remember those sunny days of my life when we used to discuss on several things of life for hours. Those moments when we used to debate on various issues over cups of tea, are still alive in my heart and will remain forever. Even the pride I felt for you on the day I came to know that you have achieved the best possible in your school leaving exam is still in my mind as bright as it was that day. It is long enough, but not so old that those memories will be erased from my heart, and I believe those days are remaining in your heart too, just as it is in mine. I not only enjoyed but feel pride of being a teacher of yours. There is no confusion in my mind that you are the best student I have ever taught and you till do also have the potential to become the best in any field you choose to perform.

We spent nearly four years as friends, yes I mean it. You came to me as a student, became no less than younger brother and at the end of the show when I am writing this letter, you are probably the best friend I have ever had.

As much as you know about this unfortunate elder brother of yours, I never expected that life will take me in such a juncture where I will have to choose between my pride and my life. Yes Sundar, my village had always been my pride but perhaps I have been cursed of leaving my pride to fulfil the oath I have taken.

You know very well what the situation in my family was and that is why finally I had to decide to accept the transfer in job which I had been rejecting for long. Currently I am going to Dhanbad and really don't know when I would return. Whether I would ever return or not, I am not sure about.

I will keep writing you letters and I know you will never fail to reply. From now onwards I will live every moments there in my village through your eyes only, I will smell the scent of the soil after first rain in the monsoon through your sense, I will worship and take the Anjali in the Durga puja through your hands, I will enjoy the bonfire in the winter through your laughter, I will do everything that I had been doing so far, but now onwards through your existence only.

Before ending I request you to take care of yourself and your education. I have a great hope and expectation for you. I know and am sure that you will never let me down.

Yours
Tara da.

Sundar was seating thunderstruck on his bed leaning his head on the wall behind. From the very first day to till date he was fantasizing every moment he lived with Tara da. As if he was watching a film of those four years of his own life.

He read the letter over and over again and stuck at the last line. He tried his best in within his mind to find out the day or the incident when respected "Tarapada da" became beloved "Tara da" to him, but nothing came in to his eyes. He even could not remind the last time when he called "Tarapada da". Really the man became more a friend than a teacher in those four years. He recalled the first day when he met Tara da.

Sundar was returning home from somewhere he could not recall now when he had to look back listening someone calling his name from behind. It was Tarapada Ghosal, a very fair complexion six feet tall well-built stature with long hair falling on his wide shoulders, an easily noticeable man amongst many. Above all the bright eyes which are always shining in enthusiasm have categorically distinguished the personality the man carries from others. A well-known person in the locality as a very bright student of mathematics who had never achieved less than hundred out of hundred in any examination he had ever appeared for. Whether it is a class test or the final examination of master degree in mathematics, Tarapada Ghosal had always been the topper in the subject. Recently he has joined a respected government job but due to his tremendous love for the subject he had started teaching mathematics to the young students of the locality. As he was from a reasonably affluent family and at the same time his own income was more than sufficient to maintain a good standard of life so Tarapada never used to ask for money from his students.

He was standing with an earthen cup of full of tea in the local tea shop when Sundar found the man calling his name. When their eyes met, Tarapada waved his hand to call Sundar. Sundar was a bit surprised and approached the man in a hesitancy in his young mind. Will you take tea, Tarapada asked Sundar and without waiting for any answer to his question he ordered the shopkeeper to serve another cup of tea to his guest. I came to know that you have achieved hundred out of hundred in mathematics in the school leaving examination, Tarapada asked spontaneously. Sundar did not get any chance to think before the series of questions hit him. Sundar nodded looking at the man standing in front of him who seemed to be happier for Sundar's achievement more than Sundar himself was. Great, after so many years somebody has again proved that we the boys from the so called backdated rural areas are no less capable than those city lads, Tarapada continued. His face was full of joy and a wide smile, as if he has achieved something great, something to cheer for. Sundar was a bit astonished as he is first time seeing someone being so happy for his success. He could well understand that by the line "after so many years" Tarapada meant the gap of nearly fifteen years between the year when he achieved the same success in his school leaving exam and now, but what he could not is what made Tarapada so happy regarding this.

The shopkeeper had already served the tea to Sundar. While sipping the earthen cup Sundar faced the next question. Who teaches you mathematics, Tarapada asked while igniting his cigarette.

Sundar replied, in the school Amalesh babu teaches mathematics and he has allowed me in his office room in case I have any doubts after the class. Tarapada's eyebrows were raised and he asked with surprise, you mean you do not have any private tutor for the subject in which you have scored the highest possible marks? Sundar did not say anything but his silence spoke it all.

I use to return from office at six o'clock in the evening, from tomorrow you will come to my home after six and I will teach you, Tarapada stated. Sundar looking at his own toe and in a low but steady voice replied, No I can't. Tarapada thought Sundar might have other engagements tomorrow so he casually replied, Okay then come from day after. Tarapada da I won't come, tomorrow or day after does not matter, Sundar replied. This time Tarapada was a bit taken aback. It was visible from his face that he was surprised and curious to know the reason of Sundar's rejection. Sundar continued and openly confessed, to be very truthful, I don't have the means to pay your fees. Tarapada was probably more surprised with the answer and could not manage himself laughing. Sundar was surprised by seeing the man laughing so loudly but he did not say anything and he was still standing quietly with his eyes fixed on the man in front of him. It took some minutes for Tarapada to control his emotion and then he asked, who said you that Tarapada Ghosal teaches to earn money? He continued, I don't take any fees from any of my students and one more thing I love spending time more with students like you who have the potential to excel than with people who always find faults in everything. You know Sundar what I believe is if young minds like you are nurtured properly then those minds will always thrive for finding solutions to every problem. Not like those old "master of all" fools who use their energy always to find problems and never a solution. He paused and took a puff and added, I dream of that day when every mind will think and everybody will work to find solution for whatever the problem be in front of them. Those minds and bodies of tomorrow should be prepared from today itself and I am confident that your generation will accomplish this successfully.

But if I get lessons from you then you will have to take fees from me, otherwise I could not come, Sundar replied.

Okay then you will treat me a cup of tea in the first Sunday of every month and that is your fee. Now from tomorrow I must see you in my class in the evening, Tarapada replied. Now you were going somewhere and I too have a job to do, and we are meeting tomorrow in the evening. He did not wait there anymore and left the place after paying of the bills he has made in the tea shop and headed for his next destintion.

For next three to four years Sundar used to visit Tarapada's home as a student. With time their relation became more a friendship than a teacher and a student. They used to discuss not only mathematics but many other things ranging from daily life situation to societal change, technological improvements to political ideologies. Tarapada was fond of reading various kinds of books and magazine which he used to lend Sundar to read also. Within this time Tarapada got married. Initially everything seemed to be fine but the situation did not take long to change. Family issues between his mother and wife that used to be internal started being public and fierce debate between the two women became a daily agenda. Sometimes even in the presence of his students Tarapada had to bear the humiliations which was beyond the imagination of those young minds about their respected and beloved teacher.

Sundar also had to be a witness of such situation for many times which finally compelled him to minimize his visits there. It was noticed by his teacher too and one day in the same tea shop where they met some years back for the first time, Tarapada asked Sundar about his absence in his class. Before Sundar could have said anything he himself said, I do understand the reason behind. He did not wait there and hurriedly left that place. On that day Sundar witnessed a great change in the same man whom he met in the same place just some years ago. The bright and enthusiast man always with a smile on his face has become a shy and introvert kind of person. The man who used to be the life of every party seems to be so lifeless. He stood there for sometimes before he left the place too. For next one month Sundar did not get any chance to meet Tarapada. Actually he avoided to visit Tarapada's house and Tarapada typically sealed himself within his office and home. And now the letter in his hand has already ransacked the peace from his mind and left some drops in his eyes for the rest of the night.

BACK HOME, LONG AFTER ...

Life never stops for anything or anyone. New incidents replace the old, new involvements replace old habits and new faces replace old faces, might not be fully but to a great extent they do. Tara da and all related to him also did not take long to become blurred in the mind of Sundar, but whenever he used to cross the tea shop or have tea there he always used to recall that first day.

Initially letters from Tara da were frequent but with time that also lost the frequency and after some years there used to come one or two letters from Tara da yearly. In the early letters he used to ask about so many things and persons of the area but gradually all the letters became oriented to him and the pains of his life only. From his letters it was clear that he was not happy with his married life. Though he did not keep any stone unturned but his wife was kind of a never ending dissatisfied person. Her father was a very rich person who actually wanted to have a highly educated and sophisticated son in law whom he will teach the urban life and culture and finally that boy will become a blind follower of his. But Tarapada Ghosal never wanted to become such a spineless creature. This created a great crack in between him and his wife. Tarapada always used to find peace in his children – an elder son and a younger daughter. These two kids were the only panacea for all his wounds and pains.

The crack broadened when Tarapada's wife finally decided to live in her father's house at Kolkata with their two kids. She cited that for the better education of the children they must be taken to Kolkata. Tarapada tried beyond his capacity to make her understand to stay with him but failed. Finally she declared that up to the Durga Puja they will be with Tarapada and then she will take her kids to Kolkata in her father's house. Tarapada had no way to resist, so he finalized that this puja he will be at his place, his home. After nearly eight years he returned home.

Sundar with Surya was talking to the decorator regarding their payments seating in the priest's room adjacent to the temple when Suren entered and said Sundar, Tarapada Ghosal is asking for you. Which Tarapada, Sundar replied with irritating voice as he was deeply involved in negotiation with the decorator. Suren replied with surprise, Tarapada da, Tarapada Ghosal. Sundar was hearing the name after a long gap of eight years. He was shocked for initial moments and then just jumped out of the room but what he witnessed simply traumatized him. For anyone who had seen this man eight years before will hardly be able to recognize him. The well-built figure has been changed to a skeleton covered with skin. The stylish long black hair is now nearly all white and above all those always bright and enthusiast eyes have lost all the glories once it had. Now it is carrying a vacant sight of utter hopelessness and frustration about life.

So how are you doing young man? Tara da asked Sundar.

It took some time for Sundar to reply, I am okay but what have you done to yourself in this eight years? Sundar's expression was clearly depicting his distress.

Life brother, this is called life, Tarapada replied with a timid smile on his lips. He continued, life is the toughest teacher who takes your exam first and teaches you the lesson through that exam, so that you never forget it. Unfortunately your Tara da failed in the exam brother. He concluded with an exhalation, for the first time ever in life Tarapada Ghosal has failed in any exam and that too so badly. There was a slime in Tara da's face that was showing his state of mind. Let's have a cup of tea, he continued and started walking towards the market holding Sundar's hand. Sundar was walking almost in an unconscious state of mind. He could not believe his own eyes. Is this real or a worst kind of dream, he was still searching the answer in his mind.

In next one hour Tara da opened his mind to Sundar. Believe me brother, I have loved and trusted that woman from the core of my soul but she had betrayed and destroyed my life, Tara da completed narrating last eight years of his life.

Why don't you come back here, we all are there to support you and you will start a life afresh, Sundar replied.

No man, I have lost nearly everything but can't afford to lose my self-respect, Tarapada replied with a smile depicting more pain and distress than happiness.

For how long will you be here? Sundar asked. Tara da replied, unless the Durga Puja ends I am here and after that I will be out again in search of life.

Come here once in a month or two, everything will be as it was. Sundar requested and received a pale smile in return.

Don't worry, until I am here I will come to meet you every day, before leaving for the day Tara da said to Sundar.

He kept his promise and for next five days. He visited Sundar's place each and every day at least once. On the fifth day when he came to meet Sundar, the man handed over two stacks of books to Sundar and said, there is no one in my family who could understand the value of these treasures so request you to take care of these most valuable assets I ever had.

Why don't you take these with you? It will help you the best to pass time, Sundar replied.

Tarapada uttered, you know Sundar, a man will always running out of time in his life unless he has to pass his time forcefully. Then only he will understand the length of every moment and at that point nothing on earth could help him passing the time. He paused for some moments and added, I am handing over my most valuable assets to my most beloved younger brother and trusted friend. I know you will always take care of these just like I did, if not more.

Sundar asked, when you are coming next time.

Tara da with a smile replied, don't worry brother I will meet you at least once before I start my last journey towards my final destination, that's a promise. Before Sundar could have asked anything else Tara da turned and left the place with smiling face and misty eyes.

Keep writing letters, Sundar shouted. Tara da did not say anything, in reply just raised his hand high.

TIME PASSED BY…

After that incident Tara da returned to his job. From then onwards for next few years Sundar used to receive a letter nearly every month from him. Mostly the letters used to be the saga of a cruelly alone person but the only thing noticeable was the post office stamps. Sundar noticed that there were hardly two consecutive letters from the same post office. As if the lonely man was travelling the length and breadth of this country restlessly from one corner to the other. In one or two of such letters there used to be some good news about him getting promotion in job or narration of the experiences of visiting some beautiful places. Out of all those letters, description in two letters shook Sundar from within, one was from Chitorgarh in Rajasthan and the other one was from Varanasi in Uttar Pradesh. He was so fanatic about Chitorgarh in his writing as if he was not feeling only, but equalizing also his own with the pathos of Maharana Pratap Singh and the tragedy the mightiest of the kings in the history of India felt of living life out of his beloved place he was proud of. The great king had to leave the place he could have died for. Regarding Varanasi he described the Harish Chandra Ghat on the mighty and sacred Ganga in such a way that he has regained at least a bit of peace of his mind about his afterlife.

Time passed by, days changed to week, week to months and months to years. The letters became a normal occurrence for Sundar which he used to read and keep in his desk, separately from all other documents and envelopes.

Within these years life also have changed a lot for Sundar. He is now in his late twenties and mostly occupied with his job and other socio-political involvements. There is no doubt that he recall those old days and the man especially when he receives a letter from Tara da but within next few minutes used to get occupied in his personal involvements. On one such day, after returning from his office

Sundar found an envelope on his desk. The postal stamp was of Dhanbad Post Office which was more than enough to understand who the sender of the letter is. He was extremely tired and kept the letter in his wallet for the next morning.

After two days he suddenly discovered the letter from the wallet he forgot to read when he was paying the bills for his tiffin to the vendor outside his office. He was in a good frame of mind and opened the letter. There were only three lines from some Dr. Arunava Dutta of Dhanbad Government Hospital but that three lines were ample powerful to tremble his soul.

Dear Mr. Sundar

One of my patient Mr. Tarapada Ghosal wants to meet you. He is suffering from Cancer for last six months and unfortunately in the last stage now. I would request you to arrive here as early as possible for you.

With regards
Dr. Arunava Dutta
Dhanbad Government Hospital
Dhanbad, Bihar

"Tara da", "Cancer" and "Last stage", for Sundar these three words were enough to repent for the delay. He made his mind that he is not returning home that day and from here going straight to Dhanbad.

The train reached Dhanbad early in the morning. Sundar took a rickshaw and reached Dhanbad hospital by next half an hour. The enquiry section was nothing other than as usually found in any government facility and more precisely in the hospitals, open but empty. Finding no one there Sundar started looking around for someone who could at least provide some information about Dr. Arunava Dutta. Fortunately he saw a sweeper busy in his work. Sundar approached him and asked, can you please tell me where I could found Dr. Arunava Dutta.

Enter through gate number two, take left and after leaving to passages again take left and you will be in the Emergency Ward, Dr. Arunava Dutta seats there, with a tremendous irritation the man guided Sundar towards the emergency ward. Crossing some tiny dimmed internal pathways full of unhygienic stuffs and many patients lying on the floor Sundar landed on the Emergency Ward.

After reaching the emergency section he found two aged women sleeping, one on a big table and the other on a bench. Out of the window there was a board with inscription – May I Help You? It took quite some time and terrific effort for the visitor to wake the helpers up and get the information that Dr. Dutta will visit at 10 AM. It was 7 AM and the three words "Tara da", "Cancer" and "Last stage" were hunting Sundar. There was no question of waiting for three more hours so he had to work a bit harder to find out the residential address of Dr. Dutta. He came out of that place and one of those few people whom Sundar asked about the residential address of Dr. Dutta showed him the way. It did not take more than fifteen minutes to reach the official quarter of Dr. Dutta for Sundar.

Excuse me, are you searching for someone, someone from behind asked Sundar as he was waiting outside the gate with hesitation whether he should disturb a Doctor so early in the morning or not. Sundar turned back and found a man at his mid-fifties was watching at him with a newspaper in his hand.

Yes, actually I am searching for Dr. Arunava Dutta but in a dilemma of disturbing him so early in the morning, Sundar replied. Sorry to say young man but unless I am not unfit, I do leave my bed as early as 4:30 AM every day, the man answered. By the way, may I know who you are and what are you searching me for?

Sundar replied in surprise, are you Dr. Arunava Dutta. The man replied, I do believe so, he added, why, you have any doubt. No, just missed it, I am sorry, Sundar replied with a smile. He continued, by the way, I am Sundar, you wrote me a letter to come here to meet Mr. Tarapada Ghosal, who is suffering from cancer and is in your custody, Sundar replied.

Hmm, yes I remind that, Tarapada requested me to write two letters, one to his wife and the other to you, Dr. Dutta answered. He continued, he was in a very serious condition when I saw him last night, let us not waste time hare. Let's go.

In next ten minutes they reached the ward. The two women who were sleeping woke up in utter urgency seeing Dr. Dutta in front of the ward and opened the door of the big room.

Sundar followed Dr. Dutta in the room, who stopped in front of a Bed. In bed number 17 Sundar found a man lying. He could not believe his own eyes. A crept skeleton of a human being covered with a skin appeared to be severely burnt was lying on the muddy bed sheet which once upon a time perhaps was white colored. Dr. Dutta probably had understood the state of mind through which Sundar was passing by. He placed his hand on Sundar's shoulder and said quietly, don't lose your strength of mind, you will need it badly very soon. He then turned to the lying man and called sympathetically, Tarapada babu look who has come to see you. After calling for second time Tara da responded with a nearly inaudible "Hmmm". Dr. Dutta pointed his finger and gestured towards Sundar to seat on the small wooden tool placed near the bed. Tara da took some minutes to open his eyes, as if he was gathering all strength he has left with to open his eyes. A smile in its weakest form appeared on his lips seeing Sundar seating by his bed. He gestured to come closer. Sundar followed the last instruction of his teacher.

Remember Sundar, I told you that I will meet you before I start my final journey. Tara da paused for moments and added, sorry brother I could not come to you, but we meet after all. I kept my promise. Tara da started respiring very fast as he has used even the last drop of his vigor to complete that sentence.

Don't worry Tara da, I have talked to Dr. Dutta, everything will be alright, Sundar tried to console the person lying in front of his eyes. He continued, we will again face life together at our village, Sundar tried his best to solace a dying man.

Don't lie when you can't, I know it all, I am not even enough fortunate to die at my own soil brother, Tara da replied. His eyes were moist. He paused and continued, once I had to leave my beloved village in search of peace and now I think it has abandoned me from all its glories and pampers.

Dr. Dutta intervened, okay Tarapada babu have some rest and Sundar come with me please. Before leaving the place Sundar took Tara da's hand in his own and said, I will come again. Tara da just closed his eyes, did not reply. Sundar and Dr. Dutta came out of the ward.

Sundar was taken by Dr. Dutta in his quarter where the bachelor used to live alone. Is he your relative, Dr. Dutta asked Sundar, who was seating on the chair in the study of doctor's quarter. Sundar raised his eyes and replied, he was my teacher, more than that my elder brother and even more than that my friend. He added, he was someone I admired, loved, have been taught by and lived with. He was my Tara da.

The doctor did not ask anymore question and left the room leaving Sundar with his memories and agonies.

Sundar returned to the Emergency Ward at 11 AM as the visiting hour starts from 11 AM. Just entering the ward he saw beside Tara da's bed a woman was seating on the same tool where he sat couple of hours before. A teen age girl and a boy was crying, seating near the feet of Tara da. Another middle aged man was standing on the opposite side of the bed. Sundar recognized the woman, Tara da's wife. He then got to understand who the teen aged boy and girl is. They were Tara da's son and daughter. He could not recognize the man but sensed that he might be someone from Tara da's in-law.

Sundar moved some steps forward to have the last glance of his teacher. There was an expression of absolute peace in the face. He came out of the room wordlessly.

Hello Sir, Sundar found one of the women whom he found sleeping in the "May I Help You" counter in the morning, was calling him from the same place but this time awake. He approached the counter. Your patient breathed last at 10:30 AM in the morning, now you will have to complete some formalities, the woman uttered.

There are family people inside who will complete those formalities, Sundar replied. He waited for a moment and then requested the woman, will you please do me a favor sister? Would you please arrange some flowers for him in his final journey? He put a ten rupee note on the table and turned back.

What should I say if they ask who you were? The woman asked.

Just tell them a student, a brother and a friend, Sundar replied without looking back and walked through those tiny dimmed internal pathways out of that place.

I don't know what he did was right or wrong. I don't know whether he pragmatically tried to change situation or not. One thing I know is that what happened to the man is absolutely not right. I don't know God whether you exist or not. I don't even know whether you could listen to me or not but today I am asking you, how many such great soul you have ever sent on this earth. And if not enough then who gave you the right to dismiss such a great life so painfully and vainly? How could you be so ruthless being God? How could you?

Can you please tell which station the train just crossed? A voice broke in to Sundar's thoughts.

Sundar looked at the man standing in front of his seat, took some time to understand what the man is actually asking to know from him and then replied, Sorry I have not noticed.

He again turned his face toward outside through the window he was seating by. The train was moving at a high speed. He was leaving so many things behind. Sundar was returning to his place, his village. He was returning to that soil which he was made up of and one day will be engrossed in to.

LET'S GET MARRIED ...

Sundar with two of his colleagues Sourabh Sil and Sourabh Sengupta was seating in the corner table beside the widest window of the office canteen. This specific table in the canteen has always been the most favorite to all the people who visit the canteen frequently because of two reasons, firstly the ample availability of the cool zephyr from the river Ganga and secondly seating here one can easily watch the entrance of the statin, more specifically the first five platforms. Sundar and the other two were almost from the same age group and the official friendship between them was no less than a personal one. Except Sundar, as the given name is identical for the other two so in the office everybody used to call them with their respective surnames, "Sil" and "Sengupta". Not the name only was identical but characteristically also there was hardly any difference between the two. They were lively, light hearted and restless almost every time, besides used to act so spontaneously without even given a second thought for anything and everything. The two impatient young men were so jovial that their deeds used to be irritating to others in the office very frequently. At the same time they were so helpful to others that they could go up to any extent to help anyone, so improvident that every month they had to borrow from their family, so irresponsible that no important works used to be sanctioned to either of the duo, so immature that sometimes their blunders used to become nuisance, but still everyone in the office used to adore and indulge the two because of their always smiling face, childlike attitudes and tremendous enthusiasm in any unproductive work. They were kind of darling to all. The two were polar opposite to their best friend and most dependable companion in the office, Sundar. For all the blunders committed by the two, Sundar was the single point of solution for them.

Today none of the two was smiling and every now and then was staring from the corner of their eyes at each other and then at Sundar, who was seating across the table and in last half an hour has not said even a single word. Sundar was staring outside the window down at the railway platform number 3. He was sipping the second cup of tea and the third cigarette was burning in between his middle and forefinger. Sil and Sengupta knew that the blooper they have committed yesterday has affected Sundar more than them and he has taken it very seriously.

From last few minutes Sil and Sengupta was talking to each other only through their eyes and both of them was trying to convince the other to say something to Sundar so that the conversation could at the least start from something. No one was ready to be the first speaker. Finally Sengupta accepts the challenge and said, Sundar don't take it so seriously man, it just another very common thing that happens everywhere and every day. I think she will forget this within two days, Sengupta in a dimmed voice tried to make up an excuse. Sil was waiting for the chance. Take it easily, it is okay, seeing Sundar not replying Sil supported Sengupta.

Sundar placed the finished cup on the plate and turned towards the two. With a slow but frightening voice he said, this is the first time in my life I am going to say sorry for something which I have not committed but unfortunately the lady has thought that I was a part of that nuisance because of you two and especially to you, Sundar pointed to Sil and continued, I personally believe that real men don't tease women and I am not ready to consider myself a fake man.

You are going to say sorry to that lady and that too in the office? Sengupta asked Sundar with astonishment. His stared first to Sundar and then his gaze move to Sil.

Yes guys, to that lady whom you teased yesterday just like street rascals, Sundar replied. He paused for a moment and added, but not in the office, in that train, he pointed to a train standing in platform number 3.

How do you know she is there, Sil asked?

Sundar with the same calm attitude replied, she generally takes the 4 PM Ranaghat local or 4:30 PM Gede local to home. He continued, today I have been watching from last half an hour and the Ranaghat local is gone but I have not seen her boarding the train or passing through this entrance, that means she must be in the Gede local, Sundar answered Sil.

Great man, so our friend has gathered so much of information about that lady, Sil pinched Sundar with a mocking tone.

Firstly it does not need great efforts to know something about one of your colleague and secondly you are again in a mood of mischief, so please mind your tone and words, Sundar replied to his friend. Well you guys either wait here or in the desk, I am going to complete my responsibility out there, Sundar stood up and left the place.

Sundar first headed towards the compartment reserved for ladies passengers only, thinking that the lady would be there, but she was not. He then decided to look for the other compartments as well.

Sundar was amazed to found the lady seating by the window of a general compartment. He supposed she will be in the ladies compartment. He entered the compartment and found it quite vacant, hardly ten to fifteen men and women were seating here and there. He directly approached the lady. May I talk to you for some time? Sundar asked the lady without any primer.

May I know regarding what? The lady looked up and firmly replied.

The train whistled to finally declare that it is time to move and subsequently moved on. Sundar had no other option but to travel at least the distance unless he could complete his words so let himself sat in front of the lady. Sundar thought for a moment and arranged his words before and then said, I know what happened yesterday in the office was no way acceptable and it was very much expected that any lady who has self-respect will obviously react against that, he paused again before continuing, but you were mistaken in one point.

I was not mistaken, the lady firmly replied. She added, I knew that you did not commit the nuisance and it was either Sil or Sengupta, I am not very sure who of them exactly it was, the lady replied casually with the same well-founded voice.

It was something Sundar had expected the least, till then he was thinking that there was a misunderstanding. Why did you chased me then? The question came automatically out of Sundar's mouth.

Otherwise your friends would never had taken it seriously, the lady replied too casually while looking outside the window with the slightest possible smile at the corner of her lips.

Whatever it was I don't want to recall, I came to say you sorry for that but now I think I don't need to when you already know that I was not the culprit, Sundar said and stood up. He planned to get down in the next station to return to his office.

By the way, my name is Rani, the lady said.

Sorry I forgot, I am Sundar, he turned back and replied. The lady smiled and in reply. Sundar smiled back before he got down in the next station.

Our respected sir who is an epitome of morality is finally back, Sengupta mocked Sundar seeing him entering the room in the office where they used to seat. Sil was perhaps busy in his work so he missed the scene and looked at the door. Let's go for a cup of tea, Sil offered. Sundar maintained a tremendous seriousness in his expression and did not reply to either of them. He came in and sat on his own desk. Sir may we please have the pleasure of having a cup of tea with a personality like you, Sil approached him and uttered again.

After half an hour at least, I have to finish of my today's quota first, Sundar replied in a profound voice. Okay, no issue, we are always at your service sir, Sil replied and got back to his desk.

So what happened sir? What did you say? Did you say sorry to that lady? What she replied? Sil did not even take a breath to ask all the question to Sundar. Though Sundar said "After half an hour at least", but it was tougher than doing anything on this planet to let Sil and Sengupta wait for more than fifteen minutes and on top of that when they have sensed something to gossip. The trio was seating in their favorite place, the corner window side table in the canteen, almost after twenty minutes from when Sundar entered his office after his short tour. Initially Sundar thought to share what actually happened in the train with the two. But then he realized that they will be instigated more to commit such nuisance again if they come to know that Sundar is not annoyed. So Sundar maintained the bitter face and replied, I approached and said sorry to her and came back. What else did you expect to happen? He completed and concentrated on the cup.

Look man, it does not take almost one hour to say "sorry" to someone and come back from platform no. 3, Sengupta enquired. We are not that stupid, he added.

Absolutely not I know. When I located her in that rush the train was already moving, so I had to take the train until the next station to complete my duty and then I came back, Sundar replied coolly.

What did you say to her, Sengupta asked again?

I am sorry for what my friends did yesterday, Sundar replied the same way. He was anyway successful to pacify his immensely curious friends about the incident.

From that day the behavior of both Sundar and Rani changed towards each other. They started greeting each other with a smile whenever they used to come across in the office, but only without in the presence of any third person. In presence of any other person they used to behave as unknown as they were before that day. It was an amazing emotion that they were adoring which they never sensed before. Gradually they started talking to each other but all the time they used to maintain the same level of concealment in front of any other office colleague. It was much easier for Sundar than his counterpart to hide their state of affair because there were only two other women employees in the office except Rani, Ujjwala and Pranati. All the three ladies not only were of same age group but they were almost inseparable from each other also. Now suddenly if Rani started avoiding them then that would easily raise the eyebrows of the two, so she had to tackle both the situations with intelligence as well as casual approach. Ujjwala was easier to manage than Pranati as she was intelligent but less critical and more a doer but the second one was a separate kind altogether. Pranati was clever and she also had a detective instinct but at the same time she used to depend on Rani for many decisions and that was the only positive point for Rani.

Sundar tried to match his shift time so that it accord with Rani's, but they never used to talk to each other in the office premise. The only time they used to talk to each other when they were returning home from the office. Rani was staying in a working women's hostel at Hooghly Ghat, which was in a separate direction from Sundar's native place. Sundar's location could also be reached via Hooghly Ghat but with a bit longer journey, so he generally used to take the longer route while returning home to spend some time together.

I think we should get married, Sundar said to Rani while discussing various other affairs in one such day when they were seating by the Ganga in Hooghly Ghat.

I can't go for marriage right now, Rani replied. She continued, as I have already told you, after passing away of my father, I am the only earning member in my family and I have to take care of my younger brothers and sisters. She continued, so it will take some time for me to manage everything, Rani concluded.

Okay, the day you think you are ready for marriage, just let me know, until then if you think in any way I could come in to your help, just ask me, Sundar replied with a supporting smile.

I understand and respect your values and tenet, but addressing all those issues might take years, Rani replied without looking at Sundar. Her eyes were fixed on the dimmed lights coming out of those tiny kerosene lamps of those trifling fishing boats that were floating on the elegant Ganga.

Absolutely no problem, I thoroughly understand the importance of duties and responsibilities towards family, Sundar replied calmly. He then paused for a moment, looked at the dignified lady seating next to him and added, I will wait until you address all your issues. Rani shifted her sight from the boats to man seating by her. It was not worthy or even required to try to find out which was more noteworthy in that sight, admiration or affection.

Situation was changing very fast for both Sundar and Rani. Sundar had been promoted and shifted to another vertical some months back. Now he was not in the platform or sorting duty anymore, he was assigned to another department. His shift time and reporting got totally changed and there was hardly any chance to meet Rani. Rani on the other hand had also shifted from her Hooghly ghat hostel to another hostel in Kolkata for better convenience to her office so that she could continue her studies as well. She has started her preparation for the final examination of her college which she stopped for sometimes after the unfortunate early death of her father. The only means of expressing the feelings was through letters and that too not very frequently. In fact they could not meet each other more than a year but both of them was more than certain about the commitment of the other.

Finally one day almost after two years from their first discussion about marriage, Rani called Sundar to meet her. They met each other after a long time. That was indeed a moment of emotion. Rani first opened her mind, I have almost completed all my responsibilities and the rest could be easily managed even after marriage. She paused for some moments and added, I believe I am now ready for that. Sundar stared at her, okay then I will inform my elder brothers and other members of my family and you do also talk to your mother on this, Sundar replied.

Within some days Rani's mother with one of her brother came to meet Sundar's family in his ancestral house and everything got finalized in the first meeting itself knowing that everything has already been firmed up by the boy and the girl. Both the family approved each other with approbation. The local priest was consulted to fix a proper date for the traditional ceremonies. After waiting so long everything happened so fast that no one even thought about.

BACK IN THE OFFICE

My family has arranged my marriage, Rani informed Ujjwala and Pranati in the office. She intentionally maintained an emotionless face to create a sense in the minds of the two listeners that there is nothing like joy or hope in her mind.

Really? Ujjwala asked with utter astonishment. I mean who is the guy? What is his name? What does he do? She took no time to shower the list of questions in excitement. She added, I mean, just don't tell us that you are going to marry, tell us in details, about everything, Ujjwala concluded.

Rani was seating with the darkest possible face she could make in such a situation. This is a good news but you are not looking happy with this, what is the difficulty, Pranati sensed that and ask. Have you seen the guy, it was Ujjwala who enquired.

Rani was just waiting for this chance. Yes, last Sunday he came to our home with his family members, Rani answered. He is in a government service, Rani concluded, perhaps in some department of the Central government.

How is he looking, Pranati questioned.

A short heighted, dark complexioned man with a bald head, almost eleven years elder than me and his name is Harogobinda Haribol, Rani replied with the same pale face that she was trying her best to maintain and to be precise, she was really performing great.

You can't marry such a man, you are simply going forward to ruin your life, Ujjwala almost cried out.

Rani stared at Ujjwala and replied, the condition my family is not so that I can tell 'No' to this arrangement, especially when they have not demanded anything and the person is in a government job.

I have never heard about any such surname 'Haribol' in Bengalis ever in my life, Pranati remarked. She continued, which caste is he from, I mean, I know you don't abide by those caste system and all, but still, I am just curious.

Rani replied, even I have never before too and as you said, Rani paused and added, I am least bothered about those caste and all, so I did not ask them. Rani continued, they said they were awarded this title by the British. Whatsoever, the date has been fixed on 15th June and both of you have to be right there with me from the morning at my home, and please don't talk about this to anyone in the office now, Rani concluded.

The two innocent girls nodded their heads in acceptance of the secrecy to be maintained regarding this is the office. They were actually sorry for their friend.

IN ANOTHER CORNER

Great man, great news, so finally we can welcome you to the married life, Sengupta almost yelled. Sundar was seating with his friends in a tea stall outside the office.

Yes, but what so amazing in it, Sundar asked Sengupta. With his signature placid expression.

This is no doubt an amazing news, how could you be so unromantic, Sengupta replied with the same voice mixed with a pinch of annoyance. He added, leave it and tell us what her name is? Where does she live? What does she do and most important of all, how it happened? Sengupta completed and stared at Sundar with a sight that was full of eagerness to get the answers. He was more interested to know everything in details.

Okay, her name is Queen, she is from Nadia, Sundar replied. He paused for moments and continued after being asked again by Sil to complete all other details, well, she is doing a job and both of our family met some days back and finalized the proposal, Sundar replied in one sentence.

"Queen", Sil mocked with raised eyebrow, then she must be very beautiful.

Just another normal Bengali girl, but yes she is educated and smart, Sundar replied. Look guys, the ceremony has been scheduled on 15th June and both of you have to be with me, Sundar completed and stood up to go.

Where are you going? Sengupta asked.

To complete my pending jobs in the office, Sundar replied coolly and started walking. The two followed him with sheer disappointment as they were in full mood to gossip on the matter for more.

Hmmm, one more thing, Sundar stopped before entering the office at the gate, turned towards his fellows and said, please don't discuss anything about this with anyone now.

But why? What the problem, everybody gets married, Sil answered.

Yes I know that part of it but there are some reservation regarding inviting you two and all others, Sundar replied. He paused and added, at least you must understand that you guys are closer to me more than any other in the office.

The two fellows nodded in affirmation and promised that they will not share the news with anyone in the office.

THE DAY

Please come inside, Didi has been waiting for you, Rani's youngest sister welcomed Ujjwala and Pranati in their house and guided them to the room where Rani was waiting for them. Ujjwala and Pranati has visited Rani's house before also so they were well-known to every member of the family. The ladies came in and let themselves sat on the bed where Rani was seating. Thank god that you are not delayed, Rani said to her friends. I was really missing you two.

So, finally you are going to marry that man, Ujjwala could not resist her to make the remark. She was still not ready to accept the decision her dearest friend had taken.

Ujjwala, facts are always stranger than fiction, and that man is not that unacceptable at all, Rani replied.

Let us see the banarasi and the ornaments you are going to wear, Pranati diverted the direction of discussion. And eventually the ladies got involved with the most interesting things on this planet, perhaps to every women, garments and jewelry.

It was nearly a journey of three hours by train from Sundar's house to his would be in-law's house, so they had to start before the afternoon to reach there on timc. Sundar was accompanicd by only six men including Sil and Sengupta. Except the two, there was one of his elder brother and his uncle was part of the team. Rest two were seniors from neighborhood. They had to change trains for three times in the journey and between every change they had to wait for sometimes on the junction points which in fact was quite a considerable chunk of the total travel time.

The bridegroom has arrived, Rani's youngest sister ran in to the room where Rani was seating with her friends and announced. She had been waiting at the outer veranda of the house and waiting eagerly for the bridegroom to arrive, so that she could bring the news before any other person to her elder sister.

Great, let us have a look at our going to be brother-in-law, you wait here for us to return, Ujjwala and Pranati jumped up and almost ran after Rani's sister.

You liar, cheat, I would have killed you if this would have some other day, but I will not let you go I promise, Ujjwala was almost furious. They have just returned after finding Sundar as the bride groom and that too accompanied by Sil and Sengupta. How could you be so mean to us? She questioned Rani, who was enjoying the scene with a naughty smile. You have crossed all the limits, Pranati remarked. By the way may we now know for how long you have been playing the game with us? She asked Rani. Rani did not reply but her smile said it all to the two ladies.

So that is why you went to say sorry to her, Sil remarked. They were seating with Sundar in another room where the arrangements were made for the bridegroom and his companions to relax unless Sundar will have to join the rituals and all the activities oriented with the ritual.

Absolutely not, this relationship started much after that, Sundar replied coolly.

Sorry to say, but do you still expect us to believe this? Do we appear so idiot? Sengupta asked to Sundar.

That is up to you whether you believe me or not but I don't lie, Sundar replied.

Really, then why have not you told us earlier about your relationship with Rani? Sengupta asked.

Not telling something is not lying, Sundar replied.

And what was the cause behind your lie when we asked the name and all details about your would be wife, Sil asked almost furiously. You even told us her name was "Queen", if I am not wrong, he added. Exactly, Sengupta supported spontaneously.

I told you everything true about her, Sundar paused and added, and by the way the meaning of "Queen" in Bengali is "Rani", so I did not lied either about this.

The two were yet to say something when an unknown but elderly man intervened and asked Sundar, please come son, it's time for the rituals to be performed and Sundar followed.

Next day in the morning the newly married couple had to perform another set of rituals before they set for the return journey to Sundar's house, to start a new life together.

A NIGHT JOURNEY ...

In such a chilled winter it will be tough for us to start early in the morning tomorrow, especially with the baby, Rani uttered to Sundar and continued, and the next train is generally used by the daily office goers and usually is crowded. She paused and added, I think the 10 AM train would be the best.

Sundar nodded his head staring at his wife and replied, I too think that will be better. He added, in any case none of us would be able to attend our office after such a long journey. We will have to take a leave for one more day, so let the journey be comfortable at least. And even if we avail the 10 AM train, we will be there before the dusk, as you know in such an anarchistic situation it would not be wise for me to travel openly after the dusk and that too with you and Mani.

Rani smiled and said, okay then let me inform my mother about this, otherwise she would be in dilemma, she completed and left the room.

TIME OF TURBULENCE

Before 15th August, 1947, the day the nation earned its independence from the nearly two centuries long colonial rule by the British, the Bengali people, especially the youth and students were one of the fiercest headache for the British rulers due to their armed revolution under the banner of Anushilon Samiti. The highly educated, cultured and motivated people coupled with the students from colleges, universities and even schools were part of the Anushilon Samiti. They were nationalist and devoted to the one only goal of their life – free India from the colonial rule of the British. They were eager to die for the cause with the gallantry that was unparalleled and implausible. Their martial expertise was unmatched and their devoutness was rare in the history. But even after so much of sacrifices, the independence we achieved divided the sacred land of Bharat in to two parts – India and Pakistan.

After independence due to the partition of the nation Bengal witnessed an enormous population from the then East Pakistan and today's Bangladesh, taking refuge here in the western part of Bengal, which was named West Bengal. Though initially the entire Bengal province was planned to be a part of East Pakistan but due to the Himalayan effort and valiant resistance from one of the greatest leader of all time in the history of Indian politics, Shri Shyama Prasad Mukherjee, the Bengal province was segregated and the western part became a state under the Indian sovereign. The people, mostly Hindu by religious faith were under attack. They were being attacked, killed, women were being raped and humiliated, their properties were being burnt and they were being forcefully thrown out of the newly created East Pakistan by the Muslims of that Muslim majority areas of East Pakistan and they had to flee to India overnight with bare hands, losing all their belongings in the hands of those fundamentalists. Uncountable number of people were hacked to death including elderly and children. It was almost impossible to find out a family which has not lost at least one of his member in that massacre. Innumerable number of women, irrespective of age, was raped and tortured brutally. It was a situation that will find only a few comparable in the history of humankind which is even worse than the Holocaust of Jews in Germany under the Nazi regime. But unfortunately the history has forgotten them and their sufferings.

This sudden change in the demographics triggered a tremendous transformation in the economies also. This huge influx raised the poverty level suddenly too high and in turn helped the leftist ideology to be established in the soil of Bengal. The utopian reverie of an equal society, a classless society with equality and so on and so forth attracted the young section of that godforsaken population living life in the slums towards that political belief.

For next twenty years form 1947, though the poverty was high and there were many issues in the society existed but the state and its people were yet to witness another violent time which they will come across shortly after almost twenty years and more specifically in the middle of 1960s, in the same fertile soil of Bengal.

In the middle of 1960s the Communist Party of India (Marxist) was divided, leading to the formation of a far-left radical group, the Communist Party of India (Marxist – Leninist) or CPI (ML) in short. On the same year when a police team arrived to arrest some of the peasant leaders, it was ambushed by a group of tribal led by a legendary tribal leader Jangal Santhal, and a police inspector was killed in a hail of arrows. The entire scene was taking place near an unknown village called Naxalbari in the northern part of Bengal, from which actually the violent movement borrowed its name and became Naxal Movement and the people followed this became termed in general as Naxal. The killing of the police officer encouraged many tribal and other poor people to join the movement and to start attacking local landlords who as per the ideology was ransacking those poor people for generations. Around 1971 the Naxalites gained a strong presence among the radical sections of the students in Calcutta and many other small towns. Some very bright and aspiring students also got attracted towards this violent revolution in the dream of changing the society overnight and freeing it from the grip of the rich people who were chewing the flesh and bones of those poor from generation in the name of as many things as possible.

The involvement of those intelligent and academically excellent people from the educated and learned strata of the society made this movement more dangerous to tackle for the government as this time both intellect and violence was being appraised by each other. Landlords, businessmen, university teachers, police officers, politicians of the right and left, more or less all except the Naxalites, were termed as "class enemies" and the killing of those people were initiated. On the other hand the government replied with the same kind of terror to stop this and in between the entire society of the state not only became terrified rather destroyed also. Some criminals also started doing crimes in the name of Naxalites so that they get a political cover. Murder, snatching, robbery became an everyday matter in the newspapers and other medias. People became tired of listening and reading about these incidents. The entire state of West Bengal and its people was living their life under constant intimidation. A fear of uncertainty shook each and every one from the core of their existence.

Perhaps out of all those people those leftist cadre who did not join the Naxal revolution and exempted from their ideology of violence were in the greatest trouble. As for the Naxalites they became traitor and stamped as "class enemy". On the other hand for the administration and law and order they became the "doubtful substances" who may be anything from a sleeper cell of Naxalites to an informer or at least silent supporter. At the best, as they were people who had been knowing about those who joined the revolution or atrocity, whatever it may be called, so they were chased by the administration for information regarding their ex-comrades. Many a time it happened that a liberal non-Naxalites became a target by the Naxalites and hacked to death as well as sometimes the police arrested and tortured a liberal non-Naxalites just on the ground of baseless doubt or to fetch information about some wanted Naxalites.

The entire society and its people were living on the edge of suspecting others, even sometimes their own kith and kin. Life was almost ruined and reliability was devastated from the core.

THREE DAYS BEFORE THE DAY

I have to go home, it is urgent, Rani said to Sundar who has just arrived at his ancestral home to meet his wife and six months old baby under the cover of the dark night. Hiding himself from the eyes of people. After taking his dinner he was seating in his room when Rani uttered him regarding the urgency that has compelled her to plan a visit to her paternal house. Today itself one of her brothers has come to meet her and has conveyed the message.

Sundar was standing by the door that leads to the open portion of the first floor holding a cigarette in between his fingers. He raised his head and turned back to look at Rani, who was standing behind him. Rani understood that Sundar was immersed in to some other thought and has missed her words. She said again what she said just a few moments earlier and added, I can't go alone with the baby. She paused for a moment and continued, in fact as my brother said, it is urgent so I think it will be even better if you accompany us too. When she completed, her face was also serious as she could understand well that the situation is not ideal for Sundar to leave the station.

Sundar thought for some moments and replied, okay I will be with you. He stopped and added, when it is urgent then we must start tomorrow itself. You go and take the train you usually take for your office and I will be following you, but you don't search for me unless I come in front.

Would it be tough for you to manage, Rani asked. She is nervous.

No, I will manage that part, Sundar replied with a smile and moved to leave the house and set for the hidden place where he spends his nights now a days. Rani closed the door behind him.

It was the winter of 1972. Sundar was really in trouble in such a situation as he did not join the Naxalites movement but still working for his political ideology being under cover. He was a well-known activist in his own as well as in the surrounding villages, which actually made him a potential target both for the Naxalites as well as for the police. Sometimes he used to be in hiding and staying outside his home. He had to spend many sleepless nights hiding out here and there leaving his wife alone with their first baby at his ancestral house. Just before six months Sundar was graced by the Almighty with his first child, a daughter. In such a tensed environment one day all of a sudden a news came from his Mather-in-law's house that out there is an emergency and both Sundar and Rani has been requested to visit there.

He first was in dilemma about leaving the station in such a condition which might raise questions in the minds of many people but finally decided to go to attend the call of his duty as in his in-law's house there was no one mature enough to handle any emergency situation. All of his brother-in-laws were too young to handle any emergency and the entire family was highly dependent on his wife for any important matter.

Early in the next morning and before leaving the station he informed all his close friends and party confidants about his leaving and then the same day in the morning he with his wife and six month old daughter left for his in-law's house. It was in a distant placc which uscd to take nearly half of a day to reach there, so when they got in to the place it was late afternoon.

It took three days to solve the situation there and on the fourth day when everything was resolved and again back in normal track then only Sundar and Rani could plan their journey return to home. They had to stay for three days there and in those three days Sundar was deeply involved in that issue so has no time to think about the situation back in his place. While leaving station, he informed his friends that he will be staying one or two days and already this was the fourth day. There was no communication possible in between to let them inform about anything. This sense created lots of tension in his mind regarding his own place and fellows for the entire time he was absent. Sundar decided that tomorrow he had to return to his place, but he did not disclosed anything to anyone. He was seating in a room and asked his wife to get prepared so that they can leave tomorrow.

THE JOURNEY BEGINS

They started late in the morning to avoid the daily rush and caught the train from there at nearly ten in the morning. They reached Rajaghat, which was nearly a journey of three hours as per the schedule and without any problem. Rajaghat was the last stop for the train they were in and is also the junction station where they will now have to change their train to the next junction. The connecting train was a long route train which was from the second division of Rajaghat and used to run almost five hours to reach Rajaghat from its starting point. Here, at Rajaghat the train stops for some time and then will move forwards.

Sundar with his wife Rani and daughter Mani was seating in the waiting room of the platform. The scheduled time of arrival of the train passed. Rani was busy in preparing the foods for Mani and did not notice that the train has not yet arrived or even there was no announcement about its arrival. Sundar has noticed that and was frequently looking at his wrist watch. Finally when the train was already delayed for almost an hour he said, I think the train is delayed.

Rani after listening to Sundar and looking at her own wrist watch asked, then what should we do.

Let me check with the station master, Sundar replied and turned to move. He stopped at the door, turned back and said, be here only unless I return, and left.

Sundar came back after fifteen minutes but that fifteen minutes seemed to be more that fifteen hours to Rani.

Due to technical fault the connecting train that we had planned to avail is late for nearly four hours, Sundar informed Rani entering the waiting room in the platform.

Rani suggested, I think we should return to my mother's house for the night and will reschedule our journey for tomorrow.

No, I need to return by today itself, Sundar was stubborn on carrying out their journey. He continued, if the next train reaches at right time to our next destination Nabohati then we would have ten more minutes extra in our hand for the second last train to Gopalpur and from there we would easily avail the last train to our native place. He paused and added, so I think we should wait. Rani nodded, but with a monumental tension in her mind.

Finally when the train was placed at the platform, the rush was such that it was next to impossible for them to board the train with a six month old baby and all the bags and baggage. So after trying hard they had to leave it. Now the situation was even worse. The last train back to Sundar's in-law's house was gone and there was no option for them to return there. They will had to wait for the next train which was scheduled to arrive after one hour.

It was nearly six in the evening when the next train left Rajaghat station. Though there were many passengers in the train but it was not crowded as the earlier one. Sundar and Rani let themselves sat comfortably facing the direction opposite to that of the train was moving to avoid the chilling breeze. It took just fifteen minutes more than the time it was given in the railway book, which in Indian railway hardly matters, but that fifteen minutes cost a lot for the couple with the baby. They have hardly chattered in the journey as both of them was separately under utter tension and was not willing to make the other one more tensed. Now they were in such a situation that they can't return to Rani's parental house and on the other hand the second last train had already moved out of the Nabohati. The only choice they left with was either to stay at the Nabohati station or to take the last train from Nabohati to Gopalpur and spend the night at the Gopalpur station. Should we stay here and request the station master to open the waiting hall for us, Sundar asked Rani.

Rani thought for a moment before answering to the question and then replied, I think Gopalpur would be better choice as a place to stay in the railway waiting hall. She paused and looked at the surrounding, except one or two beggars sleeping here and there on the platform there was none. She then stared at Sundar and said, Nabohati is a more disturbed place than Gopalpur, beside the later one is closer to our place also.

Sundar nodded his head and acknowledged her thought and said, then let us take the last train to Gopalpur. He added, there is an insignificant hope that if the last train from Howrah to Burdwan delays for some minutes more than it's usual, then there is a chance that we get that from Gopalpur.

When they board the last train from Nabohati they requested the driver of the train to accommodate them in his cabin. They depicted what they had to gone through in their journey in details. The driver was an elderly man and agreed to them, sensing the urgency of the situation. In that train perhaps there were only four persons and baby, the driver, the guard and the couple with their six moth baby.

Unfortunately the tragedy with anybody is that when for the three hundred and sixty four days a year you reach the station at right time the train gets delayed but for the single day you are delayed the train moves right at its scheduled time and you miss it. The same happened with Sundar and Rani too, when they reached Gopalpur the last train had already gone. It was nearly the midnight in a chilling winter. There was not even a single person in the station except those beggars who used to sleep on the railway platforms. The platforms were absolutely vacant. Sundar had no other option but to approach the station master on duty to request him to open the first class waiting room for them so that they can wait for next four to five hours until the first train comes. Initially the station master was in a dilemma about their identity but when both Sundar and Rani showed their railway employee identity card the man cooperated and became ready to open the waiting hall.

After being settled there they first realized that they have not taken any food for quite a long time and feeling hungry. You stay here and lock the door from inside, Sundar said to Rani and continued, let me search if I could arrange something at least for us to eat. Rani initially hesitated but then agreed. Sundar got out of the room in search of some eatables. He did not have the pleasure to go far in search as Rani would be tensed seating alone there in the waiting hall with the kid, so he as quickly as possible take a round of the area but got nothing out there.

Hey Sundar da, what are you doing here in the middle of a night. Sundar was just turning towards the waiting hall when someone asked his name from behind. He turned again around and found Abinash lying in a corner outside the station under the shed of the ticket counter on a makeshift bed. Abinash was from a poor family and when he was a young boy he got involved in to petty crimes to earn the living for his family. He had a tall and strong physic but unfortunately had lost one of his eyes one day in an accident while escaping from a police raid. Sundar then helped him to get out of that darkness and start a new life. After that Abinash started a new life as a rickshaw puller. Abinash approached Sundar and repeated his question again about his being there at midnight. Sundar told him everything that happened that day. Sundar da just inform me at any point in time if you think I could come in to your help, Abinash replied, I will be here throughout the night as I have passenger for the first train. Sundar smiled back in return and turned to get back to his family.

Sundar almost jumped crossed the stairs two to three at a time and was returning to the waiting room when suddenly his eyes fell on two boys watching him from a distance. He could not recognize the first as his face was covered with a muffler but he easily recognized the second one as Dulal.

Dulal once was a coworker in the party but when the Naxalites movement was spreading like a wild fire in the society, he switched his loyalty to that ideology. Currently there are several charges on him of various violent activities. Sundar did not react and just return to the waiting room where his wife was waiting with their daughter for his return. Rani was relieved seeing Sundar and asked, have you got something. Sundar answered with just a short "no" and swiftly took up the bags and said, we are leaving the place and that too right at that time. Rani was shocked and asked in surprise, where we are going now in the middle of such a chilling night and that too with a six months old kid. Sundar replied with the bare minimum possible, anywhere but not here, there is a problem.

They moved out of the waiting room but did not take the direct path that leads out of the station, rather they took the long route to avoid Dulal and his friend. Sundar came to Abinash who was till sleeping under the shed and wake him up. Sundar told him about Dulal and noticed a shadow of tension appeared on the face of Abinash too. Just stay here for a moment, I will be back soon, Abinash uttered to Sundar and went to somewhere. He returned within two minutes but this time he was holding two iron rods each of which was nearly four feet long. He gave one to Sundar and placed the other in the handle of his rickshaw vertically in such a manner that if needed he can any point in time pull it out very easily. Then looking at Sundar he said, it will take nearly half an hour for me to carry you from Gopalpur to your house, he paused for a moment and added, Sundar da if you could rely on me then I promise to give my best. At the same time he added showing the iron rods that if Dulal or his friends come in the way they will have a good lesson. Sundar replied, then what we are waiting for, let's move.

Rani had nothing to say about whatever is being decided by Sundar and she was just following her husband. She rode on the rickshaw with the kid on her lap. When the journey finally began it was nearly half past twelve. The kid was sleeping in the lap of her mother rapped in a blanket. Sundar and Rani was speechless and Abinash was probably extending himself beyond limit. Though there was a short route but he took the long one through the Grand Trunk road as the short route had a bad reputation especially at night and the main road used to have frequent long distance trucks travelling at night so generally with a lesser chance of criminal activities. On the way once Rani started asking a question to Sundar but Abinash very harshly asked her not to talk or make any noise. They crossed nearly eight kilometers when misfortune stroked on them. Due to something one of the tyres got leaked. Sundar sensed that but Abinash did not care to bother. Though the main tension zone was over but Abinash did not stop his rickshaw. Sundar asked him to stop as they have nearly reached the place but Abinash did not reply and carried on his duty. Finally when they reached at the house the hands of the watch had crossed the 1 AM milestone.

Sundar looked at Abinash whose face was full of perspiration even in that chilling night. He then said, you have some foods and drinks first and spend the night here at our house. He added, then in the morning first repair your rickshaw before you start for your place. Abinash initially hesitated but finally agreed to

Sundar. He was still breathing intensely. Rani knocked the door and called the family people to open the same.

Mukunda first approached and opened the door. All the others in the house had also woken up. They could not believe that Sundar had done something like that.

What the hell instigated you to do something like that? Mukunda almost screamed at his brother. He added, it would have been a separate case if you were alone but ..... You are the limit man, he could not find the exact words he should use and stopped in between.

Sundar was probably rebuked for the first time by his elder brothers in his life for doing some adventure like this. Everything is over without any problem, he just said in defense.

"Without any problem"? God knows.

EMERGENCY ...

EMERGENCY DECLARED ...

PRESIDENT PROCLAIMS NATIONAL EMERGENCY ...

SECURITY OF INDIA THREATENED BY INTERNAL DISTURBANCES ...

PREVENTIVE ARRESTS: OPPOSITION LEADRES ARE ARRESTED ...

PRESS CENSORSHIP IMPOSED ...

These were some of those headlines in various national and local newspapers on 26th June, 1975.

The nation and its citizens were shattered by the news that were coming out from various sources, some were more authentic and the rest were less but the news were hitting everyone. Irrespective of strata the entire population was under dilemma, including students, teachers, government employees, businessmen, intellectuals, journalists, professionals, political activists or even jobless vagabonds. They were unable to digest the incident or accident, whatever it was which have happened last night, that is 25th of June, 1975, the darkest day in the history of Indian democracy.

The tightest slap on the face of Indian Democracy in its history came on the 25th June, 1975 with the sudden announcement of Emergency by the then prime minister of the country Mrs. Indira Gandhi. It came in to effect just on the ground of typical self-centered thinking for mare personal political gain and rivalry. The complete misuse of power at its zenith quaked the entire nation and its citizens, if not the civilization at large. Freedom of speech banned, freedom of thinking crushed under military actions, debating the anti-people government policies were shuttered, freedom of movements became under the scanner of the government spying agencies, not the leaders of the opposition political parties only but at the same time the cadres also were arrested without any reason and thrown behind the bar without any charges against them. The law and order became nothing better than the pandemonium in the hands of the goons directly under the control of the government and leaders of the ruling party.

Indian "Democracy" had become the "Demon - Cracy" and the entire system was hacked to death mercilessly.

WHY& HOW

1970s was perhaps the gloomiest period for many democracies throughout the world. Due to causes like high inflation, unemployment and Middle East crisis, democracies across the world had to struggle with ample of existential crises. At the exact same time, India faced a much bigger existential threat under the worst of the tyrants. As Prime Minister Indira Gandhi's political position deteriorated, she brought out a slew of constitutional amendments that threatened not only the foundation of Indian democracy but at the same time it's beliefs, it's thoughts, it's intellects and finally it's existence.

In the year of 1971, the same year the Nation has gone through a war with its hostile neighbor in both the western and eastern frontier, the Indira Gandhi led government brought up the Constitutional Amendment 24 and allowed the Parliament to dilute the fundamental rights by amendments to the constitution. This was in reaction to the Supreme Court ruling that stated fundamental rights enshrined in the constitution cannot be altered. But people who were happier with the victory over Pakistan in the external territory did not even reacted against such harsh attack on the pillar of democracy and let it go unnoticed. Indira Gandhi, after the win over Pakistan and freeing Bangladesh from there, had become perhaps the tallest figure amongst all the politicians in the country.

Just next year in 1972 the government again hit back on the democratic rights of its people by bringing the Amendment 25 which allowed the suspension of the right to private property allowing the government to take over anybody's property. But again the nation suffering from huge influx of refugees, mainly Hindus who were under constant attack from the Muslims in the Islamic

Bangladesh and were fleeing to the Indian Territory, was more involved in addressing the economic crisis than the anti-people policies of the government in the central power. But, the worst was yet to come.

In 1975, the High Court of Allahabad declared that the election of Indira Gandhi as fraudulent and nullified the election. Although the nullification was based on minor charges, what followed was unanticipated. To keep herself in power, Ms. Gandhi suspended Indian democracy with a variety of steps.

She with the help of her puppets in the government brought the 39th Amendment in the year 1975 and allowed an Indian Prime Minister to ignore the courts. Thus, the Allahabad High Court order was rendered invalid. She also invoked the rarest provision of the Constitution (Article 352) to declare an emergency, which is generally beseeched only in the case when the nation is under serious threat of civil or external war like situations. Civil rights, Parliament and elections were suspended. The Prime Minister could now just rule by decree. The nightmare had happened on the 25th of day of June, 1975.

On that blackest day of Indian History after Independence, Emergency was imposed.

Overnight thousands of politicians & journalists were jailed all over the country. Protests were contained with an iron fist. Over 140,000 people were detained without trial. Censorship on newspapers was imposed. No one was allowed to write against the anti-people and undemocratic policies of the government.

Though the government and the law and order agencies in the months of emergency tried their best and even sometimes crossed the boundary of not only democracy but at the same time humanity also to make their political bosses happy and feel secure but could not kill the spirit of the nation and its people. They tried to achieve their goal by traumatizing the society, the intellectuals and also the normal people by arresting every person with a political belief other than the ruling party, but some of the leaders and cadres managed to challenge the efficiency of those state sponsored goons by going underground and carried out their political works continually. The more the law and order tried to tightened and pressurize those people probably the more uncompromising and dedicated those leaders and cadres became in carrying out their agendas and activities. The mass support was with those fighters and that helped them a lot to keep on resisting the powerful government, its agencies and machineries with the bare minimum facilities and finally the government lost the game.

BACK IN BENGAL

In one hand the people were still suffering from the violent Naxalites movements when they were forced to hold the emergency in their other hand. There was no space left for the common man to live a peaceful life.

In this part of the country as the political rival of the Congress, the leftists were under attack by the emergency as a rival political ideologue to the ruling party. Excepting one or two leaders who had an under-the-table arrangements with the Congress leaders both in the center as well as in the state, it became a nightmare for the other leaders and cadres of the party as the police and other government agencies became more than alert to put everyone related to the leftist ideology behind the bar with a charge of anti-national activity. Only except those leftist leaders who had been maintaining a good rapport with the leaders of Congress party, all the other front line leaders were arrested and thrown behind the bar except one or two who managed to escape befooling the agencies. One of them was the legendary leader Late Gopal Krishna Konar. He was from a very well to do family from a village of rural Bengal but he left everything he got from his predecessors and joined the leftist movement in the state at the early days of his college life. He was an educated person and a leader respected by all due to his sacrifices and hard works for the ideological movement. The man had a tremendous capacity of reminding people by their name and location, even for those people whom he had hardly seen or conversed with one or two times in some previous occasion, might be years back. The person was so near and dear one to the poor, mainly to the farmers and the laborers that those people were even ready to sacrifice their own lives for securing their leader Gopal da. This tremendous support from the people compelled the law and order and the spying agencies of the state to fail to catch Gopal Krishna Konar. He probably was one of those handful of prominent leaders who managed to move as per requirement throughout the twenty-one months of the emergency period and carried out the political activities without being tracked by the police ever.

Anil da has been arrested yesterday, Surya whispered to Sundar. They were seating in the club room but the main lights were off and only a slim pie of the adjacent street light was making its way to the room through the open window.

Hmm, I know, Habu told me in the morning, Sundar replied almost mournfully.

Surya stared around and said, Sundar both you and I am also under the tight scanner of the police and government surveillance agencies due to our political involvements. He paused and continued, I think for some days at least you should not get involved openly as you are after all a government employee.

I have also thought about that, Sundar replied, unless the situation changes I have decided that I will carry on my political activities in a concealed way. He added, only the handful of us who are till outside the bars should be more cautious and depict to everyone that no one will try to contact any other openly. And also convey that no one will keep or carry any document or pamphlet at home or with himself unless that is extremely needed.

Okay, Surya replied, by tomorrow I will convey the message to everyone. It's already too late and I think we must go home, Surya added.

Sundar looked at his wrist watch, it was almost eleven. They came out of the room and locked it properly. Are you going to office tomorrow or will be at home, Surya asked Sundar before leaving. Sundar replied, of course I will go to office, he paused and added, my weekly off is on Thursday and not on Sunday. Hmm, okay then, Surya said and set off.

Sundar lighted a cigarette and started moving towards the abandoned house. It was clear to him that he might be lifted by the police any day due to his past records of political involvements so he had reduced his stay at his ancestral house and used to visit occasionally only to meet his wife and daughter. He spends the day hours in his office but in the night hours he use to hide either in the tormented building beside the ground or in the club room or in another old and abandoned structure in a nearby village. Both of the old, ruined and uninhibited structures are famous as haunted places and so are actually avoided by the local people which has made those places undoubtedly better dwelling for hide out. After office Sundar generally avails the early evening train so that he could reach his place before the market is closed and the roads are empty. In the night hours somebody form his house use to take his food in a container to a predefined place and after dining Sundar use to return the container to the same person as quick as possible.

Next day was a chilling day of winter, Sundar was working in his office. In the lunch hour he went to have his food in the adjacent cafeteria when he for the first time noticed an old man was seating beside the entrance of the cafeteria. The man was seating just like another beggar who use to seat in the winter days covering their body with old tormented blankets but this man had also covered his face with the same blanket he wore on his body which was not common. The social situation was so that it created a skeptic mind in Sundar and he has started watching every person or thing with a questioning view. He tried to see the face of the man but it was impossible. After lunch he returned to office and got involved in his work again which let him forget the man. In the afternoon when he again came to the cafeteria for tea and cigarrete he pointed the same man seating till then in the same manner but overlooked this time.

At the end of the day it was totally out of his mind. Today as the workload was high and maximum of the team members were in their weekly leave so Sundar had to work a bit longer and after handing over the continuation of the rest of job to his replacement he left his office later than his usual time. After completion when Sundar reached the platform for taking the early evening train, it was already too late and the train was gone. So he had nothing to do except waiting for the next train which was scheduled nearly after one hour. As it was a Sunday so the rash was much less than any other weekdays and in reality there was hardly a few people for the train on the platform. After a long wait finally the late evening train arrived at the platform. Sundar got in to the compartment he used to travel and found only a handful of people seating in the compartment. He was indifferent unless his sight fall on a co-passenger. Sundar got stunned seeing that old beggar kind of person who was seating in the entrance of the cafeteria is seating in the same compartment but he is seating in the pavement of the gate in such a position that anybody who wants to enter or exit the compartment will have to pass through his side. Initially he thought this might be another such beggar but after noticing intensely he sensed that this one is not the same as any other beggar. The moment a thought struck him, is he following me? Who the man could be, a spy?

The train moved out of the platform on schedule. There was no one to talk so that he could divert his mind from the beggar. So many thoughts and tensions were buzzing in his mind. Sundar was feeling quite cynic about the man but he is now in such a situation that neither he could ask the man about who he is nor he was able to move out of the train without being noticed by the man. He had no other option but to be seated there, so let himself sat in his seat being highly alert.

The train was on schedule and was crossing one after another station. The compartment was becoming emptier after each stoppage as the passengers were boarding off in their respective railway stations. The way the train arrived Gopalpur in one hour. Sundar saw that the only man except him and the beggar boarded off in the station and no one boarded in. He came in to the gate and from a hawker took a cup of tea with an intension to watch the beggar from close and if that man tries to chase him or is a person from police or government surveillance then at least he could try to jump off the train to escape. He noticed that the man is still seating in the same style covering his face and body together with a single old and tormented blanket and it seems like he is sleeping. Sundar tried from many angles to see the face of the man but the way he had covered his face it was impregnable and impossible for anyone to have a glance of the face. The train generally stops for a longer period in the Gopalpur as it is the most important station after Howrah to Burdwan in the main line. Throughout the period the train halted at Gopalpur Sundar watched the man but could not see his face or get any indication or activity. The body did not even moved for an inch as if it was not a human being rather a sack covered with a tormented blanket. Finally the train started but Sundar did not return to his seat rather he stood in the opposite gate of where the man was seating. The train crossed all the stations in between Gopalpur and Sundar's native place in next few minutes.

Now when it was approaching Sundar's destination a human voice came out of the covered figure and asked, if I am not wrong, your name is Sundar, right?

Sundar was shocked and at the same time alerted to the maximum possible. He looked around the compartment to find is there any other companion of the spy present, but the compartment was empty except the spy and himself. In a moment he decided if the spy is not carrying any fire weapon then it will not be tough for him to knock him down, he is quite capable for that. Sundar is now cent percent confirmed that the man is a spy, so the time has come and he was just going to be offensive when the man slightly uncover his face. This time the shock was even bigger for Sundar, a verse came out of his lips automatically out of sheer surprise...... Gopal da. Yes it was Gopal Krishna Konar. Sundar paused for the moment and added, Gopal da, you? You are following me from the morning? But why?

The man sharply kept his forefinger on his own lips to gesturing Sundar to restrain from calling his name. Then he called Sundar closer to him by hand gesture and in a very low voice said, I had to deliver this pamphlets to Amlan and he will come to Lakshmipur tomorrow in the morning nearly at 10:30 AM at Sukanta's home. He stopped and then added, but I am being followed by a spy from yesterday so it is not possible for me to go there to deliver. Suddenly your name came in to my mind and I reminded that you work in Howrah and your place is close to Lakshmipur so I was following you. You know Sukanta right?

Sundar nodded his head and Gopal da bring out a bunch of paper from inside the blanket. He looked around spontaneously before handing over the same bunch to Sundar's hand and with the same low voice instruct him, put these in your bag and to be very careful while carrying or delivering these to Amlan.

Sundar till then was traumatized and like an obedient student followed the instructions from his mentor. The train in the meantime was approaching the station. Sundar asked, Gopal da why don't you come with me and stay for the night where I am staying? He added, you must be hungry, at least some foods and rest is necessary for you.

Gopal da smiled and said, by the night I will have to reach a specific place and that is important because some people are waiting there for me. Don't be worried. He told Sundar not to worry about him and again wore the blanket on him and came in to the same beggar's look. Sundar finally invited him at his house anytime he thinks necessary or he is free. Gopal da just smiled. The train arrived at the station and Sundar boarded off and did not look back as he was guided by his mentor.

After some years from that day Gopal da visited Sundar's house on the occasion of the fifth birthday celebration of Mani, Sundar's daughter and that was a red letter day in Sundar's life which he always felt proud to remember.

GRIHA PRABESH ...

This is really becoming harder day by day to manage within this single room and a half kitchen, Rani uttered to her husband while nourishing her youngest child and only son.

She paused for some moments and without getting any reply from Sundar she added, don't you think the time has come for us to consider about a better and at least some more spacious home, she completed and stared at her husband. Sundar was taking his evening tea and reading the newspaper seating on the bed that had occupied almost sixty percent of the space in the room. A cabinet, a table and a dressing table had occupied practically another thirty percent of the room leaving hardly any place to move around.

Are you telling me something? Sundar was engrossed in the newspaper and missed the words Rani uttered. Sensing that Rani was telling him something he raised his face and asked his wife? Rani repeated the same lines in reply but this time looking at her husband.

I do also have thought about it, Sundar arranged his words and continued, but this would be highly expensive for us to manage. He added, even if both of us pour our incomes in to it. Moreover it will not be possible for me to live in any other village except this one if I am living in this area. And as you also know that there is hardly any vacant land left for housing here, he completed.

Hmm, but in that case we have to think differently, Rani replied. She added, Mani is in the most important juncture of her education and it is really tough for her to carry her studies here within the hustle bustle of this only room. At the same time it is not also possible to ask the kids not to play or make any disturbance. Rani found Sundar was eagerly staring at her, so she continued, some of our office colleagues are shifting from their aboriginal places to somewhere near to Howrah, if you agree I can talk to them also. They were saying that those places are not yet very expensive and they are actually starting with only two rooms, a kitchen and a bath, she competed.

Okay, let me think of it for two days and let see what could be arranged, Sundar replied and left the room. Though he moved out of there and moved towards the market but his thought processes were moving around the topic he has just discussed with his wife. This is a typical characteristic of Sundar, once something hits his mind he will keep on thinking the same unless he find out a suitable solution for that. That day he chatted with his friend and met people he was scheduled to but the thought of a home kept pinning his mind.

The piece of land, just in the corner of the village road is also good, whom does it belong to, Rani asked to Sundar while rearranging the kitchen utensils after dinner. Which piece of land, Sundar asked while smoking his cigarette standing on the door that leads to the open portion of the first floor. Are you talking about that piece of land besides the house of the Chatterjee's, Sundar enquired to be sure about?

Yes, and if we can get that then all the purposes will be solved, Rani replied and added, in one hand you would have the chance of staying here in this village and the land is not only perfect for us but also very well positioned. Sundar did not answer just smiled back. Why are you smiling? Rani asked with surprise.

Sundar replied, that piece of land belongs to Atindra uncle, you know Atindra Maiti, he asked. Rani stared at Sundar, she was almost done with her job and while washing her hands she replied, yes, the tall elderly person from the Maiti family, the man use to walk with a stick in his hand. She added, I have seen him in social occasions many times. He seems to be a very good man.

Yes, he is Atindra Maiti, no doubt that he is indeed a good person but at the same time perhaps the most skeptical man I have ever seen in my life. He paused and took a long puff and added, not only me, if you go and ask anyone in the village I don't think you would get a different reply. If I request him for the land then I will probably be the third or might be the fourth person who will ask him the same thing. Sundar continued, last time he even verbally promised to someone and then turned back on the day the registry of the property was scheduled in the court. I am not going be another such idiot. Rani did not answer and the discussion was over. They went to sleep as early in the next morning both of them will have to go to their offices.

Next day in the office Rani searched for her colleague Madhuri, one of such colleagues in the office who had relocated from her aboriginal in-law's house and was building her house in a nearby place to Howrah. Finally Rani saw her in the sorting section. Hey Madhuri, can I talk to you know, Rani asked her colleague.

Yah, sure, why not, Madhuri replied instantly.

That day you were saying that you have started your house in Ballavpur, Rani paused and then added, how is that going?

I believe it would take another six to seven months at least to become habitable, Madhuri replied. She thought for a moment and then asked, you were also talking with Ujjwala about something like this that day, right. Are you also planning for one?

Yes, but not very sure about how to arrange all these, Rani answered gloomily. Actually neither Sundar nor I have any experience on this, so both of us are a bit shaky.

Don't worry, no one need to be a master of everything, even we were also shaky, Madhuri replied. By the way if you prefer Ballavpur then I can talk to people known to me for a piece of land near my house.

I think that will be better, at least you will be there to liaison, Rani replied smilingly.

ALMOST A MONTH LATER

Almost one month has passed by, Rani within this time had discussed with her colleagues regarding the places where they had either purchased lands for their future homes or they are living. While selecting she always kept in mind that the place should be near to their office and also must be well communicated. At the same time she also had kept in mind that there must be good schools and colleges in the vicinity. She had already visited some of such areas taking breaks from office in the lunch time and also noted one or two out of those places which she had found affordable as well as favorable. She had done all this on her own and decided to discuss in details with Sundar next Sunday.

Have a look at the places, Rani placed a piece of paper in front of Sundar, who was seating on the table with their monthly accounts. It was later in the morning of a Sunday when he has returned from the market and was cherishing over a cigarette and calculating the monthly expenditures that are due. She continued, I have checked almost all of those personally and those underlined are not bad and also affordable I think. She pointed to some of the underlined lines, mainly addresses written on the paper. Sundar glanced at the piece of the paper and raised to stare at Rani almost surprised. He never thought Rani could do all such material works and that too in such a matured way. There was clear appreciation and astonishment both playing on his eyes simultaneously. Out of all these listed here I think this one would be better, as it is near to Howrah as well as Vola da and Sil already live there so we will get a known neighborhood, Sundar replied pointing to a specific location on the list prepared by his wife. Vola da and Sil are out of those office associates who are more friends than colleague to Sundar. He paused and thought for a while and then said, okay then tomorrow after office I will visit the place with Vola da.

I will also be with you then, Rani replied with a cheery mind.

Next day in the office Sundar first talked to Vola da and then being assured and fixing the time of visit he informed the same to Sil just an hour before the closing time of their duty. He knew his friend from the core and was well aware that if he would have gone the other way round then until then the entire office would have known about their plan to visit that place.

Nothing like it man, if you relocate here then we all will be neighbors, what you say Sil, Vola da said jubilantly while chatting to Sundar. Obviously, Sil replied. After office Sundar and Rani was on their way to the visit the piece of land they have selected accompanied by Vola da and Sil. It took nearly one hour to reach the place from their office. You guys stay here and I am going to call the owner of the land, Vola da informed the three and walked towards a neighboring house. It took almost ten minutes for Vola da to return with a short heighted flabby man, the owner of the land who is selling his land after plotting the vast area in to smaller pieces. In the meantime Sil show Sundar and Rani the piece of land he has purchased and his new house under construction and at the same time described in details about the facilities that were available in the vicinity.

The owner of the land arrived with a wide smile on his face for the prospective customers. The place was quite good and the price also affordable so it was almost finalized on the spot.

So when I could expect for the registration and name transfer and all other legalities involved for the final sell out, the owner asked Sundar.

Sundar thought for some moments and then replied, I need some time to arrange everything as it is quite a hefty job to manage these all. He paused and added, I think by next month I will finalize, and once that arrangements are done I will let you know by Vola da or Sil. The owner nodded smilingly appreciating Sundar's plan.

After the visit everyone was happy but Rani was perhaps the most.

THE WIND CHANGER

Sundar da what am I listening? Are you really relocating to Bhadreswar? Sumanta asked entering the club room with utter surprise.

Hmmm, Sundar raised his face to listen properly what the boy is saying. He was concentrating on the cards in his hand and was almost immersed in to that. Sumanta repeated his question. Yah, I have thought about relocating, Sundar replied before going in to the cards again. He then added fixing his eyes on the cards only, but not right now, just going to purchase a land and it will take at least six months to one year more to build a house with minimum requirements to live, Sundar completed.

What? That mean maximum after one year or so from now you will be relocated to Bhadreswar, this time Dhruba, Sundar's partner in the game and a friend of Sundar's brother Anil asked him. He continued without waiting for the answer for his first question, why don't you purchase a piece of land somewhere here itself and build your home?

Look, if I will live here then I will not build my home anywhere out of this locality, Sundar replied to Dhruba, he paused and added, and here in this village the only piece of land which is selectable belongs to your uncle Atindra Maiti.

Why don't you approach him then, he will never let you down, Dhruba replied and others supported him.

You perhaps know everything about the history of the land and your uncle's deeds, Sundar said, so I don't want to be another person to be fooled, Sundar completed with a placid voice. Everybody was well known about the facts Sundar referred to and had no answer so the discussion stopped there. The mood of playing cards was gone and nobody was interested in the game anymore and it was left.

Please wake up, Dhruba is calling you and waiting outside, Rani said to Sundar. It was quite early in the morning, almost six o'clock. Dhruba, so early in the morning, Sundar surprisingly uttered to himself. He woke up and came downstairs almost in hurry to meet Dhruba. What happened? Everything okay, Sundar asked Dhruba.

A smile played on Dhruba's face. Uncle has asked you to meet him by next one hour, before he is left for the farm, he replied. Uncle.... Atindra uncle? Sundar asked to be more precise.

Yes, by 7 AM, Dhruba replied and added by the way he leaves for the farm sharp at 7 every day. He turned to return.

But why? Anything important? Should I come with you right away? Sundar asked Dhruba.

No need to be tensed, just take your time and come to our house by 7 AM and I will also be waiting there with my uncle, Dhruba replied and moved forward.

Any problem, Rani asked her husband. I don't know, Dhruba did not disclose anything, just told me to meet Atindra uncle by 7 AM, Sundar replied and moved on to the way to the washroom.

Got to know from Dhruba that you are planning to relocate to Bhadreswar, is it true?

Sundar was seating in the big classically styled hall in front of Atindra Maiti after half an hour from Dhruba left, when he was asked to answer the question by the same man. Dhruba was standing behind the chair his uncle was seating on.

Actually there is a tremendous space crunch in the existing home and it is really tough to manage there with three kids, so I was thinking of making a new home, Sundar avoided answering directly.

Hmmm, Dhruba was telling that if I sell you the piece of land beside Chatterjee's house you will stay here in this village, the voice of Atindra Maiti roared in the room. Sundar did not answer the question just nodded his head. Okay then, I am selling you that, schedule a day for registration of the land in the court, now I will leave, Atindra completed and left the chair.

Then let us do it day after tomorrow, by tomorrow I will arrange a lawyer and complete other arrangements, Sundar replied.

Atindra stopped, "let us do it day after tomorrow", he mocked Sundar. Have you checked with the temple priest whether that day is good for such job or not, he replied? You young boys, what do you think of yourselves? He added, everything could not be done every day, everything has a rule to be followed. He paused, thought for a moment and then again said, okay, you leave it, I will arrange and let you know. Atindra left the room. Both Sundar and Dhruba was stunned to the maximum.

Dhruba informed Atindra uncle last night that we are planning to relocate to Bhadreswar and could only stay here if he sells us that piece of land to build our home. He has assured me that he would sell the land to me, Sundar replied to his wife who was eagerly waiting to know what happened. He himself will manage the legalities and will let me know about the date of registry of the same in the court once everything is done, Sundar completed.

All plans of relocation was cancelled out and in next two weeks Atindra Maiti categorically arranged everything required, completed all the legal formalities and sold the land to Sundar. Everything happened so fast that it seems to be a dream. The man who had promised too many people about that piece of land and ultimately ended up with harassment for the buyers suddenly changed his mind and he himself arranged for everything needed to sell the same to Sundar. It was destiny, nothing could explain it in any better way.

Within next three months the foundation ceremony was done and the building started coming up. A very young and new masonry contractor, Sunil was hired for the job. He was a man of highest dignity and used to respect Sundar as his own elder brother due to the help once he received from Sundar. On the other hand Sundar was working day and night to support the expenses and his wife Rani was also supporting him all-out. Initially they planned for just two rooms, a kitchen and a bathroom, the minimum that is required but with time suggestions started coming from various well-wishers regarding additional things. Finally one dinning and a balcony was included. The expenses was exceeding the expectation and the savings fall down to zero but the couple did not look back and carried on their venture against all odds. They always used to console themselves that once the house is ready everything will be managed and proper again. In next eight months the building was more or less complete and in a good enough condition to relocate. This time Sundar did not forget to discuss with the priest to schedule a perfect day for arranging the religious rituals for relocating to his new house. The priest after consulting his religious scriptures and calendars fixed a date after fifteen days for *"Griha Prabesh"*.

THE DAY

The arthritis pain has become a nightmare for Sundar. He had been suffering it for almost last five years. Many physicians have already been consulted but yielded no result. The same pain has resurged suddenly just two days before the day of Griha Prabesh and made Sundar almost incapable of doing any hard work. Inevitably the entire responsibility of transferring all the fixtures, furniture, utensils and other important things from his ancestral house to the new one has fallen on his wife Rani. There is no doubt that she is capable enough to manage these sort of jobs but managing three kids at the same time has made the task more critical for her. Especially their youngest son who has just started walking and every now and then loses his balance and fall on the ground due to his heavy weight.

On the scheduled day Sundar anyhow reached his new house in the morning. His wife was busy in arranging all the necessary items that will be required for the puja and their elder daughter Mani was helping her mother. I am going to the old house to bring some items, unless I return please take care of the boy, Rani said to Sundar and placed her son near him. Sundar's brother Kuntal and his wife was arranging things there too. Everyone was busy and the boy being unnoticed stood up and started walking towards the colorful flowers kept in the plate for the puja and the inevitable happened. Before anyone could hold him, the boy slipped on the floor and fall by his face. A tremendous cry moved everybody towards that. His lips were severely injured and bleeding intensely. The entire scene took place in front of Sundar but he was not in a condition to move due the pain which has almost paralyzed him. Kuntal's wife ran towards the boy, took him on her hands and started searching for some first aid, but found nothing in the new house. She started running towards the old house taking the boy on her hands expecting some first aid there.

Rani while coming out of their old room on the way back to her new house with some items in her hand saw her son getting treated by one of his uncle and aunty by the wale in the lawn. She promptly joined the treating party and everything became normal within some time. Within next few minutes she came back to her new home with his son.

I understand your condition but expected you will at least manage the kid for some time, returning to the new house Rani uttered to Sundar in a low voice only audible to the listener. When have your son listened to me, Sundar replied in the same tone. Yah, whenever he is naughty, he is my son, otherwise yours, Rani replied smilingly.

The puja and rituals were completed successfully without any more problem. Finally Sundar was in his home, his own home made up of his blood and sweat.

NEVER ENDING PROJECT

It was no less than starting life as a new one. Every time Sundar and Rani had to work hard even after managing their respective jobs to arrange and rearrange each and every small things to make the new life complete, but they did it cheerfully. Very soon they understood that just building a house is not enough, you need to arrange many other things too. You have to arrange a water connection, paint the house, establish a boundary wall so on and so forth and all these things required investment of resources. They invested every bits and pieces of their income behind fulfilling their dream. It took almost one year to complete the house in all respect with availability of all required amenities to live a comfortable life.

The hard fact of life is, as the time passes by the requirements increases. Initially a deep wale was dig as a source of water for daily uses. Water for drinking and cooking used to be arranged from the public hand pumps in the village. So the first addition of resource came as a private hand pump in within the boundary of the house. Next within one year that hand pump was replaced by motorized pump with a water reservoir on top of the roof.

After that for some years there was no more addition. Now after three years Rani first wished for an additional room in the first floor. Initially it took some time to agree Sundar but at the end he agreed. Again Sunil was called and after estimation of cost involve he was given the job. Rani wished for one room but finally after one year when the construction ended up there were three rooms and a bathroom. Sundar was then at his early fifties, a perfect family man with all the responsibilities.

The phenomenon did not end up there. After some years when all the kids grew up and especially the eldest daughter got married, necessity of another room surged up. So finally the last room was added to the existing structure in the ground floor. That was the last addition to the house incorporated nearly twenty years from the year it was started. The people within family used to laugh at discussing the building up of their house. Sundar's son used to call this a "never ending project", but it was decided that no more addition will be made in the house.

Decisions are probably made to be changed. The decision of no more addition of infrastructure in the house changed almost thirty years from the year the house was started and ten years from the day the decision was taken. The boundary wall when constructed was made with minimum possible resources due to crunches of funds. Now, after standing so long against all the natural atrocities suddenly one day, a part of it fall down. There was no other option but to rebuild that part but Sundar decided to replace the entire wall with new construction. All the family members opposed the idea but he did not bother. He replied that at his late sixties, this is probably going to be the last time he is investing on this house so he will do it properly and employed masonry for the same. At the same time he also ordered to repaint the house as the paint had got patches in various places and the walls were getting exposed. The work took two months to be completed.

Now it's looking just like a brand new house, Sundar looked at his house and remarked.

The building once he started with minimum resources and maximum will power, the building which was no less than a heaven for him, the building he loved and adored just as his own child, the building that was his "Home" was really standing tall.

THE NAUGHTY SWEETHEART ...

Go and bring some water from your mother, Sundar asked his three years old son......

Sundar has just returned from the market and quite opposite to his character has parked his bicycle in the middle of the lawn, without properly placing it in the place where it is parked. Bring in a plate and not in a tumbler, he continued. The boy failed to understand what his father meant to say and stood still there. In the mean while Sundar brought a small puppy out of a bag and placed it on the mattress. A puppy of dark black color with long white patch running from its forehead to the nostrils. A very feeble hardly of a month old puppy, was looking so tired and suffering as if it won't survive any more. The puppy tried to sniff the mattress but it was probably needed more energy that it could gather so it fell upon the mattress helplessly. Go and bring some water in a plate for it from your mother, Sundar repeated looking at his son who was watching what his father is doing with extreme curiosity. The boy now could make out what his father is asking for and after understanding became so excited that he hurriedly ran to the kitchen to follow what his father has directed.

Mom please give me some water in a plate and not in a tumbler for the puppy father has taken home, the boy completed in one breadth. What, his mom was busy in household job so could not made out what her son is talking about. The boy repeated the same line but this time perhaps in a tone that was more effectively expressing the urgency and also in a speedier way than earlier. Your father has taken home a puppy? Rani asked her son but it seemed she is asking to herself. The boy reiterated the same words. This time his mother gave him what he was asking for and next moment the boy disappeared from the kitchen almost with the speed of an airstream.

After managing and arranging her jobs in the kitchen when Rani came to see what actually has happened, she found her husband and son seating on the ground and trying to feed a puppy some water. Though Sundar was trying his best but his inexperience of handling such kind of job was quite visible. His son was seating by his side and his eyes were glowing in energy. Do you understand what kind of responsibilities you need to accept when you get a pet and what amount of time you would need to devote for the animal? Rani uttered to Sundar in a very serious tone. Till then Sundar was so busy in managing the puppy that he has not noticed Rani standing behind him and watching. From the voice and tune Sundar could well understand that the weather is not so soothing and could anytime turn in to a stormy one. I understand but at the same time can't witness a life ends up without food and water in front of my eyes, Sundar answered. He chose not to answer her question directly rather twisted his reply in describing why he had accepted the responsibility of this small animal. What do you mean by that, she asked, this time the tune was more enquiring and the voice was more lenient.

This is the chance Sundar was waiting for to present himself. He started narrating, do you remind I told you two days before that a car has collided with a truck in the main road. Rani nodded her head, yes she could recall that Sundar has told her about a deadly accident that has taken place. Sundar continued, unfortunately neither the driver nor the other person who was seating beside the driver in the car survived but this puppy was not injured, it was probably in the back seat. The investigating police officer took it with him in the police station but he could not manage it. It was not taking any food or drinks. Sundar paused for a moment and arranged his words correctly and then continued, now the situation was such that he thought the puppy will not survive. The officer is a regular visitor of the tea shop where we meet and also known to me. He was discussing it in the tea shop and actually requesting if someone could do something. I don't know why but I could not resist myself and asked him if I could see it once. He willingly took me with him and when I saw, it was not possible for me to be indifferent about the small life and I accepted the responsibility. Let's see if I could do something for the puppy, Sundar said. He then after a long gasp added, now if you think I should return it to the police station then I will, but in that case I can assure you that this life won't survive even two more days, he completed.

It was clear from the facial expression of Rani that the Sundar had succeeded in his job. She looked at the puppy and found his son trying to play with the puppy but it was so feeble that it was not in a position to reply. She intervened, please don't disturb it now, it is too week to play with you at this moment. She found a silent disagreement in her son's eye and so she assured him, let me take care of it now and once the puppy becomes well you will play with it. She lifted the puppy and took it with her.

In next two days the condition changed. The small life started regaining its strength and liveliness by the motherly care taken by Rani. The young boy in the house got so involved with his new friend that he even forgot to go outside to play with his other friends. It became a tough job to separate the boy from his new friend and vice-versa.

Sundar thought that he must consult with someone who is knowledgeable regarding what to be done about the vaccination of dogs. As he once heard that the animals need to be vaccinated but he did not have any prior experience of having a pet so he decided to talk to Suraj. It took three days and next Sunday Sundar called his friend Suraj who was not only a pet lover but at the same time was owning a kennel also. He was a bachelor and already had nearly ten pet dogs of different breeds in his kennel. When Suraj came to Sundar's house, he first took the puppy on his hand and after watching the tiny animal for quite some times what Suraj told was amazing. He said, as per my understanding the puppy by race is a German shepherd but it needs to have some vaccines and other necessary treatments. Then he asked for a piece of pen and paper and listed some vaccines that would be needed for the puppy.

But where would I get all these, Sundar asked Suraj. Suraj recommended a veterinarian. Suraj then asked his friend, by the way is the puppy had already given a name. Sundar shook his head mention that no name has yet been given to it. Finding that no name has yet been given Suraj suggested "Lusi" for the new female member of the family.

It took some days though, but then slowly Lusi started replying when called by name. Within a year or so from a tiny little puppy fighting for his survival on this planet, Lusi grown up to a sizable dog. Motherly care from Rani helped that little life to become a demanding child. It became a sweetheart for all the members of the family and the best friend for Sundar's son.

Time passed by and Lusi now is four years old and a mature dog. The adjacent garden and lawn area within the boundary walls of the house has become her kingdom and she doesn't like to allow any unwanted intruder in her kingdom. Lusi used to be the coolest type of animal unless there is any intrusion in her kingdom but any such attempt by anyone used to make her perhaps the most furious one. Uncounted number of rats had lost their lives for their infiltration in to the area. Two of such cases actually made Lusi famous in the neighborhood also.

One day a goat from a neighbor's house unfortunately intruded within Lusi's kingdom without knowing what is waiting for it. Lusi was lying on the lawn when she sensed some intrusion. It did not took more than a moment for Lusi to jump on to the intruder. The situation became so that the goat was cornered in a place near the hand pump and Lusi was standing just one or two meters away facing the goat. Lusi was staring to that intruder with fire in her eyes and just waiting for the proper time to jump on it when Rani, who then was busy in the kitchen heard some outcry. Someone was calling her son probably in the highest human voice. When she came out to the lawn she found their neighbor is shouting and actually drawing her attention towards the corner where Lusi and that helpless goat was standing facing each other, one with a killing instinct and the other probably with the sense of losing its life. Rani was dumbfounded when she saw Lusi standing in an attacking mood in front of the inoffensive animal afraid of the final misfortune. Thank god she was not late. She started calling Lusi back with all her strength and at the same time started moving step-by-step towards Lusi. Lusi was in an absolute dilemma as she was in no mood to spare an intruder but she could no way disregard the lady calling her to retreat. In the intervening time the scene had attracted some passersby also. Finally Rani approached the place and in a pampered way got hold of Lusi. The goat got the chance it was probably never expected and ran out of the place within twinkling of eye. Lusi in her own way showed some irritation initially but it did not take long for Rani to neutralize Lusi's anger.

The second incident had become a tremendous scene for those who had witnessed that and will probably never elope from their minds. It was an evening of October and there was no one in the house except Sundar's son and his youngest brother Babu. All had gone for shopping for the incoming Durga Puja. Sundar's son was playing carom with his youngest uncle in the inner most room of the house. Have not seen Lusi for long, where has she gone, suddenly Babu asked to Sundar's son. This youngest brother of Sundar was another close person to Lusi and used to take care of her so much.

Probably roaming in the garden, the boy who was asked the question answered. Nobody knows why but Babu's mind did not succumb to that logic and he left the game and started moving towards the main door while calling Lusi. Lusi....Lusi, Babu called and wait for some minutes but Lusi did not come or even responded, which was unusual. Now it was a concern, the duo stood up leaving the carom board there. They came out in the lawn. The lights in the lawn were on and what they saw in that light was literally shocking. Two animals standing face to face. In one side Lusi was standing placing all her body weight on her back legs and balancing with the front left leg. The front right leg she was swaying very slowly. All her killing weapons, the dangerous nails are out at the maximum and was looking at the opposition without blinking her eyes. On the opposite side there was a snake, clearly showing its skin prints in the light that it is a cobra. Nearly one and a half feet in length and a blackish rope like figure, half of it lying on the ground and the frontal half is erected straight from the lying half with its head spread out maximum in both sides looking like an umbrella. It is also swaying the erected portion of its body slowly from one side to the other. Sundar's son was just wanted to call Lusi when Babu stopped him and said, don't call her, she will lose her concentration. Babu added, we have nothing to do unless the duel is over. Lusi was waving her front right leg very slowly to distract her opponent and the snake was actually sensing the moving object only and targeting to hit that. Lusi was leaning back and every time the very moment the snake was trying to hit the waving leg she was easily backtracking. That was actually leading to a false hit by the snake on the ground. The moment the snake was hitting the ground Lusi was striking back on the head of the snake with her free leg and injuring it to the maximum possible by her sharp nails and at the same time was changing her own position to distract the opponent. It was a breathtaking situation for the spectators. The snake tried for long to hit its opponent but could not succeed in any of its attempts and ended up in bleeding condition. Understanding that the opponent is much ahead in tactic it started backpedalling but Lusi was in no mood to spare her enemy. The moment the snake was trying to move back, Lusi was snatching it back by its tail. The battle last for nearly an hour and finally the brutally injured and extremely bleeding body of the snake was lying in the lawn lifelessly. The duel was over and the winner was showing its achievement by waving its tail.

After being fully satisfied that her enemy is dead, Lusi came back with a winner's pride to her family members waiting for her with bated breath. Her joyous mood was being reflected from his posture and especially her waving of her tail. Babu and Sundar's son grabbed her and checked whether there was any sign of injury in Lusi's body but nothing such was found. After some time when the other members of the family returned home and got the details from Babu and especially the boy who was probably more excited than Lusi, they were taken aback. Let us burn it, Sundar said to his brother after checking the dead body of the snake.

Lusi is in danger, please come right away, Nisha almost cried to Rani. Nisha was a neighbor and used to pamper Lusi a lot. Lusi was so naughty that incidents were more or less a regular matter but one day the situation reversed. The street dogs used to bark on Lusi from the outside of the closed gate and Lusi also used to reply on the same tone. It was a strict direction from Sundar that the gate must never be kept open and everybody from the family obeyed that. One day unfortunately the gate was kept open by the boy who used to drop newspaper. That small mistake became severe. Rani was busy in her household job when Nisha approached her.

What happened, Rani asked while following Nisha towards the gate? Her anxiety was clearly visible on her face. The gate of your house was probably left open, Lusi went outside in the road and some street dogs had attacked her, Nisha completed in one breadth. The situation is totally a mess, she completed.

Lusi has actually sneaked through the open gate to the roads and a bunch of street dogs have attacked her. When Rani reached the place she was shaken by the visual. One of the street dog was lying dead and the blood flowing out of its wound in the neck has created a pool. Another was trying to survive from the fatal attack of Lusi. Two or three other dogs were barking on Lusi, who was also roaring. Lusi was injured lethally too on the backside of her head. There were blood all over the place. Rani and some other people present there jointly had to put effort to get the street dogs out. Lusi was taken back to home but she was severely injured, very critically.

Immediately a veterinarian was called and after watching the wounds in details he said, apply these ointments and medicines as I have prescribed but one thing I must say that the wounds are lethal and at present condition I can't say anything definitively. Though medical care was provided but the injury behind Lusi's head turned in to a serious one. Rani was trying her best with everything possible but the desired result was not being achieved. Finally another veterinarian was consulted. This time the situation developed and slowly things started changing. Every day Rani used to clear that injury with medicated lotion and redress the place with fresh and clean cottons and cloths. That was really hurting for Lusi and she used to make a crying like sound but never disregarded Rani. The scene was probably more hurting to Rani but she had no other choice but to carry on her duty towards the affectionate member of her family. Many people thought Lusi would not survive but Rani did not lose heart and was giving her best try with a confidence that those people will be proved wrong. It took nearly three to four months for Lusi to overcome the situation and slowly she again got back to her originality, the naughty sweetheart.

Time did not wait but Lusi did not change. She rather became more lively and naughty after getting out of that lethal injury and tremendous sufferings she had to bear with. One day even Rani got her knees wounded for Lusi. Though it was not Lusi's fault as she was actually trying to play with Rani but ended up hurting her.

Every Sunday it was the responsibility of Sundar's son to bathe Lusi and for Lusi it used to be the best time to actually bathe the boy instead. She used to be calm and quite unless the soap was applied and once the bubbles came out she used to come in to her originality. She used to start jumping on the boy with her front legs so that the soap bubbles are applied reverse. This cleaning event used to run for nearly an hour or so and both the boy and Lusi used to enjoy this unless Rani intervened and make it complete by rebuking both her son and Lusi.

Lusi used to be kept under the observation of Babu every time in the month of October when Sundar and his family used to visit Rani's parental house after Durga Puja for two days. These two days used to be very tough for Lusi though she was taken care by Babu with the best possible but she was very alone within her mind. The family, when used to return from their tour the way Lusi welcomed them was enormous. She wanted to run to everyone at a time and finally used to end up with circling all the members and making their way harder to walk freely. She used to lift her front legs on the members to adore them. In happiness Lusi used to run aimlessly here and there in the garden and lawn. That was a scene.

THE FRIENDSHIP

Suddenly in the locality a monkey became very famous for its activity. Everyone was afraid of its aggressive nature and almost every other day the story of its attacking someone or other became a natural phenomenon. People named it Ramu, but nobody knows where the name came from or who actually gave that name to that monkey. Ramu was actually a monkey who was probably pet to someone but after the death of its master, Ramu became free. People of the locality used to irritate and disturb Ramu by throwing stones and aching it. Everyone, more specifically the young boys of the area used to irritate Ramu and used to throw stones at him. The irritation and attack made Ramu more furious. The more the furiousness increased in Ramu, the more the irritation and attack by those people increased. The only place where Ramu used to be treated with love was Sundar's house, especially by Rani. Rani used to offer foods and fruits to Ramu. Initially whenever Ramu used to come Sundar's house Lusi used to be irritated and started chasing Ramu. One day when she saw Rani offering Ramu foods, she understood that Ramu is not a foe rather might be a friend. And from that day she stopped chasing Ramu and the two animals almost coexisted happily with one another. Many times the neighbors used to be surprised by seeing Lusi and Ramu seating on the lawn side by side and having their foods without attacking or troubling one another. In fact Lusi got another friend in Ramu.

With time, the more Lusi was getting elderly the more she started leaving many of her naughtiness behind. She became less aggressive and pretty shy by nature. Stopped irritating Sundar's son every now and then to play with her. The favorite game was the boy will throw a tennis ball far away and she will run to collect the ball and will return with the ball in her jaws. The same will continue unless the boy became tired because tiredness was something probably Lusi was unknown about. She also reduced spending time within the rooms rather started to stay in the garden and lawn more and more. In fact she used to spend hours resting under the Jasmine flower plant in the back side of the house. Even after dinner Rani had to call her to come in within the room and she used to come unwillingly.

One day Rani was depicting the changes of behavior in Lusi to a very elderly and experienced man Shambhu babu. He was the music teacher for their two daughters. She depicted how Lusi has changed her behavior and has become so calm and quite. She also said that now a days Lusi even does not want to stay inside the rooms and always prefer to spend most of its time in the garden and the lawn and more specifically lying down under the jasmine tree. Now a days Lusi always prefer to be alone. The facial expression of Shambhu babu changed. Don't take it otherwise but generally animals can sense their last time and specifically dogs, the man replied. Unfortunately when they have sensed that the final day is close, he paused for some moments and added, they usually don't want to stay inside a room and prefer to be alone. I hope she had lived her life, Shambhu babu replied with mourning face. All present there became speechless. After Shambhu babu left no one who were present there believed him and negated his opinion about Lusi. Because it was unthinkable to anyone of them. From the next day everyone in the family tried every possible means to cheer up Lusi with all her favorite things like foods, games and all but it was clear from her response that she was no more enjoying those things.

Lusi, Lusi.... Rani called Lusi several times for breakfast, but there was no reply from anywhere. All the members of the family started searching her and within next few minutes Lusi was discovered resting in her favorite place, under the Jasmine flower plant. It was the last days of the month of December and the plant was full of flowers, some had fallen on Lusi. She was sleeping peacefully almost on a bed of flowers, sleeping forever.

I want no more pet in this house again, Rani uttered to Sundar who was standing by her side. Sundar just nodded his head sensing the pain she was feeling.

Nearly after ten days from the day Shambhu babu illustrated the unusual behavior of animals at their last days Lusi proved the elderly man right.

I DID NOT CRY ...

What happened Krishna, neither Biswas da nor Subhash da have yet arrived? Is everything okay or today I have come earlier than expected? Sundar asked Krishna while locking and parking his bicycle slanting it on the side wall the shop.

Krishna is the owner of the book shop in the market. Sundar, Biswas and Subhash use to meet there in the evening every day after office and spend nearly two hours of time chatting over various issues from personal to political, on numerous cups of tea. Krishna also likes to take part in the various discussion and to facilitate the same he has arranged for a wooden bench for those people outside his shop. The tea shop, by the side of the book shop has transformed the place a perfect gossiping point catering the most important requirement for any gossip, cups of a boiling hot tea. Except the three many other people also visit the place to have tea and to be a part of the gossip but they are not as regular as the three. This regularity has bestowed them with some extra importance as well as some more rights too.

Though the three men are not of same age group but they are friends. Originally Biswas da is the eldest amongst the three and in his early sixties, Subhash da is younger than Biswas but elder than Sundar and in his mid-fifties and finally Sundar, the youngest in the group is in his mid-forty. Except the age they also have a lots of differences, like Biswas is kind of a man who does not speak unless he is not only asked to rather compelled to speak, whereas Subhash has always been a very full volume and open minded person who gets involved in everything as easily as anything else. Sundar has always been the bridge between the two polar opposite personalities due to his intelligent nature and capabilities of managing things. The only common thing in them is that they all are either present or retired employees of Indian Railway. Biswas, originally from a distant district Purulia, used to live in the office quarter with his family and recently has built a house and settled here in this place with a plan to live rest of his life here. He lives with his wife and two children, an elder daughter and a younger son. Subhash on the other hand was in Bihar for long and used to live in the railway quarter, but after the early death of his wife he has taken transfer here and live with his two children, an elder daughter and a younger son. He never says anything about his aboriginal place but has developed many habits including his choice of foods most likely the people of Bihar. Not only foods but at the same time his habit of chewing tobacco also depicts his long stay in that region.

Sundar waited there nearly for half an hour but neither Subhash nor Biswas came. So finally he ordered for a cup of tea for himself. He had just finished his tea when he saw Subhash riding a Rajdoot Motorbike and coming from the opposite side. The face of Biswas was visible from behind him. Sundar knew that none of the two possess any motorbike and was surprised as he did also not have any prior information about Subhash or Biswas is going to purchase any. The next moment he recalled that Biswas could not even ride a bicycle so it is absolute bizarre that he will buy a motorbike, so it must be Subhash. Before he could have even completed his thinking Subhash approached the place and stopped the vehicle there. A small crowed assembled there within minutes to see a motorbike, which used to be something extraordinary in early eighties of the previous millennium and that too in a rural place of Bengal. Biswas almost jumped off the bike and his facial expression was saying the condition of his mind. He perhaps had almost lost his life and any how has regained it. The condition of Biswas was totally opposite of his companion. He was totally taken aback after the ride and sat on the bench quietly. He was still in a dilemma that he is alive or not. It was much more than his limit to bear with such a bumpy ride on the two wheeler. Subhash on the other hand was almost boiling in happiness and ordered tea for Sundar, Biswas and himself first, then get off the bike and sat beside Sundar.

Don't order tea for me, Sundar said, I have just finished.

You will surely not die if you take another cup, Subhash replied. Sundar understood that there is no way to cancel Subhash at least now. In the meantime Subhash has started describing various features of his new motorbike boastfully to the people surrounding him. He has already left his seat and standing beside the bike and almost carrying out a detailed display with description of the bike. It took some time for Subhash to answer all the curious queries of the people about the vehicle and finally to have a chance to seat with his peers. Sundar was waiting calmly without asking any question about this to Subhash till that time. He knew

Subhash and was sure that the man will not omit to mention even the smallest point about his new pride even if Sundar does not ask to know. After the tea and a cigarette Subhash gave a speech on his Rajdoot bike. To be very precise he has purchased the bike from an Ex-Army person before three days. The bike was needed some maintenance job for which he gave it to an automobile shop in the town on the same day. Today they have delivered the same back as per schedule. He wanted Sundar to accompany him but as Sundar was absent he had to take Biswas with him on the tour.

The motorbike became a passion for Subhash very soon. Every Sunday he started coming to Sundar's house and request Sundar to get out for a short biking trip. After cancelling for some days finally one day Sundar had to accept the tour. That day in that trip they ridded towards the more rural areas. While driving Subhash suggested Sundar, you should also learn how to drive a motorbike. He added, and if you want I would show you how to drive, it's quite a complex thing to manage a bike properly but I am there to help you.

I don't have any interest in driving bike, Sundar replied showing no intention for what Subhash said.

Though the answer was not what Subhash expected but for that day he did not say anything but the idea started pinning his mind that he will surely encourage Sundar to learn how to drive. As everybody knew that Subhash was a very full volume and open minded person, next Sunday he again visited Sundar's house. This time again he started asking Sundar why he is not interested to learn driving a motorbike. Sundar tried to avoid the question by many ways as he was actually not interested but it was impossible to make Subhash understand. Subhash did not stop insisting Sundar for a suitable answer.

What extraordinary is there to drive a motorbike, finally at a point Sundar replied. He added, if a man knows how to drive a bicycle, he could anytime drive a motorcycle too, just he will need to know what is what and that's all, he completed. Subhash was not ready to buy this logic and replied, it is always easy to say and tough to accomplish. Sundar was strict to his point. Okay, then drive this bike when you know how to drive a bicycle, Subhash asked Sundar. Now for Sundar it became a challenging situation and there was no other option but to accept it. Subhash had already handed over the keys to Sundar.

Well, then take the bike to the nearest field, Sundar returned the keys back to Subhash and said. Why not on road, when you know driving a bike, Subhash mocked. Sundar replied maintaining the calmness on his face, because I do not want to hurt any person or animal for any mistake if I make even unknowingly.

He paused for a moment and added, and as I will be driving the bike for the first time so there might be mistakes. So I want to test my driving skill in such a place where there would be minimum chances of striking anyone.

Okay point is taken, Subhash replied and then asked Sundar to seat behind him. Subhash then drove the bike to the filed at some distance from the place they were discussing all these.

Subhash left the driver seat for Sundar and stood by the side. Sundar first asked Subhash, tell me in details what is what and what functionality is that particular item used for. Subhash gave a brief description of all the elements like brakes, clutch, gear pedal and other things. He also described how to change the gears and usage of clutch in details and finally asked, do you need to know anything more. Sundar shook his head to confirm that he does not need anything more and let himself sat on the bike properly first. Then he coolly kicked the bike to start, pressed the clutch and pushed the gear pedal down one step. No doubt that he was feeling a thrill in his mind and also a tremendous excitement but on face he did not express anything. He slowly release the clutch and the bike started moving. Even Sundar was not sure about his success would be so smooth. He was sure that for first time at least he would shut the engine off but fortunately he did not and the bike was moving smartly and smoothly. He then pressed the gear one more time and it became easier. The initial jerking was gone and the bike is now moving more effortlessly and was totally under the control of Sundar. Within few moments he was circling Subhash, who was probably the most surprised man on earth at this point. After completing four circles Sundar stopped the bike in front of Subhash and places the gear in neutral. It was another tough job for the first-timer but this also get completed without any problem.

I don't believe this is the first time you are driving a bike, Subhash said confidently. You must have done this before also otherwise it is no way possible for a man to drive so smoothly at his first attempt, he continued.

Wait, first answer me what are the things needed to drive a bike properly, Sundar has got off the bike and now was standing beside Subhash. He continued, the functions of the items you need to know and the process of balancing yourself on the two wheels, right? Sundar asked Subhash. Now as I said if a person knows how to run a bicycle he knows balancing on two wheels. So what else he needs is to know the functionalities of the items like brake, clutch, etc. Sundar continued. So what wrong did I say before and which of the logic mismatches with what I did? This is simple and you just need to be logical to understand this, absolutely nothing else is required.

Then why you don't buy a motorbike, when you know how to drive, Subhash asked. Almost after two weeks Sundar and Subhash was seating in their specific place in Book shop and Biswas was not yet there when Subhash asked Sundar. From the day Sundar had successfully drove the bike, Subhash has started agreeing his friend to buy a motorbike. Sundar always politely refused but was unable to stop his companion from discussing the issue.

Okay, let me tell you in details, Sundar replied. I have understood that unless I describe, you won't let me go. He added, to be very truthful this is what I was afraid of. To be more precise that is why I was even not ready to let myself know that I can drive a bike, Sundar completed.

What do you mean by this typical logic I don't understand, Subhash was shocked by the answer.

Hmmm.... Sundar took a long haul and stated, Subhash da, you know that just before some years I have anyhow completed my house. It was really very expensive for me to purchase a land and then make a house. He added, I don't have the affluence to have a bike right now.

SIX MONTHS LATER

It was an evening nearly six months from the day Subhash drove a motorbike for first time and Biswas experienced the bumpy ride and vowed that he will never do that mistake again in his life. Subhash reached Krishna's shop nearly an hour later than his usual time and found Sundar and Biswas has been there already. He ordered a cup of tea and sat on the bench. Matted hair, dark spot under eyes and frustration on his face, he was looking extremely shattered. For some time he did not talk to the other two as if he is physically here but his mind is in some other place.

Is everything okay? Sundar asked first. Subhash did not notice and asked back to Sundar, hmmm... are you telling me anything? Sundar asked again.

Brijesh is no more, Subhash answered in a muttering voice.

What? How come? What do you mean by Brijesh is no more, Sundar was shocked and he asked Subhash in reply.

Brijesh was known to Sundar. He was a good friend of Subhash and a very dynamic and cheerful man. For some moments Subhash did not speak anything and after that what he briefed is, today in the morning Brijesh left his house for Chandannagore on his new motorbike to meet one of his client at nearly 9 AM. While returning home nearly at 10 AM his motorbike crashed with a truck on the main road near Chuchurah. Though local people took him to the Sadar hospital at the earliest but he could not survive. Subhash continued that he got the news of the accident in the morning and went to the hospital first and then took his mortal remain to his home. Finally now he is coming from the burning ghat after cremation. No one was in a position to say anything except Subhash who has witnessed the entire situation. The family is in a tremendous condition as he was the only earning member of the house, Subhash completed while lighting his cigarette. The next one hour, unless the people left the place for returning home, all the talks went around Brijesh and the future of his family only. Someway or other every person present there had lost the energy to chat or enjoy.

Almost ten days from the day Brijesh passed away, in a Sunday morning Sundar was reading the newspaper in balcony of his house when he saw Subhash coming. Subhash came in after parking his bike by the road. Could you arrange 5000 rupees right now, he directly asked Sundar while seating on the chair in front of Sundar. Sundar was surprised as he had never seen Subhash borrowing money from anyone. Is everything okay, Sundar asked?

Look, there is a problem, Subhash's voice was tensed. He paused and arranged his words and then continued, Brijesh's family want to sell the motorbike as they feel that is the cause of their hard luck and reason behind the accident. They have talked to me on this and requested to find a buyer for the same. Now, I personally don't want that lovely bike gets sold to anyone who might have affordability but not the love for it, so I decided you are the only person I could believe in. Subhash kept staring at Sundar after completing his words.

Sundar thought for some moments, actually he has also got the zeal of a motorbike from the day he drove the bike for the first time with Subhash. He has also seen the bike Subhash is talking about, it is an "Enfield Bullet 350". It is simply majestic and there is no doubt about that. Do you too think the bike is cursed, Subhash asked to Sundar seeing him silent?

Sundar raised his face and said, you know I don't believe in all such superstitions. He has made his mind and added, okay then when are we going? Subhash was probably happier than Sundar and he excitedly stood up and replied, why not right now? Sundar disheartened him by replying that he will have to withdraw the money from the bank and scheduled to go next Sunday. Subhash sat down and said, then treat me a cup of tea.

All the eyes were kept open for quite some times with extreme surprise when Sundar's wife, daughters and son saw him parking a new Enfield Bullet 350 in the lawn of their home. The color of the bike was a picture-perfect combination of royal blue and silvery white. The sound it was generating was so weighty that it was creating a sense of respect and pride. The symbols on the both sides of the fuel tank was so simple but magnificent that everybody will look at it with curiosity as well as affection and none the less, respect. In one word it was simply royal in all sense. Sundar's four years old son was more than exited and ran towards where the bike was parked.

Be aware of the silencer pipe, it's hot enough to scorch your skin, Sundar yelled at his son. Other members also followed the kid. The bike is nice but I don't believe these two wheelers, Rani though happy but remarked with a sense of seriousness. By that time Sundar's son and younger daughter has already started requesting him for a ride.

Not now, you may go in the afternoon, as it was nearly 1 PM now, Rani intervened. The kids could not disobey their mother so went inside the house but the excitement they were feeling was tremendous. Right at 4 PM they woke up and started demanding for the promised ride. Sundar took them to a ride in the village paths. That was enough for the kids to be addicted to the ride and their father also enjoyed that to the maximum possible seeing the joyous faces of his children. From that day onwards it became nearly a rule that in holidays whenever Sundar used to take his motorbike out for any purpose, he had to take the kids with him.

Another person who was more fascinated about the bike was Sundar's youngest brother-in-law, Sukanta. He was in military services and started spending more time in his sister's house than his paternal one to get access to the bike whenever he used to come home in leaves. Sundar's nephews from his eldest brother Satyendra, were nearly of Sukanta's age and were his peers who used to instigate him to get the keys from their aunty in absence of Sundar. Rani never said no to her pampered youngest brother. Though Sukanta was good in riding bike but might because of his young age he was a bit reckless too. Many a time for his adventurous driving the bike had to face small damages and dents. Every time after his riding the bike for two or three days Sundar had to take that to the service station to get the damages and dents repaired.

In the month of October every year the family used to visit Rani's paternal house after the Durga Puja. This year Sundar planned to go by his motorbike. The place was far away from his own place and at least a journey of nearly four and a half hours by road. One day he depicted his plan to Rani, who was more surprised than interested. His son and younger daughter supported their father which energized Sundar more but his wife was no way ready to let him take the two kids with him in this adventure. So finally it was decided that Sundar will go by road with his two daughters as the elder one was mature enough to manage her sister, but his son will accompany his mother and will take the train route. Sundar with two of his daughters appreciated the biking expedition to the maximum possible. They travelled through various villages and small towns, stopped in some of those villages and towns, had their meals, so on and so forth. The journey was remarkable to all the three. The boy on the other hand did not have any option but to follow his mother and had to satisfy himself with two cartoon books and a bottle of cold drink that Rani promised him.

Time passed by and the children were growing up. The more they grew up, the more they became attracted to the bike. Especially Sundar's son who used to ask everything about the bike to know its functionalities. Sundar also enjoyed sharing his knowledge with his son and used to describe every details of the bike elaborately. The young boy slowly became so attached to the bike that whenever he used to get time he started seating on the bike. He used to seat on it either when it is parked in the garage or in the lawn of the house, even in the absence of his father or any elderly person. It was his most favorite game to seat on the standing bike, holding the handle and making a noise like "vroom vroom", as if he is driving the bike as his father do. It was known to everybody in the house and no one had ever taken it seriously or forbidden the boy of doing so unless that day when the boy made it a show.

That day Sundar was in hurry as he had to go for some important assignment. He took the bike out of the garage and parked it in the lawn and went inside to get ready. Usually he used to park the bike in its main stand knowing that his boy might climb on it to have a mock driving which might unbalance the bike and cause an accident. His mind was perhaps occupied by other thoughts and he forgot to park it on the main stand and in hurry used the side stand. Seeing his father has parked the bike in the lawn, the nine years old boy did not lose any time to climb on the heavy bike and started his drill. The boy was unaware of the weakness of the side stand and suddenly the side stand betrayed. It actually slipped. The boy tried to manage the weight of the bike the way he has seen his father manages the bike but it was no way within his capacity. He was fighting a lost battle with the heavy Enfield Bullet 350. Finally the bike fall on the lawn and the boy beneath that. Fortunately the knee guards of that day's bullets were wider and strong enough which took the burden and also created a triangular shaped free space within which the tiny body of the boy got trapped. Though the boy was luckily not injured but was so confined that it was no way possible for him to get out of that place. Seeing no option he started calling his father to rescue him.

Sundar while getting prepared heard his son shouting for him from the lawn. He almost ran towards that direction. Seeing his only son in such a condition initially Sundar was shocked but when he realized that the boy is not injured he started calling all other members of the family to show them the scene. The humiliation for the boy lasted for few more minutes and then Sundar rescued him from the trap. Everyone was laughing except Sundar's wife, who was serious and rebuked both the father and the son. Father for his mistake and son for his adventurous activities with the weighty two wheeler.

Everything changes except the kids and their minds as long as they remain kids. After that funny incident nothing changed for Sundar's son and he continued his favorite game as it was. But someone else's mind was changed and on a serious note, it was Sundar's wife. She was worried about the repetition of any such accident. For that time by the grace of God her only son was not injured but it could have been fatal. Moreover it happened in the presence of Sundar, but if the same thing would have happened in his absence then who would have managed that? She settled her mind on her way forward, but it was really tough to ask Sundar to sell the bike off as it was so close to him.

I would sell the bike, Sundar almost barked on himself, this is limit. He added out of sheer frustration, I don't need this anymore. Finally Rani got a chance one day when Sundar was irritated on the condition of the bike. Originally just before two days Sukanta visited his sister's house and as it is he asked for the keys of the motorbike, which he was granted as it used to be. Sundar was out of station on his duty, so Sukanta used the bike to the fullest and became a bit more than needed adventurous. The bike had to pay the toll of Sukanta's deeds and got many scratches and dents on it. Now after returning from duty when Sundar looked at the condition of his beloved bike he was shattered. Out of extreme irritation he said to his wife that he would rather sell off the bike than spending on it so frequently. Rani was probably waiting for this opportunity for long so she totally supported that view and replied, I do also think that the bike should be sold out. Sundar was a bit shocked on hearing this. He never expected such a reply from Rani and asked her, are you serious?

Rani replied, day by day our son, who is now just approaching his teenage is getting attracted towards the bike. May be in some years from now he will try to ride it which I think should not be allowed. She paused for a moment and looked at Sundar to sense what he is feeling and then added, this will not only be a risky proposition for us but at the same time will create impede to the studies of the boy also as he will be more attentive towards the two wheeler than his studies. Sundar did not reply that day but it started disturbing him. His wife was also insisting him to decide on the issue, and the boy without knowing any of these was happy with his mock riding of the bike.

The happiness did not exist long for the boy as his father started discussing with his peers that he wants to sell the bike and there were many interested takers for the majestic piece of automobile.

Suddenly in a Sunday morning two young men came to Sundar's house as buyer of the bike. It was already scheduled and informed to everyone in the family except the boy who became thunderstruck after knowing the fact. He was with it for more than five years and in every moment of those five years he dreamt of riding the bike. He always used to say, one day when I will become young, the bike will belong to me only. And now some unknown people have come to snatch his most valuable asset from him, rather his dream from him. More shockingly everybody was aware of that but none have shared the fact with him.

The bike will not be ours anymore right, nonchalantly he approached his father and asked.

This is an old model now and we will buy a new one, Sundar had nothing to say in reply so he tried to change the topic. The boy did not say anything and came to the garage, opened the door and stared to the bike for some times and flee from there.

After nearly a quarter of a century the boy, now a mature man have still those moments alive in corner of his mind, riding the bike with his father, mock driving seating on the parked bike, helping his father in washing the bike. He had not even forgot the number of the bike which in fact Sundar himself had forgotten years back. Though his father kept his promise once he made to his son and bought his son a new bike when the boy was just eighteen but till now the sound haunts the boy in his dreams "vroom vroom", and will forever.

BLUNDER ...

Are not you being a bit more extravagant than required regarding this event? Rani asked her husband while serving him a cup of tea.

It is almost 10:30 at night and Sundar generally does not indulge himself with tea at this time but today is a special day. He is totally immersed in to his financial account book and planning for the expenditures he will have to afford in the upcoming event. So, he missed the words his wife uttered to him and did not reply. I am telling you something, Rani said again.

Hmmm, any issue, this time Sundar raised his face from the book of his accounts and looked at Rani. Rani repeated the question once again. A mild smile played on Sundar's lips, he took the cup, sipped the tea and then said, you know Rani, when our mother passed away I was at the age of two and a half years. I and my brothers actually grew up in a very constricted psychologically condition. Sundar stopped for some moments and then continued, we have faced tremendous crunch of means and lived with almost the minimum possible, sometimes even without that minimum. We had never been treated as we should have been. We never had a piece of new cloth at the time of Durga puja when even the poorest of the poor used to have at least one. Rani let herself sat in opposite side of the bed, she could well understand what is running in the mind of her husband. She knew him from those days when Sundar was a determined young man and how that same man has changed in to a mature person in these years they have spent together. She was well aware of that very soft corner in the mind of this strong muscular taut figure. She knew the agony this person has somehow hidden from the outer world, from even his closest friends. She knew that till now a kid cries and search for his mother in within this mature man, even after more than fifty years from the day a boy lost his mother.

Sundar again paused, arranged his words and continued what he was depicting to Rani, do you know why? Because there was none to think about us. Our existence was hardly a matter to anyone in the universe. We used to be afraid of being happy, celebrating events or enjoying anything. All of us had suffered from severe maladies sometimes or other. He paused for moments and added, you know that I personally had suffered from Typhoid, someone from Asthma, someone from Tuberculosis and someone from Psychological disorder. Believe me, none of us had the bare minimum chance to survive with the kind of free treatment from the local government health center we received. But again, fortunately we all did. I strongly believe this is by the grace of the God and blessings of our mother who must be watching her children from somewhere there. Sundar pointed his finger upwards. Rani could sense that Sundar's eyes have started turning red and to hide that he has just turned his face to the other side. He paused for some moments, perhaps to control his emotion from getting liquidated. After a long haul he continued, now after fighting the battle with life so long I and my brothers have earned some happiness which we wish to share with our family and children. They must never feel what we had felt throughout our time. Sundar stopped for a while, shipped the cup and said, this is the first such event I am going to organize in next one month, this is the marriage ceremony of our eldest daughter and I am so excited about it. Rani, I will stretch myself to the extent possible so that Mani could cherish these moments for ever. Please don't tell me to be pragmatic or something like that, at least this time I am not going to be one.

Rani was speechlessly observing at her husband and perhaps first time in all those years of her life she has lived with this man, she is witnessing this phase in her husband. His eyes have turned red and he was probably fighting with his emotions with all his will power to restrict them from coming out. She did not wait there anymore and left the place.

Back in to kitchen Rani was thinking about their eldest daughter Mani. Mani is perhaps the honest, kindest, simplest minded and the closest to her out of her all three children. From the day she was born, she had always been over pampered by them. The way she used to smile, the way she used to behave especially when she was angry, every small thing is so live in Rani's mind. It seems just a matter of yesterday, but twenty one years have passed by in between. A mild smile played at Rani's face, so we have travelled such a long way, she almost uttered to herself. That cute barbi doll like Mani is now a young lady who will be stepping in to her new life or rather a new phase of her life just after some hours. Their first child who used to be so over pampered that not only their neighbors but sometimes the family members also used to tease them. She has always been the most obedient and dutiful to the elders, at the same time most helping and responsible towards those who are younger to her. Mani has always been the most open-minded from her childhood and till date she does not understand any twisted intension of others. Suddenly the pressure cooker created a terrible noise of fume and broke in to Rani's chain of thought. Initially Rani was taken aback by the sudden harsh sound and then in a practiced way she lowered the flame of the gas oven. After showing some rage the pressure cooker again got back to its peaceful state and within few moments Rani again got absorbed in to her thoughts. The day Mani was admitted in the convent school, first ever from the family. How so early in the morning she and Sundar used to prepare themselves for their office, as well as Mani for her school. The scene of Sundar almost running to the railway station taking Mani on his lap is till now so new and afresh in Rani's mind. The way Mani used to fall asleep on the rickshaw while returning after her long day at school. Rani started smiling remembering those days and events. Now the same Mani is going to get married, she had become a lady and all these just happened so suddenly that nobody had ever thought about.

Suddenly the bitter feeling again arrived in her mind. There is no doubt that Raghab is well established and in a government service but there are differences in the life style of the two families. Though they have said that they are planning for their own house but Rani knows planning for a home and getting it through is altogether two separate arena of involvement. She had once done this and she knew very well the pain of building a home and how much it takes from a person. She knows that it can't be done overnight and unless then Mani will have to live in that confined space. Currently the family of five members is living in a small two room government quarter and Mani will be the sixth to get adjusted there. How Mani, who have spent her life in such a spacious and comfort zone would manage to live there? The same thought again started aching. Many times Rani has tried to discuss this with her husband but every time her voice has been shut by same logic, what we had when we started our life? Every time Sundar used to cite example form their own life but Rani failed to make him understand that they also probably would never had their own home if she would not have inspired. She could not make Sundar understand that the problem is Mani is not that active as Rani was. Rani tried her best to make Sundar understand that their daughter has never seen the harshness of life. Then how could he expect the same Mani would be able to establish herself and her voice to that people who are entirely new and unknown to her. Rani has tried to say that, I know my daughter much more than you, but she has backtracked in a consciousness that these words would hurt Sundar a lot. She has tried to say that Mani who being elder has never got that strength to establish her voice to her own siblings and you are expecting her to establish herself to some unknown people. She knows that Sundar loves Mani no less than she does but the problem is he sometimes can't understand what he don't want to understand.

Rani also have a feeling that there are differences in thoughts and cultures in the two families. She has also received some reports that have triggered a negative thought but at the same time she also knows that these type of reports many times are generated out of wrong intensions by some people who have vested interests, especially in case of marriages. Everybody in the family has seen Raghab once or twice and maximum of them have commented satisfactory about the behavior or attitude of the boy. There is no doubt that there is lack of modernizations in him and also in the other members of his family but that might because of their upbringing in a remotest rural society.

Rani knows that there are some voices that want to raise their concern and unwillingness on this relationship even within her own family but she can't allow them to become stronger. She knows her daughter very well. She is well aware that Mani might be the most obedient and responsible girl but she had never been interested in her studies. Rani herself and Sundar also had tried all possible means to create attentiveness in their daughter regarding studies but Mani had almost always failed them. It has always been reported by her teachers that she is quite intelligent but typically apathetic towards studies. She doesn't even have any willingness for any job or any other profession. Moreover recently she has been suffering from a typical pain in her stomach. Many physicians have been consulted, all the prescribed medical examinations have also been done but nothing has come out. The aching has become almost a regular phenomenon especially in the evening. In such a condition it is too risky to detain or cancel such an offer for any parents. The smile that was playing in Rani's lips has vanished and now the tension and dilemma she has been going through is clearly visible on her face. Sometimes in life it is more important to decide what you should not do than what you should do, Rani uttered in within her mind. It is tough, really a tough decision to take and position to manage for her.

Ma, should I start arranging the dinner? Mani asked her mother.

Hmmm, Rani raised her face and turned towards the voice that was calling her from behind. It was Mani, who has arrived in the kitchen to help her mother, which she always enjoys to do. She always feel the best when she is with her mother. Sensing that her mother has missed her words, she iterated again what she just asked.

Yah sure, Rani replied to her daughter and silently kept watching the transformation of her daughter from a girl to a woman. How rapidly the time had passed and how fast her small barbi has become a lady? Rani was watching the transformation of her barbi in to a lady.

By next two to three days the vendors who were hired for various gifts and presents for the in-laws, started delivering those items in Sundar's house. All the furniture and fixtures that Sundar had arranged to gift her daughter in her new life started occupying space before they reach their final destination.

One day was scheduled to go for the purchasing of the cloths and special dresses like Banarasi for the groom and special dress for the bridegroom used in such rituals. Costly cloths were purchased not for the groom and the bridegroom only, rather almost for all the members in Sundar's family as well as for the members of his daughter's would be in-laws. Rani had never seen Sundar so happy. He was spending without even a second thought. He was so happy that he did not even bother to say no to anybody or anything. When the family returned home in the evening after the long day, they were almost overburdened with the bags and baggage they have filled with new cloths and dresses.

I will go with you tomorrow, Sundar's younger daughter appealed to him. It was just after a week Sundar and Rani had completed their marketing of cloths. They have decided now they should procure the ornaments and other accessories for their daughter's marriage and decided to go tomorrow. Initially it was decided that they will go with one of Sundar's bother and one niche but suddenly their younger daughter has come to know about this and now she is not only willing rather decided to accompany her parents. Rani was initially not ready and that has triggered the girl to appeal to her father, who generally had never said no to any of her appeal. The younger daughter was more close to Sundar and also resembles a lot like himself. As Rani used to be more occupied with their elder daughter Mani so their younger daughter Gublu was mainly taken care by Sundar. Gublu was perhaps the polar opposite of Mani and from her childhood she was extremely serious about and attentive towards her studies. Her mark sheet has always been the best amongst all. Opposite to Mani, who used to depend on her mother for each and every decision, Gublu always had her own decision on almost everything. She depends on her father much more than anybody else and also always prefers to request anything to her father than to her mother. Sundar initially tried to make his younger daughter understand that this is a tiresome job but those tries were too feeble to stand against the appeal and finally it was decided that she will accompany her parents next day.

THE MARRIAGE

All other necessary things like ornaments, cloths and gifts for *would be* relatives had also been arranged. Sundar had accumulated the best possible quality for each and everything he will be gifting his daughter and her in-laws. The seating and other arrangements for invited guests are simply kind of never-seen-before in that rural area. He had personally checked and rechecked each and everything unless he was satisfied. The man who used to be extremely calculative throughout his life seems like had lost his mind.

Finally the day came, the bridegroom came with his family members and friends early in the evening for the marriage ceremony. The entire family including Sundar's brothers and their family members also were present to welcome the guests and guide them through the way from the gate to the hall that was decorated to comfort them. Every single thing was perfectly arranged and managed for them. As per the priest the rituals and religious processes was to be start almost in the midnight. Both the bride and the bridegroom had been fasting for day long as per the Hindu culture and was not allowed to consume anything on the day of marriage until the ceremony is over. Mani was feeling the pain of starving and started suffering from headache but for the first time in her life she knew that there is no alternative.

Though when the ritual started it was in the late hours of the night but all the members of the family including the children also were standing around the mandap and started cheering. Everyone was enjoying the event to the fullest. Sundar himself did the *Kanyadan* and it was the moment when his eyes were moist but with a smile of satisfaction on his lips. Rani was silently staring at her husband and witnessing the change. She might be was walking down her memory lane and recalling same an event that took place almost twenty-two years back from this date. That time in place of Mani and Raghab, she and Sundar was performing the same rituals. Those memories are still so new, so affectionate, so beautiful to cherish on. A sudden sound of conch broke in to her hallucinations and she found that the rituals are completed. Now it was time to guide the newly married couple to the hall where the Basar will be arranged. Everything has completed successfully, Rani looked at the sky and thanked the Almighty.

The next day morning use to be the most painful for any girl when she has to leave her home for an unknown destination where she would have to always cooperate with people never known to her before. The same pain perhaps also takes its toll on her parents when they have to let their daughter go. The daughter who is generally no less than a princes to her parents and have always been taken care of all her necessities, from now onwards will be someone who will have to take care of others in the family. The daughter, whose one cry was more than enough for the parents to have a tensed and sleepless night will now have to spend sleepless nights. The pampered little girl who has never been allowed by her parents to even carry her school bag will now have to shoulder the burden of duty and responsibilities of everyone in the house. For Mani also it was same, some women of the family wiped, some other mentally stronger than the first lot were standing with dimmed face. The only man who did not cry was Sundar, he was standing like a pillar but only Rani could sense what that man is going through. She knew that Sundar could not cry. It may because of the tough life he had lived and the hostilities he had faced from his childhood, which had made him such that he had forgotten to cry. He was standing in a corner with blood red eyes. Those dreamy beautiful and extended eyes in such a blood red condition were originally depicting his feelings. Finally the car moved forward with the bride and the bridegroom. Till the last bend of the road Mani was looking through the rare windscreen of the car. She was looking at the home and people she was leaving behind.

As per the ritual next to next day of the marriage the members from the girl's family are being invited by the family of the bridegroom to visit their house. And now it is the duty of the family of the bridegroom to extend their hospitality and welcome their guests with the best possible means. So next to next day the members of Sundar's family were invited to the house of Raghab. The cultural differences became more acute here but everybody cooperated. Everyone felt the disharmony in the mental frequencies but as it always happens in the Indian society, the family of the bridegroom is always more important so none should show them their mistakes. Finally they came back to their home only with hope and expectation that everything will be fine in future.

After three to four days Mani with Raghab return to her paternal house to carry out the ritual called *Asta Mangla*. Sundar and Rani was so happy seeing their daughter. They welcomed them and arranged everything needed. Some of the relatives were also there with them. The rituals were performed with every details. Everyone was enjoying the moments.

Though Mani from the very moment of her arrival at her paternal house, was trying to talk to her mother in a private space but was not getting the chance in the full house. Moreover she also had to be an important part of all the rituals that were being performed. Finally in the evening after completing all the jobs Rani came to Mani and asked her, so how is your new life going on there in your new home with new family?

As if a cloud was waiting for this lightening spark to burst. Rani was shattered when Mani finished her experience with her in-laws in last three days. Mani depicted how she had been treated, abused and humiliated in front of all, how she had been mentally tortured and avoided by the others. Mani's eyes were wet but Rani was boiling within herself. She was in one side giving consolation to her daughter, whom she had brought up like a princes, on the other side she was thinking how she would discuss all these with Sundar. None of the ladies noticed that when they were discussing everything another person was listening to them from the door of the room. Both the mother and daughter was fully immersed in to their own chats. One was describing the pains she has gone through in last three days and the other was feeling the pain in her neck of her soul. Sundar silently had listened to everything his daughter depicted just now to her mother. He slowly entered the room and sat on the bed. His facial expression was clearly illustrating his devastation. Mani seeing her father, burst in to tears, which perhaps was the most hurting scene for the man. Rani tried to console her husband but Sundar just waved her off by his hand. He waited there for some minutes and left the room without uttering even a single word.

The man who has been shadowed by pain and wound almost from the beginning of his life and was habituated of dealing with such things was shattered seeing his beloved daughter crying.

After the dinner Sundar came to his room without talking to anyone. Rani after managing her household came to Sundar and sat on the bed. They were staring at each other. Sundar first broke the silence, have we done a blunder? How could I be so wrong to judge a man and that to as my son-in-law? Have we destroyed Mani's life?

Rani was totally taken aback but she could well understand that Sundar was being broken inch by inch from within. He was perhaps losing the most valuable thing of his character, his self-confidence. But Rani did have any word to inspire the man as she always had before this day. Anyhow I have to manage it, Rani said to herself and then she uttered to Sundar, I think before we could decide anything we should at least talk to Raghab once on this matter. She added, tomorrow morning we will seat with him. He might not be as we are thinking. There might be some issues with the other members of that family but the boy doesn't seem like that. Sundar did not say anything, just nodded his head. Rani paused for a moment to arrange her words and then said, if required we would also ask the other elderly members of our family to help us find a solution. There are other veteran members who could help us in this.

Sundar was staring at Rani, but she could well understand that those eyes staring at her are not the same as it used to be. These eyes are of a man with broken heart.

Don't think too much and have a sleep, everything will be alright, Rani consoled Sundar before leaving the room.

The house was full of family people so Rani was sleeping with her two children on the first floor and Sundar in a single bed in the ground floor. It was nearly four o'clock in the morning when Rani felt someone is calling her. She woke up and found her husband standing by the bed. She promptly rose up, sat on the bed and asked, what happened?

I am not feeling well, Sundar said to his wife. I am suffocating and feeling a mild pain in my chest, he continued. He was breathing fast. Rani was shocked but did not lose her mind and asked Sundar, don't stand, seat on the bed until I come back. She ran to all the other family members in the house. Within a few minutes she returned to her husband after sending someone to call for a car and others to arrange medical facilities. Returning to the room she started soothing her husband. Within half an hour the car arrived and Sundar was taken to the nearest nursing home.

After some basic checking and tests what the in house doctor in that nursing home said was shocking, Sundar has gone through a mild cardiac failure. Though he has survived and now not in the danger zone but it could have been fatal if not taken to the medical facility in such a promptness.

I am not going to keep him here, I will take him to Kolkata, Rani said to one of the member of the family. You go and arrange for an ambulance with all facilities, she added. Many people tried to convince her that in such a condition it might not be wise for Sundar to travel so long distance and is not very much needed but Rani was stubborn and had already made her mind. She was well aware of the medical facilities available in that rural area so she did not delay and contacted one of her elder sister who was working in a renowned hospital in Kolkata. Within few hours everything was arranged and Rani personally supervised the arrangements to be sure and then asked the local doctors to provide a transfer recommendation. By next few hours Sundar was transferred to Kolkata. Rani's sister had already arranged everything so there was absolutely no loss of time and Sundar was submitted.

For next fourteen days Sundar remained there in Kolkata, submitted in the hospital. And for Rani, life was real tough time. It was not possible for her to leave her two children unattended in the house and at the same time she was not ready to leave Sundar alone in the hospital only under the supervision of the nurses and doctors. For that fourteen days she used to come home in the morning, work full day in the household in arranging all the necessary things for her kids and in the afternoon she used to return to the hospital to be with her husband. She literally spent restless days and sleepless nights.

Sundar returned home spending fourteen days of his life in the hospital. He survived the cardiac attack but it was manifested from his expression that he was mentally distressed. Actually the devastation that he failed to understand Raghab and his family used to hunt him throughout his life. The feeling crushed him that he had done a blunder by selecting Raghab for Mani, even disregarding the opinion of the other members of the family.

MY TRIBUTE IS PAID ...

Sundar, are you there at home, someone was calling for him from the gate.

Sundar has just returned from the vegetable market and was seating with the newspaper and a cup of tea. After his retirement from the job he is now enjoying a peaceful life. Except the issue of his daughter Mani which use to haunt him always in some corner of his mind, rest of his life is well organized. Rani was still in her job and Sundar's younger daughter Gublu has just joined her college and spends her time mostly in studies or going to her private tutors. She is as she always has been from her very childhood, almost devoted towards studies and serious in every matter. On the opposite side though Sundar knows that the matter was not that serious but still he has great anxiety for his son. The boy is going to face his final board examination in next few months but he is no way attentive towards his studies, rather more interested in games and social occasions like puja and various others. He does not possess even smallest bit of seriousness as his younger sister. This boy is always the cause of Sundar's headache, as he is neither like Mani, who may not be attentive in studies but is an obedient daughter, nor the boy is like Gublu, who is so serious about everything and doesn't waste even a slice of her time in anything worthless. In several occasions Sundar has tried to make this imprudent boy understands that he should change himself and his casual attitude towards life. But the boy as if is hell bent to spoil the most precious years of his own life. May be that is the main reason why Sundar could not have faith in this boy in any serious matter.

From the voice itself it was clear to Sundar that who is at the gate. This voice is calling his name more than last forty five years. He rose up and replied while moving towards the gate, why are you waiting there, come in. He knows it is Surya da. When Sundar reached the gate, he found Surya was standing there with a small packet in his hand. Sundar said again, why you are waiting there, come in.

No its okay here, I was just returning from the shop and thought to have a chat with you. He did not step inside and from the opposite side of the gate the two old friends started conversing with each other in various topics.

Sundar believe me I still recall those days when we used to roam around from one village to another, Surya said. It seems just yesterday. Sundar smiled in return as those days are still crystal clear in his mind also. Almost forty five years have passed, Sundar replied with a long haul, if I am not wrong.

How could you be wrong in calculation, Surya uttered to his friend, you had always been the best boy in mathematics. He continued, you know Sundar I still feel the same zeal, sometimes I think let us start again.

No.... Surya da....not again, Sundar replied. The days has changed, people has changed, in fact everything has changed, Sundar added. Not only we two but each and every one we met, we worked with, was ready to sacrifice everything for the ideology we carried but now people could sacrifice their ideology even for the slightest material gain. At that time those used to be the leader who were ready to sacrifice but now there is always a race to become a leader. And more pathetically, nowadays leadership is saleable and purchasable item in the market of politics. Politics is not an ideological war anymore, it is a business. People investing in to it to have a better return and that too in the shortest possible period of time. He stopped, his frustration was visible on his face.

Yes I agree with you, Surya replied, there are some exploiters who are seating in the power and involved in every possible means of corruption but general people are still not that bad. He continued, if we could approach those general people who are the sufferers then the system is ought to change.

Sundar shook his head in disagreement and replied, you are forgetting one thing, the people in power will never allow you and me to create problem in their lavishing life. He paused for some time and added, we will simply be thrown out. Can't you see who are seating in the power? The predecessors of those people whom we fought against with our tooth and nail, sacrificing all our dreams except one, to establish a society of equality. And what we have achieved, the same society of inequality, just with some changes of faces. Nothing else has changed.

The two old friends were standing with their heads down. I was wrong, Surya uttered, and I dragged you in the same ship.

No, neither you nor I or anybody of that time who fought for the cause was wrong, Sundar replied. Either the time was wrong or the ideology we believed in was nothing but the seventh heaven. He paused for a moment and added, do you know what sometimes I think? Surya raised his head to stare at Sundar and asked, what?

Sundar with a pale smile on his lips replied, we have given our flesh and blood to create a Frankenstein monster, which one day or other will destroy us ruthlessly.

Okay man I must go now, nearly chatting for half an hour Surya said, there are hell lot of works there at home.

What do you mean by "Hell lot of works", Sundar asked. Surya smiled and replied, I came to buy some sugar and now I will go home and clean the used dishes and utensils those are lying dirty from yesterday night. He added, then I will cook and take my bathe and then only will have my lunch. With the same old signature smile playing on his face he turned and started walking towards his home.

How could a man on earth be so happy after losing everything or should I say after disregarding everything he could have enjoyed? Sundar silently asked himself looking at the trail of Surya returning to his home. Should I call it a home, he cited a question on his own thought and get back to the room again where he was seating before Surya called him. Sundar came back to his room and let himself sat on the bed. Memoires from those old days started penetrating his mind again. Those days when Surya was the only person so affluent that everybody used to be jealous of him. Those days when Surya was one of the main sponsor for various political program. Those days when Surya did not even think twice to empty his own pocket for others. Those days when Surya always used to be pampered and taken care by his mother and maternal grandfather. Those days when almost half of the cultivating lands in this area was under his possessions. And now the same man is washing used plates and kitchen utensils by his own hands. The same man everyday has to cook for himself. Horrendous, Sundar uttered to none.

What happened, who you are talking to? A voice broke in to Sundar's chain of thoughts. He raised his face and found his son standing at the door of the room. The boy was in his room in the first floor and while coming down the stair has heard his father saying something. When he found his father was seating alone, he was surprised and asked the same to his father.

No.... nothing, just I was thinking about Surya da, Sundar replied. He then stopped and added, he has to do all the household jobs at home by himself only. Unbelievable.

Yes I know, his boy replied casually and continued, every day we all have seen him washing his plates and utensils in the pond in front of the club. He paused for a moment and asked his father, by the way why you are thinking all these. Sundar did not answer just waved his son off.

Have you taken your breakfast, Sundar's son asked him?

Yes, Sundar replied, your portion is kept in the kitchen. He stopped and added, go and complete it. The boy did not waste any time and moved towards the kitchen. In the next twenty minutes the boy finished his breakfast and was ready for going out to his club. This is the same club once which used to be the heart of his father. For which Sundar once was even ready to thrash a man who blamed the club and its members.

Where are you going, Sundar asked his son, who was in the mood of going out and was busy in wearing his sleepers?

In the club to play carom, and will be back in an hour or so, the boy gently replied, expecting a dreaded reply from his father.

This addiction of yours towards the club will ruin your life, Sundar almost screamed to his son. The boy is now at the crowning of his teenage and his typical interest in the club and various social occasions has become a headache for Sundar as a father. You are nothing better than a worthless fellow, Sundar added, I have been investing all of my time, energy and resources behind your studies and you are more interested in night guard party than your studies.

It was almost 11 in a sunny Sunday. The boy did not reply and coolly slipped out of that place.

Staring at his son going to club, Sundar smiled. He can well understand from where the boy has inherited this typical mind of involving himself in to various social occasions.

AFTER SOME DAYS

It was almost 8 in the evening and Sundar has just returned from his daily walk. Nevertheless Rani many times has requested him to carry his daily walk, but not to walk for almost 6 – 7 km every day at this age but Sundar was stubborn on his decision. He always used to cite a typical reason that without this walk he loses his appetite, which is even worse. Rani sensing that it is tough to restrain her husband, then tried to agree him to carry his daily walk but maximum up to 2 – 3 km, but she has again failed. There was no one in the house except Gublu, who was as usual immersed in to her studies. Where is your brother, Sundar asked his daughter?

He has not yet returned from the field, Gublu while going back to her desk replied and disappeared in the bend of the stair.

Sundar looked at the wall clock, it was showing 8 PM and the boy who is going to face his board examination in few months is still busy in playing games. Sundar was almost furious, today I must teach him a lesson, he said to himself silently. He then asked for his daily evening tea and retired to his room.

The doorbell rang in next twenty minutes. Sundar has just finished his tea. It must be that reckless rascal, now he has finally found time to return home. He approached the door and found his boy waiting outside. You don't need to get in to the house, get out of here, Sundar almost shouted to his son. He added, day by day the more your examination is approaching closer the more you are spending time in games rather than studies. Now you will tell me something bizarre to stand your cause, right?

The boy raised his head and said placidly, Surya uncle has passed away.

What? When? How do you know? Sundar asked the question breathlessly. His eyes were saying his disbelief. The shock he has just received was clearly visible on his face.

Yes, we were returning form field when we first came to know about this, the boy replied. Babul hurried there to confirm and we were waiting outside his home. He added, as per the doctor nearly at 6:30 in the evening he has breathed for the last time. The boy stopped for a moment and stared at his father. He was well aware of the bond of friendship and trust between these two men. Sundar was bodily standing there but he was not present. The boy continued, we all were arranging things that would be needed now. I have just came to inform you about the incident, others are waiting there in the club. He added, all of us will accompany his mortal remains to the burning ghat. Everyone in waiting for his relatives who are yet to come and pay their last regards and then by next one or two hours we will start.

Sundar left the door and get back to his room, the boy followed him. Sundar was shattered. He sat on his bed for a moment and then stood up and started wearing his shirt. Are you going to see him for the last time, his son asked him? Sundar did not say anything, just nodded his head. Then suddenly he returned from the door and again let himself sat on his bed. Have you seen anybody from the party leadership, Sundar asked his son.

Yes, some of them have come with garlands, the boy replied.

Sundar did not ask any more question and waited silently. So many things were running on the screen of his mind. From the first day he spoke to Surya da in the library to recently when he and Surya da was chatting in front of his home.

The bright young Surya da to an aged man with silvery white hair and unshaved beard. Form an improvident young boy from a highly affluent family who left his government job to carry on his passion for politics to a man who had become almost the opposite. From a man used to be surrounded by innumerous number of people to a man cruelly alone in his abode. From a man who had nothing to worry about because there were so many people for him to do that part of life, to a person who again have nothing to worry about because there was no one for him to be worried of. A man who left all the luxuries that was available to him for his political ideology but never became successful politician. A man who took decisions on the basis of his emotion and instinct and never on self-interest throughout the span of life. The man who should have been there in the top but unfortunately lived a life just like another common man. Perhaps that is what he always wanted to become one, just a common man. But one thing that never changed in that man was his smile. The beautiful, open minded, hearty smile that was the signature of the man. Sundar shook his head.

You are coming with me or you will come afterwards, the boy who has already prepared for going out asked his father. Sundar was almost lost in his own thoughts and forgot about his son's presence in the room. The sudden intrusion in his thoughts take him back to his sense again. He raised his face, looked at his son and stood up. There was some tussle going on there in within his mind. He started wagging in the room. The boy was losing his patience and repeated his question again.

Sundar stopped for a moment, stared at his son and replied, I am not going to see him this time.

This was perhaps the answer the boy expected the least. He was taken aback and with the same surprise in his eyes he asked, what do you mean? I don't understand. He added, this is the last chance to pay the tribute to the man and you had always been his companion for years. Recently even I have seen both of you were cherishing your past moments and you are not going to see him for the last time. Would you get any more chance to see him? The boy completed and waited for the reply from his father.

Sundar looked at his son and replied, I hardly believe any one on this planet knows Surya da better than me, any one feels the pain for him more than what I feel, but I am not going to see him today. He paused, arranged his words and then said again, regarding the paying of tribute that you are talking about, I will say just one thing, my tribute to that man is already paid. I would better remind that smiling lively face that I have seen for not years but decades, rather than recalling his face when it is lifeless. He had always been and will always be present alive in some corner of my memory, which I don't want to kill by seeing the lifeless face of his. He had faced many pains from many people whom he loved unconditionally, Sundar paused again probably to hold his emotion back and then added, let him experience a happy existence somewhere in my mind at least as long I am alive.

There was silence. Absolutely pin drop silence. The boy was overwhelmed by the words of emotion what he has listened just now from the most pragmatic man on earth he has ever known. He has never witnessed such emotional part in his father before. In the meanwhile Sundar had approached to the open window and was staring at the dark outside. What he was looking or searching for in that pitch black outside was only known to him. He did not even turn to look at his son. The boy tried to say something but could not manage words to console his father. He waited there for some time and finally said, then I am going, it may be late to return from the burning ghat.

Sundar did not turn back or said anything this time and just waved off his son with his hand gesture. The boy finally turned his head and looked back from the gate to see what his father was doing and found the man still standing at the window staring at the dark night outside.

Probably I won't ...

IN THE BANK OF GANGA

Sundar's son was seating on the large and wide staircase that leads to the flowing waters of the river. It was winter, the month of November and the continuous chilling cold breeze from the river was piercing through the skins of all other who were seating with him but he was not feeling anything like cold. Perhaps his sensations were not functioning properly or he might have lost them all. The ghat was full of hustle bustle but no voice or sound was strong enough to penetrate in to his mind or chain of thoughts. He did not know where his eyes were landing on to. Whether he was staring at the river at a whole or at the flowing water or at those small canoes that were sailing through the river or to those ferryboats that were navigating across the river to and fro to carry travelers from one side to the other, he can't exactly say. He did not even know what he was thinking about, so many scenes were appearing as a flashbulb in his mind and in the next moment before he could even see it properly, that was being overshadowed by another. The same thing was going on again and again and again, interminably. He was not ready to think the beautiful past as the days of the future would never be same again. Perhaps that was the very reason he was even not prepare enough to think of the incoming days of the future. He is living this specific day most painfully in his life till date.

He was thinking what happened in last five hours still seems to be a bad dream which will all being well be over in next few moments, when almost certainly as usual the affectionate voice of his mother will intrude in to his ears. His mother will just call and wake him up from the bed and he will complain that he is again late for the train today. And a run for getting ready for his office will begin as it always begins all the five working days of any week. He is now working in a multi-national company and also doing well. He is satisfied that at least he had taken his father out of the tension regarding the future of his son. He is now at his late twenties and more or less a happy young man. Sundar's younger daughter has also completed her higher studies and working in an organization of repute. She also was getting prepared to start her Doctorate of Philosophy. Everything has been settled and Sundar was busy in arranging the marriage for his younger daughter. In fact everything was settled between Gublu and Samyo, and now the two families have also cheerfully attested the choice of their respective kids.

Sundar was happy as he has almost completed all his duties and responsibilities properly. After this he will be even happier. He still reminds the way his life has travelled the long path of these years. He sometimes still wonder how the life has established him as a successful man, starting from almost an orphan child. Rani has also retired from his job some years back and now she is more involved in managing Mani's life, the only decision that still pinch Sundar. On entirety life was good for them.

THIS MORNING

But suddenly it all messed up and everything changed. Even last night when Sundar's son returned home from office everything was perfectly alright and suddenly in the morning everything changed drastically.

It was as early as half past six in the morning when his mother woke him up from bed and conveyed, please come and see, your father is not feeling well, he is suffering from suffocation. Initially for one moment he was taken aback, but just for one moment only and then rushed downstairs. Within seconds when he entered his father's room he found him seating in the corner of his bed and trying hard to breath. It is the month of November, still the fan was circling at the highest possible speed. Probably someone has switched it on with a hope that it would help the man lungful. His father's facial expression and perspirations were portraying the pain he was going through. He has never seen the strong man so helpless, so feeble looking. What happened, he asked his father. His father did not answer just gestured to express that he is feeling tremendous respiratory discomfort. There was no time to lose, he again ran upstairs to get his cell phone. He thought about the names who could be helpful in such a situation. Many names appear in the call list. He dialed Babul's number. Two things played to help him decide on the names, firstly Babul's house in nearest to his and hardly a distance of some minutes, and secondly Babul possesses a car and knows driving well so he could come with his car. The phone hardly rang for two three times when from the opposite side Babul's voice appeared, what happen, so early in the morning, any problem?

Sundar's son conveyed the urgency in few words and asked Babul to come.

Just wait, I am coming at the earliest, Babul dropped the phone down.

What is next, he asked himself. Yes the medical facilities should be arranged beforehand. Just after calling his friend Babul he dialed the number of another known person in the local nursing home and tried to depict the problem and requested him to arrange for medical facilities detailing the issue. The assurance from other side was given. All these happened within two to three minutes. As if there was a race with time. He again rushed downstairs to his father's room in the ground floor. His mother and younger sister was trying their best to soothe his father.

Don't worry, Babul is coming with a car and I have also informed the nursing home authority to arrange all the medical facilities, the boy uttered to his family. He added, by the time we will reach there, all the necessary things would be in place. Sundar tried to raise his face and raised a side of that to look at his son. There was a typical smile on his face clubbed with the agony of tremendous suffocation that he was going through.

By next five minutes, it was almost 6:45 AM Babul arrived with the car. Sundar leaning on his son's shoulder get in to the car and the vehicle moved. Within two three minutes it stopped in front of the nursing home. Everything was arranged at the gate itself. Sundar raised his face just when the car stopped and looked at his son and said, probably I won't father. He breathed and added, finally the day has come, its time. Before getting out of the car Sundar spoke to his son for the last time. He used to call his son "father" when his son was a child and again called him by the same name after so many years, for the last time in his life.

Don't talk, it will increase the discomfort more and don't worry, just hold on and everything will be alright, his son replied to him. Sundar did not say anything, just a slight smile played on his lips, as if he jested about what his son said. He was placed on the trolley bed swiftly and taken to the cabin where the physician and the medical equipment had already been organized. Within moments every equipment was attached to his body and the monitor started showing graphs.

But Sundar was true, he did not give any time to do anything, within ten minutes he started sinking and nearly at 7 AM he left this earthly world and his family behind. His mortal body was lying on the bed with the same slight smile till present on his lips.

Mangal, Sundar's son looked back, someone was calling him from behind. It was his youngest uncle. He found many people standing in the cabin, his mind was somewhere else. Everything has been arranged, we have to move the body back to home, others are waiting out there to have a last sight, one of his friend uttered to him.

Hmmm, Mangal nodded his head and stood up. He sat beside the driver of the vehicle on which the mortal remains of his father was being carried, the vehicle moved towards home.

I will never talk to you again, these were the words Rani uttered seeing the lifeless body of her life partner. She did not cry. Perhaps the more intense the pain the less the chance of tears coming out, it gets dried in within.

BACK IN THE BANK OF GANGA

Mangal turned his face from the Ganga and his eyes fall on the smoke coming out of the smokestack of the electric incinerator. The dark black smoke coming out of the smokestack was getting diluted and then slowly blended in to the sky. He tried to hallucinate the face of his father in there. The face of his father, who was lying on the bed of the nursing home just before some hours as if he was sleeping peacefully. There was no change in his physical existence except one, there was no life.

Mangal looked back feeling a hand on his soldier, come with me, you have to perform the last rite for your father. You have to succumb the mortal remains of your father in to the Holy Ganga. It was his youngest uncle and one of the closest support from childhood. Mangal stood up and followed his uncle silently.

In few hours all the rituals were over and it was time to return home.

Mangal turned back at the burning ghat, he was leaving behind his childhood, his recklessness about life, his casualness about anything and almost everything. He was leaving behind his strongest support, fiercest critic of his ideologies and thoughts, his greatest teacher, his wisest philosopher and finally the ultimate guide for whose guidance he is standing tall in his own life.

BACK IN HOME?

Late in the evening Mangal was seating alone in his room in the first floor. He was recapitulating twenty eight years of life he spent with his father. He remembered what his father used say about the last day of life.

I would never lay down on bed helplessly and none of you will ever have to serve me even a single glass of water. I have lived on my own and the same way I will leave this world behind, his father always used to say to his family members. He was so inconsiderate at the same time so confident about his final day. As if he had always been knowing what will happen and was absolutely prepared for that.

It is still not clear to Mangal even today that how could a man be so sure about the future. Whenever anyone enquired about so much of inconsideration Sundar had about death, he used to reply, I with my own hand have incinerated minimum hundred dead bodies and paid them their last rights. He used to add, I am well aware about this paramount reality of life, which today or tomorrow will certainly happen. When you can't change it, better you ignore it and live every moment of your life positively and try to do something valuable for the humanity and the society, he used to conclude with this line and a smile.

Mangal raised his face to stare at the framed picture of his father, which was hanging from the wall and uttered to himself, I don't know how would I live this life, he paused for a moment and continued, I am not as confident as you were about the last day but still I pray that the final count should be like yours only, no pain, no irritation for self or others, no becoming burden on others, no hustle at all, just a matter of thirty minutes........and it is over. The gorgeous way of living life should also be the way of leaving life behind. But not yet, not yet..... I have to carry your bequest and I will, I won't say promise because it is too feeble a word to such a prodigious task, rather for me it's an oath to you and to the life.

Mangal.......Mangal........

A voice pierced in to his line of thoughts. That is a call of duty, responsibility, affection, gratitude and emotion. He stared to the photo once again, then finally stood up and turned to leave the room.

His mother was calling him from down stairs.

Printed in the United States
By Bookmasters